I0746659

Farmed
- and -
Dangerous

An Accidental Farmer Mystery

Amy Gregg

Farmed
- and -
Dangerous

An Accidental Farmer Mystery

Amy Gregg

FOX POINTE PUBLISHING

Copyright © 2022 by Amy Gregg

All rights reserved. Published in the United States by Fox Pointe Publishing, LLP. No part of this book may be reproduced in any form or by any electronic or mechanical means, including information storage and retrieval systems, without permission in writing from the publisher.

This is a work of fiction. Names, places, characters, and incidents are either a product of the author's imagination or are used fictitiously. Any resemblance to actual events, places, organizations, or persons, whether living or dead, is entirely coincidental.

https://www.foxpointepublishing.com/author-amy-gregg-1

Library of Congress Cataloging-in-Publication Data
Gregg, Amy, author.
Olson, Sarah, editor.
Town, Scotty, designer.
Johnsen, Krista, cover artist.
Farmed and Dangerous / Amy Gregg. – 2nd printing.
Summary: A recently divorced Twin Cities-based socialite takes over her family farm and helps solve the murder of a small-town realtor.
ISBN 978-1-955743-29-7 (hardcover) / 978-1-955743-48-8 (softcover)
[1. Cozy Mystery – Fiction. 2. Small Town & Rural – Fiction.
3. Farming – Fiction. 4. Amateur Sleuth – Fiction.]
Library of Congress Control Number: 2 0 2 2 9 4 0 9 2 8

Dedication

To
Bernard & Adeline
and
Glenn & Leona

"**Are you sure this is the right place?**" Lilly Rhodes asked again as her Kia Soul rolled to a shuddering stop. Slender fingers flexed and gripped the steering wheel in rapid succession. "I don't remember it looking quite like this."

"This is it!" Mrs. Maggie Swenson beamed.

Lilly's companion's enthusiasm grated down her spine. She shot her a hard look, an incredulous expression that escaped the middle-aged woman.

Lilly looked beyond the windshield and hood to the farmhouse, a square, sprawling two-level with a wrap-around porch. If it had been well-maintained, which it had not, this farmstead would have graced the cover of *Better Homes & Gardens*. In its current condition, Lilly placed it as a featured overhaul on one of the popular HGTV fixer upper shows.

Bare spots on the roof revealed missing shingles and holes which promised attic issues. The house needed many new coats of paint and re-hung shutters. A screen door swung haphazardly out onto the slanting porch. To Lilly, the building looked tired, ready to let time and the elements finish what they'd started.

Maggie exited the vehicle as Lilly surveyed as much of the property the windshield allowed. She knew behind the house stood more buildings, sheds, and a barn. She watched as Maggie loped up the stairs to the porch, dancing to one side as her New Balance sneakers sunk through a rotten board. Lilly was secretly impressed with how swiftly and elegantly the woman moved about the porch and worked on unlocking the main door.

With a heavy sigh, she opened the car door and went to join the realtor.

Lilly's kitten heels crunched on the gravel driveway as she made her way slowly toward the house and the spritely woman. She clutched her MK handbag close, as if expecting a thief to jump from the unkempt peony bushes and make off with her purse.

Only two short months before, she had been sitting in her Lowry Park loft, sipping a Surly Furious IPA, glaring at the stack of manila folders scattered across her coffee table. Little 3M Post-It flags marked where her signature was required; the splatter of pastels clashed with the seriousness of the papers on which they were attached.

One pile of folders held copies of her grandparents' Last Will and Testament, attorney notices, and more legal jargon Lilly was unable to wrap her head around. Her lawyer relayed the message buried in these papers was that her grandparents had left her their old farmstead in Lone Tree, Minnesota, southwest of the Twin Cities in Brown County.

The other pile contained divorce papers.

"Mrs. Rhodes, you need to come and take a look!"

Maggie's voice drew Lilly back to the porch before her. Unconsciously, she flinched at her name. Her old name. Why did it take so long for one silly little name change to go through and become official?

Final.

"Coming, Mrs. Swenson."

"Oh, enough with the 'Mrs. Swenson!'" The realtor laughed as she swatted playfully at the air. "I told you back at the office, call me Maggie. Everyone does."

Lilly sighed and made her way up the sagging porch steps to follow Maggie, but the other woman had already moved on to the interior of the house. Lilly cringed at the shriek and explosive bang of the screen door opening and closing. With a deep breath, she readied herself before stepping over the threshold.

How long had it been since she last stepped foot in the old farmhouse?

As she walked into the main entry, hardwood floors glinted in the warm sunlight. Before her rose a large wooden staircase, complete with an intricately carved banister, naturally drawing her eyes up toward the second floor where she could just barely see a recessed, rectangular outline of a closed attic door. Off to her left, a wood-framed entrance welcomed her to a sitting room furnished with chairs, couches, love seats, and coffee tables that were made by a loving, old hand. To her right, a twin entrance opened to a dining room filled with more wood furniture.

But it was all clean. Hardly a hint of dust or cobwebs in sight. Perhaps the only fault Lilly found was the stuffy smell from the home being closed up for so long. It was as if she had stepped into her own home after a long vacation.

"Oh, thank God!" Lilly's relief gushed from her before she could control herself.

"What, Lilly?" Maggie called from beyond the dining room. The realtor hustled back to the front entry, her face frozen in a perfect customer service smile. Lilly noticed another doorway behind Mrs. Swenson, teasing of a large, white, and clean kitchen.

"Nothing, Mrs. Swenson, uh, Maggie," Lilly cleared her throat as she turned and ventured further into the sitting room. "I just wasn't expecting to find the place furnished."

Why wouldn't it be furnished? Her grandparents hadn't died that long ago. No other family came forward to claim anything from the house. Where else would their possessions go?

"When your grandparents, uh," Maggie's voice faltered. Lilly found it amusing that the chatterbox realtor was finally speechless. "When your grandparents passed, they left everything that was in the house, barns, any of the outbuildings to you. They wanted to make sure you were comfortable here."

Lilly noticed the "didn't you read the will?" tone in Mrs. Swenson's voice. But that would explain why there was no estate sale, no auction, why none of her aunts, uncles, or cousins came clamoring for their piece of the inheritance. Her stomach sank as the words of the will she'd been staring blankly at for weeks solidified in her mind.

She got it *all*.

Lilly stood at the foot of the stairs and turned slowly, taking the time to drink in the once familiar sights around her. The position of chairs, knick-knacks, and pictures hadn't changed in the near two decades since she last stepped foot in the farmhouse. Memories long buried struggled to the surface; ghostly remnants of children running through these very rooms, their laughter tumbling down the stairs. Lilly shivered as the last peal of giggles faded.

"Come on, we'll have more time to explore the house later." Maggie's cheerful voice drowned the last memory as she grabbed Lilly's hand and pulled her through the house. The immense kitchen whirled past as she hustled Lilly through a back door and onto the wrap-around porch. "Let's check out the barns!"

Lilly regained control and pulled her hand from Mrs. Swenson's. "Um, not right now, please."

Mrs. Swenson stood on the ground, looking up at Lilly, who was still on the porch, her words hanging in the space between them. "Why not, dear?"

She cleared her throat and tried to put on her best smile. "I'm not dressed for trudging through barns," Lilly hoped that would stop any more questions. "And I'll have plenty of time to go through them tomorrow."

A knowing spark lit up the realtor's eyes. "Not if you don't want the cows to starve."

"*The what?*"

Lilly knew for certain the will hadn't mentioned livestock.

A quick march across the backyard brought Lilly to the main barn, a large nineteenth century construction with fading red paint that loomed before her. She coughed as the strong smell of hay, dirt, and manure wafted out of the barn doors. Mrs. Swenson eagerly opened one of the doors and the assault on Lilly's senses intensified. Lilly had noticed the lingering aroma of manure and animals when she arrived at the farm, but she'd figured it was merely a lingering scent, like towels that never lost their musty odor no matter how many times you washed them. The cows, hidden in the bowels of the dimly lit barn, moaned and bellowed.

Lilly stared helplessly into the dark, smelly building.

"If my grandparents have been dead for two months, who has been feeding these cows?" she demanded, holding a hand over her nose and mouth. She remembered now that she had always hated the barn, even as a little girl. This smell was not a memory she wanted to relive ever again.

"The lawyers made arrangements with one of the locals." That "didn't you read what you signed?" tone returned. Maggie seemed at ease with the barn and walked into the structure, leaving Lilly alone.

"Who is this local?" She groaned and followed the woman into the barn, gasping as her heel sunk into a suspiciously soggy patch of straw.

"Watch where you step," came Mrs. Swenson's late warning.

Great. Just great. These were her favorite shoes. She begrudgingly followed Mrs. Swenson deeper down the main walk of the barn.

"Mrs. Swenson—Maggie, who is the person that has been taking care of the animals?" Lilly asked as she goose-stepped her way closer to the realtor.

"I'll give you his contact information when we get back to the house," Mrs. Swenson replied with a dismissive wave as she stopped in front of a row of stalls. "Here they are. Aren't they beauties?"

Lilly collided with the older woman trying to avoid a particularly foul smelling section of straw-covered path. She lost her balance—kitten heels are not meant for barns—and tumbled forward, landing in a large pile of hay. Thankfully, it was cleaner than what was strewn about the cement walk.

"Oh, Lilly!" Maggie gasped. "Are you alright?"

Lilly pushed herself up onto her hands and knees, instantly regretting looking down at her clothes. Besides pieces of hay and other assorted grasses, there were dark spots that she prayed were just mud. She searched the hay pile for her purse, lost in the ungraceful fall.

Why did she decide to wear Armani jeans and a Chanel blouse to a farm? A farm of all places! The soles of her kitten heels proved to be no match for the wild outdoors. Some stupid need to show that she was someone of importance. Someone who had left this small town and made something of herself.

But had she?

A large black and white mouth appeared by her head, opened, and let loose a spittle-laced MOOOOOOOOO.

Lilly raised her eyes and found herself face to muzzle with a large cow, wet mouth chewing lazily mere inches from her own. She screamed as she scrambled backwards away from the noisy beast. The cow answered with another mournful bellow before plunging her mouth back into the hay.

"Oh, Mrs. Rhodes, Lilly—" Maggie stammered, fumbling over which name to address her by.

"Schmidt," Lilly corrected forcefully. She blanched, the feel of her maiden name still foreign on her tongue. "Lillian. Lilly."

"Lilly, dearie, are you alright?" Mrs. Swenson clumsily helped her stand, swatting at the hay and straw that clung to her clothes and hair. Lilly cringed as the woman's helpful gestures only managed to spread the mystery splotches on her clothes.

"Yes, yes, I'm fine," Lilly awkwardly side-stepped away from Mrs. Swenson. She turned toward the stalls and the cows in hopes of hiding her reddening cheeks.

Before her, each in their own little stall, stood five black and white cows, each chewing her cud. The one that made the rude introduction stuck her neck through the iron bars of the stall, straining to get closer to the newcomer. Her neighbors weren't nearly so curious, each busying herself with eating or settling in to sleep.

"So, those are the cows?" Lilly gestured toward the small herd, flinging muck-covered straw from her fingers.

"Holsteins, to be more precise. There's twelve in the herd at the moment, the rest must still be out in the pasture," Mrs. Swenson reached forward and patted the first cow on the muzzle. "This here's Dandelion."

"Dandelion?"

"And her daughters, Daisy and Daffodil. As you already found out, Dandelion can be a bit of a handful. She's got a mind of her own. So be mindful around her, and also around any of her daughters—she sure is protective of all her calves." Mrs. Swenson went on, patting the two smaller cows in the stalls next to Dandelion. "These other two are sisters, Peony and Poppy, but not related to Dandelion. And Emerald, Magnolia... but I don't need to bombard you with all their names, you'll get acquainted with all the other ladies soon enough."

"How do you know their names?" Lilly looked at each cow in turn, not sure if she could tell either of them apart.

Mrs. Swenson smiled. "Your grandparents always had a calf or two available to any of the Four H-ers who needed a project. Many of my own nieces and nephews have used a Schmidt Holstein for a fair entry. These ladies, and the ones that came before them, are well known in the county."

Lilly hugged her arms closer, ignoring the sticky squish of her shirt. This woman she stood next to was a realtor by trade, but as Lilly watched her move about the barn, interacting with the cows, she seemed to be coming home.

"Now, when you have more calves, you'll have to keep the flower names going," Maggie instructed. "Beverly just loved flowers and Harold couldn't stand to see her unhappy, so he allowed her to name each calf. As much as he griped about it, we knew he'd do anything that woman asked of him. Of course, they're not all named after flowers, some are named after gemstones..."

The reminiscent ache to Mrs. Swenson's voice gripped something deep in Lilly's chest and twisted. How well had this woman known her grandparents? Why does she sound like she's grieving more than their own granddaughter? She knew nothing about her grandparents or their life on the farm over the last fifteen years.

"Ms. Schmidt?"

Lilly jumped as she felt hands gently guide her toward the barn door. The use of her maiden name—her grandparents' name—eased the constriction in her chest with each step toward the main house, as if affirming that she did, in fact, belong back on the farm.

"Come, Ms. Schmidt, let's get you cleaned up,"

Maggie insisted that Lilly take a shower while she prepared them a light snack. Lilly wasn't sure what type of food would be in a house that was supposed to be vacant for two months, but she was too dirty to argue with the woman. Thankfully, along with her moving boxes, she had brought an overnight bag on this adventure; she wasn't sure if bank officials, lawyers, and the like would need her to spend the weekend instead of the day.

Lilly stepped from the shower and relished the plush bath mat between her toes. How she had loved to lay on this mat when she was a little girl after her baths. She wondered if it was indeed the same bath mat or if her grandmother had bought them in bulk. She wrapped an oversized terry cloth towel around her still-steaming body and wiped the mirror clean. One thing she'd make sure to do would be to get ventilation fans and heaters put in the master bath. Her grandparents had kept the old building up to date for the most part over the years, but some necessities were still lacking.

The faded tile of the counter and walls brought back more hidden memories of her time spent on the farm. As strange as it was to be back, rummaging through cabinets and closets like before, it was even more strange knowing that her grandma wouldn't be ascending the stairs asking if everything was alright and if she needed anything else, and by the way, there are fresh chocolate chip cookies if she'd like some. She felt like an intruder, an unwanted house guest snooping through medicine cabinets.

How long will it take before I start thinking of this place as mine?

Lilly dressed in silence to be attentive to the old house, not wanting to miss what stories it planned on telling. She had quite a bit to catch up on. Maybe the tales the house revealed would drown out the chatter in her head.

In fresh jeans and a V-neck T-shirt, Lilly quickly brushed her long hair. Her once meticulous auburn braid was deemed a complete loss after her barn performance. She thought about redoing the braid, but she wanted to get downstairs and see what Mrs. Swenson was getting into. Maggie. Lilly needed to let go of such formal titles this far in the country. She relented and opted to let her hair fall naturally down her back as she hurried down the stairs.

"You clean up pretty good, Lilly," Maggie grinned as Lilly entered the kitchen.

The kitchen, expansive by nineteenth-century standards, appeared even larger due to the white tile floors and crisp white ceramic countertops. To break up the white, the cabinet doors were trimmed in barn red paint, connecting the outbuildings with the homestead. Pots and pans of copper and cast iron hung from the ceiling just within reach while standing at the large island. Lilly smiled as she relived family Christmases, the faint scent of vanilla and bread filling her nose.

"I made some tea, would you like a cup? I couldn't find anything much to eat. Looks like the fridge, pantry, and cupboards were cleaned out." Maggie placed a tray with her grandmother's tea service on the island.

The spiced tea mingled with her memories and brought back the ache in her chest.

"You were going to give me the contact information for the person who has been taking care of the animals?" Lilly returned, wanting to get back to business. If she stuck to the matters at hand, she'd be able to ignore the unease that steadily grew inside.

"Oh, yes." Mrs. Swenson nodded as she placed an empty teacup in front of herself and Lilly. "That's Ryan."

Lilly waited for more to come after the stated name, but only received a full cup of tea poured instead.

"Does Ryan have a last name? Phone number? Address?" Lilly pressed.

"You'll need to go to Fritche's and stock up on groceries," Maggie continued as she took a seat on a stool next to the island.

Lilly sighed and followed suit, knowing this wasn't going to be as short as she'd hoped.

"Mrs. Fritche will make sure you get everything you need. They're still semi-full service, which is hard to find nowadays," Maggie said. "Although, I do like the deli selection at the larger grocery store across town. The prices are more reasonable, but the service can't match Fritche's..."

Lilly let her eyes and mind wander around the kitchen as the realtor continued her tale of the local grocery store feud. She allowed her mind to recall more family dinners prepared, she and her cousins chasing each other around the island, narrowly avoiding ruining Thanksgiving when her cousin Tammy collided with the turkey on the edge of the counter.

"Swenson."

Lilly blinked back to the present. "Excuse me?"

"You asked for his last name. Ryan Swenson." The realtor took a tentative sip from her tea, then smiled. "Beverly always had the best taste in tea."

"This was still here...?" Lilly stopped the cup a few inches from her lips.

Of course this was still here, what realtor would bring tea to a client's house?

"Oh, goodness, yes." Maggie laughed, swatting at the air again. "Tea doesn't go bad, dearie. It's just dried leaves. And I checked the date on the box. This was bought just before... well... you know."

Lilly convinced herself to try the tea. The aromatic drink spread comforting warmth through her body and slowly worked at her frayed nerves. Even as she felt herself relax, Lilly couldn't shake the odd twinge of memory that came when Maggie mentioned the hired hand's name. Ryan Swenson. It felt strangely—painfully—familiar.

The mug almost fell from Lilly's suddenly numb fingers when the pieces clicked into place.

"*Ryan* is the hired hand?" The question blurted out before she could stop herself.

Maggie gave her a puzzled look. "Yes, Ryan. I'm surprised it took you that long to remember him, dear."

Memories erupted in Lilly's brain like fireworks, some she'd thought long forgotten to the sands of time. She inwardly scolded herself for taking so long to put the pieces of the puzzle together. The Swensons were the closest farm to her grandparents', and the closest thing to neighbors out here amongst the cornfields and barns. Maggie's face finally registered in her old memories, though she hadn't spent much time with that branch of the Swensons as she did with Ryan's family.

Lilly amazed herself at how well she blocked out memories of her old high school boyfriend.

"How are you related again to Ryan?" Her face flushed at the bluntness of the question.

"He's my nephew. His father is my husband's brother." Maggie nodded. "Robert, my husband, and his brother, Matthew, grew up on the farm just down the road from here. The Swensons and the Schmidts farms were started up within years of each other, back when the original family members came over from the Old Country," Maggie chuckled as she said these last words. "Matthew and his boys still run the family farm. Robert and I moved into town after we got married. Bob's never been much into the animal side of farming, really. He likes to work more with his hands—machinery, tinkering."

Lilly nodded mutely, sipping her tea and listening to the woman drone on.

Maggie added, "Bob works at the John Deere dealership in the repair shop. Though now, he's gotten into volunteering at the high school to help build sets for the drama department. I think he's gotten a touch of that 'mid-life crisis' you hear so much about."

As much as Lilly would like the woman to just write down Ryan's phone number and leave, it was nice to get a little view into the town's happenings. Why not get some intel on the natives? It would be needed in the future. Lilly supposed that if someone gave a woman like Mrs. Swenson a willing ear, they'd be given more than just a little run down on the town.

"Mrs. Swenson—sorry, Maggie—I don't mean to be a pest, but if you could get me Ryan's number, I'd really appreciate it."

"Oh, yes." The realtor nodded deeply. "I suppose it has changed since you were last here. You kids with your cell phones and all. I suppose you two didn't have your own phones when you were going together in high school, did you? And I should probably get out of your hair, anyway. You've had a big day already, and there's still more to do!"

Lilly's well-practiced, polite smile drew tighter at Maggie with each word.

Maggie rifled through her purse and brought forth one of her business cards and a pen. She scribbled on the back and slid it across the island. "Here's his cell. He always has it on him, so don't hesitate to call him whenever you need help. He'll be here tonight for the last feeding of the cows and probably the morning's. Will you be staying or going back to the Cities?"

"I guess I'll be staying the night." Lilly picked up the card and slid it into her jeans pocket. "I had planned on heading back to Minneapolis tonight, but like you said, I've had a big day. And I have some boxes to unpack."

"Unpack?" Maggie's eyes sparkled. "Oh good! I was hoping you'd be staying on the homestead! Will Mr. Rhodes be coming soon?"

The question slipped out before the woman realized what she said.

"Oh goodness!" Her hands covered her mouth. "I'm sorry, Lilly."

Lilly nodded, understanding the slip-up. Much like her grandparents' deaths, the topic of her divorce was glazed over from the moment the two women met at the realtor's office earlier that afternoon.

"No, Mr. Rhodes will be staying in Minneapolis. He got the loft in the divorce since I came into land so soon before proceedings and division of assets were finalized."

A small wave of shock spilled over Maggie's face. "You weren't planning on living here, then?"

"No. I wasn't sure what I was going to do with the land and house when I found out I'd inherited it, but my dear ex-hubby decided that for me. So here I am."

Mrs. Swenson rose and came to the other side of the island. She took one of Lilly's hands in hers and gave a firm squeeze. "Don't you worry about that now. We'll be glad to have Bev and Harold's granddaughter back home where she belongs."

"Thank you, Maggie." Lilly gave the woman a warm smile and surprised herself when she genuinely meant it. "Just give me a moment to get my purse and I can drive you back."

"Oh no, I'll text Ryan to come pick me up." Mrs. Swenson grabbed her phone from her purse and tapped the screen furiously. "He's got nothing better to do since he busted his leg up."

Lilly watched as Mrs. Swenson gathered her belongings and headed toward the front door. The realtor switched into surrogate mother mode, giving Lilly instructions on how to care for the tea service so it wouldn't get water spots, and advice that, even though the house was in the county, she shouldn't forget to lock her doors. Remembering her grandma's stern words about seeing a guest to the door, She followed after Maggie while agreeing to follow each of the woman's directions.

"Ryan's on his way. He was at the farm down the road." Maggie announced as she pulled open the door. "If that boy was using his phone while driving again, I'll have his uncle talk to him."

"Your husband?"

"Ryan's other uncle. His mother's brother," Mrs. Swenson answered, as if that made everything clearer. When the silence from Lilly drew out longer than expected, she answered her puzzle: "His uncle is the sheriff."

The throaty growl of a diesel engine roared from the yard. Maggie's face lit up as she exited the house.

"Oh, Ryan's here!" Maggie bubbled. "Come out and say hi, Lilly!"

"Do I have to?" Lilly asked, ashamed at the edge of desperation in her voice as she saw the rusted green Chevrolet truck bounce up the gravel drive. She'd have to get that driveway fixed soon before she had to pay for everyone's body shop bills.

Lilly followed her out onto the porch as the truck pulled up next to her burnt orange Kia, dwarfing her vehicle. The man in the cab, Ryan, stayed in the vehicle as his aunt descended the stairs amidst her good-byes and future promises to check in again soon. Lilly gave a small wave and a smile from the doorway. So what if they had dated back in high school? And that she had mercilessly ended things with him in the least effective way possible—if there was an effective way to break someone's heart. That was nearly a lifetime ago; Ryan wouldn't hold onto a teenage broken heart for this long. Would he?

"Hi, Ryan," Lilly called from the porch.

Much of Ryan's face was obscured by a John Deere cap and the shadows within the truck, but Lilly knew the returned expression was anything but neighborly.

Lilly spent the rest of the afternoon moving the boxes from the back of her Kia into the house. She didn't have much in the realm of belongings, which turned into a blessing with the discovery that the house was still furnished. After a handful of trips, her move was complete. She sat in the living room, her heart sinking slightly at the sight of so few boxes clustered around her. Most of her marital assets were taken care of by Alec during the divorce.

Her whole life was stored in fifteen UPS Store boxes.

Some of her friends told her she'd been railroaded by Alec and his lawyers, her own lawyer should have fought harder to make sure it was an equal division of property. Lilly didn't want to drag out the divorce with fighting and negotiating over who got what. She wanted to be done with everything that pertained to Alec. Frankly, the majority of the stuff in their Lowry Park loft was Alec's. He had insisted on decorating their home and she allowed him. As long as she was able to have a small workspace of her own, she was content.

The announcement of her sudden inheritance made the decision to let Alec have whatever he wanted out of their loft all the easier. She took her books, computer workstation, pictures, clothes, laptop, and favorite coffee mug and bid the loft goodbye. Let Alec and Olivia redecorate how they wanted.

Her grandparents not only left her the house but a sizable trust that paid for property taxes and utilities, which explained why she still had electricity and water. For the time being, she was set. But eventually, she'd have to look for a job.

Back in Minneapolis, she held a part time, almost volunteer, position as a graphic designer for an up-and-coming environmental non-profit, but it didn't pay a living wage. And it didn't need to, since Alec had brought in most of the money in their relationship. That freed Lilly up to spend most of her time with the other socialite wives partying their way around the Twin Cities. And since Alec brought home the bacon, he reasoned he was in charge of decorating the loft, deciding what should be bought, where and how their living space was to be arranged.

His money equaled his rules.

And she had let him set the parameters of their roles in the marriage. He went to work each day at Wells Fargo while she had a role not much more than a trophy wife—arm candy for corporate functions and holiday parties. She worked for the pure enjoyment of helping others, offering her services for a nominal fee in return for the greater good. That nominal fee allowed her to partake in mimosa brunches.

Ugh... was that all I did?

But now she would need to make her talents bring home her own bacon.

Her drafting table, which Alec was more than willing to let her take, sat in an unassembled pile in the entryway, her computer tower and monitors alongside. She wasn't sure where she wanted to put it. How much of her grandparents' home did she want to completely change? Lilly needed an office, a creative place all her own. Perhaps in the morning she'd explore the house more and get ideas of how to make it more her home. There were plenty of rooms in the old house, certainly one could be easily converted to suit her needs.

The crafty country chic motif that her grandmother had spent her whole life curating throughout the house pulled at Lilly in two directions. One led her down a nostalgic path, the warm scent of sugar cookies and hot chocolate mingled with a long-lost sense of belonging and love. The other shouted at her that all these paintings of barns, covered bridges, and little Amish girls in fields needed to go.

Now.

"I don't need to decide on anything tonight," Lilly spoke to the empty house, as if to ease its worries. "I've got all the time in the world to get things how I want them."

She paused and sighed as only the tick-tock of the grandfather clock down the main hall broke the silence. The clock chimed six o'clock and reminded Lilly she was starving. She had barely eaten most of the day. A local pizza place shared the same block as Mrs. Swenson's realty office, perhaps they delivered. After a quick Google search for the phone number, Lilly ordered supper and knew she worried the employee when she excessively thanked them for delivering all the way out to her farm. With food on its way, Lilly unpacked another box in silence.

She missed hearing the city noises, trucks and cars moving about Downtown Minneapolis, the muffled chatter of tenants outside the door. Her ears hurt at the lack of sound outside.

"I'm going to be talking to myself just so I don't go crazy from loneliness and silence," she smirked as she stood and stretched.

Twenty minutes later, the pizza arrived. Lilly found herself so starved for not only food but human contact that she bit back an invitation for the delivery boy to join her. Certainly, the high schooler would think this was the start of a low-budget skin flick, so she kept her mouth shut as she handed him the money. She sat amongst her meager belongings and ate her pizza in contemplative silence.

Lilly glanced through the large living room to the back of the house. She could see the barn in the growing dusk. A muffled moooooo drifted toward the house.

Could she actually run a farm? The thought seemed outlandish. She was sure her grandparents left enough money for her to care for the cows' needs, bedding, feed, medical care—do cows need medical care?—but could she run the farm? Earn a living off the meager herd? There was no mention of any cropland in the will, only the building site, so she was certain she couldn't make a living off raising any sort of crop.

Lilly didn't have the slightest clue on how to run a lawnmower, let alone a five-ton tractor.

Perhaps Ryan could help her out. What was his number again? Lilly dug Mrs. Swenson's business card from her pocket and looked at the name and number scrawled on the back.

Ryan.

Yes, un-neighborly Ryan. She frowned as she shoved the card deep into her back pocket. What was his problem, anyway?

Apparently, she was his problem.

The amount of daggers thrown her way by his glare assured her that he, in fact, remembered her and the events nearly fifteen years ago, and that he did, in fact, hold tightly to the pain she had unwillingly caused.

On top of being newly divorced, Lilly now had to deal with a resentful ex-boyfriend.

Wonderful.

Another cow voiced her annoyance over something. Lilly glanced in the direction of the barn and bit her lip. It had to be after their supper time, should she go out and feed the cows? What time did they need to eat? More importantly: what did they eat? Was Ryan coming to tend to them tonight, or did seeing the new owner of the property mean he was off the hook?

"I should call him," Lilly muttered as she walked into the kitchen with the pizza box. Half the pizza remained and would be a welcomed breakfast in the morning. Or perhaps she could heal old wounds between her and Ryan with the promise of cheesy goodness if he came to help with feeding the cows. What was that phrase her mom used constantly? The way through a man's heart is through his stomach.

She stared out of the back door at the barn. The idea of attempting to feed twelve cows made her blood run cold. "I should call him. Just to double check he is coming..."

Lilly exhaled loudly as she punched in Ryan's number.

It rang twice before, "What."

Though now a little deeper and graveled over the years, the sound of Ryan's voice transported her back a lifetime ago, startling her with visions of school lockers and Homecoming dances. She almost pulled her phone away from her ear at the sudden flood of memories.

"You there?"

"Is... this Ryan?" Lilly asked, fearing the response.

"You called me," he snapped. "What do you want?"

Oh, this is going to be fun. Lilly took a calming breath before she spoke. "This is Lilly Rhodes, I'm back now... living at the Schmidt farm—"

"I know who you are."

Seriously? She cleared her throat. "I was just checking to see if you were planning on coming over to feed the cows toni—?"

"I'm on my way now. I'll be there in five."

The line went quiet.

"What the—" Lilly gripped her phone in both hands and let out an exasperated scream at the blank screen. "What an absolute jerk!" She stormed out of the kitchen and down the porch steps, her feet carrying her to the barn before she fully realized where she was headed.

Maybe she'd dodged a bullet by dumping him in high school and leaving town.

"The first chance I get, I'm going to get a new farmhand! I don't care how nice his aunt is, he's gone. How could my grandparents like someone like that?"

She stopped before the closed barn doors, the building cast in shadow as the sun started to set. Inside looked more foreboding than it had that afternoon. Lilly cursed herself for not grabbing a flashlight in her march out of the house. She went to the door and slowly pushed it open, surprised that the smell still didn't get any better.

"I can do this," Lilly assured herself. "I don't need jerky Ryan to do the job. This farm is my responsibility now."

Dandelion bellowed out a welcome—or was it a reprimand?—as Lilly felt along the inside wall for a light switch of some sort. Her fingers brushed against rough wooden walls and studs, what she was hoping was only some sort of linen instead of cobwebs, but she finally found something that felt like a switch. She flipped it and a harsh yellow light came from behind her. It was the switch for the yard light on the outside of the barn. Lilly sighed, thankful for some sort of light, and went back to her search.

"What are you doing?"

Lilly spun around at the barked question. She instantly knew the voice and her lingering annoyance from their previous conversation flared once again. "I'm trying to find a light switch," she returned.

A heavy sigh came from the shadowy barn. She saw a black mass move around the opposite side of the barn doors. Suddenly the interior exploded in a wash of light. Lilly grunted as she tried to shield her eyes.

"Light switches are over here," Ryan grunted again.

"Thank you." Lilly lowered her hand, hoping to get a better look at Ryan. His back was to her as he bent over the front of the cows' stalls. He wore the typical uniform of a farm boy: jeans stained with God only knew what, an untucked flannel shirt to guard against the growing chill of night, and the faded green baseball cap she recognized from earlier.

"And to answer your question, I'm checking on my cows," Lilly took a step toward him, trying to see what he was up to. If she could figure out what he was doing, then she could dismiss the farmer from any future duties and be rid of his rudeness.

He snorted. "Your cows."

He lifted a bale of hay from a stack next to the stalls. Without another word, he broke it into sections and fed one to each cow. Their moaning ceased as the food was placed before them.

Lilly put her hands on her hips. "Yes, my cows."

Ryan tossed the last hay chunk to the final cow, brushed his hands off on his jeans, and turned around. Despite being hidden under the cap brim, his brown eyes sparked with a dangerous, taunting light. "What are their names?"

Oh, crap, Maggie said them earlier...

"Dandelion," Lilly pointed to the first cow. She was never going to forget her. "And her daughters..." Oh, crap, what are her daughters' names...?

Ryan arched a brow expectantly.

Lilly felt her cheeks burn under his hard stare. Why did he care if she knew what their names were? Was this some sort of stupid country test? If you didn't know all your cows' names, the cow police would come and take them away?

"Daisy and Daffodil."

Was that a tiny glimmer of pleased surprise that passed over his face?

"And those two?"

"Peony..." Lilly's voice faltered as she looked at the two cows, who chewed contentedly on their supper, "and Poppy. I don't know the names of the rest of the herd, your aunt didn't tell me."

"Hmmph." Ryan brushed past her and went around to the back of the stalls.

Lilly followed him, her anger overpowering any need to watch where she was stepping. "Hey! What is your problem?"

"I have no problem," Ryan shrugged. He took a large metal shovel from the far wall and began to push the manure from behind the cows into a deep gutter just at the end of their stalls.

"Yes you do! I have been nothing but polite—oh, dear God," Lilly gasped and stopped short, her breath and stomach stuck in her throat. She abruptly turned away.

Ryan continued to clear out the stalls, moving around Lilly as if she weren't there. She certainly caught a smirk under his hat. He was enjoying her discomfort!

She watched him work in silence, neither making an effort to continue any conversation. After he cleared the manure and soiled straw from the stalls, he went to a large panel on the far wall and flipped a large switch. Lilly thought it looked more at home in Frankenstein's laboratory than a barn. The clatter of grinding gears and swinging chains filled the barn, drowning out any noises from the cows. Lilly saw a conveyor belt move along the gutter, pushing the straw and manure down into a hole.

"What's that doing?" Lilly shouted.

"Clearing the manure." Ryan pulled a large straw bale from a stack near the Frankenstein switch. He broke it apart and tossed fresh bedding into the stalls.

"Where does it go?"

Her question was lost in the noise of the gutter cleaner. Lilly crossed her arms over her chest and waited for him to finish his chores. She wasn't going to waste her breath trying to talk over this noise if he wasn't going to be civil enough to answer. She also needed to keep the pungent stench of freshly churning manure out of her nose and mouth.

After the new straw was in place, Ryan turned off the gutter cleaner. He barely looked at her as he walked back out to the main walk. He went down the walk to a door Lilly hadn't noticed earlier and disappeared into a sort of back storeroom. Ryan emerged with two contraptions Lilly could only describe as scuba tanks crossed with a squid. Four metal nozzles hung down from a plastic cup that attached to a longer hose that went to the tank.

One more memory unlocked itself as she stared at the contraptions. Their names and functions sat on the tip of her tongue. Her former life seemed to amuse itself by tormenting her so.

Lilly watched him in silence and amazement, astonished at how swiftly he maneuvered the machines. Ryan slid the two metal attachments into a steel pipe above the cows' pens and hung the tank from a thin wire. Once that was in place, he took a blue paper towel from his back jeans pocket and wiped off each of the teats on Dandelion's large udder, then attached the four nozzles. He stood, pushed a sequence of buttons on the tank, and walked to the next cow to repeat the process on the second tank.

"What are those things?" she asked.

"You used to do this all the time, City Girl," Ryan grumbled. "Figure it out. Or did all that city living wipe your brain clean?"

She stared at him, mouth agape and her face flushed with humiliation.

It was bad enough to be thrown back on the "old homestead" after being absent so many years. She practically grew up on her grandparents' farm, born and raised in Lone Tree. Up until she turned fifteen, she had known the barn and all the outbuildings on the farm like the back of her hand. As Lilly gazed upon all the instruments and equipment in the barn, they all rang with dim familiarity, like trying to remember something from a dream. The very fact that she was back in the place she had spent so much of her childhood and couldn't recall something that had been so second nature to her at one time ate her up more now than when she'd signed the divorce papers.

Lilly jumped as the tank attached to Dandelion whirred to life and milk began to suction out of her udder into the tubing and into the pipe.

"Milkers," she finally spoke as her foggy memory parted enough to pull out the right words. "Tie stall milkers."

His silence didn't surprise her anymore, only added to her growing dislike for the man. She jumped out of his way as he moved from cow to cow, shifting the milking machines down the row as each cow's milk ran out. Lilly noticed how once he had hung a milker on one cow, he immediately was crouching by the next and wiping her udder. If he wasn't going to tell her how to milk a cow, she was damn sure going to figure it out on her own.

If Lilly was timing things right, the whole milking process took about ten minutes for each cow. Lilly watched intently, taking mental notes on how he handled himself around each animal, how he placed the milkers on the udders, and what buttons he pushed to make the machines work. It seemed to Lilly that Ryan's years of this routine and knowledge of each cow probably expedited the whole process.

Once more, without a word, Ryan gathered the milkers from above the cows and returned them to the back storage room. As the door closed behind him, Lilly caught a quick glimpse of a large silver cylinder. Now that milking was done, she went back to watching the man who went about his business as if she wasn't there. There was something peculiar about him, but she couldn't quite put her finger on it.

"How many times do the cows get milked a day?" She asked as he brushed past her. Again her question went unanswered.

Lilly followed him. She finally realized what was odd about him as he moved. Ryan limped slightly on the left side as he walked. What did Maggie say before, he busted his leg up? That could mean a myriad of injuries, especially for a farmer. She watched him in silence, wondering if she could ask about his injury. *No, he'd probably storm out of here*, Lilly told herself. Although, right now, that wouldn't be a bad thing.

He inspected the water cups that stood at the end of each stall. She didn't remember seeing them before, but she was too busy falling face first into muck to notice. Each cup had a piece of tubing that let out a stream of water whenever a cow nudged it with her muzzle. Ryan tightened one that sprayed little Daffodil right up the nose. The little cow went back for a drink, hesitant for a moment at the thought of another impromptu shower.

Lilly hugged her arms across her middle. She felt nervous. Why? Why was she so nervous around Ryan? They had grown up together, spent nearly every waking hour at this very farm, even dated... She knew Ryan. Right? It's never easy reconnecting with an ex, especially one you weren't prepared to run into. Lilly understood that. What had she expected of this abrupt interaction with Ryan? Not butterflies and rainbows and a cutesy reunion certainly, but one a little more civil than the arctic cold shade he was throwing her way.

"It's... it's good to see you again,"

Ryan leveled a withering glare at her, and she immediately wanted to flee to the house.

He walked past her and out the barn door. Lilly scrambled to catch up with him. The sun had just set, and the night grew suddenly cold. Her annoyance with Ryan was enough to keep the chill at bay, though. He was almost to his truck, parked once more by her Kia, by the time she caught up.

For someone with a bad leg, he moves fast!

"Ryan," she called as she jogged to walk beside him. "I think we got off on the wrong foot. Let's start over."

"No need." Ryan dug in his pocket for his keys.

Lilly took advantage of this as his pace slowed while he extracted his keys. With a few hasty skips she placed herself in between him and the driver's door. His eyes widened, then narrowed at her little stunt. She smiled up at him, her best impersonation of his aunt's realtor smile. In the harsh glow from the yard light next to the house, Lilly saw the scowl form under his five o'clock shadow.

"Please, Ryan." Lilly held up a hand. She stopped herself from placing it on his chest. That would be too intimate of a peace-offering for someone who had decided to hate her before they were even reacquainted. "I'm just trying to be friendly. We're going to be working together, and we used to be—"

"Working together!" Ryan interrupted. "We are not going to be working together. I'll come twice a day to milk, feed, and bed the cows and let them out on pasture. You'll be inside, keeping your designer ankle boots dry and your fake nails clean. You couldn't even find the light switch, how do you think you'll be of any help to me?"

Her cheeks burned, and she felt her calm demeanor slip away.

I am done with this!

Lilly stood up straight, matching his height. She fought the urge to whip his stupid John Deere hat off his jerk head. "Mr. Swenson, I assume my grandparents set up a method of monetary compensation for your work before they passed?"

"Do you think your big words are going to scare me?" Ryan snarled. "That the poor, country bumpkin will bow to your will if you use words with more than two syllables?"

"You didn't answer my question," Lilly narrowed her eyes. "I know you're being paid to take care of my cows—yes, my cows." Lilly jabbed a finger at him as he began to open his mouth. "But my grandparents aren't in charge anymore. I am. And if you wish to still have a job here, as I'm sure you do since I'm certain no other farm will hire you in your condition—"

His eyes narrowed and darkened.

"I can just as easily find someone else to come and take care of my cows. I've tried to be nice to you, tried to learn about the cows, and from the start you have been rude to me and dismissed me. I'm sorry about what happened fifteen years ago but if our past is going to be a problem for you, if we can't act like civilized adults to each other, let me know now so I can make new plans." Lilly hoped her voice relayed the confidence she was faking.

Ryan gripped his keys tighter in his hand.

She crossed her arms over her chest, prepared to wait him out.

"Excuse me, Mrs. Rhodes, but I need to get going." Ryan's words were clipped. "I need to get some rest before I come back in the morning."

Lilly backed away from the truck and allowed him to climb inside. She kept her eyes on him as he started and maneuvered the vehicle to leave. He kept his eyes averted from hers, though she knew he must have felt her gaze burning into his skull. Not until he was half way down the driveway did Lilly exhale a shaky breath.

She walked back to the house, her arms and legs quivering with adrenaline and what she hoped was triumph in taking a stand against the bad-mannered farmer. As she mounted the stairs and entered the house, her elation wavered suddenly and her stomach dropped.

She might have won this battle with Ryan, but what type of war had she just brought down on herself?

Chapter Three

After a long night of fitful sleep, Lilly's alarm jolted her into an unfamiliar world of gingham and lace. For a moment, she felt like Dorothy waking up in Oz and trying to process the brilliance that was Technicolor. Maneuvering around the farmhouse still felt like a dream, flashes of memories slowing her adjustment to her new living arrangement. In the haze of a poor night's sleep, she found it hard to tell what was a memory, a dream, or reality.

As she got dressed in jeans and a light-weight cardigan set, Lilly contemplated putting her clothes away in the dressers and closet. She opened the drawers and smiled thinly at her grandmother's clothes still folded neatly, silently waiting for her return. Lilly brushed her fingers carefully over a sweater, the delicate lace around the collar appearing as pristine as the day it was purchased. A dull ache formed in the pit of her stomach as memories of her grandmother wearing that sweater flickered in her mind. It had been close to two decades since she'd last seen Grandma Beverly, and the fact that she still wore that old garment gave Lilly an odd sense of peace.

If she didn't give up on this old sweater, then she surely hadn't given up on me.

Lilly gently closed the drawer and tapped the top of the dresser absently. She'd have to move her grandparents' things out eventually, to make room for her life in the farmhouse.

But not quite yet.

Lilly finally made her way into the kitchen, her stomach leading the way. An empty pantry greeted her, making her stomach growl louder. Yet the thought of the remaining pizza in the fridge made her hunger sour. One can only handle so much pizza in a twenty-four hour period. Taking a trip into town moved up on her list of things to do that day as she regretfully snagged a piece of cold pizza and made her way toward the front door. She grabbed her purse and keys from the front table and exited into the early morning.

Springtime outside in the country, even in the morning, is never truly quiet. Lilly heard her cows lowing in the barn as they started to wake, along with the distant calls of neighboring herds stirring. Low rumbles, almost like thunder, drifted through the grove of trees to the north and east of the farm, signaling the beginnings of field work. Lilly glanced at her watch and shook her head; she wasn't much of a morning person herself, but after years of marriage to a man who regularly saw both five o'clocks in a day, she'd become a reluctant early riser.

Given that it was a quarter to eight by the time she made her way out the door, she wondered when exactly farmers started their days around here. She didn't remember when her grandfather started his morning chores. He'd started to do less around the farm when she and her family still came around. She couldn't remember the last time she saw the farm actually functioning.

She yawned, stomped down the porch steps, and added coffee to her mental grocery list. A quick Google search last night had revealed the nearest Caribou Coffee was 25.6 miles away, and Starbucks even further out at 28.9 miles. However, Lone Tree did host a small café. Lilly made a note to check out the café later that day.

I thought Starbucks were everywhere, this is unacceptable, Lilly mused as she hoisted her purse higher on her shoulder. I must obtain an adequate coffee supply out here in the sticks.

The rusted green Chevy parked next to her car caught her off guard for a moment before her brain registered that Ryan must be doing his morning chores. Lilly looked at the old truck then over to the barn, biting her lip as she fought with the idea of going to the barn to say good morning. It was a shame they'd had such a rocky first meeting. She wanted to at least reach a civil peace with him.

However, after how he had treated her the night before, and how she had also threatened his job, she figured keeping a healthy distance from the hired help would be a good thing for now. She started up her Kia, turned around in the driveway, and headed toward town.

At least, what she thought was the road toward town.

The gravel roads outside of town were laid in a large grid pattern, and an intersection was normally a sign of the end of one field or property line and the beginning of another. Lilly followed the road as long as it went straight, vaguely remembering that town was due west from her grandparents' farm. Long stretches of cropland blurred by on each side of the road. The fields were black with freshly plowed soil. Large farming equipment, foreign to Lilly and certainly not resembling any tractor she'd even seen, chugged along the rows of dirt, preparing for planting. Lilly allowed herself to be gently lulled by the rhythmic rumble of the gravel under her tires, her gaze softening as she took in the sights around her.

Suddenly, her due west road stopped at the fork as a large irrigation ditch cut through the road. The gravel split to the left and right, either direction curving along the winding course of the ditch.

"Which way is town?" Lilly muttered as she glanced at either fork. She tried recalling Maggie's directions from the day before; however, nothing came to mind. Vague memories of driving out to the farm with her parents from Lone Tree intermingled with the return trip made by her grandparents.

And who decided not to name country roads?

Lilly took a deep breath and aimed her Kia to the right fork. She wasn't sure which direction the road would eventually send her in, but her smart screen on her dash stated she now headed northwest.

"The fork must loop around the ravine a bit and go back straight west toward town," Lilly assured herself as she followed the winding gravel road, the ravine to her left.

The road continued to follow the ravine until she crossed a small bridge. Her dash compass read due west. Town was only a few minutes away.

Twenty minutes passed and no town met her gaze, only acres and acres of what would soon become corn, bean, and hay fields. The sporadic farmsteads dotting the landscape grew even further apart as she drove on. The once soothing soundtrack of gravel churning beneath her car shifted aggressively. Large chunks of stone popped against the undercarriage of her Kia, pieces of stone exploding against the wheel wells and below her feet.

"Great. I'm lost," Lilly fumed as she pulled over to the side of the gravel road.

She glanced down at her purse lying in the passenger seat next to her and instantly felt the fool; her phone had Google Maps on it. She could open up the app and, without even having an exact address, the automated voice could direct her to where she needed to go.

Lilly dug through her purse and withdrew the forgotten device. She opened her navigation app, plugged in her location, and hit the search icon, but the screen went blank with only a small white turning circle in the middle.

"Oh, no you don't," Lilly shook her phone. "Don't tell me you can't find me!"

The white circle chugged along, growing slower with every rotation.

"No, no, no, no!" Lilly grunted as the screen flashed to reveal a stylized radio tower with the words "NO SIGNAL, TAP TO TRY AGAIN" underneath.

Lilly tossed her phone back onto the passenger seat and stared out beyond the windshield. She could possibly turn around and follow the road back to the original split, try taking the left fork to see if that would get her to town. Or she could try to get back to her grandparents'—her farm— once more. The sea of cropland around her seemed to swirl and spin.

"Great, just great." Lilly thumped the steering wheel with the heel of her hand. "Got lost my first time leaving the farm."

Lilly grabbed her phone once more and opened her car door. She reloaded her GPS app and held her phone up at arm's length, willing the device to find some sort of WiFi or 4G signal. Over and over again, she restarted her app, walking around her car.

Before she realized it, she had wandered down into the grassy ditch along the gravel road. Her foot sunk down into dead grass growth left behind after the snow melted, muddy water squishing up over her shoe.

"Great," she muttered while attempting to free her foot.

The mucky ground held onto her shoe like glue, her other foot at risk of being sucked into a soggy fate as well. Lilly trudged back toward the gravel, feeling the mud and dead grass wrap around her feet as if the ditch intended to trap her. No matter where she put her foot, she couldn't seem to get a hold of solid ground. Finally, the grasses released her and Lilly stumbled up the side of the ditch, landing unceremoniously on her back side in the dirt with a wounded cry.

Lilly stared at her soggy feet and watched as water ran out of her shoes and socks. She crossed her elbows over her knees and let her forehead rest on her arm. She tried to take a few calming breaths as her yogi had instructed her many times, but she found it difficult to obtain the inner peace she sought at that moment.

"At least I have some flip flops in the car," Lilly consoled herself. She rose stiffly to her feet, grimacing with each squelch of her shoes. She opened the back passenger door and rummaged around the floor for the pair of flip flops she had thrown back there a couple of months ago after her best friend Katie had taken her to get mani-pedis after Alec had served her the divorce papers.

I wonder if there's a nail salon in town. Lilly sat on the cluttered back seat and tore off her soiled shoes and socks, threw them all to the floor, and slipped on the plastic sandals.

What else can go wrong? She asked herself as she wiggled her toes. Her bright blue nails glinted in the sunlight, revealing a few chipped spots in the polish. Finding a nail salon bumped up a few notches on her mental list of necessities, a close second to coffee shop.

"Maybe I should just head back to the farm..." She pressed the heels of both hands over her eyes and let loose a cathartic noise of exasperation. "If I could only find it!"

A knock on the car window nearly sent her out of her skin. She gripped the seat back and faced the source of the noise. Just outside her car door stood a man dressed in jeans and an untucked button-down Oxford. He bent down to look into the open door and gave a wide smile, his bright white teeth in contrast to the tan of his face.

"Good morning, ma'am," the man smiled again, "might be a stupid question, but are you lost?"

Lilly could only nod, her patience and dignity running thin.

"Name's Maxwell Carpenter," he extended his hand into her car.

Lilly slowly shook his hand. "Lilly Rhodes."

"Rhodes..." Mr. Carpenter gave her hand a firm squeeze. "Say, you're not the same Rhodes that took over the Schmidt farm, right?"

"That's right," Lilly found herself nodding again. She took the time to take in Mr. Carpenter a little more. His business-casual attire seemed at odds with a man out for a walk in the middle of the country, though his tanned skin said otherwise. He looked to be in his late forties, close cut blond hair that seemed to be thinning and graying. His smile was warm and his eyes appeared friendly.

"Then you must've worked with Maggie on that deal," Mr. Carpenter went on. "We all had a pool going to see who'd be able to sell that place first when it went on the market."

"On the market?" Lilly twisted in her seat to better face him. "I'm sorry, I didn't think it was ever on the market."

Mr. Carpenter nodded, a sheepish smile slipping across his face. "Sorry, Ms. Rhodes. Slip of the tongue. True, it was never on the market in the normal sense. There was a time limit on the will for when the next of kin had time to claim it. Then, it'd be put on the market if that window closed."

"How do you know Mrs. Swenson?"

And how do you know so much about my farm?

"We work in real estate though for different companies." Mr. Carpenter dug into the breast pocket of his shirt and produced a business card. "Prairie Pine Realty."

Lilly took the card, politely looking it over briefly before tucking it into her jeans pocket. "To answer your original question, Mr. Carpenter—"

"Please, call me Max, all my friends do,"

"Yes, well, Max, I am lost." Lilly returned the smile, though a little strained. "I'm trying to get to town and I think I took a wrong turn. And my phone's not getting any signal for GPS."

"That's easily done around here," Max nodded. "This part of the county is a cell phone dead zone. Seems like every other week, they're putting up a new tower somewhere out here. You'd think with all those towers, we'd avoid having a dead zone, huh? It's this little triangle sliver that's just out of the range of the nearby towers. People can drive right through it normally and never notice a change in service. But I guess most people aren't on their phones out here, so they never even notice, you know?"

Lilly looked at him with a blank gaze. *Does everyone around here just ramble?*

"Sorry," Max smiled again. "You'll want to turn around and head the way you came. You'll follow the ravine so it stays on your right hand side, alright? You'll get back to the split in the road that got you here in the first place, and you'll want to keep going straight. That would have been the left fork if you'd turned left at the first place. Follow that for about, say, ten minutes and you'll be at the northern end of town."

Lilly climbed out of the back seat and followed the quick gestures that accented his almost spit-fire directions. Suddenly the pathway to town appeared clear and obvious. She turned from Mr. Carpenter, as if to inspect the field behind her car, hoping that he wouldn't see her flushed cheeks. She wondered how many lost city folk he'd rescued from the corn fields and knew she was a sad member of that tally.

"What are you doing out here in a ditch by an empty field?" Lilly asked.

Max smiled. "It's plowed, recently planted. Not entirely empty."

Lilly arched a brow.

"Sorry, sorry." Max cleared his throat. "I have a client who is interested in purchasing some farm land, and I came out here to double check property lines."

She glanced around the sparse landscape. "I don't see any for sale signs."

"Agriculture real estate doesn't always use those garish for sale signs. Most land ads are placed online or in agriculture magazines. Keeps the inexperienced prospects down to make room for the quality investors. Now, do you remember how to get back to town?"

She tried to reconcile his landmarks with what she remembered of her spotty mental map so that clarity of the way out of the field remained crystal clear until she got to the main road. If it was as easy as turning around, and going straight through the forked road, then she should be able to follow those directions out of the backlot for Children of the Corn.

"Thank you, Max, I think I should be able to make it to town from here."

"You're welcome, Ms. Rhodes." Max stepped back from her car and gave a wave. "We'll see you again soon!"

Lilly rolled up the window and threw her car in reverse. After some awkward K turns, Lilly finally got her Kia facing the right direction. She glanced in the rearview mirror and saw Mr. Carpenter standing in the middle of the road, still waving.

"What a weird place, random people just hanging out in vacant fields waiting for stranded people," Lilly muttered as she focused once more on driving. She snuck a glance at the rear view and almost slammed on the breaks.

Mr. Carpenter was no longer in the middle of the road behind her. In fact, she couldn't tell where he had gone.

"Great." Lilly shook her head and continued back to the fork split. "Now I'm imagining random people offering help to stranded drivers."

Lilly pushed that thought from her mind as she focused on getting back to town. She followed Mr. Carpenter's directions and went straight through the fork—going on the left split, as he'd said—and continued straight. She hoped that she'd finally find town and get to a grocery store. Her one slice of pizza almost an hour ago hadn't held her over as long as she would have liked. On top of nerves from being lost, her stomach started to grumble again.

Mr. Carpenter's directions proved surprisingly simple, and Lilly found her way into town in less than ten minutes. The gravel road she followed into town suddenly turned into pavement as it fed into the heart of the town. After a short jaunt through a residential section, her road came to a stop sign at a larger street, marked with Junction County Road 45. Lilly glanced to the right and left, noticing that this road was also marked Main Street, and store fronts and business marquees hung from the brick façades. With a smile, Lilly turned left and found a parking spot along the main drag.

She stepped out of her car, hopped onto the large sidewalk, and felt as if she had been transported to Mayberry. The quaint storefronts boasted unfamiliar names, only a few major chains of banks and investing firms popped up in between the mom-n-pop stores. Lilly shouldered her bag and continued on down the sidewalk, amazed at how few people she had to maneuver around. In downtown Minneapolis, the sidewalks and Skyways were crammed with people, in attire running the gamut of thousand dollar business suits to homeless shelter Lost and Found. Here, she met the middle ground, plenty of jeans and flannel, John Deere green and Carhart brown.

Lilly scanned the stores, seeing what matched up with her memories. A lot can change in a small town in almost twenty years, about as much as it wouldn't change. More than a handful of store fronts were dark with FOR LEASE/SALE signs hanging in the once vibrant display windows, and almost all of those signs were from Prairie Pine Reality, Maxwell Carpenter's company.

She shook her head, unsure if she had really met the realtor or if she'd had one of those experiences straight out of a tabloid, with the angelic figure leading the stranded motorist to safety only to disappear when the traveler turned to thank them. Of course, these stories always ended with the motorist finding out the person they'd seen had been dead for years. Lilly shivered despite the mild spring morning.

If that turns out to be the case, Lilly stopped in front of another abandoned storefront with a Prairie Pine Realty sign, *I'm burning rubber back to Minneapolis.*

A familiar smell piqued her nostrils, distracting her from the possibilities of paranormal encounters. She took a deep breath and exhaled loudly. "Coffee!" Lilly exclaimed, spinning on her heel toward the delectable aroma.

A woman walking by shot her a concerned glance and gave her a wide berth as she passed.

Next to the empty business was a sight for sore eyes and stomach. A café that boasted all day breakfast seeped wafts of fresh drip brew and something drenched in cinnamon. "Grandma's Attic Café" was painted on the front windows in bright blue. Lilly hurried into the café and allowed herself to soak in the welcoming smells.

Along the street-facing windows were small booths full of likely regulars, elderly couples having their daily coffee outing while planning to spend a good portion of the morning in their sunbathed seats. Past a row of tables was the counter, where the patrons either sat at bar stools nursing their coffee or stood waiting impatiently for their order to go.

A woman about Lilly's age manned the counter, calling out confirmations of refills or pastries to go, shoving tangles of brown hair from her face with the back of her hand. At this hour, the morning rush must have ebbed, but the kitchen and the front counter still ran at high speed to ensure the customers were satisfied.

"I'm home," Lilly sighed as she slowly made her way to the counter.

It definitely wasn't a Starbucks, or even a Caribou. The décor screamed small town in farming country with tractor tin plaques and metal milk jugs with the type of patina that would make an American Picker drool. The eating area was adorned with mismatched tables, chairs, and place settings that certainly were acquired from yard sales, flea markets, and grandparents' basements.

Which would explain the name of the place. Lilly couldn't help the smirk tugging at the corner of her mouth. *If it wasn't so heavy on the country chic, I'd think I was in one of those indie coffee shops in Minneapolis.*

"Can I help you, ma'am?" The woman behind the counter called out as she wiped down the counter as a large man in overalls lumbered off his bar stool.

Lilly glanced up at the handwritten menu on large chalkboards hanging behind the front counter. "Yes, I was wondering if—"

"If I never! Lillian Schmidt, is that you!?"

She froze as her name shrieked out from behind the bar. A handful of people called her Lillian, normally when she was in trouble, and she knew none of them were in that café. Two of them were also dead.

The woman raced down the counter to a hinged section, shoved it up, and didn't stop to keep it from slamming down behind her. All eyes in the café turned at the noise and focused on the two women. Lilly could only stand still as the brown haired woman wrapped her in a tight hug.

"Oh, Lillian, I'm so glad you stopped by!" She squeezed Lilly tighter.

"Um," Lilly swallowed. "I'm sorry..."

"It's about time you showed up back here, Lillian." The woman released her and shook a playfully admonishing finger at Lilly. "You've been in town, what, a day and you finally make it to my place? Ma said you were back and I was waiting for you to stop in for something to eat last night since that old house you're in now is emptier than church on Super Bowl Sunday."

"What?" Lilly's mouth hung open.

"So, what'll it be? You seem like a caramel latte to me."

"Um, I'm sorry, but I don't—"

"It's on the house, Lillian." The woman started to turn back to return behind the bar, but Lilly grabbed her hand. "You're going to love my caramel latte. I think this recipe is the best one yet, right Earl?"

An older man, dressed in clothes that looked as if he walked straight out a Steinbeck novel, sat hunched on a stool farther down the counter. He raised his head at the mention of his name, tipped his faded and frayed John Deere hat, then went back to his coffee.

"I'm sorry, I'm going to sound like a horrible person but I—"

"Don't remember me?" Pale blue eyes sparkled. "Don't worry about that. You didn't remember Ry-Ry right away, either. I know it's been a while since you've been to the old haunts."

Lilly watched in dumbfounded silence as the woman scurried behind the counter and started to make her drink.

"I'm sorry, you're going to have to back up." Lilly finally blurted out.

The espresso machine roared to life as the woman started to steam the milk and prepare the shots. Lilly could see her mouth moving but couldn't hear a word over the noise of the machine. Given the racket it made, Lilly figured it was a hand-me-down from a chain coffee shop.

The woman returned with a steaming, foamy mug that released sweet caramel and vanilla swirls into the air.

"But it's so good to see you again, Lillian." The woman completed her unknowingly one-sided conversation.

"Back up, back up," Lilly held up her hands. "You know I don't remember you… please… remind me? I couldn't hear you over the espresso machine."

"Certainly! Faith Fischer. But you probably wouldn't know that name, I married Tobiah Fischer after high school."

That means nothing to me, Lilly fought the urge to roll her eyes. What she did remember from her time in this small town during her childhood was how the adults always made sure one knew who they were married to or related to, as if one's identity could only be validated through one's extended family.

Faith replenished a stack of napkins on the counter. "But you'd probably remember me better as Faith Swenson."

Another Swenson.

"You wouldn't happen to be related to Maggie Swenson?"

"Did you bump your head and have one of those soap opera level amnesia episodes?" Faith laughed. She wiped her hands off on the apron tied around her hips. "Maggie is my aunt!"

"Maggie is your aunt," Lilly repeated as she took a sip of her latte. The creamy sweetness burned with just the right amount of heat and acidity. It almost rivaled the lattes she'd grown used to in the Cities.

"I guess a lot has pushed us all out of your memories over the years, huh?"

Heat rose in Lilly's cheeks. "I'm sorry, it's been quite a few years since I was last back in town," she replied, her words checked. "I can't be expected to remember everyone I met fifteen years ago."

Faith placed a small plate piled high with sugared donuts in front of Lilly. "Don't be so serious, Lillian. I'm just giving you some good natured ribbing. Make you feel at home."

"Thanks." Lilly hesitantly lifted a donut off the plate. It was still warm and the sugar melted between the dough and her fingers. She bit into it, thankful for the lull in conversation and a homemade confection. She scoured her memory, trying to place Faith in a flashback. When she visited her grandparents, there were a couple of kids from the neighboring farm that would stop by occasionally...

"We did hang out when we were younger, when I visited my grandparents," Lilly said slowly as the pieces fell into place.

Faith leaned her elbows on the counter in front of her and smiled warmly. "We did."

"I'm so sorry, Faith," Lilly looked down at her lap. "It's just been a really rough couple months, with Grandpa and Grandma passing, then my divorce, and last night didn't make it any better—"

"Yeah, Ry-Ry told me all about it." Faith grinned as she walked out from behind the counter. She held a coffee pot in each hand and went to each occupied table, offering refills on drip brew.

"Ry-Ry?"

"Oh, he'd kill me if he knew I called him that in front of you!" Faith beamed as she returned to her spot by the espresso machine.

"Ryan Swenson is your brother..." Lilly muttered as she gave a small grimace. Faith was Ryan's older sister; she and Faith hadn't interacted much when they were growing up. Something about being too cool to hang out with the little siblings and their dorky friends. Lilly smiled, remembering Faith as the too cool teenager. Apparently, the two women had interacted enough for Faith to give her a positively glowing welcome.

"You sure gave him a scare last night."

"Oh, I did?" Lilly's grimace exploded into a grin. She allowed herself a few moments to bask in that small victory. "I hope he's not too mad about me threatening his job, I was just upset—"

"Don't worry too much about Ryan." Faith said, her tone softening. "It's good for him to have someone put him in his place now and then. The family hasn't had the best of luck trying to reign his temper in, so it'll do him good to have you to keep him in line. No offense, Lillian, but all these five years working for your grandma and grandpa probably did more to enable his current mood more than anyone. Harold and Bev really let him have his way running the farm. He's hell to live with if things don't go his way."

That would explain his hostilities toward me last night. Lilly chewed on her donut thoughtfully. *I've upset his status quo.* "Can I ask what happened?"

"Nothing that hasn't happened around here a hundred times," Faith shrugged as she plucked a donut off the plate and bit into it, continuing her explanation around the sugary confection, "boy grows up around cows all his life, thinks he's invincible. Then, one day, he grows careless and the lughead lets a bull pin him."

Lilly winced as she sipped her latte.

"He's been just miserable to be around since then." Faith shook her head. "But enough about Ry-Ry, catch me up on you, Lillian!"

She smiled, amazed at how quickly this woman could switch gears. "I go by Lilly now, for one."

"Lilly?" Faith arched her brow. "Lilly. Yeah, that'll do." She tossed Lilly a conspiring wink as she whirled around to stock supplies behind her.

A pleasant silence fell between the two women as Faith tended to behind the counter and Lilly concentrated on her caffeine and sugar consumption. Lilly wasn't ready to "catch up" anyone on what she'd been through the last fifteen or so years, especially not her most recent past. Her split and divorce from her husband still burned bittersweet.

A bell jingled above the main door, signaling more customers. An elderly couple shuffled up to the counter and bid good morning to Faith. She greeted them by name and asked questions about their grandkids and a recent trip, but didn't ask for an order. She immediately went to work pouring two drip brews and pulling three chocolate frosted pastries out from the below counter display case.

Lilly watched in amazement as, through the whole transaction, from entrance to payment to departure, Faith continued to talk non-stop, barely allowing the couple to answer her questions, let alone proffer their order. The couple had to be extreme regulars.

"You said that you were glad I stopped by your place," Lilly began as Faith finished waving goodbye to the elderly couple. "Do you own this place?"

Faith nodded, a girlish smile spreading across her face. "I do. Toby and I bought it a few years ago when the original owners, Mr. and Mrs. Baumann, decided to become permanent snowbirds in St. Augustine. It's been my baby ever since."

"That sounds wonderful," Lilly raised the last donut to her lips. She'd often had wild schemes of owning her own business, but each time she'd come up with a business plan for a graphic design firm, Alec shot her ideas down with a long list of reasons why it'd never work: she shouldn't risk leaving her current position over a pipe dream; if she went into business for herself, she'd never be home and their marriage would suffer—it ended up suffering anyway, though, hadn't it?

"That one's on you, you jackass," Lilly's whispered words dripped acid.

"What was that, sweetie?" Faith looked over her shoulder as she refilled Earl's coffee.

"Nothing," she waved her hand absently. "Just thinking aloud."

Faith opened her mouth in reply, but it snapped shut. "Oh Lord," Faith whispered, eyes staring hard over Lilly's shoulder.

"What?" She turned to see a familiar face walk into the café.

With movement that could only be described as an overconfident saunter, Maxwell Carpenter entered the café. Lilly watched Faith and the other patrons as the man walked further into the eatery. *Please let the rest of them see him, too!* Lilly pleaded silently.

"Morning, Faith," Maxwell called out with a wave.

"That damned idiot," Faith hissed.

Lilly shrank back from the counter. "Faith?"

"Your usual to-go order, Max?" Faith called out, her expression melting into a beaming smile in an instant.

"The usual, yes, but I'll stick around for one of those mouthwatering scones, Faith my dear." Maxwell settled onto a stool one away from Lilly.

At least Mr. Carpenter is real. Lilly eyed the realtor as she finished her latte.

"Mrs. Rhodes, so great to see you made it into town!" Maxwell slapped the counter. "Soon you'll be traversing these backroads like a local in no time."

"Thank you, Mr. Carpenter. Max."

To Lilly's right, a stool clattered to the floor. She and the remaining patrons started at the clanging metal. She hesitantly turned toward the commotion and saw Earl turn to glare past her and fix his burning gaze on Maxwell.

"Carpenter!" Earl's voice boomed in the small café. Lilly was certain his voice gained its deep tenor from years of being out in the dusty fields and smoking at least a pack a day. She swallowed as the two men stared each other down, and she found herself unwillingly in the cross hairs.

"Earl, good to see you," Maxwell nodded. Faith set a cup of coffee in front of him. He kept his eyes focused on the older man as he raised the coffee to his lips. "How's Mavis been?"

"You get away from that young woman," Earl rumbled as he moved closer.

"He's not bothering me—" Lilly began.

"You know to keep your distance from the Schmidt farm," Earl continued, either not hearing or choosing not to hear Lilly.

"Earl, please, let's not start this again," Maxwell sighed and set his coffee down in its saucer. "Let's just enjoy our coffee and be neighborly, no?"

The elder man now stood behind Lilly. "I know you were out pokin' your nose around the lines again. I've told you many times to lay off the lines."

"Lines?" Lilly looked from Earl to Faith.

Faith gave a slight shake of her head and pursed her lips.

"Earl, you know I have many clients out in your neck of the woods who are looking into alternative land agreements." Maxwell swiveled on the bar stool to face the counter.

"Don't turn your back on me when I'm talking to you!" Earl thundered as he reached out to grab at Maxwell's coat sleeve.

Lilly scrambled off her stool, wanting to be as far from the potential brawl as possible.

"Earl, please," Faith pleaded as she placed both palms firmly on the counter.

The café was silent, though Lilly was certain everyone could hear her heart thud inside her chest.

After a long, controlled breath, Maxwell turned his head slightly to look at his sleeve gripped in the old man's fist.

"Mr. Graves, I strongly recommend you remove your hand from my jacket." His voice was measured and icy. Lilly involuntarily shivered at the professional, yet threatening tone to his words. "We don't want to involve Sheriff Heimdall again, do we?"

Earl narrowed bushy gray brows at the realtor. Then, with a muttered curse, he released his grip. "This isn't over, Carpenter." He growled. Earl took a couple steps back then whirled to face Lilly. She stiffened against the counter like a deer caught in headlights.

"Don't you listen to a damn word that man says, y'hear young lady?" He snarled, pointing an arthritic finger under her nose. "You'd do right and do what your grandfather promised."

With that cryptic message, Earl turned sharply and left the café. Lilly focused her gaze on the old man, watching as he walked past the front window and out of view. Slowly, the remaining patrons returned to their conversations, now full of murmured recollections and speculations over the scene that unfolded.

Do what my grandfather promised?

A hand on her arm brought Lilly back to the café. She gasped and saw Maxwell leaning over, patting her arm gently.

"Let me apologize for Mr. Graves," Maxwell sighed. "He's not known for running with all cylinders, if you get my meaning."

"What did he mean by 'do what your grandfather promised'?" Lilly asked, resting once more on her stool. Her donuts and latte suddenly settled heavily in her stomach.

"He was old friends with Harold and Bev," the realtor answered. "He's been taking their passing pretty hard. Who knows what the old codger means?" Maxwell finished the last of his coffee in one long gulp. He stood, adjusted his coat, and turned toward the door. "Great coffee, Faith, as always. I'll get that scone next time."

"Thank you, Max," Faith said.

Lilly noticed the slight tremor in her voice.

"If you ever want to revisit that proposal of expanding your locations, don't hesitate to give my office a call!"

Lilly watched as Maxwell left with a clatter of bells. She noticed the pivoting heads of the elderly couples in the window booths, sneaking glances in her direction then quickly huddling together to converse in hushed tones. Her breakfast did another flip in her stomach.

"What was that about?" Lilly finally turned to Faith.

"He did take your grandparents' deaths pretty hard." Faith shook her head.

"Not that! The whole thing with him threatening Mr. Carpenter!"

"That's a feud that goes back years."

"And I got sucked up into it?" Lilly sputtered.

Faith traced her finger along the plate that once held the donuts. She held her sugar encrusted digit up and gave a rueful smile as she sucked the sweetness from her skin. "Welcome back, Lilly Schmidt."

Chapter Four

Lilly spent the rest of her morning putting her groceries away and reorganizing the kitchen. After the eventful morning at Grandma's Attic, she made a stop at Fritche's grocery and picked up what she hoped would be a month's worth of food. Maybe more like two weeks. Her first day was turning out to be more than she bargained for. As she walked around the store, she decided that she needed to do some investigating into what Earl Graves had said to her. She didn't like the idea of some disgruntled old man nursing a grudge, either real or imagined, against her.

His words repeated in her head as she stacked canned vegetables and pasta sauce in the spacious pantry. *"You'd do right and do what your grandfather promised."*

What was that supposed to mean?

"I don't know what my grandpa promised you, you crazy old man," Lilly muttered, setting a gallon of milk in the stainless steel refrigerator. "I hadn't spoken to my grandparents in fifteen years, and you think I'm supposed to know about what you and he may have talked about at some point in his life?"

To alleviate some of the stress that churned in the pit of her stomach, Lilly straightened pots, pans, and kettles in the various cabinets around the kitchen. The tidying helped take her mind away from Mr. Graves. She didn't remember her grandmother's kitchen being this elaborate when she was younger. She discovered utensils, crock pots, and cooking contraptions that she couldn't recognize, let alone guess at their use. One whole cabinet next to the pantry contained dozens of cook books, many well-used and dog-eared while others looked as if they had just come from the bookstore shelves.

"I'm going to have to make a map of where everything is in here." Lilly sat on one of the island stools and gazed around the sparkling clean cabinets and counters in a bit of a daze. She glanced once more at the cookbook library. "And I suppose I'll have to learn how to cook?"

The silence of the kitchen grew to be too much, especially after such a strange morning. Lilly considered going up to the second floor and continuing her rearranging streak, maybe working on converting one of the extra bedrooms into her office space, but she knew the crushing silence would only follow her.

She looked at the island counter and reached out for her phone, only to withdraw her hand. Who would she call? She knew no one in the area and her friends in the Twin Cities would be busy working. Even if they had the day off, would they travel the almost two hours to come and spend the afternoon with her?

A long, loud *Mrrrrrrrrrooooo* filtered through the windows and into the kitchen. Lilly turned toward the barn and made a face. She glanced at her watch and discovered it was almost noon. Ryan's truck was absent from the driveway when she returned from town and she wasn't sure when he would return to feed the cows for the second time, or if he'd show up sometime before their supper. With all the excitement from her trip to the café, Lilly was glad he wasn't still around when she came home.

"I suppose I could go for a tour of the grounds." Lilly slid off the stool and walked out of the kitchen through the back door.

The brisk spring morning had turned into a pleasant day with a light breeze. The tiny new leaves on the trees barely rustled with the breeze. Thankfully, the wind came from the south so the house was upwind and any unpleasant barn odors were carried in the opposite direction.

Lilly stood in the backyard and spun in a slow circle, soaking up the sights of the farm. She didn't remember much from Mrs. Swenson's hurried tour of the building site from the day before; her brain was caught up in trying to make sense of her new "normal." And her memory proved to be less than reliable at the moment.

The farmhouse sat at an odd alignment, the front door due south and the back door due north. The out buildings framed the main house in a pattern that reminded Lilly of the fifth side of a six-sided die. Off to the left, or the northwest corner as her grandpa called it, stood what she remembered as the machine shed.

Much like the house, the siding and shingles needed repair. Lilly could only assume what tractors, plows, and other farming equipment still stood on the dirt floor, and in what condition her grandparents had left them. Toward the northeast corner was the barn, which, after a quick Google search the night before, Lilly learned was a Gambrel style barn. Painted the traditional red with white trim, neglect and the elements had faded the once brilliant colors to something only slightly better than dingy gray.

Closer to the south side of the property and the front of the house stood the unattached garage in the southwest corner together with the old chicken coop in the southeast. She decided to investigate those two buildings at another time, for Dandelion and her small herd had begun to voice their demands.

Lilly walked slowly toward the barn, finally taking in the subtleties of the barnyard. The barn had been built into a slight rise in the yard, an earthen ramp leading up to what could be called the second floor of the barn. Lilly vaguely remembered from her childhood numerous afternoons spent playing in the mountainous stacks of hay and straw bales. Below the hay loft stood the main area for the livestock. At one end of the lower level stood a giant tank; the other led out to a little pasture.

She paused before entering the barn, taking a moment to allow her brain to process her current surroundings one more time. Despite spending her childhood amongst these buildings, groves, and fields, Lilly felt a hollow void spread throughout her gut as the warm, familiar tingle of nostalgia failed to blossom in her chest.

Perhaps those Hallmark Channel movies lied, Lilly thought with a frown. The girl who returns after years in the big city doesn't always feel right at home immediately upon stepping foot on the old family homestead.

The mournful laments of the cows grew louder, with more of a demanding tone.

I'm going to have to send a strongly worded letter to Hallmark about their lack of truth in advertising, Lilly decided with a sigh as she trudged towards the barn.

The cows were complaining for a reason, and she was unsure if she'd be able to assist in meeting their needs. Her brief observation of Ryan and his chores didn't offer any contingency plan for non-primary meal concerns.

Lilly entered the barn slowly to allow her senses to acclimate to the barrage of smells. The cows fell silent at the long creak of the barn door. The sudden silence threw her off guard, a heavy unease settled at the pit of her stomach.

Dandelion broke the eerie silence first, her loud and distinct bellow seeming to rattle the old barn to its foundations.

Once Lilly's eyes adjusted to the dim light of the lower barn, she sought out the main light switch. The illumination from the overhead bulbs didn't improve the situation drastically, although she now felt she could maneuver around the barn in relative safety.

She did not want a repeat of the poop face plant incident, even though none of the potential witnesses would have been able to say anything if it did indeed happen again.

Lilly walked down the main aisle of the barn, taking mental stock of the small office, milk tank room, and supply closets to the right, just across the main walk from the cows. To her left stood the tie-stalls with their bovine inhabitants. The wall with the assorted doors stood along the side of the barn built into the hill, placing these rooms under the earth ramp. This also meant they had no natural light besides through the slits that passed as windows. The left side, beyond the cows, held glassless windows covered only in chicken wire that brought in fresh air as well as views of the small-looking pasture.

"What do you ladies want?" Lilly asked the small herd as she stared Dandelion straight in the eye.

Dandelion responded with a noise that sounded like a sneeze strangled by a wet belch.

"Lovely..." Lilly groaned, turning from the cow. "I can't help you if you're hungry. Ryan didn't show me how to feed you. Or milk you, if that's the problem. So, if that's what is bothering you, you're going to have to wait until that grumpy farmer gets here."

Dandelion bellowed again, suddenly pulling hard at the chain that tethered her neck harness to the stall supports. Lilly paused and watched the cow, growing more concerned with each terrific yank the cow subjected her neck to. The large cow pulled at her tether with such force Lilly worried she was going to hurt herself.

"Hey, you crazy cow, knock that off!" Lilly scolded. She immediately felt foolish trying to admonish a beast that easily outweighed her by a thousand pounds. Mere words were not going to calm Dandelion down. She moved toward the upset animal, unsure of how to calm the beast. "It's alright. I'll get you food..."

Lilly glanced up at the ceiling, picturing the hayloft beyond.

"I'm sure I can get some hay for you," she smiled back at the cow, confident in her new plan.

Dandelion strained at her neck harness, eyes wide and nostrils flared, then bellowed as Lilly turned away.

"She's going to be the death of me," Lilly muttered, grateful to be leaving the noisy cow behind.

Lilly managed her way up the ramp to the hayloft doors. She reached out to grab the large metal handles, then stopped. She didn't know if there was even hay still left in the loft. She had never seen Ryan go up there; all the food he had given to the cows had already been in the barn. For all she knew, Ryan brought the food from off farm.

Lilly traced a finger along the outline of her phone in her jeans pocket. Should she call Ryan? He'd most likely yell at her for upsetting the cows, and they wouldn't milk right for weeks. She snickered at her own joke, suddenly remembering her grandma saying that to her grandpa. Looking at the large handles, she gripped them with both hands, her brow creased.

This was *her* farm. These were *her* animals. She should be able to tend and feed them as needed without assistance from "Ryan the Curmudgeon." If she was going to figure out what her future held at the farm—whether she could stay and make a go at this way of life—she needed to be able to actually perform the necessary tasks.

With many near-starts, shouted swear words, and one broken nail, Lilly managed to work the large wooden door along its long-lost groove. Slowly but surely, she was able to make an opening large enough for her to slip through.

Much to Lilly's surprise, the hay loft held fresh-looking bales, stacked into a tidy pyramid-like mound. The mound was in the middle of the floor, surrounded by the remnants of vintage bales gone by. As the straw broke crisply under her feet, Lilly wondered if some of the golden stalks were indeed older than her.

The sweet, earthy smell of grass hung about her in stale clouds of dust, the particles shimmering in the shaft of light coming from the doorway. Her Timberland boots thudded dully against the aged wooden floor as she wandered around the bale stack. Below, she heard the cows' bellowing and moaning travel up through the rough hewn boards.

"I found your hay," Lilly called down to the cows. "You can stop your belly aching!"

Lilly stood in front of the bales, eyeing up the ones closest to the outside of the pyramid, attempting to judge which would be easiest for her to move. The large rectangular bales, measuring at least one foot by three feet, loomed before her as dense and daunting. She dug her fingers into the closest bale, grasping onto the tattered, red twine holding the hay together. With an undignified grunt, Lilly pulled at the bale.

The block of grass barely budged.

After adjusting her grip, Lilly took a deep breath and tugged once more at the bale. The bale shifted a few inches, the slight movement enough to knock her off balance. Lilly cried out as she landed unceremoniously on her behind in the thin layer of straw. Dust and debris billowed around her, causing her to cough as she sputtered out curses. She rose, brushing straw and dirt from the seat of her jeans, glowering at the stack of bales.

Dandelion's distinct *mrroooooorrww* echoed up from the stalls below.

"Shut up, you old nag." Lilly positioned herself in front of the bale she had budged. She wound her fingers around the twine once more. It appeared as if she were dancing as she tried to find the perfect placement for her feet. The flickering yellow strands of straw on the worn wood made for a slicker surface than what Lilly hoped to find.

She paused and almost laughed at herself awkwardly planted in a Warrior II yoga pose. She doubted this was what Swami Piper intended for her yoga students.

"Set your intention, ground your Muladhara..." Lilly took a slow, deep breath and exhaled slowly, trying to connect with her Muladhara, or root chakra, as well as hoping her years of yoga would be able to transfer to this real world situation. Like word problems in grade school math.

"One... two... THREE!"

Lilly heaved against the twine. To her amazement, the bale moved farther than before. She grinned as she remained upright. With a reset of her previous stance, Lilly tried once more. She was too excited about moving the massive bale to bother thinking of how she was going to get it down to the cows.

Lilly pulled as hard as she could on the bale, and it came away from the stack. As did the one below it. And the bale above.

In an instant, Lilly found herself managing not just one hay bale, but three.

The intended lower bale tumbled down from its unbeknownst precarious perch, crashing into her legs. As she lost her balance, the higher bale slid off the target bale and landed on her arms, wrenching her hands from their holds.

In a blur of hay, dust, arms, and bales, Lilly collapsed backwards once more. Only now, Lilly's attention was split between crashing to the floor and dodging massive blocks of compressed hay. She managed to escape being completely trapped by the three bales, thankfully only having one bale come to rest on her legs. She lay on the floor, coughing at the newly disturbed dust, and gazed up at the vaulted roof of the barn, taking a few moments to collect her thoughts.

The one bale laying across her legs wasn't as heavy as trying to move it had led her to believe. However, if all three had landed on her, she might not be staring up at the roof, she'd be crushed. And no one would know she was in the hay loft until Ryan came to do chores in a few hours.

"I'm such an idiot," Lilly muttered as she slowly sat up and glanced at the vaulted roof.

After the shock and humiliation of the bale avalanche wore off, Lilly finally recognized the strange objects hanging from the various support beams, rafters, and walls of the barn.

Heavy knives, short- and long-handled scythes with sharply curved blades, claw topped hammers, hand saws, and what could only be extra blades for plows hung from large iron nails around the hay loft like macabre Christmas decorations. A collection of hand-sized scythes hung directly above her, their deadly metal crescents glinting in the dusty light.

Lilly quickly dislodged herself from the bale and moved from under the beam. She brushed herself off as best she could, knowing she'd be discovering pieces of hay and straw in her clothes throughout the rest of the day. She winced as she moved; although she hadn't been crushed, heavy-lifting and falling on the floor had taken their toll. Lilly sighed and frowned at the three errant bales scattered around her feet. One bale had partially broken in half as a result of its tumble, its carefully packed contents spilling out onto the floor.

"Great, now how do I get these downstairs?

Dandelion bellowed from below.

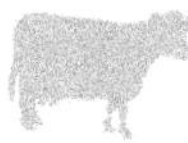

"What the hell happened in here?"

Lilly winced as the shouted words filtered through the hay loft's floor boards down to the cow stalls. "Well, hello to you, too."

Peony and Poppy answered the enraged question with mournful moans.

"Shh," Lilly hissed, tossing handfuls of hay in front of the cows. "I cleaned up the mess. Not my fault his standards are stupidly high."

She managed to get most of a bale down into the stall area of the barn. Lilly took large handfuls down at a time, and after six trips she discovered a dilapidated wheelbarrow just inside the door of the hay loft, conveniently hidden behind some long-handled scythes. The bale soon lost its shape as she transferred it into the wheelbarrow.

It didn't have to look pretty, it just had to taste good enough to shut the cows up for a while.

Lilly finally made her way down the row of cows, stopping in front of Dandelion. She held a large, semi-intact chunk of hay, paused in front of Dandelion. The large cow huffed through her nostrils, the wet breath disapproving of being made to wait. The bovine pulled at her neck harness, wiggling and stretching out thick, black lips until she succeeded in snatching her prize from Lilly's hand.

Foot falls thudded above her head, causing dislodged cobwebs to rain delicately down on Lilly. She glared up at the shadow that crossed the ceiling. Heavy boots paced back and forth across the hay loft. Lilly knew Ryan was assessing the situation she had left in the hayloft, taking stock of any damage done.

"I leave this place for a couple of hours..."

The voice and footsteps faded away, a relative silence filling the barn stalls. Lilly had just picked up on some incoherent cursing and ranting, muffled through dirt and centenarian wood, when the large barn door swung violently on its hinges.

Lilly jolted upright at the explosion as the heavy wood met an iron support column.

Ryan stood in the doorway and Lilly swore she saw the disdain roll off him in waves as his dark eyes locked on her. Again, his face was mostly hidden behind the worn brim of his John Deere cap. His larger frame was sheltered beneath a bulky canvas jacket. He took a couple steps beyond the doorway, his gait halting.

As if he could tell she watched his gait, Ryan stopped.

"You."

The one word stung her and she forced herself to not flinch.

"What did you do to my hay?"

Lilly had prepared an apology speech, knowing that the current hired hand might have a reaction like this. She knew she had left the hay loft in a relative state of disrepair; it wasn't that disastrous, though. Nothing that warranted the level of anger Ryan's voice and stance displayed.

Even through their divorce, neither she nor her husband exuded such animosity towards one another.

"I got some hay down for the cows." Lilly stood tall, knowing a fine layer of white dust covered her skin and clothing. She wore her disheveled appearance, with barn grit and cow slobber, as a badge of honor. Farm cred, as it were.

"You got hay..." Ryan's hard voice didn't waver.

"Will you let me try to explain before you crucify me?" Lilly began. "After feeding, I was going to go back up there and clean up more. I know I left a mess—"

"Who said you could go up there?" He moved into the barn. As he spoke, he made his way to the wheelbarrow. Lilly dropped a hand to a wooden handle, laying claim to it and the hay inside. "There is nothing up there for you—frankly, there's nothing outside the house for you here. What put this notion in your head you should go up there—"

"My grandparents!" Lilly shouted.

Ryan stopped mid stride, mouth frozen open, ready to spew more harsh words.

"My grandparents thought I should go in the barn, the loft, and everywhere else on this farm when they gave it to me." Lilly held his gaze, though found herself unable to control the slight shake in her voice or her hands.

"What is your problem anyway?" Lilly continued, filling the silence between them. "I moved some hay around, broke some bales, but I'm feeding them to my cows. My. Cows. You act as if I set the barn on fire or killed a cow. It's just hay. This is my farm now, and I'm going to try my best to figure out how to run it, how I can be helpful. I've had a crappy winter finding out my husband cheated on me and served me divorce papers in the same week. I've lost my home, I moved away from my friends and job and... and... and I had a crazy idea that starting over here would help, so I'm not just sitting around the house feeling sorry for myself."

Ryan remained silent.

"I would think of all people, you'd know what that feels like."

Lilly's hands gripped the handles of the wheelbarrow to keep herself upright. She took a deep breath, unsure where all that had come from. But it felt good to finally voice it.

One of the cows moaned softly, breaking both Ryan and Lilly from their silence.

Ryan cleared his throat as he adjusted his cap over his sandy brown hair. Even in the chaotic lighting of the barn, the flush under his stubble was clear.

"Don't get all bent out of shape," Ryan finally spoke, his voice gruff. "You don't need to tell me all your problems, I ain't your therapist."

An undignified cry erupted from Lilly's throat as she dug her hands into the pile of hay before her, pushing Dandelion's muzzle out of the way in the process. She threw the clump of hay at Ryan, who stood no more than six feet away from the wheelbarrow.

The silage missile sputtered out in the air, spreading out like a cheap firework, the bulk of the hay barely reached Ryan.

His mouth curled as a chuckle escaped his lips.

Lilly, embarrassed by her impromptu confession and humiliated by the ineffective retaliation, felt heat rise from the pit of her stomach and spread like wildfire. She swallowed a grunt and pushed past Ryan.

Hot tears pricked her eyes as she stomped up toward the farmhouse. She kept her gaze down on her feet, hoping she was headed in the right direction. She couldn't handle another humiliation in front of Ryan.

Her foot touched the steps to the back porch before she heard the voice calling after her. She half turned and saw Ryan making his way up to the house, his limping exaggerated by the uneven ground.

"Ms. Rhodes," Ryan called to her, his voice still gruff.

"Yes, Mr. Swenson."

"Ms. Rhodes, uh, Ms. Schmidt..." Ryan came to a stop at the bottom of the steps. "I, back there, I, uh..."

"Yes?"

He scratched at the back of his head, disrupting his cap. "I'm..."

Lilly sighed. "I don't have all day, Mr. Swenson,"

She noticed the tiny pull of a grimace at his formal name.

"I've been tending to this farm a long time," Ryan began haltingly. "Not used to having other people poking around here."

Is this his version of an apology? Lilly turned to face him fully, arms crossed over her stomach. *It might be the best I get from him.*

"I'm more concerned with why you were taking the blades and scythes down—"

"I didn't take any of those things down," Lilly cut in.

Again they locked gazes.

"There's some missing."

"Missing?" Her eyes flicked to the hay loft doors. "How do you know there's any missing? It's an absolute mess in there,"

"No thanks to you," Ryan muttered.

Lilly narrowed her eyes. "Excuse me, I will clean up your precious hay loft."

"I make it a point to know the number and the location of all the farming equipment, especially blades," Ryan continued. "There's no shortage of teenaged farm boys around here who aren't above raiding farms for dangerous equipment on a dare."

"I take it you know from experience?"

"I was raised on a farm, wasn't I?" He almost looked proud.

Lilly couldn't help the smirk that pulled the corners of her mouth. "Why would you think I took those tools?"

Ryan shrugged. "I don't know. You got some hipster, eco-social-justice warrior bull in your head and you wanted to rid the place of those evils PETA brainwashed you about?"

Her jaw dropped. A fiery wave spread through her body and she wasn't sure if she was more hurt by what he said, or afraid that's what he thought of her. Why did his opinion of her matter? Lilly stood straighter, making sure to climb one stair to put some extra height between the two—a symbolic gesture of taking the high road to ease her flustered mind.

"I did not take any tools, Mr. Swenson," again, the faint twitch at the formality, "and I can assure you that I never would take any tools from anywhere on this farm without at least asking you first. I know you've been running this farm for a long time, and I don't want to disrupt your little ecosystem. With that being said, I own those tools now, I own this farm, and I want to be part of its everyday work. That's why I was up in the hay loft."

Ryan rolled his eyes, appearing to fight the beginnings of a grin. "Alright, alright." He lifted his hat and immediately placed it firmly on his head. "Do you have to talk so much? I don't remember you talking this much when we dated."

She stared at him as the flustered feeling surged anew in her stomach.

Why did she talk so much? What was it about this aggravating man that made her mouth run away with her? She owed him nothing—not an explanation or a glimpse into her back story. Yet here she was, babbling on about her right to be there and how she needed to prove herself.

Damn him.

Perhaps her loose tongue came from being lost in her new normal and trying to find her footing. She certainly didn't need accusations from the cranky hired hand. Being accosted by a random old man at breakfast surely hadn't helped matters either.

Speaking of the old man, Lilly remembered she needed to take her newbie farmer hat off and put on her amateur sleuth hat.

"Let me know what you find out about the missing tools," Lilly climbed the remaining porch steps. "I have some info to dig up. Excuse me."

"Info about what?"

She pursed her lips as she opened the kitchen door. "Nothing you need to concern yourself with, Mr. Swenson." Lilly knew he flinched again at the formal address and she allowed herself to smile.

Before she let the screen door slam behind her, she called over her shoulder, "Oh, and don't forget to finish feeding my cows."

Lilly walked straight through the kitchen, down the main hall, and out the front door, only realizing where she was when she heard the front door slam behind her.

All the words Lilly wished she'd said and the ones she had regrettably uttered pinged around her skull, adding insult to injury as she stepped down to the driveway. The gravel crunched under her shoes. She imagined each large chunk was Ryan's big stupid face.

"I'm just trying to help out," Lilly muttered as she walked down the driveway. To her left sat Ryan's truck, and she glowered at it. Her foot struck out at the tire before she could stop herself. The dull thud of her shoe against the heavy rubber of the tire wasn't as satisfying as she'd hoped. Lilly continued on her way, still muttering to herself, needing to release her frustration in a healthy way.

The driveway was a long stretch of gravel raised up on a low grade from the rest of the field land on either side. Deep in the recesses of her brain, she remembered her grandmother stating it was almost a fourth of a mile from the main road to the small horseshoe turnaround at the top of the yard. Lilly trudged her way down the gravel path, not sure what her plan was once she got to the main road. She'd worry about that once she got there. Now, she just needed to put some distance between herself and Ryan.

Her first thirty-six hours back in Lone Tree were anything but welcoming. Other than Mrs. Swenson—Maggie—and Faith, most of her interactions had been found wanting to say the least. The realtor she met at the side of the road, Mr. Carpenter, wasn't too bad, though she had felt a bit uneasy around him. He reminded her a bit of a sleazy used car salesman.

The afternoon air cleared the further from the farm she walked. The bare fields of rich black earth laid untouched, remnants of last year's corn stalks sticking out from plowed-over curves of soil. Lilly stared at the expanse of field, flashes of brilliant green corn stalks returning to her memory. How many times had her mother and grandmother yelled at her for wandering into the fields? Any warnings or threats of getting lost or being eaten by the combine fell on deaf ears as she, Faith, Ryan, and their other brothers went gallivanting through the fields.

She glanced back toward the main house. How did she ever get along with that pig-headed man? Lilly didn't remember him being so stubborn and impossible all those years ago. What happened to him to change him so drastically? Faith mentioned an accident, and it wasn't hard to ignore his limp. Perhaps he had a reason to be so grumpy?

"No, no one has a reason to treat people like that," Lilly told herself as she continued to walk.

The end of the driveway drew closer, as did the main road. The ditches were full of dried long grass and cattails from the previous summer, newer grass pushing its way through the dead overgrowth. Lilly stopped at the junction of the drive and the road, glancing each way, as if checking for traffic before crossing the street. On the other side of the road was her new mailbox, a battered gunmetal box with a faded red flag on one side attached to a rough, square wooden post.

Lilly considered the mailbox with an amused look. She hadn't considered checking the mail yet.

"I suppose I'll have to do a change of address," she muttered to herself as she crossed the gravel road to the mailbox.

The dirt road squelched beneath her feet due to the spring melt. She surprised herself remembering that gravel roads were prone to frost pockets, or what her dad called "frost heaves," that would leave either depressions or bumps in their wake as the weather grew warmer.

She flipped open the battered metal door and discovered a distinct lack of mail. Lilly snapped it shut and fidgeted with the alert flag, figuring she'd delay her return back to the farm. The less time around Ryan, the better, she decided.

A glimpse of denim and leather caught her eye at the base of the mailbox's post. The dead grass was thicker around the mailbox, though Lilly noticed clumps of the grass appeared to have been trampled.

Lilly sighed as she crouched to inspect further. "Some farmer lose his clothes? What the h—"

Her voice stuck in her throat as her hand touched the leather. It turned out to be a leather shoe. And not just any leather shoe. Given a quick glance, Lilly recognized the style of shoe; though, the exact brand escaped her. Alec favored that style of shoe which was normally found at Neiman Marcus. The last time they traveled to New York, he had bought several pairs.

What was a shoe worth thousands of dollars doing in a ditch in rural Minnesota?

She had seen this exact pair of shoes before but where...?

Lilly watched as her fingers gripped around the shoe, not minding the few traces of mud and grass stuck to the sole. She gasped and released the shoe as she found it had a decent weight to it. Something was inside it.

She pulled again on the shoe, hoping that the something was only mud, maybe even a field mouse who had decided to upgrade their spring lodgings. The shoe came towards her, the shift causing her to lose balance and topple backwards on her seat. She steadied herself and pulled again.

More denim followed the shoe. Attached to the shoe was a pair of jeans.

Lilly's mouth grew dry as her eyes scanned upward. Her fingers grazed a patch of pale, chilled skin between the shoe and the jean cuff. The skin belonged to the foot in the shoe she was holding, as well as the leg that fleshed out the jeans. She leaned forward and pushed aside the compacted grass.

As her vision telescoped, she saw the body lying in the ditch, limbs at haphazard and painful angles. A bright splash of red streaked down the front of an Oxford shirt. Blond hair sat atop a head bent in a very wrong way. Pale eyes stared off into the distance.

Maxwell Carpenter...

She fell back and scrambled out of the weeds and back onto the road.

Max Carpenter was in the ditch. And he wasn't moving.

"Mr. Carpenter?" Lilly called, her voice barely a whisper. "Max? Are...
are you..."

She knew the rest of her question was futile. Before she completely registered what her body was doing, Lilly ran back up her driveway,
screaming, "Someone help! Please, help! Call 911!"

Chapter Five

The farmyard was awash in blue and red lights. Sedans and SUVs in various combinations of black and white with "Lone Tree Police Department" emblazoned on the sides littered Lilly's driveway all the way down to the road. She watched the action from her porch steps, her heel kicking absently at the rotten hole Mrs. Swenson's New Balances had sunk into just yesterday.

I should get that fixed...

Police—regular officers, some in suits who Lilly believed were homicide detectives, and crime scene investigators—canvased her driveway and the road surrounding her mailbox. First responders and rescue vehicles had left almost an hour ago after it was deemed their services wouldn't be required.

Maxwell Carpenter was dead.

She closed her eyes against the image of the realtor's pasty face amongst the dead grass and weeds, glassy eyes searching for something they'd never see. The first officer on the scene had dragged her from the relative safety of the porch, making her take him to the site where the body... Mr. Carpenter... was and explain what happened.

There wasn't much for her to tell. She had gone to go for a walk and check the mail, and found a shoe in the ditch. She remembered the disapproving look the officer gave her when she said she touched the shoe.

How was she supposed to know there was a dead person attached to the shoe!

Even though the medical examiner, who arrived almost an hour after the initial 911 call, had stated that the estimated time of death of Mr. Carpenter would most likely remove Lilly as a suspect, she still felt like every glance she received from the various law enforcement officials wandering around her property was laced with suspicion. Other than her finding Mr. Carpenter and her inadvertently contaminating the bottom of his shoe, there really wasn't anything for her to worry about.

Or was there?

She caught movement from the corner of her eye and caught Ryan leaning against the long side panel of his truck, arms folded tightly across his chest. With his John Deere hat pulled down low over his face, it was hard to get a reading from the man. He'd been minimally supportive when she first came running up the driveway, screaming and on the verge of passing out. He forced her to sit on the porch, told her to put her head between her knees and take slow breaths—"I don't need you passing out on me when I have to deal with an actual emergency!" he barked at her as he thrust his phone in her hand—and hurried back down the way she had just come.

She'd lost sight of him after the police started to arrive. She assumed he had gone back to chores after the authorities took over. This was the first time she'd seen him since he left her on the porch.

"What are you looking at?" He called over, brimmed head facing the driveway.

"Can't you say *anything* nice to me?" Lilly snapped back. "There's a freaking dead person by my mailbox. Doesn't that automatically mean you're supposed to quit being a jerk?"

She caught a shadowed smirk across what she could see of his face.

"When do you think they'll let me go?"

"Let you go?" Lilly kicked angrily at the porch step. "There's a crime scene at the end of the driveway, not everything is about you! Sheesh, get a little perspective."

Again, he only grinned.

She kicked the stair again.

"Hey, if you make that hole any bigger, I'm going to make you fix it," Ryan pointed a grease covered finger at her.

"Then make yourself useful and fix it now!" She shouted back.

He grunted.

Lilly turned away from the frustrating farmhand, chin pressed firmly against her palms. She found her thoughts circling back to poor Mr. Carpenter; she couldn't shake the image of his prone body being lifted onto a stretcher.

Who would want to hurt Mr. Carpenter, let alone kill him?

The question bounced around her head as she watched the police cruisers and crime scene SUVs begin to vacate her yard. A man in dress slacks and a long overcoat strode purposefully over the gravel turnabout toward the house. Lilly frowned, knowing it was another police officer coming to ask her more questions.

Sheriff Brandford was in his late fifties with thick salt-and-pepper hair. His serious brown eyes seemed to be perpetually narrowed, causing his forehead to hold permanent creases. Lilly decided he'd be an attractive man if he lightened up a little. Although, being law enforcement at the scene of a murder, she doubted he had much to be happy about.

When he had introduced himself upon first arriving on the farm yard, the name and face struck Lilly as painfully familiar. During the official interrogation about the incident, Sheriff Brandford confirmed Lilly's suspicions—the sheriff was a second cousin on her mother's side.

"Lillian?"

"Yes, sir, uh, Mike—Michael." Lilly straightened as he approached, like a student being caught by the teacher goofing off. How do you address an officer of the law who is also family? "Do you know what happened?"

"You can call me Mike,"

"I call that a conflict of interest!" Ryan called from his truck.

Mike paused, his eyes fighting to stay on Lilly and not acknowledge Ryan's comment by glancing his way. "We're still determining what happened. Appears blunt force trauma to the head, but the coroner will figure that out after the autopsy."

Lilly blanched with a shiver. "Who did this?"

"That, we won't know until we process the evidence we collected," Brandford replied, sounding tired. Or perhaps he was tired of people asking that so soon in an investigation.

"Can I leave yet?" Ryan shouted from his truck.

Lilly gaped at him, wanting to sink down through the porch steps. "Oh my God..."

The Sheriff's calculating eyes flicked over to Ryan. "Mr. Swenson, correct?"

"The same," he replied, lifting his head to meet Brandford's gaze.

The two men sized each other up in silence, two alpha personalities determining how to proceed with the rest of their encounter. "We're finishing up with the scene as we speak. You'll be able to leave in about a half an hour."

Lilly hid her smile with her hand as Ryan gave a disapproving grunt. She decided she liked Cousin Mike just on that interaction alone.

Sheriff Brandford returned his attention to Lilly. He had a little notebook in his hand and pen in the other. "Before we leave, is there anything else you'd like to add, anything else you remember?"

She remembered how hysterical she had been during her initial interview with the police and Sheriff Brandford. It had been unbecoming and almost a waste of time. He had told her he'd give her some time to compose herself while he gathered preliminary information from the MEs. As she sat trying to calm herself, there wasn't much more she felt could be added.

"I met Mr. Carpenter earlier today. I'd gotten lost getting to town and he gave me directions." Lilly chose to ignore the belittling chuckle from Ryan. Didn't he have anything better to do?

"Where did you meet Mr. Carpenter?" The Sheriff started writing in the notebook.

"In a ditch?" Lilly offered. The Sheriff arched a brow. "I don't know where the ditch was exactly... he said he was checking out some prospective properties that would be coming up for sale soon."

The Sheriff nodded. "Anything else?"

"No, it was a brief encounter..." Lilly frowned, her addled brain working to sort out details she knew were missing. She noticed that he was putting his notebook away, a subtle hint that he felt they were done.

"Mr. Graves!" she blurted out as the idea exploded in her brain.

"Mr. Graves," he repeated. "You mean Earl Graves?"

"Yes," Lilly nodded furiously. The sheriff slowly pulled his little notebook from his inside coat pocket. "Earlier this morning, at the café, he was yelling at me and Mr. Carpenter."

Brandford's pen stopped writing. "Yelling about what?"

"He told me that I needed to do right by him. I have no idea what that means. I just met the man today!" The words tumbled out of Lilly's mouth almost too fast for her to say them. "And Mr. Carpenter was there, and Mr. Graves started yelling at him."

Brandford made a noncommittal noise as he continued to scribble on the paper.

"Maybe Mr. Graves hurt Mr. Carpenter!" Lilly blurted.

The scrutiny from both Ryan and Sheriff Brandford was swift and palpable. Lilly shrank away under the pressure of the Sheriff's gaze.

"Thank you for your time, Lillian." Sheriff Brandford gave a curt nod before turning toward one of the waiting sedans.

He paused at the base of the porch stairs. Lilly watched as the gears churned behind his eyes. "How are your folks?"

The question stunned her into a moment of silence. "They're doing good, I guess. I haven't talked with them in a while."

Mike nodded stiffly. "When you talk to them next, tell them we say hi, alright?"

Lilly nodded mutely as she watched the Sheriff leave. Her stomach sank at the forced pleasantries from the sheriff. How many people had her family hurt when her family decided to leave town?

Her stomach growled before she could ponder that thought more. She glanced at her cell phone. It was just after two in the afternoon. How hadd the morning passed by so fast?

Oh yeah. *Dead body and a police investigation have a habit of eating into one's day,* Lilly thought bitterly. Thankfully, she had put away her groceries before the excitement started. She would have otherwise returned to the kitchen to find room-temperature deli meat and half-melted ice cream.

"About time," Ryan remarked louder than necessary.

Lilly glared at him as he sauntered—well, sauntered as well as a man with a limp can—to the driver's door of his truck. "You can't leave yet, he said in about a half an hour," she reminded him, then cringed when she heard the high school mean girl tone in her voice.

His hand froze above the door handle. "Then what am I supposed to do until they're done?" he called over his shoulder. "I'm done with all the barn chores and the cows are out for the afternoon."

Lilly dropped her heel onto the broken porch step. The resulting thud seemed to fill the front yard. She glanced down, praying she hadn't added another hole to the step. The weakened wood held up, though.

"I've got something for you to do while you wait!" she called over to him. She wasn't going to deny herself that tiny thrill of seeing his shoulders slump as his eyes narrowed in on the step.

She found herself strangely energized after leaving Ryan on the front lawn. The best she felt all day. So energized, in fact, that she dug through her few moving boxes until she found her laptop and set up a temporary command center in the back sitting room. Her phone was out of commission while it charged; waiting for police to conclude their preliminary investigation meant a lot of Candy Crush and social media scrolling and a drained battery.

The old farmhouse was built in a large square with the formal dining room and kitchen off to the right side of the central staircase, and a formal sitting room taking up most of the left side of the house. Tucked back in the far corner was a smaller sitting room, what Lilly guessed could have been a den or maybe a study at one point in the house's history. Her grandparents squeezed the less attractive, yet more comfortable, furniture into this small room. Overstuffed leather chairs with well-worn cushions and cracked arm rests accompanied built-in bookshelves that were pushed well beyond their capacity.

Lilly pulled an old leather ottoman over to its matching armchair, using the ottoman as a makeshift desk for her laptop. As her computer powered up, she brushed the worn leather and smiled, faint memories of sitting on her grandpa's lap reading Nancy Drew or The Farmer's Almanac at night while her parents, aunts, uncles, and grandmother had yet another squabble in the kitchen.

Who would want to kill Mr. Carpenter?

She brought up the search engine on her laptop and couldn't help but do a little hip wiggle of anticipation over the information she was about to uncover. Her fingers hovered over the keyboard, flexing as she thought over what to type into Google's waiting search bar. Lilly stared at the screen and her shoulders slumped. The cursor blinked at her, mocking her.

She had no idea what to type to begin her search.

Why would Earl Graves want to hurt and/or kill Maxwell Carpenter?

How does one start searching for information on motives for murder?

"I could start with just his name?" Lilly bit her lip as she slowly typed "Earl Graves" and hit search.

The screen went blank for barely a second before it repopulated with the search results. Her eyes scanned over the offerings, hundreds of variations of "Earl" and "Graves". Lilly scrolled through and found everything from grave sites and burial services, White Page listings for anyone with the first or last name of Earl, to music videos for the song *Goodbye Earl* by the Dixie Chicks.

"That was helpful." Lilly flopped back on the chair, the old cushions voicing their displeasure by *whuufs* of air from the various seams and cracks.

She stared at the unhelpful links and chewed on her lip.

"Seriously, what is wrong with me?" Lilly smacked herself lightly on the forehead as she sat up quickly.

She went back to the search bar and began typing "Earl Graves" once more, though this time she added "Lone Tree, MN" after his name. How could she have forgotten the number one rule in internet searches? Be as specific as you can with the information in the search bar. A couple days on the farm and she apparently forgot everything she ever learned about computing.

Google thought for a millisecond before producing another selection of search results. This list was much smaller than the previous, and from a cursory glance, Lilly could already tell she'd been more productive this time around.

There were a handful of searches that contained both "Earl Graves" and "Lone Tree, MN", while others focused on the town. Lilly found herself drawn to the links about the town.

The Lone Tree Chamber of Commerce had their own webpage dedicated to the history of the town and surrounding area, as well as all the fun activities families and tourists could enjoy in southwest Minnesota. Like many towns in Brown County, the name of the small town was derived from the Native American name. One of the closest cities to Lone Tree was Sleepy Eye; that town's name was taken from a Dakota chieftain, Ish-Tak-Ha-Ba, or Chief Sleepy Eyes, who lived in the area. Lone Tree borrowed from the Dakota name Bde Çaå Waåoeidaå, which translated to Lone Tree Lake. The European settlers declared the town and the lake, on the shores of which the town was built, Lone Tree and

Lone Tree Lake respectively.

Lilly attempted to pronounce the Dakota name and found her ancestral Scandinavian tongue just couldn't handle the task. She smirked as she recalled sitting with some friends around a high-top at the coincidentally named Dakota Jazz Club in Minneapolis, each taking a turn attempting to pronounce Lake Calhoun's new name, Bde Maka Ska, which had only officially changed two months prior.

Looking back on that particular brunch, Lilly was certain that Bde Maka Ska was easier to pronounce than they had made it out to be and their struggles likely came from one too many trips to the Bloody Mary bar.

Lilly shook her head, bringing herself back to the task at hand. She could learn more about the vast history of Lone Tree another time. Now, she needed to figure out if Earl Graves had done anything noteworthy to end up on the internet.

Even with the added qualifier of the town, she found nothing more than online phone book listings for the Earl Graves who lived in Lone Tree, as well as other Earl Graveses who did not.

"This is getting me nowhere," Lilly muttered as she closed out of Google and stared at the blank laptop screen.

She wasn't even sure what she was hoping to find. Between the divorce, her grandparents' death, and the move, her poor rattled brain jumped into crime drama murder mystery TV show mode. The strange, and frankly over-the-top, manner in which the old man had spoken to Lilly had tricked her into thinking there was more beneath the surface. Something sinister, cloak-and-dagger, a clandestine pact made between her grandfather and Earl Graves. But this wasn't a TV show, it was real life.

Her new—although some-assembly-required—life.

Lilly's eyes glanced over the den-slash-study, marveling at the books and their ancient, well-maintained spines. Their gold embossed lettering of titles and authors glinted in the early afternoon sunlight that filtered through the muslin and lace curtains. The grandfather clock in the main living room began to chime, the resonant tones echoing throughout the main floor of the house. She winced, realizing that she'd have to get it looked at by a professional to get the chimes back in tune.

Thinking about fixing the clock triggered a cascading list of other things that needed to be fixed or updated around the house and the farm outbuildings. From the outbuildings her mind wandered to the fields surrounding her, a sea of black dirt and crops. Then the ditches.

And the ditches brought back more images of Mr. Carpenter's lifeless body.

As she sat there, Lilly's chest constricted as each new item added itself to her mental list. The golden book spines dimmed suddenly, the once soft light from the window grew crushing.

With barely a thought, Lilly bolted up from the leather chair, grabbed her laptop, and left the sitting room. She continued down the front hall, snatched her purse and car keys from the entry table, and bounded through the door. For a brief moment, she second guessed if she had indeed shut the heavy front door behind her.

Lilly didn't acknowledge Ryan's Chevy truck trying to leave at the same time, nor did she see him slamming on his brakes to narrowly avoid her orange Kia Soul as she tore down the driveway, kicking up gravel.

Long-dormant muscle memory took over as Lilly drove and she found herself back in Lone Tree and parked in front of Faith's café, Grandma's Attic, once more. She stared out beyond her windshield at the quaint eatery's front windows and tried to trace her path from the farm to town. All she could recall was, this time, she took a far more direct route, even more efficient than that given to her by Mr. Carpenter.

She tried, and failed, to push any thoughts of the deceased realtor from her mind.

Before her sudden departure from her grandparents' lives, Lilly had started her driver's education training on those very same gravel roads that now seemed a labyrinth of dirt and barely plowed fields. Perhaps being on those roads once more awakened something that she had forgotten over the last fifteen years.

As she stared at the front door of Grandma's Attic, her stomach growled loudly. Lilly glanced at the clock on her car's dashboard and realized she hadn't eaten since that morning. Between getting lost, trying to feed the cows, surviving another run-in with Ryan, and dealing with a dead body, Lilly had barely stopped to take care of herself. She grimaced as she thought about going into the café twice on the same day; however, Lilly figured that the regulars in Lone Tree visited more often.

Upon opening the door, Lilly was greeted with the homey smells of beef roast, fresh baked bread, and what she figured was wild rice soup. Her stomach rumbled once more.

"Lilly! You're back!" Faith waved at her as she handed a credit card back to a customer. "We'll see you tomorrow for coffee, Jimmy," she called after the man as he left.

Lilly tried to stand next to the counter and found each stool occupied. Most of the tables and booths were also regrettably occupied with groups of elderly patrons who were near identical copies of the groups that filled the café that morning. Lilly worked her way up as close to the counter and Faith as she could without inconveniencing someone paying or eating.

"Is this place ever empty?" Lilly asked over the din of the crowd.

"Only when the doors are locked," Faith grinned. "What can I get you?"

Lilly stared helplessly at the chalkboard menu above the bar. The grainy white lettering suddenly blurred together from hunger. "Whatever that soup is, it smells wonderful," Lilly blinked her tired eyes.

"Oh, that's a good choice!" Faith's eyes lit up. "You go find a spot and I'll bring it out."

Lilly turned from the counter and scanned the dining space. The more comfortable and secluded booths already held elderly occupants who looked like they intended to stay awhile, and the tables crowded into each other with boisterous farmers, factory workers, and construction crews.

She started to lose hope of finding a table when a pair of construction workers vacated their table. Lilly didn't wait for someone to come to clear the dirty dishes or wipe the table down, she scurried over to the mismatched chairs and claimed it as her own. Busying herself with stacking the used dishes into a manageable pile on the table, Lilly could feel eyes slowly flicking in her direction.

Word of the new girl in town spreads fast, Lilly thought as she kept her eyes focused on the chipped Formica table, as if the faded yellow and gray boomerang designs really were that interesting. The tables and booth nearest to her didn't bother to hide their rubber necks, and for those out of her periphery, she could feel their stares burn into her back.

How much of the news of her arrival was spread by Maggie Swenson? The good-natured, well-meaning realtor more than likely told all her coworkers, any real estate clients, and anyone else who would listen about Harold and Beverly's granddaughter finally coming home. Or word spread after the morning's run-in with Earl Graves. Lilly was certain that most of the town's busy bodies sat in those booths during his ranting, and after they finished their scones and coffees, talk of the incident must have spread like wildfire.

Thinking about the surly farmer brought back the recent unpleasantness of only hours ago. She shivered. That's why everyone was looking at her. Not only was she the new person in town—the estranged granddaughter of one of their own—there was now a dead body on her land. Well, almost on her land. Did the ditch that held her mailbox constitute part of her property?

Coming here was a bad idea. Lilly took a deep breath. Her earlier panic had barely subsided; now, the unwanted attention from the towns-folk threatened to tip it over the edge once more.

"Hey, are you okay?"

Lilly started in her seat, her eyes rising from the 1950s table to see a pair of dark blue pants accompanied by a black holster, complete with glinting black pistol.

She swallowed hard and scooted her chair back.

"It's the gun, isn't it?" The same voice continued, chuckling behind the words. "Everyone's always a little jumpy around the gun."

Lilly blinked once more and finally raised her eyes to take in the source of the voice and owner of the gun. Wedged between her table and the neighboring table full of farmers stood a policeman in a crisp blue uniform, buttons, badge, and accessories gleaming in the dim café light. A warm smile eased the sharpness of his nose and jawline, both strong and—heaven help her, Lilly couldn't deny—extremely attractive.

But she did always like a man in uniform.

"Mind if I sit?"

"Oh, yes, yes, you can sit," Lilly blurted as she fussed with the stack of dishes to make room for him.

"Don't worry about them, Travis will be around to pick them up." The policeman smiled again as he maneuvered into his chair.

Lilly looked at him hard, her initial shock wearing off. "I'm sorry, why are you sitting with me? Is there something wrong?"

The man laughed, hazel eyes crinkling at the corners. "Oh, no. Nothing's wrong. Faith just sent me over to make sure you were feeling okay. Said something about you having a rough last few days?"

More like last few hours.

"Faith?" Lilly turned, trying to spy the woman behind the counter. "Are you Tobiah, Faith's husband?"

"Toby!" He laughed once more. "That's rich. No, sorry. I'm Joshua, Faith and Ryan's cousin." He held out his hand across the table.

"Lilly Schmidt," she accepted his hand, surprised at how strong he gripped hers. She smiled back, taking a few seconds to glance over his uniform. His golden badge held the town seal, stating LTPD above a smaller pin that read J. HEIMDALL.

"I know who you are."

"Oh, you do?"

"I was out at your place earlier." Officer Heimdall's voice tightened. "You probably didn't see me with all that was going on."

Lilly nodded politely. Besides the first responding officer and Sheriff Brandford, she didn't get a chance to see much of the other officers.

"But I know you from before today," he added.

She straightened in her chair, heat rising in her chest, her throat tight. "How do you know me?"

"Faith said your memory was pretty bad, I didn't think it was this bad!" Joshua smirked. "We played all the time at your grandparents' farm. You, your cousins, Ryan, Faith, and me."

Her apprehension faded a bit. How much of her childhood had she been repressing for the past fifteen years?

"I'm sorry I don't remember you very well, Officer Heimdall." Lilly gave a forced smile. "I was away for a long time."

"Why were you gone so long?"

Lilly's mouth tightened as she searched her mind for an answer. Thankfully, a young man who she assumed was Travis stopped by the table and took away the stack of dirty dishes. "Faith said she'd be out in a bit with your soup." He hurried away as quickly as he'd come, providing a welcomed distraction from Officer Heimdall's question.

"So if you're a policeman, that must mean your dad is one of the county sheriffs?" Lilly asked.

"You don't remember me, but you can remember that?"

"Maggie gave me a quick rundown on the Swenson family tree yesterday while showing me around the old farm."

Joshua nodded. "Aunt Maggie means well, just be careful around her."

Another twinge of apprehension crept up her spine. Today was not the day for cryptic questions. "Why?"

"Do you always take things so seriously?" He laughed again. Lilly found herself liking the fact she could make him laugh, even if it came at her expense. "I just mean if you get her going, she'll talk your ear off. Poor woman doesn't have much to do around the house now that Uncle Robert is retired and the real estate market's not what it used to be—"

"I knew you two would hit it off!" Faith's cheerful voice drowned out Joshua's words. She materialized next to the table and placed a steaming bowl of wild rice soup and a little dish with a dinner roll in front of Lilly.

Joshua cleared his throat. "Hey, Faith."

Lilly noticed Joshua pushing away from the table, even though she knew he tried to be nonchalant. Faith's smile deepened as he moved.

Now what is Faith up to?

"You were looking a little pale there for a few moments, Lilly," Faith continued as she pulled over a spare chair from a recently vacated table and sat down. "I thought I'd send Josh over to make sure you didn't need any immediate assistance."

"Thank you, Faith." Lilly forced a smile, looking from cousin to cousin then back to her soup. "I'm doing alright now."

"You came in here like the devil himself was chasing you. You were white as a sheet. Did Earl spook you a little?"

"Earl?" Joshua's brows arched at the name.

"No, he didn't. Well, what he said was a little odd," Lilly fumbled for words around a spoonful of soup. "Haven't you heard about what just happened at my farm?"

"Word's been trickling in about Max," she nodded. "Nothing's really a secret for long in a town this size."

"Earl Graves?" Joshua asked, his eyes narrowing at Lilly.

"He spoke to me this morning," Lilly began.

"You spoke to Earl Graves?"

"Yes, Josh, Earl Graves." Faith rolled her eyes. "Sheesh, keep up."

He narrowed his gaze at his cousin briefly. "What did Mr. Graves say to you?"

Lilly swallowed hard, her soup settling like rocks in her stomach. "He told me that I should do what my grandpa had promised him. I have no idea what he's talking about. Mr. Carpenter was there, Earl yelled at him too."

"Carpenter," the officer scoffed, leaning back from the table.

Lilly glanced at the cousins with wide eyes. "Can someone tell me what's going on around here? I feel like I've been dumped into the middle of the Hatfield-McCoy feud, and everyone thinks I'm on the opposite side. And now someone is dead!"

Faith gave a small laugh. She tore apart a roll and popped a piece in her mouth. Lilly gaped as she realized that Faith was helping herself to her roll.

"In small towns, there's feuds everywhere. It'd be a cold day in hell if there wasn't a feud," Faith spoke around her ill-gotten bread. "Everyone here is involved in some little tiff with someone. Lots of people are related here by some manner, be it blood, marriage, worker-employee, someone's got beef with someone."

"Do these feuds normally end up with someone dying?" Lilly's hard gaze caused Faith to put the roll down.

"No," she answered, the word drawn out.

"Then why does the name Earl Graves seem to ruffle more feathers than others?" Lilly prodded. "I mentioned him around Ryan earlier and he looked like he'd seen a ghost."

"Mr. Graves has a, well, long history with a lot of people in Lone Tree," Joshua said, his tone and words clipped. Lilly figured he had subconsciously slipped into "cop mode." "And not just minor tiffs, as Faith calls them."

Lilly swallowed one last bit of soup, finding it unpalatable. "Is he dangerous?"

"No."

"Yes."

The cousins spoke as one, though not in agreement.

"He is not dangerous," Faith elbowed Joshua in the arm. "He's just a cranky old man with no family around and few friends, and thinks the world owes him for a lifetime of trouble."

"Not according to official records." Joshua twirled the salt shaker.

Faith made a dismissive noise. "Don't listen to him, Lilly. Earl is just a crank old man who's had a hard life and now can only make those around him as miserable as he is. He's not a threat."

"He seemed prone to violence this morning." Lilly shuddered at the memory of the old man stabbing his gnarled finger in her face, yelling about old promises to be kept. "And now, the person he was aiming that anger at is dead."

"Earl just took the death of your grandparents hard." Faith flicked the last bit of Lilly's roll in her mouth. "They really were some of the last people in town who were friendly to him. Max dying is not related to Earl."

Joshua pushed back from the table. "Earl just likes to make others around him as miserable as he is, he's no killer."

"I mentioned him to the Sheriff that was at the scene today. He didn't seem too worried about Mr. Graves..." Lilly felt her certainty in the man's involvement shaking.

"See, nothing to worry about. Just a cranky old fart blowing a lot of hot air." Faith gave a decisive nod.

"Well, as interesting as the conversation and company have been," he gave a courteous nod to Lilly as he rose to his feet, "I, regretfully, have to get back to work. Ms. Schmidt, it was a pleasure. Faith, behave."

The two watched him leave the café. Lilly's mind spun, churning over the new little bits of information about Earl Graves. If he'd been as notorious around town as the cousins made him out to be, and Joshua had certainly hinted that he had a criminal record of some kind, why didn't anything like that show up on her Google search? Most minor crimes and run-ins with the law were public record.

There was more to this Earl Graves than she thought.

"He seemed nice." Faith's voice brought Lilly back to Grandma's Attic.

"Seemed nice?" Lilly frowned at the other woman. "Of course you think he's nice. He's your cousin."

Faith only smiled.

Fragmented memories skittered through Lilly's mind, dredged up by Joshua's comment about all of them playing together as kids. She remembered Ryan, Faith, and their elder brothers, but Joshua's presence didn't stick as well. "And how is he your cousin?" Lilly pulled her plate closer and continued eating her soup despite her stomach turning. If she didn't, Faith would probably steal the rest of it.

"He's a cousin from Aunt Maggie's side. One of her younger sisters, I forget her name, had Joshua and was unable to take care of him so Maggie and Robert became his guardians when he was like five or something."

"Really. What happened to Maggie's sister?"

Faith shrugged. "I don't know. That's one of the few things Aunt Maggie won't talk your ear off about."

Lilly narrowed her eyes. "Now that's hard to believe."

"It's true." Faith held up her right hand with fingers extended in what Lilly could only assume was some scout salute.

"Were you actually trying to hook me up with him?" Lilly demanded with a soft edge to her accusing words. "I've just been through a very traumatic experience today—two of them to be exact! I'm not looking for a matchmaker!"

"And why would you jump to that conclusion?" Faith shot back, a hand dramatically fluttering to her chest. "He could be married for all you knew."

"He didn't have any rings."

"Ha! So you did look! You wouldn't have looked unless you were interested!"

Lilly sighed with a tired smile. "Faith, please. I appreciate the gesture, but I just got divorced. The ink is barely dry…"

"Say no more, say no more." Faith held her hands up in surrender. "I thought I'd just help you… make a few friends in town. Being new and all, it's hard to meet new people."

"Thank you, I guess."

"And besides," Faith leaned in and dropped her voice, "you heard the fuzz—I'm supposed to behave."

Chapter Six

Lilly found herself wandering the main street of Lone Tree after slipping past Faith in the chaos of the afternoon rush in Grandma's Attic. The tables and booths were filled with early birds getting their post-lunch coffee and pastries. The restaurateur had taken it upon herself to pester Lilly in between orders, especially about what she thought of Joshua. Lilly wasn't in the mood to discuss any future relationship plans with Faith. She wasn't even to the point of talking about them with herself.

She halted her walk at an intersection, the stoplights signaling that pedestrians weren't allowed to cross. Lilly vaguely registered the passing cars and lumbering trucks as they made their way along the street. She thought about Faith's questions and strong hints that she should go after her single policeman cousin. Why shouldn't she take a chance and pursue him? She could tell there had been little tingles of attraction between the two of them as they'd sat in the café.

The light turned and she made her way across the street, no clear destination in mind. Why didn't she feel as if she could be interested in Joshua?

In Lilly's mind, she and her ex-husband were barely separated. Her heart was still getting used to the fact they were divorced, too. Everything had happened so fast: one minute, her marriage was intact—far from perfect, but happy. Then she'd found out about him cheating. Within the week, he was serving her papers while the "Other Woman" hung possessively on his arm.

Six years of marriage, no matter how it ended, wasn't something to just brush aside when the next handsome face came along.

Although recently, she felt she could take a page out of Alec's playbook. Hadn't he moved on to the next pretty face while they were still married? Why shouldn't she allow herself a little fun now?

And besides, daydreaming about a cute police officer was much better than spending all her time thinking about a dead body.

She mounted the opposite sidewalk and glanced around the intersection, wondering if she should keep walking or possibly head back to her car.

Suddenly Lilly shuddered, feeling a chill tumble down her spine despite the mild spring day. A nagging voice at the back of her mind insisted that she was being watched. She feigned checking her watch and digging in her purse as she caught the periphery of the street and sidewalk around her. Living in Minneapolis had helped hone her surrounding-awareness and self-defense skills. She never figured they'd come in handy outside of downtown.

Across the street, not quite directly opposite from her, stood a hunched over figure. Lilly risked turning toward the figure, even with her attention supposedly on the contents of her wallet.

The figure lurched towards her on the sidewalk. Lilly pretended to answer a phone call, standing close to the stop light and crosswalk. The hunched shadow across the street mimicked her position by the crosswalk button. She turned, making one-to-two-word responses to a one-sided conversation, and caught a full look at who had spiked her "Spidey Sense."

Earl Graves.

He wore stained overalls and a well-worn Carhartt jacket. A trucker's hat that had seen better days sat haphazardly on his equally disheveled gray hair.

Lilly flicked her eyes to many points around her, shop doors and parked cars, but she could feel the old man's eyes burn into her every movement. She ended her fake phone call and started to walk down the sidewalk once more, away from Grandma's Attic and certainly away from her car. She didn't need Earl following her and figuring out what her car looked like.

He already knew where she currently lived, no need to give him any more information he could use later.

Lilly kept her eyes focused on the sidewalk and store fronts ahead of her, fearing what she'd see behind her with a quick look over her shoulder. Her "Spidey Sense" was still sending thrills up her neck, all the proof she needed that the crazy old man still followed her with at least his eyes.

"Good afternoon, Lilly!"

She jolted to a stop at the sound of her name, her attention rushing back into the present. Lilly looked up from the sidewalk and noticed she was stopped in front of a real estate office. Maggie Swenson stood outside the office, adjusting a sandwich board displaying new properties for sale and lease.

"Oh, good afternoon, Maggie."

Maggie gave her a well-rehearsed smile and wink. "Out exploring this fine day?"

Lilly cast a quick glance over her shoulder. Earl Graves was nowhere to be seen. Either he had been scared off by the presence of Maggie, or he felt he had scared her enough for one day.

"Uh, yes." Lilly willed herself to relax. "Just had to get off the farm, you know? Get around people again. I never realized how lonely it gets in that big house."

Maggie nodded, sagely. "Definitely. There's nothing quite like city living."

"I wouldn't call Lone Tree 'city living,' exactly." Lilly gestured to the sparsely populated street and sidewalks.

"I heard about what happened earlier, poor dear. Finding Mr. Carpenter like that. How are you doing?" Maggie continued to fuss with the sandwich board. "Blasted concrete," she muttered.

"How did you hear about Mr. Carpenter already?"

She gave up on righting the sandwich board, leaning it against her leg as she turned to Lilly. Now that she was starting to calm down and come back to herself, Lilly noticed how Maggie was dressed. Unlike their first meeting, she had on a pair of crisp, dark blue slacks and an expensive looking button-down popping out from under a cashmere sweater. Lilly had a passing thought that the realtor would look more at home amongst the corporate types of downtown Minneapolis. Lilly wondered at the sudden shift in wardrobe; it didn't fit the "Maggie Downhome Brand."

"Old Merlin Ridges has a police scanner, heard it over at the Attic just as it was happening." Maggie shook her head.

Lilly smirked. "Aren't police scanners illegal?"

"I believe so, but don't tell Merlin." Maggie shot her a mischievous wink. She suddenly sobered. "It is a shame about Max, though. I might not have liked what he was planning for the town, but he was a decent man."

Lilly narrowed her eyes, confused as to this sudden confession. "What did he have planned for the town?"

"I suppose by now you've heard about some of the property development deals he had in the works around town, no?" she asked. When Lilly shook her head, she continued, "Lone Tree is a quaint little town, yes. However, there is nothing keeping the people here. No businesses to offer jobs, no retail or dining to keep money in town. Most of the people your age and younger are heading to Mankato, New Ulm, and even St. Peter for jobs and to meet their basic needs."

Maggie paused; Lilly figured she was waiting for her to ask a question or to seem surprised by this fact. She decided to play along. "I had no idea the people of Lone Tree were hurting so much."

"Agriculture, the family farms, and the mills for processing the crops can only go so far. More residents are leaving town, or using online shopping for their needs, taking their hard earned money out of Lone Tree and out of the coffers of the small businesses still trying to make a go of it here," Maggie continued, hitting her busy-body stride.

"Max was planning to bring some of the big box stores into Lone Tree, like Target, Walmart, Cub Foods, stores that will fill the basic needs of families for groceries and goods, as well as giving jobs to residents to help build the stores and to work there."

Lilly suppressed a smile, realizing Maggie had found a new pair of ears for her vast knowledge of the town gossip. She wondered how quickly the residents of Lone Tree tired of her lengthy pitches. She remembered the friendly warning Joshua had given her about his aunt and couldn't help but finally smile. Lilly glanced down at the sandwich board, noticing the properties for sale were all fields and former homesteads. "Where will these big stores go?"

"Mostly on the northeast part of town, just a little hop away from Lone Tree." Maggie answered. "And with the business boom, so will housing developments. More people will want to stay in Lone Tree. At least that's what Max is—was hoping for."

Northeast side of town? Lilly tried to align a mental map of the area. *That's where my farm is... and where Earl Graves' farm is?*

That explains why the old man was so hostile toward Mr. Carpenter...

"That seems pretty straight forward. Almost too good to be true," Lilly said with a raised eyebrow at the older woman.

"That's what everyone in this town says." Maggie's mouth turned down sharply. "People here are resistant to change. Always have been, always will be. I can see that some of what Max was planning would be a good thing for the town..."

"But what?" Lilly prompted at the abrupt silence.

"I like the way Lone Tree is now," Maggie replied with an almost apologetic smile. "It's so hard to keep small towns small nowadays. Either they turn into ghost towns or get overrun with corporate greed."

"What Max was proposing does seem like a lot of change to happen at one time," Lilly offered.

"This town doesn't have as big a problem as Max thinks." Maggie's voice grew hard. "For years, this town has been struggling, but we have survived all the things that Max said would kill us off."

Lilly remained silent and gave a clueless shake of her head.

"Max had been butting heads with most of the Chamber of Commerce and the city council members over this silly expansion idea of his." Maggie took Lilly's silence as the cue to continue. "I know Lisa Hayes would get quite livid at the Chamber meetings whenever Max showed up with yet another reason why the big box stores would benefit the town."

"Wouldn't the Chamber be looking to add more commerce to the town?"

"Not that type of commerce, dearie." The realtor shook her head. "They like small town stores, mom and pop shops as it were. Keep the money here in town instead of some big corporate office in New York or

China or some godforsaken place—"

Maggie cut herself off, looking taken aback by her own outburst and yet like she wanted to say more, but remained quiet. She patted a hand over her hair and stood a little straighter. "But no more talk of that now. We mustn't speak ill of the dead."

Lilly nodded as Maggie's words sank in. Some of what Max proposed for the town made sense. She wasn't sure how it would work with the size of the project he was hoping to advance.

"I think Max was on the right path for the town. Maybe needed to scale it down a bit, though." Lilly kicked at a stone on the sidewalk. "The town would really benefit from that type of expansion, if it pans out."

Maggie cleared her throat.

"It'd just be a shame if it did hurt the small town feel of Lone Tree," Lilly added with a quick smile. "Being back here, I'm realizing there's a lot of memories."

Maggie eyed her, then flashed a million dollar smile. "It must be nice being back at the old farmhouse again."

"It is," Lilly said as she shoved her hands in her pockets.

"Any plans for the old place?"

Lilly's eyes flicked from the realtor to a vacant shop front across the street, suddenly remembering her earlier panic attack.

Maggie must have sensed Lilly's unease and she gave as comforting a smile as a salesman can give. "If you need any advice, don't hesitate to contact me at my office, or even on my cell, alright?" With the stealth of a magician, Maggie's hand shot out with a business card.

"Thank you," Lilly said as she stuffed the card into her back pocket. "I haven't made any long term plans yet. I'm still trying to get settled in. I think I have some time to explore what to do with the farm. I've had a lot of big changes in my life recently, and I don't think I need to add anymore."

"Your big move after the divorce?"

Lilly's eyes narrowed. "Yes—"

"It's been great having Harold and Bev's granddaughter back to town." Maggie gave a motherly smile.

"I hope I can live up to everyone's expectations."

"Don't you worry about them, Mrs. Rhodes." Maggie halted. "Oh, goodness, I'm sorry."

"It's alright—"

"Should I still use Ms. Rhodes? Or should I switch to the maiden Schmidt?"

Lilly licked her lips. "I'm still figuring that out. Neither name sounds quite right to me at the moment."

"I just hope Mr. Graves didn't give you too much of a fright," Maggie offered.

The switch in topic threw Lilly off guard. It took her a moment to form a reply.

"It certainly surprised me, almost scared me. I feel bad for him, I can't give him what he wants because I have no idea what he's talking about."

"A little helpful advice, don't listen to a word that man says. He's a delusional drunk who tries to scare people into giving him what he wants because he believes the world owes him," the older woman said, giving a decisive nod.

Some more clues... Lilly nodded knowingly.

"Having been in Lone Tree longer than I have, and certainly having had more interactions with Mr. Graves, I don't suppose you'd know what he wants from me, would you?" Lilly ventured.

The realtor shrugged. "I don't know what that man could have said to you, but like I said, he's just a lonely old man. Who knows if anything he says is founded in reality?"

Lilly pressed her lips together and let out a slow breath. "You must know something. Any information is better than what I have now. Maybe if I had an idea of what he was talking about, I could help him?"

Maggie muffled a scoffing laugh. "Help him? You sound like your grandmother."

Instantly Lilly's ears perked up and she found herself leaning closer to the realtor. "What do you mean by that?"

"Your grandma Beverly was one miracle away from sainthood, truly. She'd help anybody who came to her, no matter how trivial their problem was. Give the shirt off her back."

"How did she try to help Mr. Graves?"

Maggie let the sandwich board clatter to the sidewalk with a disdainful look. "He never married, and his siblings all dropped him like a bad habit. It isn't too hard to figure out why they'd do that. I suppose your grandma felt sorry for the man. She'd buy groceries for him, go over once or twice a week, and do his laundry for him. Go check on him every so often to make sure he was eating, taking care of things around the home."

"Sounds awfully nice to do for someone no one seems to like."

"Again, one miracle away from sainthood."

"Oh no..." Lilly felt the blood drain from her face. "Does Mr. Graves want me to continue to check in on him like Grandma did?"

That drew a genuine belly laugh from the realtor. "Oh lord, I pray not for your sake!"

"Then what?"

Maggie shrugged, kicking a wingtip shoe absently at the abandoned advertisement. "I wish I knew. Again, half of what he says you can be pretty sure he twisted it a mile away from the truth, and the other half, you can't be sure he didn't just flat out make it up."

"Then what do I do about him?"

Maggie picked up the dejected sandwich board, pulled open the door to her office, and shrugged. "Just ignore him, Lilly. Ignore him and he'll just go away."

Lilly continued on her walk, her mind churning over Mrs. Swenson's words. She slowed her pace and glanced around the current section of Main Street where she found herself. The store fronts were fewer now, and more residential buildings popped up in between the business signs. She glanced behind her and found herself only two blocks away from Lone Tree Realty, yet it felt a world away.

A sprinkling of Tudor and Victorian style homes added a quaint feel to the street. Lilly felt strangely at home, as if she had just walked into a neighborhood in Northern Minneapolis.

One pale yellow Victorian with faded cream trim caught her eye across the street. It looked familiar... The grand house stood almost three stories above the sparse foot traffic below. A segmented bay window jutted out into the well-manicured lawn with an arch of celestial-colored stained glass catching the eye. Lilly marveled at the brilliant glinting from the panes throughout the upper two stories as well, though the third level was likely more a partial attic or extra room.

The colorful house stood out among its neighbors, the last bastion of a long-forgotten era. Lilly glanced up and down Main Street, and, finding the coast clear, jay-walked over to the grand Victorian.

Hey, if I get arrested, hopefully it'll be by Officer Josh! Lilly smirked as she loped across the pavement.

As she paused on the sidewalk before the house, Lilly took in the careful landscaping. A large rough-hewn wooden sign stood amongst a bed of azaleas and hostas. In bright red paint, "Lone Tree Public Library" was hand-painted in large letters.

Lilly ascended the walk to the front porch, seeing displays of books arranged expertly in the window sills and bays of the first floor. Next to the ornate glass front door hung another hand-painted sign informing patrons of days and hours of operation.

She opened the glass door and pushed the secondary screen door, a cacophony of bells jingled above her head, and she passed over the threshold. Lilly cringed as she slinked away from the door, feeling self-conscious over causing so much noise in a library. She was certain a stern, paper-thin, and old librarian would descend upon her from the dusty stacks, admonishing her for disturbing the peace.

No dowdy spinster guardian of the books accosted her as she made her way further into the library, however. She began to relax and take in the sights around her.

The house-turned-library was laid out much like her grandparents' home, only on a smaller scale. Instead of a dining room, living room, and sitting parlor full of turn-of-the-century furniture, each room was full of rows of low bookshelves. In the larger dining room, a handful of tables were set up, ready to welcome any patron that needed space to study or spread out. At that moment, a group of elderly couples sat quietly around one of the tables, one energetic senior dealing to the rest from a battered deck of cards.

More shelves bordered the room instead of cooking appliances and cabinetry in what would have been the kitchen, creating a sort of literary fortress around the circulation desk. Much to Lilly's surprise, a young woman sat behind the desk—no spinster school marm with sharp features and an even sharper voice with which to shush people.

The young woman, with blond hair pulled back into an unruly bun at the top of her head, glanced up when a wooden floorboard creaked beneath Lilly's shoe. Large brown eyes peered at her over a pair of black, thick-rimmed glasses. This young woman would have looked more in place on Nicollet Avenue than in rural Minnesota.

"Hello and welcome to Lone Tree Public Library!" The librarian's bubbling voice rivaled the jingle of the doorway bells.

"Uh, hi." Lilly weakly waved, then instantly cringed.

"Is there anything I can help you find today?" the woman asked as Lilly took a few steps closer to the desk.

She saw a name tag with "Allison" etched into the white-coated metal.

"Not really, uh, Allison. I was just walking down the street and saw the house—uh, library, and wanted to check it out. I haven't been here in years."

Why did I add that part?

"Come back for spring break, eh?" Allison nodded. "Do you go to Mankato State? Or are you up in the Cities?"

Lilly bit her lower lip to keep from smiling. Or was it to keep from grimacing? She was well beyond college at this point, and the idea that someone thought she looked to be in her early twenties was the little boost she needed that day.

"No, I'm already out of college. I went to the U in Minneapolis," Lilly replied.

"I'm hoping to transfer to the U, maybe to the St. Paul campus," Allison offered. "I'm not doing so well at Mankato. Hopefully, being in a larger city with more enlightened people will suit me better."

"You think so?" Lilly fought a grin.

"You seem like a worldly woman. From the Cities, right?" Allison's voice dropped down to what Lilly assumed was supposed to be a confiding tone, as if Allison had found another member of the resistance. "Between you and me, this town is so backwards. I want to get to the Cities to find more progressive, forward-thinking individuals, you know?"

Oh, yes, she would fit in so well on Nicollet Ave. Lilly couldn't help her smile from forming.

"I understand completely," Lilly nodded, leaning toward the young woman. "I hope you get your transfer."

"So do I!" the young woman gushed in an anguished drawl.

A buzzing sound coming from the desk by Allison's elbow caught both women's attention. Allison looked down and a flush spread over her cheeks. She picked up her cell phone and gave Lilly a giddy smile. "I have to, uh, take this. You can look around all you want. Upstairs are the research computers if you're interested."

Before Lilly could say thank you, Allison pushed back from the desk on a wheeled office chair, spun around so Lilly could only see her back, and started talking into her phone with hushed tones.

"Gotcha." Lilly nodded to herself and continued her exploration of the library.

She meandered through the shelves, taking note that the children's and teens' sections took up the majority of the first floor. A small sign at the back of the first floor indicated that general fiction, nonfiction, and reference could be found up the adjacent stairs. Lilly ascended these stairs, each creaky footstep sounding like a bomb in the silent library. Given that it was later in the afternoon on a weekday, Lilly figured most patrons would be at work or at school, unless they were on spring break, like Allison had thought she was.

Once on the second floor, the squeaks and groans of the old house subsided some. Lilly took a moment to breathe in the musty air, the newly-familiar smell opening the floodgates for once-forgotten memories. Her Grandma Beverly would bring her and her cousins to the library almost every time they came to visit. Sometimes, she'd even invite the Swenson children along, Faith and Ryan. Eventually, the trips to town consisted of her, sometimes her cousin Tammy, Faith, and Ryan. Then Ryan stopped coming along, possibly not wanting to seem "too girly" to his elder brothers.

Why am I remembering all of this now? Lilly walked through the rooms of the second floor slowly, noticing how each former bedroom now held its own genre of book. The master bedroom now housed general fiction, including the subgenres of mystery, sci-fi, and romance. Autobiographies/memoirs, science, and art were split between three children's bedrooms. A large sitting room attached to the master bedroom held the main reference section and two older model flat-screen computers.

Lilly sat in front of one monitor and jiggled the computer mouse to life. The screen flickered awake to reveal the Lone Tree city crest set as the desktop background. Lilly clicked open the library's search engine and poised her fingers above the keyboard.

Again, she found herself at a loss of what to type in to get the desired result. She wasn't even sure she knew what she wanted her desired result to be. She stared at the flickering computer screen in silence, hoping that the universe would just throw something in her lap.

She remembered her first failed attempt at searching for information about anything in this town online and pushed away from the monitor. This town was just Mayberry-esque enough to not be capable of internet-worthy news. Lilly knew that any further searching online would be futile. She'd be able to gather more information from the locals. Her brief conversations with Officer Joshua and Maggie Swenson were prime examples.

She was growing more confident that the townsfolk would be willing to tell her what they knew when she mentioned Mr. Graves; they definitely wouldn't hold back how they felt about the man. When dealing with someone so widely reviled, Lilly just wondered if she'd be able to discern fact from opinion.

Lilly made her way down to the main circulation desk. She found Allison no longer disposed of with her cell phone. Now, she stared at the computer monitor with half-closed eyes.

"Allison?" Lilly announced her presence as she rounded the corner. The young woman barely moved. "Just wondering, does this library have any historical records of land titles and ownerships?"

Allison's blank expression answered Lilly's question before the young woman opened her mouth. "I don't know. I just started here..."

"Is there someone here who could tell me anything about land titles?"

A slow blink was added to the vacant stare.

"Mrs. Krzmarzick would know."

"Mrs. Kritmahzeck?" Lilly's mouth fumbled over the name.

"Chris. Mar. Zik." Allison exaggerated each syllable's pronunciation, with what Lilly deemed the faintest of eye rolls.

So much for being comrades in progressive arms...

"Sorry, Krzmarzick." Lilly knew she still wasn't saying it right. "Is she in?"

"Not until Friday. She's still out on some medical leave. Had her hip replaced or something."

"Friday..." Lilly ticked the days off in her head, shifting her plans slightly with the new information. "Thank you, Allison. I'll be back in on Friday."

"Okay, have a good day."

Lilly left the moody pseudo-librarian, reconstructing her plans as she walked back to the entrance. Did she want to go to the farm right away? Alone out in the near-middle-of-nowhere so close to the scene of an alleged crime?

Lilly rounded a shelf of books and skidded to a stop. The area with all the tables was suddenly full of people. She hadn't heard any of them enter the library; either they were really stealthy, or Lilly had imagined the chiming bell at the door when she first entered.

At each table sat a pair of elderly women and a pair of equally elderly men sat on their respective sides. Laid out before each group were intricate patterns of playing cards. Lilly had spent many nights in her grandparents' living room playing all manner of card games: Five Hundred, Rummy, Hearts... This particular card game proved foreign to Lilly, however.

She recognized a few of the players from Grandma's Attic and the other morning when Earl Graves had screeched at her like a barn owl. A few peeped up from their hands and gave her a quick glance over, not wishing to break their concentration for too long to give a proper rural greeting. Lilly returned the gesture with a small wiggle of her hand.

"Take a picture, it'll last longer," an old man with a green and yellow John Deere hat groused.

Lilly took a small step back, surprised by such a comment coming from an elderly man.

"Pssst, Eddie, leave the girl alone and play that losing hand," the woman across the table scolded.

"I am not losing, Wilma," Eddie snapped back.

"We all know what you're holding, so hurry up and put it down so we can move on." Wilma grinned, her jowly chins jiggling with suppressed mirth.

Eddie glowered at the woman as he slammed his cards face down on the table.

The neighboring three groups all responded with what felt like a well-rehearsed *sshhhhh!*

Eddie's face flushed beet red.

Wilma turned to Lilly and beckoned her over with a slender yet knobby-jointed finger. "Did you have a question, dearie? Would you like to play Sheep's Head with us?"

"Sheep's Head?" Lilly echoed.

"She don't want to play no Sheep's Head, Wilma," Eddie growled. "Hurry up and deal the next hand, will ya?"

Wilma turned a laser focused glare at him. "How do you know she doesn't want to play?"

The two began bickering, ignoring the other tables' shhh! warnings.

"Please, no, no thank you!" Lilly called over the noise. "I-I don't know how to play Sheep's Head."

"Let her play then!" a man from another table called. "Then Eddie might finally win a game!"

Eddie's face flushed a deeper shade of red as the other card players joined in on the raucous laughter.

"Maybe another time." Lilly couldn't help but smile.

"Aren't you Bev and Harry's granddaughter?" the second woman on Wilma and Eddie's table asked. "Lillith... Lucy... Leslie..."

"Lillian. Yes, Bev and Harold were my grandparents."

"So you're the one who found the stiff, eh?" Eddie barked.

The other eleven seniors fell silent and stared at their fellow player.

It's just not Eddie's day... Lilly thought while fighting back a smirk.

"Yes, I did find Mr. Carpenter's body," she replied.

"Someone finally did him in, eh?"

"It was only a matter of time."

"Poor thing, but I suppose that's the end someone like that is bound to have..."

The peanut gallery began talking at once, each wanting to voice their opinion on the death, figuring Eddie had already broken the ice with his crude comment. Lilly wondered how long the waiting period was in a small town before news like that was freely discussed amongst the gossip mills. The once quiet card club now bubbled with rumors, gasps, and relieved keepers of salacious tidbits—true or not—about the deceased.

"He's the one who got himself on people's shit lists, so why should it be a surprise that he's finally discovered in the ditch dead?"

Lilly narrowed in on the speaker of the last comment. A small, unassuming woman in a teal polyester track suit with a matching flower pinned in her hair continued to shuffle her hand of cards as Lilly studied her. The other card players noticed Lilly's fixed attention and soon followed suit.

"Elvira, whatever are you talking about?" a female tablemate asked.

"He's the one who got himself on people's shit lists, so why should it be a surprise that he's finally discovered in the ditch dead?" she repeated.

"Elvira!" another woman gasped. "How could you say such a thing?"

"It's true, ain't it?" Elvira returned, her voice even and with a touch of amusement.

"Who would possibly hate him enough to want him dead?" Wilma asked as she dealt out the new hand to her table. Eddie greedily snatched his cards off the table, scowling at each new card he added. "Good thing we're not playing poker, Eddie," she added with a grin.

"Who didn't do it is the better question," another man at Elvira's table chimed in. "He wasn't the most moral of men. Just ask ol' Perry about the underhanded things he did to him."

"Perry?" Lilly asked.

"Matheson Trucking, on the east side of town on County 45 on your way to Sleepy Eye," the man explained. "Poor guy is still trying to rebuild after all these years."

"What happened?"

"A land deal went sour real quick." The man shook his head as he assembled his new hand. "Of course Max would never own up to it, no matter what Perry threatened."

Lilly stood there, absorbing these new nuggets of information as the groups slowly quieted down and went back to focusing on their cards. The time for gossip and chitchat was done. She realized she had been forgotten by the card club so she slipped silently around their tables and toward the front door. Her mind churned with all the information she had just picked up without even trying, segmented and piecemeal though it was.

She checked her watch as she walked down the flagstone path, realizing that Ryan would be back around five or six to start the evening milking and get the cows ready for the night. Given he'd had extra time earlier that day waiting at the farm for the police to clear the road, he had already completed his other afternoon chores ahead of schedule.

Slowly, thoughts of Max Carpenter and the possible murder slipped into the recesses of her mind to simmer until the time was right. Now, she had other matters more pressing to consider. Mrs. Swenson's questions pinged around her head as she made her way back to the farm. What was she planning to do with the farm now that it was hers?

Could she see herself fitting into a modern, yet very strange, version of Green Acres?

She glanced at the time again as she navigated the gravel roads back to the farmstead. Lilly needed to find answers to the many questions and "what if"s at once. She tried to remember what her father used to say about teaching someone how to do something new. Something like "the best way to learn to swim is to just jump off the pier"?

Lilly smiled as the farm slowly came into view. Her fingers danced on the steering wheel as excitement and nerves fought for dominance as she passed the mailbox. There was no sign of the police presence from just a mere couple hours before, which was good, because she didn't have time to focus on the macabre events of earlier..

Lilly needed to set concrete plans for the farm and she needed to be quick about it, before Earl Graves interfered. Whether that interference would manifest as a chronic annoyance or something more deadly, Lilly didn't want to know. She was going to jump into this whole farmer thing, and get sweaty and dirty along with the cows.

And Ryan would teach her, whether he liked it or not.

Chapter Seven

Lilly parked her car near the farmhouse, brain still churning over the barrage of ideas for the farm. The drive back from town had given her time to start brainstorming and to make a mental list of keywords to scour the internet for later. She smiled when she spied Ryan's rusty green Chevy down by the barn. For wanting to leave the farm so badly, why was he back so soon after leaving?

For a flitting moment, Lilly wondered what the grouchy farmhand did when he wasn't at the farm.

She made her way down to the lower level of the barn, going over her well-practiced speech one more time before confronting Ryan. Lilly reworked a few major sentences, ensuring her chosen words conveyed a more confident tone. She may not be an active graphic designer at the moment, but she still had the gift of weaving marketing magic.

Too bad she didn't have time to create a corresponding PowerPoint; then, she'd really be in her persuasive prime.

The barn was quiet and the stalls vacant when she entered. The tether chains hung from the iron bars of the stalls, creaking faintly in the breeze from the barn windows. As disconcerting as the cows' moans and bellows were, the palpable silence she walked into now was more alarming. With each step, Lilly's stomach tightened.

Where are my cows?

She retraced her steps back to the office and supply room doors. Finding those rooms to be empty, Lilly strained to hear any noises from the hay loft.

Ryan's truck was here. Where was its owner?

A deep baritone honk, like an out-of-tune saxophone, blared in through the windows, drawing her attention over to the open side of the barn. Beyond the windows, she spotted a handful of black and white spotted shapes running and jumping. She stood next to the windows and watched as the small herd frolicked in the pasture. In spite of weighing nearly a ton each, the bovines kicked up their hind legs and bounded across the small field. Lilly smiled, pleased to see the herd enjoying the spring weather and also pleased to see that they all were let outside. Why had only a handful been let out before and now the whole group was out? She made a mental note to ask Ryan about the herd's pasture schedule.

Dandelion's distinct bellow echoed from the pasture. Some of the younger cows began twitching their tails and swaying their heads. Again, Lilly noticed a frantic tone to the matriarch's deep tones.

The double doors crashed open, ushering in a gust of spring air...and one disgruntled farmhand. Lilly bolted at the noise and coughed at the cloud of dust stirred up from the straw. Ryan hurried over to the supply room door, carrying what looked like a canoe paddle.

"Where have you been?" he barked when his gaze landed on her.

"Well, hello to you, too!" Lilly called back through a final cough.

"The cows are out," Ryan snapped as he jerked open the supply room doors and disappeared.

"As they should be!" Lilly returned when Ryan reappeared. "It's a gorgeous day out. They should be outside."

"No, you daft heifer." Ryan stomped over to her. He held the odd-shaped canoe paddle in one hand and a broken broom handle in the other. Lilly opened her mouth to counter his insult when he abruptly thrust the canoe paddle toward her.

"They're loose. The pasture fence broke and some got out into the grove." His hard eyes held her gaze from under his John Deere hat while the tone of his voice kept her silent. "I got some back, but they keep slipping through. I need help."

He slammed the supply room's door and went outside.

Lilly hurried to catch up with him, the strange paddle rattling as she moved. *So that's why he was back so soon. With the cows breaking out of their fence, he never had the chance to leave the farm.* Her voice returned. "If you needed help, why didn't you call me an hour ago?"

He glared over his shoulder.

She followed him into the pasture and through a large metal gate. They continued along the wire fence to avoid the scampering cows in the middle of the enclosure. Lilly cast wary glances at the cows, suddenly realizing how large the animals were when not in their stalls.

Ryan led Lilly to the far end of the paddock where the grove began on the other side of the fence. Still littered with dead leaf material, brown grass, and barren trees, the grove was slowly coming to life as spring charged on. The grove surrounded the farmstead on two sides, offering what her grandfather called a natural snow fence and windbreak.

As they neared the back fence, Lilly noticed a section of wire missing between two wooden posts.

"You stay here and guard this section. Keep the other cows from getting out. I'm going to go get the others still left out here," Ryan said as he walked past her into the grove.

"Wait!" Lilly screeched.

A small chorus of cows replied with their own frantic cries.

"How am I supposed to stop them?" Lilly's voice shook.

Ryan's shoulders slumped as he trudged back to her. His hand shot out and grabbed the paddle's long handle and raised it—along with her arms—up to her face. The strange contraption rattled again like there were little plastic beads or beans in the hollow end of the paddle.

"With this." He shook it aggressively, exaggerating the noise. "Cows get spooked by noises and motion easily. If a cow comes too close to this gap, just shake this at them. Wave your hands. Make noise. It's that simple." He opened his hand to release the rattle, causing Lilly to almost drop it. He turned and walked through the dead undergrowth of the grove.

"Is that it?" Lilly shouted after him.

"You could also just keep talking," Ryan called over his shoulder. "I'm certain hearing all about how hard your life has been will make a few of them fall asleep."

Lilly gasped as he disappeared into the murky grove.

"Big stupid jerk." Lilly turned to face the pasture. The realization that almost a dozen near-ton animals were within a stone's throw of her and all she had to protect herself was a rattle stick settled heavy between her shoulders.

She studied the herd and kept track of where the cows were and how far away they were from her. Counting to make sure that she had nine out of the twelve cows in the pasture proved more challenging. The black and white splotches blended together, making it near impossible for Lilly to distinguish one cow from another.

Save Dandelion. She was the largest and loudest of the herd. Dandelion moved deliberately around the paddock, swinging her massive neck back and forth, gently head-butting the rest of the herd away from the barn and toward the far end of the pasture, in a spot away from the hole in the fence. A few of the more frisky cows received a sharp nip on the hind quarter from the elder cow before they begrudgingly moved.

Lilly watched in silence, not sure if she should believe her eyes. Was Dandelion helping to herd the other cows for her? If not that, she certainly was keeping them in line. Dandelion walked around the pasture, still bobbing her head up and down and calling with her deep voice. Could she also be calling to the three wayward cows in the grove?

Her feeling of imminent danger subsided. She amused herself with shaking the rattle paddle, not really in earnest, and vaguely wondering how long Ryan would be.

Not all the cows paid heed to Dandelion's ministrations. Two cows, smaller than Dandelion though still formidable animals in their own right, began an ambling march toward the back part of the paddock.

And right toward Lilly.

She stopped, the faint rattle halting. She watched them advance on her. Lilly swallowed hard, fists clenching then easing up on the long plastic handle, feet rocking back and forth.

Lilly waved the rattle-paddle in a wide arc about her head. The two advancing cows paused for a moment and then continued their slow progression.

"Shoo cows, shooo!" Lilly called to them, now waving the stick in front of her in fast strokes. Still, the rattle hardly lived up to its name. "Go back to the barn!"

The Holsteins moved closer to her. Lilly backed away from them, keeping the paddle between her and the animals. She pressed her back against the rough wooden post and watched as the cows crossed the pasture line and stepped into the woods.

"No! No! Go back to the barn!" Lilly stabbed the air between her and the cows with the paddle. It finally made enough noise for the cows to hear. The one closest to her stopped and swung her head toward the racket. To Lilly's dismay, the cow licked at the paddle, then continued with her friend into the grove.

"No, no, no, no!" Lilly watched helplessly as they walked further into the woods and then turned back to the others still in the enclosure.

Dandelion had stopped moving the herd toward the barn and now laid down in the grass, lazily chewing her cud with her eyes half closed. The others, who Dandelion had worked so hard to corral, were free once more to creep toward the open part of the fence.

"Much help you are!" Lilly shouted. She shook the stick at the cow. It still didn't give off much noise.

Lilly gave an undignified cry and threw the stick toward the grove. "Stupid stick!"

It finally gave a healthy rattle as it clattered to the dirt.

She shifted her stance, unsure of her next move. Did she dare go after the two cows or should she stay and watch the rest? Ryan would be coming soon with the other three. Five cows would be easier to deal with than if the whole herd of twelve escaped into the grove. Lilly quickly goose-stepped over to where the rattle had fallen and snatched it from the damp earth before reclaiming her spot at the fence gap.

Something rustled behind her. Lilly whirled around, rattle paddle brandished like a baseball bat. She scanned the dimly lit grove, the hazy spring sunlight unable to add much distinction to the winter debris. She whirled back around to watch the cows. They had settled down from whatever burst of energy they'd had earlier. Most nibbled at the new growth grass or laid down for a quick early evening snooze.

Behind her, a branch snapped loudly. Lilly faced the grove again.

"Ryan?" Her voice was small compared to the expanse of trees.

A black blur moved along the dead undergrowth.

"Ryan?" Lilly called out louder.

The sun dipped below the horizon, casting the grove into murky shadow. Trees and their branches blended together, bushes and shadows becoming one. The more she looked into the trees, the deeper the grove appeared. She remembered it wasn't that big of a grove, so why did it seem so massive now?

As her anxiety spiked, Lilly tried to recall what she'd learned in her first year of college in freshman art class. What was that depth perception thing? *Atmospheric perspective. That's why all the trees are blurring together... the color getting lighter the farther away something is...*

Another branch snapped to her right. Closer this time.

When did the grove get this creepy? I don't remember it being this scary when I was little...

Something screamed in the bushes to her left.

"Ryan!" Lilly shrieked and jumped behind the fence post, rattle-paddle waving above her head wildly.

A raccoon scurried from behind a tree trunk, raced to a neighboring tree, and disappeared up into the bare branches.

The woods around her fell silent. All she could hear was her blood pulsing in her ears and her own ragged breathing. Behind her, Dandelion gave a soft, mournful mooooo.

"What are you doing?"

Lilly gave a strangled scream, then saw Ryan trudging his way out of the grove. His jeans and Carhartt jacket were muddier than usual, all signs of his solo efforts to wrangle the cows. His John Deere hat was pushed back from his face, allowing her first decent look at him since she arrived on the farm. Normally, his features hid beneath hat brims. Blue eyes, once believed to be dark, appeared bright blue through the dirt and grime on his face. He still sported a five o'clock shadow that accented a strong jaw. The most out of place thing on Ryan's face was the playful smirk tugging up one side of his mouth.

That same rascal smile that twisted her insides all those years ago.

"Ryan—" Lilly gasped as heat rose up her neck.

"You're trying to contain cows, not signal passing ships for help, Gilligan." He walked up to her and took the rattle-paddle. "Give me that before you hurt yourself."

Lilly's words exploded out in one breath. "Where are the cows? Two more got out and I couldn't stop them, and I thought about finding you or going after them, but then I'd leave the fence open and—"

"Why didn't you call me?" Ryan mimed holding a phone up to his ear.

Lilly's eyes narrowed. How dare he throw her words back at her.

"The two cows that just got out—no thanks to you—were the daughters of one of the ones that got out." Ryan rested the paddle over his shoulder. "They found us back in the grove and, thankfully, I got the heifers in line. All five are some of the calmer cows on the farm. Was able to get them out up closer to the main gate by the barn instead of coming down through the trees again and getting someone lost or hurt."

Lilly gaped at him, looking at the grove and then the pasture. She hadn't even noticed any activity up by the main gate. From her position, however, the dimming evening light consumed much of what she could see.

"Did you scare me on purpose then? Running around the bushes?"

Ryan grinned. "No, that wasn't me. Though, I wish it was me. I think you screamed loud enough for old Earl to hear you on the other side of the fields. Maybe gave him that heart attack that'll do him in finally."

"The raccoon, then."

"What about it?"

"Did you spook it to come at me?" Lilly demanded. "It could have had rabies! It could have bit me!"

Ryan laughed, scratching the back of his head. "Again, wish it had been me."

"Then who—"

"C'mon. We have to get this fence fixed." The gentler tone to his voice silenced any further accusations from her. "You go to the supply room, get the wire on the blue spool, and bring it back here. It's on the first rack to the left when you enter the room, middle shelf. I'll stay here, lest any more rabid animals decide to attack. Grab a headlamp, too."

She wanted to lay into him with the perfect comeback, but the idea of being away from the grove and the cows was too good to pass. Lilly turned and took the same path they had used on the way from the barn, making sure to keep as much distance between herself and the cows.

"Wire's on the first rack, middle shelf..." she mockingly repeated Ryan's instructions. "How am I supposed to know when one rack starts and one ends?" Lilly muttered to herself as she slipped through the main gate and up toward the barn. She continued to repeat his instructions, afraid of messing up, certain Ryan would snap at her if she returned with the wrong wire. His patience with her was surely running low.

"Really, what is his problem?" Lilly kicked at a rock as she turned to the lower barn doors. Her rush of confidence from earlier had certainly deflated since her return to the farm. Now that she had failed to properly contain cows, he'd be harder to convince to allow her to help around the farm. Although, only two cows escaped during her watch. That had to count for something, right?

The blue light of late dusk had finally turned to thick blackness as Lilly reached the barn, fumbling her phone out of her back pocket for light. She reached her other hand for the barn door's metal handle but drew her hand back quickly when it was warm and sticky instead of cool and smooth. "What, did one of the cows lick the door on the way to the pasture?" Lilly muttered as she flicked her hand to get the wetness off. As her phone's light burst through the liquid night, she saw her palm and fingers were a bright shade of red.

"Did Ryan have time to do some painting while I was trying to use that stupid jingle stick?"

She raised her eyes and light to the door and took a staggering step backwards.

The faded white of the doors was marred with an angry slash of red, the same sticky mess that had dripped onto the door handles. In the middle of the red was a black object. For a moment, she told herself it was just a stuffed animal. Lilly's vision faded for a heartbeat as she forced herself to look away. The thing hanging from the door was small, furry, and splashed with the same viscous red. Something bright and metallic glinted from the back of the thing's head.

"Ryan!"

Lilly barely remembered screaming his name before everything toppled into blankness.

The strong aroma of freshly brewed coffee drew Lilly out of the comforting oblivion she had been in. She blinked and was half surprised to find herself laying on the plush couch in the farmhouse, propped up with pillows. *Of course I'm in the house, there's no coffee maker in the barn. Lilly pushed herself up onto an elbow. Unless that's something else Ryan is hiding from me.* She looked about her surroundings and found the couch was separated from her dirty clothes by a bedsheet.

"Aunt Maggie was adamant about putting the sheet down first."

Lilly nearly fell off the couch at the voice; only once she recognized Faith's form lounging on a recliner opposite from her did her heart rate lower.

"Faith, what are you...?" Lilly rose to a sitting position, careful not to move too quickly. Her head felt heavy and she feared shifting positions at regular speed.

Faith gestured to her clothes. "You're very muddy. She didn't want Ryan to put you on the couch in such a state."

"Ryan?"

"Too bad you were unconscious. You'd have gotten a kick out of hearing their back and forth," Faith continued, eyeing Lilly closely. "According to Ryan, you're a lot heavier than you look."

"He said what?" Lilly immediately regretted her outburst, as her head responded with a painful throb.

At his name, Lilly's heavy mind cleared. She recalled attempting to help him get the cows in and fix the broken fence. She remembered heading toward the barn to get wire. Then the bright red stain on the door...

Lilly leaned back against the couch with a groan, feeling queasy again. "What happened?"

"You fainted."

"I got that part," Lilly sighed. "What happened after that?"

"From what I got out of Ryan, you screamed. He ran up to the barn and found you out cold on the ground." Faith leaned forward in the recliner. "Once he saw what was on the door, he called the police and then called me. I was at the café chatting with Aunt Maggie, and she insisted on coming with me."

"The police are here?" Lilly glanced around the living, taking in the relative silence of the main floor. "What did they find out?"

Faith shrugged. "Don't know much yet. Ryan brought you into the house before the first responding officer arrived. Informed him that you didn't need medical attention."

Lilly rubbed at the back of her head, finding the tender spot that was causing her headache. "And what medical degree does Ryan have that makes him an authority on the matter?"

Faith smirked. "You fainted at the sight of blood, Lilly. There's not much to do for that other than make you comfortable, make sure you don't swallow your tongue, and wait for you to wake up."

Lilly frowned. "Fine."

"And yes, the police are still here. Ryan's chatting to Joshua and his partner right now down at the barn. I suppose we should let them know you're awake in case they want to talk to you." Faith plucked her cell phone off the recliner arm rest and started to text.

"Where's Maggie now? Did she go home?

"No, she's in the kitchen." Faith didn't raise her eyes from the phone screen as she pushed away at buttons. Lilly turned toward the entryway from the living room to the main hall. She was able to make out faint noises from the kitchen. Maggie was talking, her voice muffled through the doors and distance.

"Who is she talking to?"

"Probably herself." Faith grinned, still focused on her phone. "There, Ryan let Josh know you're awake. They'll be up in a few minutes."

"We could just go down to the barn," Lilly offered.

A cacophony of falling silverware crashing in the kitchen reached their ears just as Maggie shouted down the hallway, "No one is going down to the barn!"

Lilly and Faith caught each other's glances, pausing to listen as the clamor in the kitchen died down. Faith sat straighter in the recliner, a faint grimace pulling at her mouth. "Uh oh, we said her name too many times, here she comes."

"No one is going down to the barn until the boys say it's all clear." Maggie burst into the living room carrying a large serving tray. Lilly wondered vaguely where she'd found it in her kitchen. Maggie Swenson glanced over to the couch and plopped the serving tray onto the coffee table in the middle of the room. "Oh, Lilly dear, how are you feeling? Anything I can get you?"

Lilly glanced at the tray and took note of the carefully arranged finger sandwiches, cheese slices, crackers, and sliced strawberries. She gaped at the spread. "Where did this all come from? I didn't have any of this in the kitch—"

"Aunt Maggie made me stop at Fritche's on the way over." Faith shot Lilly a sideways glance.

"I wasn't sure if you'd had time to get anything since you arrived, dear." Maggie leveled a harsh, yet motherly, glower at Faith. "I wanted you to be prepared. Now, hang on. I'll go get the beverages."

Maggie turned on her heel and disappeared back into the kitchen.

"Prepared for what? The whole Lone Tree Rescue Department to show up?" Lilly pointed to the alarmingly large amount of food.

"You know church ladies, they always make too much food even when they know how many people will be in attendance, and then complain when there's leftovers." Faith stretched precariously out of the recliner and snagged a sandwich from the tray.

"Who are the boys?" Lilly asked as she plucked a couple strawberries from the tray.

"She calls any of the male cousins and their friends 'the boys,' no matter their age." Faith picked at her sandwich, inspecting what her aunt had put in it. "Last I knew, it was Ryan, Joshua, and his partner Lance."

"Partner?"

A devilish look flashed across Faith's face. "There's no need to be jealous of Lance. He's Joshua's police partner, partner in crime fighting. He's still very much on the market and looking for someone of the female persuasion."

Lilly's cheeks burned as she grabbed a strawberry. "That's not what I meant—"

"Are you ladies thirsty?" Maggie materialized in the living room, carrying a smaller tray full of mugs and a small tea kettle.

Where is she finding all this stuff? Lilly watched as she arranged the mugs and the kettle on the coffee table.

"I figured I'd make tea, Lilly, in case you weren't feeling up to something stronger quite yet." Maggie set a cup in front of Lilly, put a tea bag in, and poured steaming water into the mug.

"Stronger? Were you going to bust out the hard liquor, Auntie?" Faith chuckled. "I'm sure there's still plenty in the house for when Lilly needs a good shot."

"Shush, you," Maggie hissed as she set the kettle down.

The aromatic tea was pleasing and calming, helping Lilly's mind and nerves settle. She muttered a thank you to Maggie and sipped cautiously. She wished Ryan and Joshua would come in already. Not knowing what had happened and what she exactly saw on the barn door unnerved her more with each passing moment. That, and not knowing who had done it.

The front door creaked open, followed by the slamming screen door.

"Oh, the boys are back." Maggie scuttled out into the entryway. "Ryan, Joshua, please, this way. Lilly is awake."

The living room seemed to shrink as the three men entered. Ryan, still clad in his dirt-encrusted jeans and jacket, was the odd man out standing next to Joshua and Lance, both dressed impeccably in their crisp uniforms. Lance, or Officer Braun per his badge, appeared a few years older than Joshua, his face darkened and lined from years spent outdoors. Dark eyes peered about the room, the consummate cop always on the watch for the smallest clue. Both had taken off their hats and tucked them under their arms when they entered the house, save for Ryan, whose hat seemed permanently attached to his head.

Joshua stood in front with Lance standing at his right and Ryan far behind on the left. "Faith, Aunt Maggie." Officer Heimdall nodded to his relatives. He then turned to Lilly and his scope of interest narrowed. "Lilly, nice seeing you again."

She forced a smile, though she knew it wavered. "I just wish it wasn't under these circumstances." Just within her field of vision, she caught Ryan mouthing "Again?" to Faith, who dismissed him with a sly smile and a subtle wiggle of her fingers.

"Did you guys figure anything out?" Lilly asked, looking from Joshua to Officer Braun.

Joshua shifted on his feet. "Yes and no. Are you up to a few questions?"

Maggie shuffled closer to the couch. "I don't think she's quite up to interrogations, Joshua. Poor thing has had a terrible fright. Why don't you boys have a bit of a snack first?"

"Aunt Maggie..." Ryan groaned, his head rolling back.

"Auntie, do you need any help with the dishes?" Faith leapt up from the recliner, swiftly snaking her arm through Mrs. Swenson's. "Let's clean the kitchen up so Lilly doesn't have to later."

"Oh, that's a splendid idea, yes..." Maggie nodded vigorously as her niece led her out of the room.

The two cousins remaining in the living room waited until the kitchen door swung shut before either took a breath.

"You'll have to excuse Aunt Maggie," Joshua said with a lopsided grin and a quick glance to his partner. "She gets herself all worked up over any police related talk."

"Doesn't approve of your profession?" Lilly asked.

"What she thinks of as police work, she gets off the cop shows on TV," Ryan answered from the corner. "She firmly believes that Josh is going to get gunned down by a ruthless drug lord one of these days."

Lilly smiled as Joshua rolled his eyes.

"My first question is, what was pinned to the barn door?" she asked, looking at each officer in turn.

"You're not going to faint again?"

"Ryan, please." Joshua turned quickly to shoot his cousin a withering look. He turned back to Lilly. "It appeared to be a, well..."

Lilly's nerves couldn't handle the long pause that followed, nor could she understand why Joshua suddenly started to crack up.

"Seriously, Josh, grow up." Ryan kicked at his cousin's rear with a foot, though he appeared to be fighting a smirk as well. "Act like a cop for once."

Lilly watched the two and wondered if this was some sort of inside joke the two shared. Why they chose now to break into a fit of giggles was beyond her.

"Fine, fine." Joshua swatted Ryan's foot away. "It was a dark brown toupee."

"A... toupee?"

The living room fell silent—well, mostly silent, as Ryan's snickers could barely be contained—as the four let the word sink in.

"So it wasn't an animal."

"Never alive."

"Well, not that we know of," Ryan chuckled.

"Ryan," Joshua hissed. "And what you thought was blood is some sort of paint."

"Paint." Lilly looked from the two policemen to Ryan and then back to Joshua. "That wasn't any paint I've seen. Who would nail a toupee covered in paint to my barn?"

Joshua sat on the recliner that Faith had occupied. "First, tell us what happened at the barn earlier."

Lilly let out a long breath and told the officers about her afternoon, coming back from town and going into the barn, Ryan and her bringing the cows in, and finishing with what she remembered seeing on the barn door before fainting.

Officer Braun diligently wrote down notes of her account, giving just a hint of a nod as he finished writing. Lilly watched him finish, amazed at how silent the man was.

"You didn't see anyone around the yard?"

"No... I was in the back by the pasture until right before I found the anim—the toupee. Didn't hear any cars, people, nothing. Ryan brought the cows up by the main gate not too long before I went up to the barn and he didn't mention anything either." Lilly pressed her lips tightly together as Ryan nodded in agreement. "Do you think this might have anything to do with Mr. Carpenter?" Lilly asked, glancing at each policeman.

"We don't believe it has anything to do with Mr. Carpenter," Joshua replied slowly. "Although, we'll certainly be comparing evidence from both scenes to see if there is any overlap. Has there been anyone else on the farm today, or the last couple days?"

Lilly narrowed her eyes at him. "Just Crabby McCrabberpants over there."

Joshua scratched his nose, trying and failing at hiding his smirk. "Well, that's a whole other investigation."

Ryan snorted. "Back to the hair kabob, Josh."

"Other than me, Maggie yesterday, and Ryan, I haven't seen anyone else on the property." Lilly bit her lip, realizing how much of her land she couldn't readily keep an eye on. Who knows how many people trek around the fields and grove without her knowledge?

Would security cameras be feasible out on the farm? Or maybe she should look into getting a farm dog. She couldn't call herself a legit farmer if she didn't have at least one dog running around barking at everything that moved.

"It was probably some high school kids playing a prank." Ryan scratched at the back of his head. "Think it'd be funny to be linked to the Carpenter death somehow."

"Why would they do that?" Lilly asked.

He shrugged. "High school kids do stupid things."

Lilly couldn't help but hear the double meaning in his words. *Really? You're going to be petty about old history now?*

"Earlier, you mentioned some farm tools missing," Lilly explained before adding details about her earlier adventure in feeding the cows and Ryan's accusations. She saw him cower in the doorway, crossing his arms tighter across his chest, refusing to meet her gaze.

"According to Ryan, one of them was found," Officer Braun said once her tale was complete, not looking up from the notes he was scribbling. "A scythe was used to, uh, well, attach the toupee to the barn door."

"How many were missing?" Joshua looked at his cousin.

"Three wrenches and the scythe." Ryan's voice was hard.

"I told you. I didn't move your precious tools." Lilly leaned back on the couch. "So whoever stole the tools did this? The Sheriff said Mr. Carpenter's cause of death was likely blunt force trauma to the head. A wrench could certainly kill a man."

"We can't be a hundred percent certain that the two incidents are connected, though it is possible. We're still figuring that out," Joshua answered. "We'll take the scythe back to the station, see if we can find anything on it. Fingerprints are almost impossible to get off a wooden handle as ragged as that, but there might be something else this guy left behind."

"Any other odd things happen over the last couple days?" Officer Braun asked.

Lilly shrugged. "The only thing I can think of is Earl Graves getting up in my face at the café today. But I told that to Sheriff Brandford."

"How do you know Mr. Graves?" Braun asked.

"I don't know him." Lilly ran her hands through her auburn hair, wincing as her fingers caught unruly tangles. Most likely the remnants of her escapades in the pasture and with the raccoon. She made a face as she picked bits of leaves and straw from her hair. "We had a run-in at Grandma's Attic and he started yelling at me about promises my grandpa made him and…"

Lilly felt the color drain from her face. "He did this, didn't he?"

Both policemen exchanged looks. Braun started making quick notes once more as Joshua turned to Ryan with a stony expression. Ryan, in turn, shrugged at his cousin and shook his head, raising his hands in a brief "wasn't me" gesture.

"We can't say that yet," Joshua said carefully.

"You guys know something about Earl that I don't." Lilly sat up, pointing at Joshua and then to Ryan. "Everyone's been telling me he's harmless, and I knew he wasn't. He made it look like he killed an animal and pinned it to my barn! He probably killed Mr. Carpenter, too!"

"We have no evidence of that," Braun offered as he continued taking notes.

Lilly narrowed her eyes at him, wanting to grab his pen and break it in half.

"He's never done something like this before, so it's unlikely he's the culprit," Joshua said.

"Every serial killer has to have a first, Josh," Ryan added.

"Not helping, Ryan," Joshua growled over his shoulder. He turned back to Lilly. "We'll talk with him and see if he knows anything. His farm is next to yours. He may have seen something."

Lilly looked each officer in the face, not sure if she should say anything else. Of course, they wouldn't be quick to point blame to Earl Graves; proper police officers gathered all the evidence, spoke to witnesses, and made sure to have all the pieces of the puzzle together before they started accusing and arresting. Lilly wasn't sure she could be as unbiased as the police. She hadn't liked the old man since she'd met him that morning and he'd yelled at her; his cryptic words still continued to haunt her. If Earl was unhinged enough to accost her in a public restaurant, why wouldn't he try to send a more deadly message her way?

"What am I supposed to do now?" Lilly asked. "Am I allowed to clean the door off? I don't know if I can stand knowing that mess is out there. I might not leave the house if it has to stay up for a lengthy investigation."

"I took some preliminary pictures. The crime scene guys came not too long after we got here," Joshua explained. "They got everything they could, but I'll check when we get back to the station and let you know when you can clean up."

"Thank you," Lilly sighed. It wasn't exactly what she'd hoped to hear, but at least she didn't have to stare at a bloody barn for days or weeks.

"Are you going to be okay out here?" Joshua asked.

"I don't know." Lilly looked at him, not certain if he was still in official cop-mode. "I'm suddenly not a fan of staying here by myself tonight, but I don't know anyone around here, really."

"I'll check in on her tonight," Ryan offered. Lilly started, having forgotten he was still in the living room.

"Neighbors are closer than you think out here, though it might not look it with all the open fields. Just keep the yard light on, doors locked, windows shut, all that typical stuff." Joshua gave Lilly a reassuring smile. "If anything weird happens, call 911 right away."

Lilly followed the two officers to the main hall and entryway, thanking them once more before she shut the door. She hugged her stomach and wandered back into the living room, at a loss for what to do next. She could faintly hear Faith and Maggie's voices down the hall, both women still working in the kitchen. Lilly would have to thank Faith for distracting Maggie. Lilly wasn't sure how much of the woman's frantic energy she could handle at the moment. Thinking of those two reminded her of the food still displayed on the coffee table. Her stomach churned at the sight, her nerves too frayed for her to enjoy the idea of eating.

"You okay?"

Again, she had forgotten about Ryan. She jumped at his voice, nearly tripping over the decorative floor rug.

"No, I'm not." Her words came out sharper than she intended. "And why didn't you let a medical professional look me over before you moved me?

His jaw slackened slightly. "What?"

"I fell. Hit my head. I could have a concussion. Injured my neck. Don't you know the first thing to do for someone who hits their head with un-confirmed neck injuries is to not move them?" Lilly fought as her words came out faster and faster. "By moving me, you could have permanently damaged my neck!"

Ryan gazed at her for a moment before shaking his head. He pushed away from the mahogany entry with an odd chuckle. "Alright then."

He turned and walked toward the door.

"Where are you going?" Lilly demanded, taking a step toward him.

"I'm going to make sure the fence repair is holding, and then go home, maybe get into some cleaner clothes, eat some supper, and then come back for my chores," Ryan responded. "If that's not going to spook you and get the cops called on me."

Lilly opened her mouth, stopped, and then opened it once more. "M-Maggie made sandwiches, you—you could have some if you're hungry."

Ryan waved a hand, dismissing the offer. "I wouldn't want to hang around and risk damaging you further."

He yanked the front door open and kicked the screen door out into the early evening. It slammed shut behind him, eliciting a concerned call by Maggie from deep within the house. Lilly watched him go, dumbly wondering how it had gotten so late.

What time was it? The day's events blurred together, skewing her concept of time. Somewhere down the hall behind her, the grandfather clock chimed. Lilly counted the chimes to herself and realized she had awoken well after seven o'clock.

The angry growl from Ryan's diesel engine jolted Lilly out of her stupor. She walked to the front door and slowly shut it as his truck disappeared down the driveway.

"Now what crawled up his butt and died?" Faith appeared next to the door, peering out the windows.

"I don't know." Lilly turned away from the door and walked into the living room.

"He's always had his moods." Faith followed Lilly and plopped back into the recliner. "Another one of his 'all the world's against me' pity parties. So typical of the youngest brother, really. He'd get them all the time when we'd play here, remember?"

Lilly sunk into the couch and hugged her knees, lowering her chin onto them. "No, I don't, really."

"That soap opera-level amnesia strikes again," Faith joked as she assembled a cheese and cracker sandwich.

"No." Lilly shook her head. She closed her eyes. "After the falling out between my parents and grandparents, I had to stop mentioning anything about Lone Tree around them. I guess, after enough time, I started to forget stuff in a way."

She did remember. Nearly everything from her childhood on the farm had been creeping its way back to her consciousness. It was easier at the moment to play dumb than to be constantly reminded of all the pain—hers and what her leaving caused to others. Seeing Ryan each day didn't make their falling out easier, either.

Faith chewed noisily on her crackers, raising her brows as a silent push to continue.

"It's all there, really. Being here now is bringing a lot of those old memories back." Lilly gave a small smile, knowing that was all she wanted to share at that moment even if Faith wanted more. "It's hard being somewhere that was once so familiar but seems so foreign now. And everyone here knows so much about my family that I don't..."

Faith nodded knowingly. "How'd your parents feel about you moving back to the old farmstead?"

Lilly gave a sheepish smile. "They don't exactly know I'm here."

"Really!" Faith laughed.

"They just know I relocated after my divorce."

Faith shook a finger at Lilly. "They're going to be furious with you coming back here."

"I'm going to tell them... eventually..." The color started to drain from her cheeks. "But why would they be?"

"You know." The conspiratorial tone edged back into Faith's voice as her brows arched meaningfully.

"No, I don't know."

Faith's eyes searched Lilly's face and her mouth fell open slowly. "You don't know what caused the fall out?"

"No. I was fifteen when it happened," Lilly said defensively. "Even if my parents told me, I doubt teenage me would have paid it much mind."

A scheming grin spread on Faith's face. "Do you want to know?"

"How do you know?" Lilly cried. "This is exactly what I'm talking about. Everyone in this town seems to know more about my family than I do. How do you know what happened between my parents and grandparents?"

"Because your grandparents told my mom. All our families are... were... are incredibly close. And Mom, against her better judgment, told Aunt Maggie. So the whole Swenson-Heimdall clan knows." Faith sat back in the recliner. "And if Maggie knows something, I'm pretty sure that most of Lone Tree knows, too. Not much is secret in this town. Although, you do have to know the right people to get any information."

"And who would this secret society of secret keepers be?"

"Don't you remember anything about little towns?" Faith grinned. "The church ladies, of whom my aunt is the leader."

Lilly grunted and let her head fall against the back of the couch. "Unbelievable."

"You didn't answer my question."

"Which was?"

"Do you want to know?"

Lilly raised her head and leveled a hard stare at the restaurateur. "You're serious. You know everything that happened?"

Faith raised her right hand as she placed the other over her heart. "I'd never lie about family drama."

Lilly matched Faith's smile. "Tell me."

Maggie shuffled loudly into the room, breaking the conspiratorial spell. "You barely ate any of these sandwiches, Lilly! Are you sure you're alright? Do we need to take you to the hospital in Sleepy Eye?"

Faith groaned as Lilly shook her head. "No, Maggie, I'm fine. Just not hungry at the moment. So much excitement and all that, I'll have something to eat a little later."

Maggie scanned her with a critical gaze. "I suppose if you say so."

She turned to Faith. "Faith, dearie, it's getting late. We should leave Lilly to rest. And you need to get back to the café."

"Lucas is more than capable of running the café without me, Aunt Maggie." Faith tilted her head. "He's only been my head manager for five years."

"Nevertheless, we've intruded on Lilly for too long." Maggie turned and went to the entry, collecting their bags and jackets. "Now, Lilly, you can keep the food we brought. I noticed your fridge was a little bare, as was your pantry. If you need any help with shopping, let me know and I can run to Fritche's for you."

Faith and Lilly stood, eyeing each other as they watched the older woman scuttle about the main hall, continuing to talk about shopping lists as well as other stores to visit when in town next.

"I suppose I'll have to do my big reveal later," Faith whispered.

"You can't just bring up something like that and then leave!" Lilly hissed.

"I can't tell you in front of Auntie, she'd skin me."

"If you told me something this important about my own family!?"

"Okay, come on, Faith, let's get out of Lilly's hair now." Maggie all but dragged Faith to the door. "Lilly, you call me if you need anything, you hear?"

Lilly smiled and followed the two to the door. "I'll be sure to do that, Maggie. Thank you for all your help today."

"Don't mention it, dearie." Maggie patted her shoulder softly. "Do get some rest, okay?"

The trio tumbled out onto the porch as Faith and Maggie each fought to pull their jackets on, the younger hindered by the unrequested assistance from the elder. The early spring evening was proving to be a cold one. Lilly hugged her arms tightly against the damp chill. Beginnings of frost were forming on the grass and metal porch furniture. Even if it was late spring, April in Minnesota still held the threat of snow at any given moment.

"Oh, Lilly." Faith turned to her, pulling her own arm out of her aunt's grasp. "If you are looking for something to do tonight, I'm certain there's something for you in grandma's attic."

Lilly furrowed her brows. "I'm not up for going into town anymore tonight, Faith…"

Faith cast a quick glance at Maggie, who was hurrying toward Faith's car, then leaned close to Lilly as her aunt called her name loudly. "Trust me. You'll want to check out *grandma's attic*."

Chapter Eight

After Faith and Maggie left, Lilly sat in the living room, allowing her brain to churn over the events of the last few hours. She was halfway through a finger sandwich before Faith's last words made any sense. *Trust me. You'll want to check out grandma's attic.*

She bound up the stairs before the half sandwich hit the platter. Now, she stood on the second floor, facing the top of the stairs, her eyes aiming up. She stared intently at the thick white string hanging from the ceiling. Above her, the drop-ladder for the attic was framed in roughly painted repurposed wainscoting.

Lilly reached for the string. Her heart thudded in her chest and into her ears. Was she ready to find out what happened all those years ago? Did she even want to find out?

What's that old saying? "Ignorance is bliss"?

She took a shaky breath and finally pulled down on the ladder's string. Calling it a string was being generous. Lilly was certain her grandpa had used a piece of bailing twine as the pulling mechanism. The ladder didn't budge. Lilly took a firmer hold of the small wooden toggle at the end of the string and put more effort into her tugging.

The string snapped in half.

Once she regained her footing, she threw the broken string to the floor with an undignified grunt. "That's just perfect."

She stomped down the stairs and headed straight into the kitchen. She opened the myriad of cabinet and pantry doors, unsure if she'd find a step stool. What farm wife didn't have a step stool in the kitchen? The cupboards were certainly hung higher than what her just-over-five-foot tall grandma could reach. She had to have a step stool.

Lilly searched the kitchen and the dining room to no avail. She stood in the middle of the dining room, fists on her hips, running through a list of possible alternate storage spots her grandparents could have squirreled away a step stool. Maybe it was out in the barn. Lilly shuddered at the thought. She wanted to keep as much distance between herself and the barn as possible for as long as she could.

She put her hands on one of the ornate dining table chairs, rocking it gently from side to side. It didn't feel too heavy. Lilly bit her lip and begged her grandmother's forgiveness as she lugged it toward the stairs.

Lilly discovered the truth in "easier said than done," a favored phrase of her mother's. The solid wood chair revealed its honest weight and cumbersome maneuverability halfway up the staircase. As she struggled to get it to the top step, she kept reminding herself that she was just slightly out of shape and her difficulties came from the awkwardness of lifting a chair up a flight of stairs. She had never been expected to lift or move large pieces of furniture. Alec always saw to having a legion of men from a moving company arrive and schlep their larger pieces around when they had moved from St. Paul to Minneapolis after they'd gotten married or whenever they would acquire a new piece for their loft.

She also didn't take any furniture with her after the divorce. Alec had promised the divorce proceedings would be smoother if she kept their loft as is. Apparently, Olivia, upon seeing the loft, loved the overall décor, declaring the special resonance phenomenal. She felt her chi flowing freer than ever and didn't want one piece removed, lest it disrupt the Zen.

The memory of the pretentious words of her husband's mistress slid down her spine, and she suddenly wanted a shower. Or to throw up. Lilly couldn't leave the loft fast enough after hearing that. She also didn't believe that the day the divorce was finalized was Olivia's first time stepping foot in the place.

After what felt like an eternity, Lilly made it to the top of the stairs. As if adding insult to injury, the chair snagged on the carpet runner as she dragged it under the attic doorway. She ignored the rumpled carpet and stationed the chair under the broken pull string. Lilly also ignored the ominous creaking of the chair as she stepped up onto the plush seat. She apologized to her grandma once more, hoping the fact she only had socks on would lighten the affront. How many times did her mother, aunt, and grandma yell at the cousins to get off the nice furniture? And Heaven forbid if one of them had shoes or boots on.

She stood straight with arms outstretched to maximize her balance on the chair. The frayed end of the string hung mere inches in front of her face. Lilly tugged on the twine with both hands, thrilled to hear the encouraging creaks and groans of the wooden trap door. She pulled down harder, blocking the sound of creaking wood as she focused on getting the blasted attic door open.

"Well, if you didn't have a concussion from earlier, that's a damned good way to ensure you'll get one."

Lilly's stance on the chair faltered as the voice came up behind her. She tried to turn around and almost toppled the chair in the process. Balance once more restored, she turned at the waist to see the unexpected visitor.

"Oh, it's just you," Lilly sighed as Ryan's form ascended the stairs. "How did you get in?"

"Front door's unlocked." He jabbed a thumb over his shoulder. "For someone who just had a dead body and a toupee kabob, I'd expect you to be barring the door."

Lilly looked down at him and bit her lip to keep the snarky remark at bay. She felt heat rise in her cheeks at this news of her mistake. Faith's tantalizing promise of information about her family had distracted her from basic safety.

She watched as he made his way up the stairs, his gait halting at best. He was dressed in a cleaner version of what he'd left the farm in, jeans and a button-up flannel. His ever present John Deere hat was now pulled down over damp brown hair, a sign that he had in fact cleaned up since leaving. *Why shower if you're going to get dirty again doing chores?* She then caught sight of his mismatched socks and almost laughed.

"Do your own laundry, I see?" She jerked her chin toward him.

Ryan stopped at the top stair and looked down at the floor. "They don't need to match. They just need to be clean and warm."

"I'm surprised you even took your boots off to come inside." Lilly turned back to the attic string.

"I may be a country boy, but I still have manners," he retorted. "Beverly would box my ears from the beyond if she caught me anywhere but the entry or the kitchen with my boots on."

She smiled, remembering her grandma doing exactly that to her and her cousin when she was younger. And even the Swenson and Heimdall kids when they came over to explore the farm. "I'm surprised to see you here—in the house, I mean."

"I said I'd come and check on you," Ryan grunted, standing next to the chair on her left. "And I'm glad I decided to come in before I went to the barn. You're going to get yourself killed trying to open the hatch like that."

"I'm fine," Lilly huffed as she pulled on the twine once more. "I got this."

"Why do you need to go in the attic, anyway?"

"Just... uh... curious... that's all..." Lilly said between tugs.

Ryan let out a heavy breath. "There is nothing that important in the attic that you need to kill yourself over. Get down."

"Stupid thing's stuck, I just need to work it loose, that's all."

"Right." He crossed his arms over his chest as he watched her. "Get down off the chair."

"Don't you have cows to feed?"

"They can wait. I'm not leaving until you either get up into the attic or abandon this crazy venture."

She cast a skeptical look over her shoulder. "How noble of you—"

Her words were cut off by the sound of fabric and wicker rending. Just as Lilly looked down at the chair, her left foot sunk into the cushion. Her body tilted before she registered that she was falling.

"Ooof!" The air rushed out of Lilly's lungs. Her descent was halted by something solid. She blinked and looked around, surprised she wasn't laid flat out on the floor but half supported by arms as sturdy as small trees while her feet stuck into the chair seat. She glanced over her shoulder and stared dumbly up into Ryan's face.

"Ryan, what—"

"You broke the chair." Ryan's voice was thick as he quickly lifted her legs out of the chair and settled her onto the floor.

"I..." Lilly looked from Ryan to the chair. The woven wicker seat support had given out under her weight. The ancient chair hadn't been designed to withstand the full weight of a standing person, especially one exerting increased downward pressure.

"Oh..."

"Bev's gonna be so mad when she finds out about this." Ryan shook his head. "Finally, someone else's ears are going to get boxed for once."

"I doubt my grandma's ghost is going to come back to avenge a busted chair." Lilly tilted her head toward him, eyes narrowed.

Ryan chuckled. "You must not remember your grandma very well."

The two stared at the broken chair. Lilly stepped to the side, wanting more space between her and Ryan. Her traitorous female side liked being that close to the farmhand too much. She could still smell his odd yet alluring mixture of soap and lingering hay. Lilly would freely admit that the man was attractive—in that rugged, good ol' country boy kind of way. They had dated for a reason. She knew plenty of her Uptown friends who would be throwing themselves at him.

Lilly would have counted herself among them upon coming back to Lone Tree, but then he went and opened his mouth.

Ryan smirked. "I told you to get off the chair."

Lilly fixed her gaze on the attic door, biting absently at her bottom lip. "Do you know if there's a ladder or step stool around?"

He shook his head. "No, and I'm not letting you bring any more chairs upstairs."

"Great." Lilly slumped. She felt herself deflate. Panic settled in her chest and radiated out. She almost felt herself trembling. *Maybe delayed shock from the sickle incident? I was so close to answering a fifteen year old mystery...*

Lilly hugged her arms tightly, hoping Ryan didn't see her shaking. "Now how am I going to get up there? I need to know..."

Next to her, Ryan let out a heavy breath. "You really want to get up there, don't you?"

Lilly turned toward him, startled by the tone of his voice. "Yes, but I—what are you doing?"

Ryan thrust a pocket knife into her hand before he lowered himself into an awkward squat. He held his arms out as if waiting for an embrace. Bending his neck to catch her gaze, he nodded his head toward his outstretched arms. "C'mon, get up."

"What in the world are you doing?" Lilly gasped again, looking from him to the pocket knife and back again.

"Climb on up and use the knife to pry the ladder loose."

She shook her head. "I'm not climbing on you!"

"You want to get up to the attic or not?"

"No, no, this can wait until tomorrow, after I find a ladder or something. This is crazy! Get off the floor, Ryan. I'm not going to have you hoist me like a bag of cow feed and that's final! If the chair wasn't sturdy enough for me, then certainly you—"

"Lillian, get over here!" Ryan shouted.

She pressed her lips into a thin line, staring down at her socks. Her full name startled her, especially coming from Ryan. "Okay," she replied meekly.

As if she hadn't already filled her awkward Ryan moments quota for the week, climbing his arms topped them all. Any skin showing above her shoulders flared a brilliant red as his arms wrapped around her thighs, his forearms settled firmly beneath the seat of her pants. With a movement that was liquid smooth, he lifted her from the floor and bounced her higher in his arms. Now, her knees rested against his arms as her midriff met his turned face.

"Okay..." Lilly breathed as she drew her feet under her, finding his sturdy thighs to rest them on. "I'm going to put my feet right here..."

"For the love of... I don't need a play by play! Just get a move on!" Ryan grumbled.

Lilly frowned. She slowly, quietly shifted in his arms to get into a better position. Using another human for support was awkward and disorienting. The chair had been sturdier than this. Other than a grunt as she shifted her weight, Ryan remained quiet. She reached up toward the attic door and fumbled with the pocket knife to get a blade out. Her foot slipped and she almost cried out in fear, but her toes found purchase along Ryan's inner thigh.

"Hey, watch where you're putting things," Ryan grunted.

"Sorry, sorry." Lilly swallowed again, feeling her whole body burn. She was thankful Ryan couldn't see how deep the blush on her cheeks and neck was. She pushed the knife blade between the frame and the attic door, unsure of what she was exactly supposed to do to jar it loose. She slid the blade along the groove, hoping to dislodge whatever gunk had built up over the years. A fine trail of dust and debris followed the knife, signaling that whatever she was doing was working.

"You done yet?" Ryan growled.

"Hey, this was your bright idea," Lilly shot back. "I'm getting some gunk out, so hopefully it'll work."

She flipped the blade closed and tried pulling on the frayed twine again. The ladder budged slightly. "Okay, I got one side freed up a bit. Now the other side."

Lilly dug the blade into the opposite side of the ladder, rewarded with another thin spray of dust bunnies and debris. "Okay, I think I got it." Lilly pulled on the twine again.

Ryan shifted, careful not to topple her. "Get down and we'll—"

The ladder pulled free of the ceiling abruptly, clattering and unfolding above her. Lilly ducked and covered her head with her arms. The pocket knife flew, skittering on the floor somewhere. She screamed as the ladder, opening like an oversized accordion, whizzed past her head and crash landed against the floor. Her sudden dip to get out of the way of the ladder caused her sock-covered feet to slide on Ryan's jeans. Before she knew it, Lilly fell in a very unbecoming manner and found herself straddling Ryan's waist. In a heartbeat, he collapsed to the floor underneath her with a great exhalation of breath.

"What the hell!" Ryan shouted, his voice hampered by her crumpled form and waves of auburn tangles. He wriggled, trying to dislodge himself. "Get off!"

Lilly was almost too stunned to move. She stared down into Ryan's eyes, his face as red as hers felt. Though, she doubted it was from embarrassment. She regained her senses quickly, extracted her legs out from under Ryan, and crawled away from him until her back hit the hallway wall. She watched as he slowly picked himself off the floor. He coughed and winced as he drew his left leg up and rolled into a sitting position. His John Deere cap had been lost in the kerfuffle.

The two locked eyes, lingering dust from the attic ladder falling about them. Lilly braced herself for a verbal barrage. *Even if this was his stupid plan,* Lilly reminded herself. The intense look in his eyes startled her. After everything that happened today, she didn't know if she could survive a berating from this corn-fed lunkhead.

Ryan reached behind him and jammed his hat back on his head, never breaking eye contact with her. As his features descended into shadow once more, a lopsided grin spread over his face. He draped his arms over his knees and started to laugh.

Lilly watched him laugh, her panic subsiding a little. She didn't know if she was still in trouble with him or not. *This could be a diversion,* Lilly warned herself. As he laughed, however, she couldn't fight a small smile.

"Are you okay?" he asked as his mirth faded, his features softening. She nodded. Ryan narrowed his eyes at her. "Are you okay?" he asked again, and Lilly noticed the concern in his voice.

"I'm fine."

He sighed and struggled to his feet. He walked over to her and extended a hand. "C'mon, get up."

She eyed his offered hand. "I'm not sure I should, given what happened last time you said that."

"I'll admit that wasn't one of my more stellar plans." He smirked and gestured again with his outstretched hand. Lilly took hold and he pulled her to her feet as if she weighed nothing.

"Are you okay? I'm sorry I fell... I didn't mean to... you're not hurt or anything?" Lilly asked, looking him over. Her eyes lingered on his left leg.

"I'm in one piece." Ryan turned slightly, pulling his leg out of her gaze. "But you're heavier than you look."

"Excuse me?" Lilly cried.

"I can't help it if you weigh a ton." Ryan held his stomach and gave her a big grimace. "Good thing I didn't offer to have you sit on my shoulders, you'd have snapped my spine."

He laughed as Lilly moved to swat his arm. He tried to dance away from her, but still got a hearty slap.

"Well, the ladder's down. You should go up and find what's so important." Ryan hobbled over to the ladder.

Lilly winced with every step he took. "Don't you think you should sit down?"

He locked eyes with her, his own darkening under the brim of his cap. "I'm fine."

She lowered her eyes and followed him to the ladder. He climbed up the shaky ladder, each foot fall echoed by a high pitched creak. Lilly waited until he stepped onto the attic floor before she ascended the ladder. It didn't creak as much under her feet, giving her a little pick-me-up.

So I'm not as heavy as you say, Lilly bit back a smirk, knowing Ryan watched her intently as she climbed the ladder.

She stood, Ryan uncomfortably close to one side, the sharp drop off of the ladder to her left. She swayed, feeling the beginning spins of vertigo. Lilly tried to step away from the opening, but her path was blocked by Ryan and piles of boxes. Ryan shuffled over to the other side of the ladder and stomped on the floor.

The ladder collapsed in on itself, folding back up into the ceiling—floor—plunging the attic in dim light. Lilly opened her mouth to protest when a bare bulb burst to light above her. Ryan stood below it, a pull string in his hand. A faint, sad smile played at the corners of his mouth.

"Why are you doing all of this for me?" Lilly finally asked.

"Because Faith wasn't the only one your grandma told things to," Ryan said, his words strange in the cavernous attic. The swaying bulb cast him in a series of eerie shadows that made Lilly shudder. "And it's about time you knew the truth."

The house was quiet once more with only the distant tick tock of the grandfather clock echoing down the hallway. Lilly sat in her grandpa's den, staring blankly at the large cardboard box placed in the middle of the floor. Within its beige, battered confines sat piles of papers and manila envelopes, the ones Ryan promised would answer all of her questions.

Ryan had helped her bring the box down from the attic before he went to start the evening's chores. She almost asked him to stay with her while she went through the box, certain he would know what she was looking for better than she did. Lilly decided against it and let the farmhand continue with his duties.

After further thought, she wanted to face these answers alone. He had already confessed that he—and most of his family, it seemed—knew some of the details about what had happened within her own family, so it wasn't that she worried about him learning about a delicate family secret.

No, Lilly didn't want to run the risk of ugly crying in front of the emotional black hole that is Ryan Swenson.

What was his deal, anyway? From their first encounter he barely spoke to her, and when he did, his words were anything but cordial. Save for their more recent exchange; there, he actually laughed. Should she ask him about the hostility?

Well, I did sort of kind of threaten his job a couple of days ago... Lilly bit her lip at the memory. Perhaps her gambit to establish dominance in their employer-employee relationship backfired. What employee hasn't made life miserable for the new management, afraid that the "old way of doing things" was going to be drastically changed?

It wouldn't be the first time a grand scheme of hers went awry.

He wasn't as understanding as his sister that she was away from the old family farm and Lone Tree for fifteen years. Faith, Mrs. Swenson, and a handful of other locals seemed to not mind her long-term absence and welcomed her back into the fold as if no time had gone by at all.

Or maybe it was because she had up and vanished fifteen years ago with barely a word of explanation. Boyfriends tend to frown on their girlfriends leaving. It certainly puts a strain on the relationship.

Lilly looked down at the box and took a deep breath. Would she be mentioned amongst these papers? Perhaps the answers before her would also shed light onto Ryan's less than warm reception and why her family had gotten the H-E-double hockey sticks out of Dodge.

She reached down into the box and brought out the topmost pile of papers. They had yellowed with time and limited exposure to the elements in the attic. Like most attics in century farmhouses, hers had the barest of insulation. She was also certain one of the windows had a crack in the frame that allowed drafts, rain, and snow into the attic space. The box before her bore more than enough evidence of water damage.

A brief paging through the papers on her lap didn't reveal any earth shattering secrets of her grandparents. Most were saved newspapers from back before her father was born, detailing entrants into the local county fair and weddings of who she believed were friends or distant relations. Lilly set that pile aside and lifted up a heavy manila envelope. Age had weathered the envelope into almost a velvety suede, the ribbon tie barely holding on to the clasp it had been carefully wrapped around. From the heft and thickness of the envelope, it felt like a book.

Old ledgers? Did my grandparents have money problems? Lilly's brain skipped from one theory to the next. She unbound the envelope and slid its contents into her lap.

A leather book with a blank and worn cover rested on her legs. Lilly stared at it, afraid to move. Once it plopped into her lap, she felt a short thrill charge through her body, a strange energy leaching from the old book.

Lilly opened it carefully, its cover and binding creaking from being closed for so long. She flipped through the book, scanning the compact script on each page. On the upper right corner of each page was written a date. The earliest date in the book was May 1965, the year her grandparents married.

It was her grandmother's journal.

Lilly dug through the box, finding more heavy manila envelopes similar to the one in which the journal was kept. She opened envelope after envelope, finding matching journals, all written in her grandmother's small cursive hand, each containing a year's worth of entries. After her search was complete, Lilly had unearthed forty-five journals. She spent the next hour putting the journals in chronological order. Lilly did some quick calculations and realized there wasn't quite one journal for each year her grandparents were married. As she skimmed through the books, she discovered some years didn't have as many entries as other years. The journals in the more recent past held shorter years, with numerous days, if not months, unaccounted for. One whole year—1970—was omitted entirely.

Lilly paged through 1969 and 1971, making sure she hadn't missed a shortened year.

What happened to 1970?

Her father was born late in 1969. Nearly every year before then was documented in such detail it might be called obsessive. Why hadn't the new mother immortalized her firstborn's first year?

Lilly's brain buzzed with questions and theories. She pawed through the journals again, picking out the ones that contained the years 1969,

1971, and 2004—the year her grandparents and parents had their mysterious falling out, and the last year she could remember anything about the farm.

She gathered those three journals and moved her sleuthing into the kitchen. Her stomach had finally decided it was hungry, and its growling distracted her from the project at hand. Lilly brought out the platter of finger foods Mrs. Swenson had so generously laid out and nibbled on a small sandwich, mindful to not get any food remnants on the journals.

As Lilly skimmed through the journals, her appetite waned and she wished she hadn't opened the attic.

On the snowy night of December 21, 1969, Harold and Beverly Schmidt welcomed their son, Christopher Eugene, and daughter, Christine Elaina, into the world. Due to the near-blizzard conditions, the babies barely made it to the Sleepy Eye Medical Center in time. Beverly made a rather off-color comment in the days following the birth, stating that the children's journey began in the backseat of the Studebaker so why shouldn't it end there?

Lilly couldn't help blushing at her grandmother's racy words, but that was soon overshadowed by her father's sister.

She didn't have another aunt. Her father and mother never mentioned any other aunt save her father's younger sister Ellen, mother of her cousin Tammy.

She had an Aunt Christine...

Who's Aunt Christine?

Lilly read through the next pages carefully.

Entries followed documenting the twins' first Christmas and plans for their Christening in the weeks to follow and visits from family and friends to the farm to help the new parents. As the year wound down to 1970,

Beverly's entries became shorter and vague. Lilly re-read each passage numerous times as she tried to decipher her grandmother's cryptic words.

On New Year's Eve, her grandmother wrote about her struggles with both babies, how the offers of help began to run dry, and how Harold brought whiskey home again in the most recent grocery delivery.

The next time her grandmother wrote in her journal was January 15, 1971.

What happened in 1970 that grandma didn't want to remember?

Lilly scrambled through the 1971 journal, the entries at the beginning of the year were happy and short, mundane even in their reports of how the crops were growing and how the neighbors did in county and state fair entries. Lilly frowned as she barely saw a mention of her father or aunt. Compared to the previous journal entries, the words put down by her grandmother seemed almost forced, as if she was making herself journal again after a year's absence.

May 1971 brought back longer entries. Lilly read each word with baited breath, wondering if her grandmother would finally reveal to the reader why the style shifted so suddenly in her journaling.

May 20, 1971

Harold hasn't made it out into the fields yet this year. The likelihood of getting a decent crop doesn't look very promising. Earl has offered to help plant the acreage that borders his land. He seems to be more functional than Harold, I don't know why that man has waited this long to accept his offer.

I will go over to Earl and make an official offer for him to run our land. Harold is in no condition to be on a tractor. He can barely handle the cows. I'm certain they will be going soon if Harold doesn't stop.

Lilly sat back from the island counter and stared dumbly at the refrigerator's door. This shed a spotlight on the ramblings of Earl Graves. Her grandmother had Earl run their fields for them while Grandpa was... incapacitated somehow. Was he ill? Was he helping care for the twins? And why hadn't the twins been mentioned in over a year?

Risking the possibility of missing crucial details, Lilly flipped through the journal to the middle of June. She caught mentions of Earl agreeing to run the land for them, but not much could be done for the corn fields anymore that year. He'd work on the hay and alfalfa fields until the season was done. They'd have to talk more next spring if the situation with Harold had changed.

More cryptic entries. Lilly's frown deepened as she flipped page after page, eyes trained to zero in on a handful of words. Was Grandma purposely keeping whatever was going on with Grandpa out of here, just on the off chance someone read these?

Mention of Earl dropped off as the summer turned to autumn. Lilly jumped past Halloween and hoped the entries nearing the twins' birthday would be more revealing. Her father and aunt would be turning two in December 1971.

Lilly's eyes started to blur as she scanned the pages, the delicate cursive hand steadily becoming more erratic. Soon, Grandma Beverly gave up cursive altogether and the rest of 1971 was written in hectic print.

December 1, 1971

It's getting closer to Christopher's birthday. Can't believe my little boy is going to be two soon. He's gotten so big over the last year, thankfully. I was beginning to worry after the unpleasantness with Christine.

Christopher doesn't mention her as much anymore, which surprised me he remembered her at all, since she passed so young. Thankfully he doesn't say her name around Harold. I can distract him with his new brother or sister coming in three short months.

It looks like Earl will be running the land this coming spring. Harold isn't up to working the fields anymore. At least he's keeping busy with the cows. That's all he has motivation for during his good days. I hope that this passes with Harold soon. Losing Christine has been hard on me, as well; I don't know why he gets all this special attention.

Lilly shut the journal and pushed it across the counter.

"Dad had a twin sister," Lilly murmured, a hand going up to the base of her neck. "Grandma and Grandpa kept her a secret from him, that's why he never mentioned her..."

The kitchen felt too warm suddenly, too close for her liking. She slid off the stool and made her way out to the back porch. She dropped hard onto a wicker chair, the seat creaking under the sudden weight.

Lilly stared out at the farm yard, the barn and other outbuildings growing dim in the evening light. The darkness hid any evidence of the unpleasantness from that evening in dark shadows. The muffled calls of the cows drifted up from the barn, followed by the occasional sharp command from Ryan as he finished his chores.

Her grandparents had lost a daughter. She'd have to go back through the journals to see if the cause of death was ever revealed. Death records wouldn't be that hard to obtain from the county or hospital if she really wanted to find out. Lilly gnawed at her bottom lip, her brain churning as it processed the long kept secret.

Grandpa Harold had taken the death of his infant daughter hard, harder than Beverly it appeared. He could barely operate the farm after Christine died. The bitterness in her grandma's last entry was palpable.

He couldn't function because he was drinking. Lilly's brain filled in the missing piece, causing such a shock that she started in her seat. Piece by piece, the vague references in the journal entries found their proper place.

He brought whiskey home, Lilly recalled a passage from her grandmother's journal.

Heavy footfalls on the porch steps bolted her from her thoughts. She blinked in the growing shadows and light from the kitchen windows. Ryan's dark form emerged from the night and sat in the wicker chair next to her.

"You found the journals?" It wasn't so much a question as an affirmation.

Lilly nodded, keeping her eyes from him.

"And you read them?"

Again, she nodded.

Ryan leaned back in the wicker chair and let out a long breath. "Don't hate them."

"Don't hate them?" Lilly echoed. She was shocked by the acid in her voice. "They lied about my aunt even existing. My dad had never mentioned her, even before they stopped talking. He probably didn't remember he had another sister. They lied about Grandpa's drinking, too!"

Ryan was quiet. "Being open about losing a child and alcoholism wasn't done back then. And especially out here. Rural folks keep their personal lives hidden. Tragedies and demons aren't meant to be fodder for the local rumor mill."

Lilly shook her head, frantically wiping at her cheeks. "He drank himself stupid while his wife mourned the loss of their daughter. She couldn't even mention her name around him!"

"I'm not commending his actions." Ryan's voice was soft, barely above a whisper. "It's just what it is."

"Bullcrap," Lilly spat.

The two sat in silence. Lilly refused to look over at Ryan. The mere fact he knew more about her family's history than she did burned almost as hot as the anger she felt toward her grandfather.

"You didn't get to the parts where Bev goes through the big showdown between your dad and grandpa yet, did you?" Ryan's words came out measured, respectful even.

Lilly shook her head.

"I'll save you some reading and pain and tell you what went down, since you know about the drinking." Ryan leaned forward, elbows on his knees, and fingers loosely clasped together. "Your grandpa never went back to working in the fields. He couldn't handle that level of work when he hit the bottle hard, so he stuck to the cows. I guess feeding and milking the twenty some cows by hand back then wasn't so bad if you were three sheets to the wind or trying to crawl back from a hangover. Tractors... Well, Bev said there were a few close calls with augers and the hay chopper, so she got Earl involved."

"Earl took over running the cropland," Lilly broke in.

"Yeah, and that temporary agreement became an indefinite arrangement. It worked out fine for years. Earl rented the land from Harold and Bev, they shared the profits from the crops, it suited Harold fine. He didn't have to crawl out of the bottle too much to tend to his cows."

"Ryan, please," Lilly hissed.

"Sorry." He cleared his throat. He took his hat off and let it hang between his knees.

"Can we skip to why my parents stopped talking to my grandparents?"

He took his hat off and let it hang between his knees. "Bev said the drinking never got better as the years went on. He was able to hide it better as your dad and Ellen got older and when you and then Ellen's kids came along. Then, I think it was around your dad's thirtieth birthday, Harold got really drunk when you and your parents were visiting. The next five years Harold and Chris battled it out about his drinking, got into some pretty heated fights about it. Your dad was able to arrange something with a local treatment center and gave your dad the ultimatum: treatment or he'd leave."

"Grandpa didn't go," Lilly concluded after a pause.

"Bev said Harold told your dad to leave the house and never come back." Ryan shook his head. "So at the end of that visit, they never saw you again. We all never saw you again."

"They didn't talk for fifteen years because grandpa wouldn't stop drinking." Lilly took a ragged breath. "I didn't get to say goodbye to my grandparents because he wouldn't give up drinking?"

Ryan's hand reached for hers and held it gently.

After a long pause, she drew a ragged breath. "How did they die?"

He was silent.

Lilly caught his eyes in a hard stare. "If you know, you better tell me."

"Complications of acute alcoholism." Ryan answered bluntly. "Bev passed not even a week after him. Perhaps she couldn't live without him, or she was just relieved it was all over."

The tears burning at the back of her eyes finally spilled down her cheeks.

"I'm sorry, Lilly."

Once more silence fell over them, each lost in their own thoughts.

Lilly passed her hand over her eyes and took a deep breath. She glanced down at Ryan's hand still enclosed around hers, and she gave his fingers a tight squeeze. She didn't trust herself yet to speak a word of thanks to Ryan.

It was a lot to let sink in. Fifteen years' worth of silence broken in one evening.

"So what do we do about Earl?" Lilly cleared her throat, voice still choking with tears.

"What about him?"

"He threatened me yesterday, remember?" Lilly narrowed her eyes. "He stapled an animal to my barn door."

"Allegedly," Ryan chimed in. "And it was hair. Fake hair."

"Whatever." She shook her head. "He's got some bone to pick with my grandparents, something they promised him."

"He was indefinitely running their land when they died, most likely it's about the acreage," Ryan ventured.

Lilly's mind buzzed as she continued putting pieces of the puzzle together. "They must have said something to him about running the land after they were gone. Something that wasn't in the will, the official will that I got after they died."

Ryan shrugged. "Just let him keep working the land, as if nothing changed."

Lilly stood up suddenly, pulling her hand from his. "No, if it was as simple as that, why would he make such a dramatic proclamation?"

Ryan watched as she began to pace the porch. "Because he's a crazy old man?"

"Grandpa or Grandma must have said something to the effect that he'd be getting the land when they went. Who else was going to run it? Their only son wanted nothing to do with them." Lilly paced faster, warming up to her theory. "However, that agreement didn't make it into the finalized version of the will before they died... or it was never meant to?"

Lilly turned to Ryan, eyes sparkling. "He wants the land. He wants me to follow through with their verbal agreement. Grandma must have written about it in her more recent journals. I'm certain I can find proof of the verbal agreement. Wait, are verbal agreements legally binding?"

She paused and tapped a finger against her lips. "He still thinks he's getting the land. He doesn't know what the will actually says, and believes I'm keeping the land from him." Lilly concluded, "He's threatening me to make sure I follow through. I mean, I am the daughter of Harold's 'evil son,' so why wouldn't I keep the land from him as some sort of last dig at his alcoholic father?"

"Whoa, whoa, whoa, hang on." Ryan grabbed hold of her hand as she passed, jerking her to a halt. "Slow down there, Nancy Drew. You've had a pretty disruptive day today. Let's keep the conspiracy theories to a minimum until you've had time to think this all through."

Lilly pressed her lips together as she yanked her hand free from his. "Why won't anyone believe me about Earl being dangerous?"

Ryan sighed and stood, stretching his arms over his head. "Because he's not dangerous. Earl Graves is just a cranky old man who has a chip on his shoulder and thinks the world owes him. He's not trying to scare you off your land, he's not trying to get you to pay up on a debt he thinks is owed to him. You just need a good night's sleep, and you'll realize why this all sounds crazy in the morning."

"But—"

"Get to sleep." Ryan jammed his hat back on his head. "I'll be back in the morning for chores and I'll check in on you to make sure you've come back to reality."

Lilly frowned as she watched him walk off the porch and head to his truck. Why was no one believing her? She couldn't shake the bad feeling she got—and continued to have—about Earl. He was trying to get her off what he believed was his land.

And no matter what it took, she was going to prove it.

Chapter Nine

Lilly sat in the kitchen, finger tracing the rim of her coffee cup as she watched the sun's rays creep higher on the horizon. She hadn't bothered to go to bed, instead spending a restless night in the den. Her grandfather's leather chair, once so inviting and an icon of warm memories, turned cold and rough during the night. Eventually, she moved to the couch in the living room to spend the remainder of the night. Now, she found herself sipping luke-warm coffee before dawn.

She was certain she'd even beat the cows waking up.

The three journals still laid on the counter before her, untouched from the night before. She knew they'd have to go back into the box and then to the attic, where her grandmother had secreted them away from prying eyes. Lilly couldn't bring herself to look at them, let alone move them.

Lilly glanced around the kitchen, eyes searching the cabinets and appliances for any signs of her family's past she could have missed through the years. She had vague recollections of the fights her parents and Grandma would have in the kitchen while she and Grandpa played in the den or on the porch. How many times did she hear their raised voices all the way out in the chicken coop when she played with the neighbor children?

She was a child then, how would she have known about hidden pains of alcoholism and child loss? How was she possibly supposed to be on the lookout for the tell-tale cover phrases adults use to keep such troubling information away from children's ears? Adults argued and disagreed. She fought with her parents about various things, so why wouldn't adult children continue to disagree with their parents as they got older?

Lilly raked her fingers through her tangled hair and screwed her eyes shut. She wanted her brain to settle down enough so she could think. The back door opened slowly, but the stealthy entrance was thwarted by the screen door slamming shut. Lilly knew who her guest was before he spoke. She lowered her head to her arms and listened to his boots thunk against the tile floor.

"Morning."

She smirked faintly at the hesitant tone. Lilly raised her head and gave him what she knew to be a half-hearted smile. She was too tired to fake anything more.

Ryan flinched as he sat across from her at the island. "Holy cripes, you look like hell."

"Are you always such a charmer?"

"You caught me on a good day." His smile matched her feeble attempt. "Did you get any sleep?"

"No, not really." Lilly pushed her words through a long yawn.

Ryan eyed her half-full coffee. "The truth hit you that hard, huh?"

"There's more in the pot, not sure if it's still hot." Lilly waved a limp hand toward the kitchen counter. "I'm not sure what's worse, knowing the truth about my grandparents, understanding why my parents cut them out of our lives like that, or just being generally pissed off at every-one for lying to me."

"All completely reasonable reactions." Ryan returned with a full mug of coffee. He took a testing sip, grimaced, and continued to drink the dark brown liquid. "It'll take time to come to grips with your *new reality*."

New reality? Lord, help me...

She rolled her eyes, pushing her own mug away. "Thank you, Dr. Phil."

After a brief staring contest, he took a deep breath. "I'm certain Faith has mentioned my accident. I've caught you looking at my leg over the last few days."

Heat spread across her face. "Sorry."

He waved her off. "I was at Ludeson's farm, helping him and his boys castrate and de-horn the calves, moving some of his bulls onto trailers for shipping—"

"Shipping? Where do cows get shipped to?"

His brow shot up. "Where do you think your Big Macs come from?"

Lilly's face contorted and Ryan smiled.

"As I was saying, I was helping Ludeson. His son Mike and I were in the pen with one of their bulls trying to get him on the trailer. Sampson was his name. Ludeson had him as the herd stud for the beef cattle. He was an old bull, ornery as hell, and old man Ludeson was done dealing with him, so off he was shipped. I knew that bull's reputation, I'd seen him pin a few of the other hired men before this. But I was young and thought I knew everything. And I had Mike in there with me, so what could go wrong, right?"

"He pinned you." Lilly wasn't sure she wanted to hear the whole gruesome tale.

"Ludeson hadn't de-horned Sampson when he was a calf. One of the handful left on the farm that still had their horns, and his set was massive. I swear he had some Texas Longhorn in him somewhere."

Ryan scratched under his hat. "Anyway, the bull wasn't wanting to be led anywhere, especially a trailer, so he started throwing his weight around. He shouldered Mike into the fence and then went after me, head down and horns ready to do some damage. Horn got me right in the thigh, messed up a bunch of muscles, barely missed my femoral artery, and broke my femur."

"My God, Ryan."

"After more surgeries than I can remember, the docs patched my leg up the best they could, given the amount of damage that bastard did to everything." Lilly noticed his hand drifted down to his left leg. "Then came the physical therapy to get me walking again. Over a year of exercises, stretches, pain meds... I think I even had a couple smaller surgeries to go in and fix stuff, take out scar tissue. After all that, I still don't walk right. Nerves didn't heal right, I guess. The docs and therapists explained it to me but I think I was in too much pain and denial to listen." His resignation was thinly veiled by a shrug.

"You seem to be walking well, now," she offered.

Ryan gave an undignified grunt. "It's been almost ten years since that bull ripped my leg apart. I walk well enough, sure, but it still hurts with every damn step. Some days are better than others."

Lilly's stomach dropped. "Ryan... I'm sorry about what I said that first day..."

"Don't. You didn't know." He held up a hand and cleared his throat as a flash of sheepishness glinted in his eye. "That was one of my worse days, when you showed up."

They fell into an uneasy silence. The sudden intimacy settled awkwardly around them. Ryan looked down at his coffee and brought the mug halfway to his mouth before he set it down again.

"I told you that, to tell you this: you were dealt a big blow yesterday.

Your family did things they felt were helping you at the time. Though, those choices weren't much better than the things that hurt. Now you have to figure out how you're going to move forward."

"Move forward?"

"I can't go back and stop my leg from getting busted; my future in farming changed and I had to figure out how to make a living with a bum leg. It's been hard, not a lot of people will hire someone who can barely get around the yard most days."

"But my grandparents did."

Ryan nodded. "I accepted their help, knowing full well all the rumors and stories that came along with the job. Did I want to work for an ailing, cranky alcoholic? No. Was your grandfather still a decent man? Yes. Everyone has their flaws. I continued to work with cattle, even though I know exactly what they are capable of. Am I going to let one stupid mistake keep me from working with the animals I love? No, I'm going to learn from my stupidity and move on. Just because your family isn't perfect doesn't mean you can or should forgo all the good stuff. This isn't an all or nothing situation—it rarely is when it comes to family."

Lilly lowered her eyes, fidgeting with a thumbnail. She bit her lip, fighting to find a proper response. She just smiled and finally met his gaze. "You're very smart, Ryan."

"You mean smart for a farm boy?" A grin pulled at his permanent five o'clock shadow.

She shook her head. "No, just smart."

"Right," Ryan snorted before he took a drink.

"No, I mean it."

Another pause descended around them, although less awkward than the previous one. The two fell into their own thoughts, allowing a comfortable silence to grow. Only the steady ticking of the wall clock alerted them to any passage of time. For the first time since she'd arrived at the farm, Lilly felt at ease in the silence of the house.

Dandelion's distinct bellow broke the strange spell between them and set both into motion at the same time. Each fell over their stools and their words as they sprang from the island. They filled the silence with rushed words, hoping to dissolve the unintended familiarity and restore the status quo.

"I should get back to the barn—"

"It's getting late, er, early, no late—"

"There's some feed I need to pick up—"

"Shouldn't waste more of your time—"

"I'll get out of your hair." Ryan moved toward the back porch and opened the screen door. "I'll be back for afternoon chores."

"Ryan, wait," Lilly called as he stepped out into the morning air.

He paused, keeping his gaze focused on the brass handle.

"Th-thank you."

A throaty grunt as the screen door slammed was his only reply.

Lilly found her mind racing yet her body unable to keep up with her scrambled thoughts. Nevertheless, she was unable to sleep when she attempted to lay down. The only thing her mind and body could both agree on was sitting on the couch and watching daytime television.

She'd had enough with adulting and decided the only cure was a pint of moose tracks ice cream and Price is Right.

Instantly, Lilly was transported back to her childhood, which seemed more than one lifetime ago, enjoying food choices that were most definitely parentally-disapproved but grandma-endorsed. The nostalgic feeling solidified with each spoonful of ice cream she ate. She added frosted cereal and chocolate milk to her internal shopping list, amazed that such cravings from her youth were so strong now. Foods she thought she had long outgrown and which would certainly send her more health conscious friends into a tizzy if they knew she planned to purchase said items on her next grocery run.

As she lay on the couch, watching the next contestant come on down, Lilly's mind drifted back to her former life. Her city life. Her married life.

What doors opened to her the day she said "I do" to Alec Rhodes. Born into old money and a silver spoon to rival the sculpture with the cherry, he could trace ties to the more affluent families of the Twin Cities through the centuries; some even boasted named mansions on Grand and Summit Avenues in St. Paul. Lilly had had no idea of the levels of wealth flowing between the two cities along the Mississippi, the quaint Midwest charm hiding the ruthless past.

Being the wife of a Rhodes also carried certain expectations. Thrust from rural Minnesota into the upper crust of Minneapolis, Lilly enjoyed the glamorous life: the bustle of fundraising galas and corporate functions, calling upon fellow members of the upper echelon with her mother- and sisters-in-law. She felt like a modern Elizabeth Bennet, making social calls just to see and be seen.

After a while, even silver tarnished and the cherry soured.

What had Alec seen in her to think she'd fit into that world?

A hefty rap on the front door jarred Lilly back to the game show and an unexpected visitor. It certainly wasn't Ryan—he'd just let himself in like he owned the place. She peeled herself from the couch as she shoved a large spoonful of cream and chocolate into her mouth, and greeted her caller.

Cousin Sheriff Michael Brandford stood on her front porch, his uniform crisp and flawless even after having been shoved into the cruiser. He gave a small smile, one Lilly understood to be a gesture well practiced and much used when visiting those involved in a case.

Michael gave a short nod. "Good morning, Lillian. I hope I'm not interrupting something."

Lilly tried to speak but realized her mouth was occupied with stubborn ice cream that refused to melt. She forced herself to chew and swallow the frozen concoction, wincing with each bite. "No, not at all," she ground out as an epic brain freeze threatened to shut down her basic executive functioning. "Please, call me Lilly. We're family and all."

We are?

She swallowed and blinked away the icy pain. "Please come in. I think I have some coffee in the house still."

"No, thank you. Maybe another time. I'm just here for a quick visit," Michael replied as he glanced around the porch.

"Looking for something?"

The sheriff appeared sheepish when he turned back to her, like a child caught with his hand in the cookie jar. "It's nice to see the Schmidt farm without so many uniforms around."

"Tell me about it," Lilly groaned.

An awkward pause settled between the two.

"Why are you out here then? Any leads in Max's case?" Lilly's words blurted out, unable to bear the silence for one more second.

"Nothing I can say at the moment, sorry to say." The sheriff's voice was clipped, too professional for Lilly's liking. "Though, we did make a little headway with your murdered toupee."

Lilly wasn't a fan of his smirk. She could just imagine the fun the officers were having at her expense, having to make a report on an assassinated hair piece. "And what is that?"

"It had a label sewn into the lining. *Property of the LTHS Drama Department.*"

"A drama department toupee?"

"Part of the props and costumes the kids use when putting on shows, I suppose."

"So... I'm being targeted by a drama teacher?"

"Not the teacher, most likely a student or group of students at the high school who are part of the drama department or have access to the props closet." Michael corrected.

"Still doesn't answer *why*?"

"That part we're still figuring out. Kids in small towns like Lone Tree don't have a lot of things to do to keep them out of trouble. Pranks and stunts are a commonplace nuisance around here." He took a measured breath. "Most likely a group of students heard about Max's death or even the simple fact that a new person moved to town—"

"I'm not new," Lilly stressed.

"—and they dared themselves to pull some stunt at the crime scene. Not very often we have one of those around here."

Her mouth parted, prepared to stress again that she was not, in fact, new to Lone Tree, when her voice caught in her throat. Quickly, her mind shifted gears. "Crime scene?"

Michael sighed, realizing his slip too late. "Max's death has been listed as a probable homicide." He relented.

"Probable? What's probably about it? He had a huge gash in his head!"

"The M.E. is still determining if that was indeed from a malicious object or an accident. Max could have knocked his head on a number of things at home or the office—a cabinet, door, a falling box—and not realize how bad the blow was until it was too late."

Lilly chewed on her bottom lip as she mulled over the new theory. "Possible..." she muttered. "Then why the crime scene label?"

"I'm not taking any chances." Sheriff Brandford stood a little straighter.

"So what about the toupee murderers? What do I need to do now?"

"We're conducting interviews around the school. It's toward the end of the school year; the seniors always come up with a prank to pull. We're seeing if anyone has heard things around the halls."

"And when you find out who did it, then what happens?" Lilly felt a rock form in her stomach.

"You can press charges of trespassing and vandalism, if you want."

As tempting as that sounded, the likelihood of a high school student ratting out a fellow student was a long shot. Seniors in a small town high school formed surprisingly strong bonds.

"Oh, there was a question I had for you." Michael patted the front pockets of his uniform shirt until he produced a small note pad. "What do you know about *La Scarpa*?"

"*La Scarpa?*" Lilly blinked as Michael flipped through pages of his notepad. It was a name she'd never thought to hear in Lone Tree. "The Italian shoe company? What about it?"

Michael handed her the notebook, opened to a page with a taped Xeroxed copy of a photograph. She stared dumbly at the photo for a few moments until her eyes adjusted to the poor image quality. The copied photo showed a section of dirt and grass with a distinct heel print embedded in the muddy ground.

Within the heel print sat an outline of a lion's head. The Lion of Venice snarled back at her with fangs bared and paw raised to strike, the tell-tale symbol of the Italian shoe company. Modeled after the bas relief sculpture in Venice, Italy, where the company was based, the logo paid homage to the Renaissance era art which helped influence many of the company's shoe designs.

"Why am I looking at an imprint of one of the most expensive boots in the world?" Lilly asked.

"We found that near Mr. Carpenter's body." Michael deftly lifted his notebook out of her hands. "This shoe company doesn't make men's shoes, does it?"

She shook her head. "No, only women's shoes..." Lilly snatched the sheriff's notebook back and brought the photo closer to her face. "This isn't a high heel, it's too wide. This print must be from one of *La Scarpa's* limited boot lines."

"Limited?" Michael narrowed his eyes and took his notebook back. He opened to a fresh page and began scrawling notes. "When did it come out?"

"Early 2010, I think." Lilly tapped her chin as she searched her internal fashion database. "Only ran for the spring season, debuted at New York's Fashion Week that February."

"Uh huh..." the sheriff muttered as his pencil flew over the page.

The crunching of gravel under more tires took their attention off the porch and beyond toupees and footwear. Maggie Swenson's tan and rust sedan pulled up next to the sheriff's pristine cruiser.

"Well, looks like you have another caller." Michael backed down the porch steps.

Lilly had instant flashbacks to her upper echelon days and felt nauseous.

"Thanks for your help on that shoe. I'll keep you informed of any other developments," her second cousin twice removed called to her as he passed by Mrs. Swenson. "Maggie, good to see you."

"Good to see you too, Sheriff!" The woman bubbled.

"Thanks, Sheriff... uh, Michael," Lilly stammered as her mind became a jumble of murder, cheesy hair pieces, and expensive Italian leather.

She and Mrs. Swenson watched as he turned his cruiser around in the driveway's horseshoe and left the yard.

"What was that about, dear?" Maggie asked. "Are you alright? I hope nothing serious happened."

Lilly dismissed the concern with a little wave. "Just a possible lead for the toupee killing."

She was more concerned with any updates pertaining to a certain deceased realtor.

"And to what do I owe this visit, Maggie?" Lilly switched to her old "holding court" voice too quickly and her stomach churned. She gestured for Maggie to head up the stairs to the front door.

"I just wanted to stop in and see how you've been holding up, dear. With everything that has happened, it hasn't been a very welcoming few days for you in Lone Tree." Maggie let herself in through the front door and down the hallway. Lilly watched and followed the realtor navigate through the hallway to the kitchen, intrigued at how everyone seemed to be at home in her grandparents' house. Which was now her house. Were her grandparents so welcoming to the residents of Lone Tree that everyone treated this house like a second home? Or were the citizens of Lone Tree expecting everyone to have a "what's mine is mine, what's yours is mine" mentality?

I'm going to need to remember to lock my doors...

Lilly made a mental note to check the local hardware store for new doorknobs; she suddenly feared that, even if she locked her doors, there might be copies of the Schmidt's keys strewn all over town.

Once in the kitchen, Maggie settled at the island, perched on a stool as if it were her own home. "I do hope you've been able to find some good in Lone Tree since arriving. Really, this is the most excitement we've seen in decades."

Lilly sat across from Maggie and remembered her bowl of ice cream in the living room and the TV she left on. She could faintly hear the mid-morning news drift down the hall. She mourned her melted ice cream for a breath.

"I just hope that my coming to town didn't open an evil portal or anything," Lilly offered. "I wouldn't want to be a harbinger of bad omens."

"Oh, goodness, don't say things like that!" A hand fluttered dramatically to Maggie's bosom. "We have one of those in town, one of those Wickerns."

"Wiccan," Lilly corrected softly, hand concealing a smirk.

"She moved to town a few years ago, and I swear devilish things have happened since she showed up. I just hope that what happened to Maxwell isn't part of her and her kind."

"I doubt Wiccans want to kill a realtor. And if they did, it wouldn't be with a blunt force to the head. They'd cast a spell or hex or something." Lilly enjoyed how uncomfortable Maggie looked after that last remark.

"But Wiccans and murders aside, I am strangely enjoying my time back at the farm." Lilly decided to limit the amount of shock she inflicted on the woman. No sense in turning one of the few friends she had in Lone Tree over an inappropriate joke.

"I'm glad, dear." Maggie settled back into a less aghast continence. "So you'll be staying then?"

"I haven't really thought about it. I might stay a few months, I suppose. Since the divorce, I don't have anywhere else to go but back with my parents." Lilly picked at her thumbnail absently again. "I don't think they'd like to have me back, they were so used to being empty-nesters."

"You have a home here in Lone Tree as long as you like," Mrs. Swenson smiled. "I do hope you'll decide to stay. It would be a shame for the old homestead to leave the family."

"I'm not much of a farm girl," Lilly admitted with a pang in her chest. "I've been so removed from everything... I don't know if I'll be able to keep the animals and everything. I'm not a farmer."

Maggie beamed, reaching across the island to pat the top of her hand. "Ryan will certainly help you find your country legs again!"

"Right."

"Oh, don't be so hard on him. I know you two had your rough patch, but that's water under the bridge! He'll be happy to help an old friend relearn what it means to be a farm girl!"

An old friend, sure. But what about an ex-girlfriend who just up and left with barely an explanation?

"I'll think about it. I still don't think Ryan is too keen on me being here. I disrupted his natural groove, I think."

"Pssh!" Maggie waved the comment away. "Farmers and Lutherans don't appreciate change, you know that. And when you have a Lutheran farmer who's a man on top of it, you're bound to run into some pigheadedness. Just give him some time and he'll get his head out of the mud and be our sweet Ryan once again."

Lilly laughed in spite of herself.

"I suppose the change of ownership of the farm on top of losing my grandparents was pretty hard on him."

Maggie nodded. "He and your grandparents were really close, yes. After their death and while the will was being sorted out, the future of the farm was so unknown."

"He feared losing his job," Lilly ventured. "And he could still fear losing it. He doesn't know what my intentions for the farm are. I could have very well put a 'For Sale' sign at the end of the driveway or kicked him off the farm the moment I drove up."

"Very logical assumptions, dear. But we know what happens when we assume..."

"I know, I know."

"Have you given any thoughts to what you'll be doing with the farm? The fields? The whole town has been hearing nothing but speculation about the farm's fate."

"From Mr. Graves, I suppose," Lilly groaned.

"He's not the only one interested," Maggie cautioned. "Remember, this is the most excitement Lone Tree has had in years, and it's family drama so it's even more enticing."

"I've been doing some research online about small farms and I stumbled upon something called ag-tourism."

"Ag... tourism?"

"It's basically a fancy term for cottage industries, homemade items, farm to table stuff." Lilly leaned closer to Maggie, eager to share what she'd learned. "Like local on-farm milk bottling or cheese making, farm-to-table produce, eggs, even products made from things on the farm. I discovered milk soap and lotion."

"Milk soap?"

"I have a lot more homework to do on these topics, but they sound promising. It'll bring a lot of business to the farm as well as Lone Tree."

"You sound just like a certain someone."

Lilly paused. "Who?"

"Maxwell Carpenter," Maggie answered. "He had big plans for Lone Tree, too. Not all of them went over very well with the people in town."

"I'm not talking about big box stores, just something local that's made at a local farm. How more anti-big box store can I get?"

"Just don't bite off more than you can chew, dear." Maggie wagged a warning finger at her. "Though I may not fully understand what you were just talking about, it's nice to see you excited about ideas for the farm. That means you plan to stay a while."

"I guess..." Lilly shrugged. "Say, kind of off topic but not really, does Lone Tree have a farmer's market?"

"It does. Or, well, it might still have one?" Maggie fumbled. "Your grandmother was part of the group that started the farmer's market, and they were planning on starting it up again this summer, but now that Bev's passed... and the field they held it was bought by a land developer... I'm not sure they'll have it this year."

"Hmmm." Lilly fidgeted, overflowing with ideas and fresh worries.

Maggie glanced down at her watch. "Oh, goodness, I need to get back to the office! I'm sorry to run out on you like this!"

"Not at all, Maggie, it was good to see you and talk about anything but murdered toupees and Max for a few moments."

The two made their way down the hall once more to the front door. "You call me if you need anything, okay, dear?" Maggie insisted as she opened the screen door. "And I mean it—anything."

"I'll keep your number on speed dial if I have a problem," Lilly assured her.

"You take care of yourself, okay? No offense, dear, but you look ragged." Maggie called from her car, "Make sure you take a nap sometime today, please? And make a good meal. If you need me to come over and fix you something, I'm just a ring away!"

"I'll be fine. Thank you, Maggie," Lilly replied with a wave.

As the realtor left the farm yard, Lily thought of her wasted ice cream in the living room and was glad Maggie went to the kitchen and not there. Seeing what she deemed a "good meal" would keep the well-meaning woman there even longer, and all Lilly wanted was some quiet for once. The influx of advice from nearly everyone she came in contact with was growing tiresome.

Although, the idea of a nap sounded too good to pass up.

Chapter Ten

She awoke after noon, this time from the comfort of the master bedroom. After a quick shower and polishing off a couple more of the finger sandwiches from yesterday, Lilly sat in a wicker chair on the back porch. The farm was quiet except for the occasional lowing from one of the cows and birds chattering in the trees around the house. The horseshoe of the driveway that crested near the barn stood vacant; she had picked up on the hired hand's tendency to park his truck in the same spot every time he showed up.

Most likely picking up that feed he needed to get, Lilly mused to herself as she gazed over the empty yard.

The windows and metal on the roofs of the outbuildings blazed in the midday sun. The heat of the day crept up on Lilly, unusual for late April. Beyond the protective wall of the grove, the rumbles of tractors and other farming equipment eventually reached her ears.

She remembered now the gentle peace of the farm from her youth. In spite of the revelations of the night before, Lilly couldn't find it in her to hate the farm and her grandparents. Nor her parents, for that matter. Ryan was right, they all did what they thought was best at the time.

Though, it didn't make it hurt any less.

And it didn't make her decision about what to do with the farm any easier. She knew she wanted to try and make this new situation work. Knowing the hardships her grandparents had trudged through sparked in her the need to keep the farm going for as long as possible. Lilly didn't want it to fail now, after everything else.

It survived in spite of child loss, alcoholism, and family estrangement. She'd be damned if the farm collapsed after the urbanite granddaughter took over.

Urban...

Lilly gnawed at the corner of her mouth as she mulled that word over in her mind.

Her girlfriends back in the Cities raved about their excursions out into the 'country' for wine tours. And how many times had she begged Alec to go apple picking in the autumn? Urbanites and suburbanites seemed to be finding ways to venture forth from the concrete jungle and bring a little bit of a simpler life back home.

What would happen if she brought a little urban to the rural?

Lilly jumped from her seat and tore into the kitchen. She rushed around the kitchen and entry hallway collecting her purse and keys, stopping in the den for her laptop, and then was out the front door.

Lilly drove into Lone Tree and waited at the light along County Road 45 for her chance to turn toward Grandma's Attic. She needed to clear her head and an afternoon in a semi-crowded café to pour over her odd research into farm-to-table business ideas was just what she needed. She watched with a disinterested gaze as the stream of evenly spaced traffic chugged down the main thoroughfare. She noticed the crosswalk counter steadily tick on toward zero, meaning the light would soon give her the right of way to turn.

County Road 45.

Lilly suddenly reversed the direction of her blinker. She bit her lip and almost squeaked when the light turned green and she made a hard left at the traffic light. Her little Kia headed down the county road in an eastern direction, toward the edge of town.

She didn't have a clear reason or plan, but something told her she needed to ask Perry Matheson some questions about Maxwell Carpenter. The name has been lurking at the back of her thoughts ever since the card players at the library had mentioned it.

Does this mean I think he's a suspect? Lilly chewed on her lower lip as she neared the edge of town. Houses and store fronts grew sparser, making way for more industrial looking buildings with signs marking them as mechanics, farm implement parts, and one dive bar.

"No, he's not a suspect..." Lilly muttered to the empty car as a large sign proclaiming MATHESON TRUCKING & SHIPPING came into view. She slowed her car and turned into the parking lot, her stomach suddenly auditioning for Cirque du Soleil. "Just want to talk to him about Max..."

Matheson Trucking sat along the very edge of town. After the turn lane into its driveway, the county road stretched long into the distance. Not only did the county road serve as the main drag through town, it also symbolized the only major road that led anywhere out of town. Lilly wondered how many residents of Lone tree pointed their cars east and never looked back.

"Ugh. That sounded like a really bad country song," Lilly muttered with a grimace. Her family would also be included in that total.

She parked her car in what she assumed was the customer parking area. The gravel lot rested between a metal shed and a large garage structure, pickup trucks, farming trucks, and long-haul semi cabs scattered around in what could have posed as rows. Her Kia—and herself—felt more than just a little out of place as her kitten heels crunched across the gravel toward the smaller shed.

A neon OPEN sign hung in a large window, the "N" flickering at a chaotic rate. Lilly pushed through the heavy steel door into the trucking company's modest office. A ragtag selection of chairs surrounded a coffee table covered in piles of car, truck, and farming magazines. Poking out from under the masculine reading was a pristine copy of *Women's Home Journal* and Lilly couldn't help but chuckle.

"What do you want?"

Lilly jumped at the grizzled voice. Turning, she found a middle aged man with short-shorn hair. It was so short it was impossible to tell if he was blond or had gone gray.

"I'm looking for Perry Matheson," Lilly announced as she walked toward the counter. She would have grinned at the sound of her confidence and professionalism, but that would have been a dead giveaway that she didn't belong.

"Perry's out in the garage under a rig." The man jerked his thumb over his shoulder.

Her eyes followed the gestures and she nodded, as if she understood completely what the man meant. She focused back on the man, whose faded blue work shirt proclaimed him as "Bud."

"I see. I wonder if I could bother Perry a moment for a quick chat."

"You can wait until he's done with his rig," Bud grunted. "Unless you're here to hire on a rig."

"Well, not exactly…" Lilly felt her veneer of confidence crack.

"Then you can wait or leave, take your pick."

Lilly frowned as her window of opportunity started closing. She didn't want to hang around the dirty office more than she had to; it smelt of stale oil and exhaust. Also, Bud might start questioning more about her supposed business with Perry.

She didn't want to explain to the employee that she was going around playing amateur sleuth and possibly suspected his boss of murder.

Yeah, that'd go over well.

Then, an idea struck her like divine lightning. It was risky, but if it worked, she'd give old Nancy Drew and Jessica Fletcher a run for their money.

"Well, Gary from Christensen told me to see Perry right away when I got here." Lilly made a show of pulling out her cell phone from her purse. She began opening apps and scrolling, making tsk tsk sounds as she scrolled, her brows furrowing with each swipe.

"Christensen?" Bud muttered. Lilly swore she could see the lightbulb sputter to life above his cue ball head.

Christensen Farms was one of—if not the—biggest farming operations in the county, perhaps all of Minnesota. They were known for their pig farms that supplied pork products to most of the Midwest and beyond. Lilly remembered it being "kind of a big deal" back when she still lived in Lone Tree.

"Yeah." Lilly nodded absently as she scrolled the phone screen. "Oh, yeah, here's that email... here, let me open it up..."

She made another dramatic display of tapping open the supposed email. Bud would never know she was checking out her Instagram feed. "Okay, it was in here somewhere, there! Something about a trucking contract? Short term. Could turn into something bigger..."

She let the sentence trail off, to ensure Bud took the bait.

Christensen Farms also had most of its own tractor trailers and long-haul trucks for transporting their product to and from the plant in Sleepy

Eye, about fifteen miles away. Lilly hoped such a prize dangling in front of what looked to be a struggling business would be too good to pass up.

"From who?"

"From who... who?" Lilly echoed before she caught herself.

Another crack.

Bud nodded, his eyes darkening. "Who from Christensen sent you?"

Before, she had said a name and now she couldn't remember it for the life of her. Surprising even herself, her face remained stoic as she answered: "Gary."

Bud held her gaze for what felt like an eternity. Finally a ghost of a smirk broke his granite face.

"Well, that son of a gun." Bud shook his head. "About time Gary came to his senses. Sure, go right on out to the garage. Perry's workin' on a Peterbilt in bay five."

"Thank you." She gave a brisk nod and hurried out to the parking lot, lest she blow her cover by squealing for joy.

She had placed a large wager on sorely outdated local knowledge hoping that she hadn't lost the farm, so to speak. Saying a large cooperation like Christensen was looking to expand their shipping fleet was beyond risky; it was downright stupid. She could have been laughed out of the office before she even had a chance to test her detective skills.

Thank John Deere it paid off.

Eat your heart out, Nancy Drew.

She forced her heart back into her chest as she made her way across the gravel lot to the garage structure. The gravel abruptly turned to cement stained with black grease and oil as she entered the large open bay door. Before her stretched an assortment of tools, piles of tires, and parked semi cabs. Lilly guessed the building to be twice as long as her barn, but not much wider.

Six semis took up most of the space, lined up neatly in what Lilly assumed were the "bays" Bud mentioned. She couldn't help but be reminded of the cows in the barn back home in their stalls.

Back home?

"Does everything around here have to be lined up in ordained spots?" Lilly muttered under her breath. "Now... what's a Peterbilt?"

She didn't have to wonder for long. The sharp click of her heels against the cement floor had caught the attention of the man she'd come to see. Perry walked out from between two semis, or rigs, about two semis down from where she stood.

Perry Matheson proved to be a striking figure, perhaps as aged and gray as Bud, with the same stained blue-striped coveralls with knees worn almost clean through, but he certainly carried himself better.

"What do you want?" Perry asked as he wiped each finger in turn with a rag that was more grease than fabric.

Lilly balked at the question and tried to recover quickly. "Mr. Matheson?"

He slung the rag over his shoulder. "That's what it says on the sign out front. Still doesn't answer who you are."

"I'm Lillian Rhodes—uh, Schmidt. Bev and Harold's granddaughter."

"Huh, I'll be damned. The prodigal son finally returned."

"Excuse me?"

"Your dad finally come crawling back with his tail between his legs?" Perry's grin was a strange mix of good-natured ribbing and vindication.

"Oh, no, um, no it's just me—just me that moved back," Lilly stammered. "My parents still live in Minneapolis."

"Hmm." Perry's mouth straightened. "Shame. I went to high school with your parents. It would've been nice to see them again."

"I'll pass that along."

He turned on his heel and disappeared between the two semi cabs. Lilly followed dumbly, like a lost puppy.

"So, Lillian Schmidt, what can I do you for?" Perry started tinkering on something within the opened engine panel on what Lilly believed was the rumored Peterbilt.

"I was wondering if I could ask you a few questions, if you have the time." Lilly inched as close as she could to the man without getting in the way of the toolbox next to him. He moved between engine and tools swiftly, wrenches and ratchets flung over his shoulder blindly to land askew on the tool tray.

"What sort of questions?" The engine block echoed his grunted question. "I'm not hiring right now, and no offense, I don't think you know your way around an engine."

Lilly didn't join in his laughter. "No, I'm here about Maxwell Carpenter?"

His hands paused in their work for the span of a breath, then continued to crank on the wrench. "And here I had half hoped that Gary did send you."

"How did you—?"

Perry shot her an icy glare. "Bud texted me while you walked over here. Or do y'think us country folk ain't got yer fancy tech?" He accented the sarcasm with an exaggerated southern drawl as he wrenched at a bolt again. It snapped with an improbable three dimensional noise that Lilly felt in her chest. "I don't have time for your questions," Perry concluded.

"It won't take long, Mr. Matheson," she pleaded.

"I said I don't have time," he growled as he tossed the broken bolt onto the floor. Lilly watched as it skittered out of sight under another semi. "Why do you even care about Max?"

"I found him..." Lilly began.

He pulled away from the side of the semi's engine and leveled a silent, studying gaze on her. "That's right, I read about that in the paper, and heard from Merlin's cop radio." He paused in thought. "Sorry you had to go through that."

Lilly gave a small smile, silently thankful that his voice softened a degree. Perhaps she could still pull this off after all. "What was your relationship like with Mr. Carpenter?"

Perry shook his head and dug through the layers of tools. The clangor of the metal almost drowned out his bitter laugh.

"Old cronies have been spreading the rumors around town before his body went cold, I see. Didn't think I'd get caught up in it." He chose a larger wrench and started working on another section of the engine deep within the side of the truck.

"I don't mean to imply you had anything to do with his death—"

"Then tell me, Ms. Schmidt, why are you here?" Perry turned on her suddenly, wrench in hand and pointed at her face.

Lilly stepped back involuntarily. "I'm just trying to find the t-truth. The man died basically on my doorstep. I feel I owe him and his family that much."

Perry narrowed his eyes and lowered the wrench. He turned to his toolbox and threw the large tool in with a weary grunt. "There certainly was no love lost between Max and I. That don't mean I was rejoicing when he died."

Lilly remained quiet, hoping her silence would prompt him to continue. She managed to get her foot in the door this much; she didn't want to risk him shutting it completely on her.

"No doubt you know he worked in real estate. Not just selling homes and such, but also commercial land and farm land. Five years ago, Max and I were working out a deal for me and my company to buy the vacant lot next door, so I could expand my business. I was looking to add five more rigs and needed the space for housing the trailers and to expand the loading dock."

Perry sighed, picked up a pliers, then let it slip through his grip back into the toolbox. He gestured to the garage structure around him. "As you can see, that didn't happen."

"Why not?"

"Max sold the property out from under me." His voice matched the stony consistency of the parking lot. "Found some other buyer, one of those partners of his in that blasted modernization of Lone Tree scheme of his. They outbid me, the bank liked their financials better than mine... and they got it."

"Did you sign a contract or something with Max? How could he go behind your back like that?"

"Almost signed. I was on my way to the bank to sign on the loan before heading over to Max's office to finalize our paperwork. I'm barely out of my drive here when I see that smug S.O.B. roll up and slap a 'sold' sign on the lot." Perry scratched at the back of his head.

"Why hasn't anything happened with the property?" Lilly asked. "Seems like a lot of work to just have the lot sit empty..."

Perry dug through the toolbox once more. Lilly saw the shadow fall over his eyes. He was debating how much to tell her. She didn't blame him, given her less-than-truthful methods of gaining access to him.

"There has to be a partner," Perry finally spoke. He lifted a screwdriver out of the box, then lowered it down again. "Carpenter had to have at least one other partner in his land deals, maybe two. All his scheming couldn't have been done by one man alone, no matter how highly he thought of himself."

"Another realtor at his office?" Lilly asked, trying and failing to keep the excitement out of her voice. She had noticed Perry didn't comment on the lot sitting empty, but the idea of a partner was more interesting.

"He's the only realtor at Pine Prairie. Chased all the other decent ones to work with Maggie Swenson or straight out of town. There's only so much ego one office can handle." Perry shook his head. "For all I know, this other partner could be halfway across the world now, with all the trading and business that is done online."

The little hope that Lilly had for a new lead withered as quickly as it sprang up in her head. She could check with Maggie's real estate company for any double agents, as it were. Who better to partner with than a local who is familiar with Lone Tree, the residents, and properties? Though, with what Perry speculated about an outsider, an online partner made sense as well.

"Five years. And nothing has happened with that lot or Max's expansion dealing. So, insult to injury, I have to stare at that damned empty lot of weeds every day for five years, knowing it was rightfully mine," Perry grumbled. "I can only imagine how difficult that must be," Lilly said. "Must have made you pretty mad seeing that lot over there."

Perry leaned in close to her, another wrench materializing in his fist. He jabbed it under her nose. "I didn't kill him," he spat.

"I didn't say—"

"You didn't need to." His eyes darkened. "And now, I'd ask you kindly to leave my garage."

Lilly made good time back to her car. She didn't register the crunching of gravel beneath her feet or the slamming of her car door over the pounding in her ears. Lilly threw her car into gear, tires spitting gravel as she exited the lot.

What was she thinking? Going to a random garage and interrogating someone she suspected of murder? Alone! And without telling anyone where she was going! All she had learned in self-defense class had gone right out of her head. He may have killed before, he could do it again! Did she even get any useful information with this stupid stunt?

Perry, much like many others in this town, didn't like Max Carpenter's plans for the big box stores and housing developments. Did she just inadvertently lengthen her suspect list while risking her life accusing a man of taking another's?

Lilly needed to construct plausible motives for murder. Establish a plan of attack before her next interview. Did she even have a next interview? What was that name Maggie Swenson mentioned, from the Chamber of Commerce? Lilly's brain went blank as she drove west on County Road 45 toward town. She'd remember the name later. Now was the time to regroup. She needed a Watson to her Holmes.

Preferably one that could make a killer caramel latte.

She parked as close to Grandma's Attic as possible, but it appeared she had arrived in the middle of a rush. With her laptop tucked safely under her arm, she entered the crowded café and searched for an open seat. All the tables and wall booths were full, many occupants appearing to still be mid-meal while others sat and chatted as harried busboys took dirty dishes away. Lilly caught flashes of Faith behind the counter, refilling coffee while trying to close out tabs.

The restaurant patron saints must have been looking down on her, Lilly decided, as a group of elderly ladies rose from their booth and shuffled their way to the door. She dashed through the packed dining area to the booth and slid onto a cushioned bench, muttering an apology with just the right amount of shame after she bumped into one of the women in the process.

Lilly started up her laptop and brought up her search engine as a familiar form plopped into the booth across from her.

"Was wondering when I'd see you here." Faith tapped the back of the laptop. "Are you doing okay?"

Lilly arched a brow at the concerned tint to the normally bubbly restaurateur's voice, yet continued typing. "Why wouldn't I be okay?"

"Ryan told me you went into the attic last night."

"We did."

"And that you found out."

Lilly met Faith's gaze and smiled, unable to hide her amusement at how open ended Faith's comments were. Given the fullness of the dining room, Lilly knew there had to be a few gossip mongers in the crowd and that Faith knew who they were, as well as their hearing radius.

"Yes, I did." Lilly nodded, lowering her eyes back to her screen. "I'm doing as well as I can, thank you."

Faith mirrored the nod. "Should I grab you a plate for lunch?"

"No, thank you, I had some more of the sandwiches your aunt brought yesterday. Although, a caramel latte would be lovely while I research."

"Certainly." Faith left the booth as quickly as she entered.

Lilly smirked at the high-energy woman and worked on checking her email. She was scared to look at her inbox, now that she wasn't on her computer as much as she had been before she arrived in Lone Tree.

"What are you researching?" Faith placed a large mug next to Lilly's laptop. She sat down and shoved a wire basket around the other side of the screen. Nestled in the basket was white-and-red checked wax paper heaped with still sizzling fries.

Not one to question free food, Lilly popped one in her mouth before she answered. "New business ideas for the farm," Lilly managed around piping hot potato. She breathed in deep the caramel and espresso scents rising from the mug next to her.

Faith coughed, a fry catching in her throat. "You're not going to sell the cows, are you?"

Lilly looked at her through her lashes. "I wasn't planning on it, no."

"Good, because Ryan would be devastated."

"I'm not planning on subtracting anything from the farm quite yet. I know the cows meant a lot to my grandparents, and definitely mean a lot to Ryan. I'm trying to see what else I can do with it." Lilly explained as she continued to type keywords into the search engine. She frowned as her searches came up wanting.

"Good." Faith grinned as she grabbed the ketchup bottle from the end of the table. "I was hoping you'd say that, especially after your guys' talk this morning."

"This morning—" Lilly paused as the ketchup bottle farted its contents over the fries, "how do you know about this morning? Did you bug my house?"

"Ha! No, I wish though. I tried to bug Toby's sister's house once with my daughter's junior spy kit she got for Christmas that year, because I know her husband is hiding something from her, but Josh took it away. Crushed my poor little Marie until he gave it back a month later."

Lilly blinked, waiting for the rest of the answer.

"I do talk to my brother, Lils." Faith dragged a fry through the lake of ketchup on the red-and-white wax paper. "And you've been sleeping for half the day. A lot of stuff happens in seven hours. I can't believe he told you about his accident like that. I don't think he could believe he told you. I knew it was a matter of time, though."

Lilly lowered the laptop screen so she had a clearer view of her farmhand's sister. "What are you talking about?"

Faith's eyes widened and her jaw dropped, revealing her half-masticated French fry. "Ryan still wants you."

Now, it was Lilly's turn to gape at Faith. Then, she laughed as she reached for her latte. "He's barely tolerated my existence since the moment I've stepped on the farm. He just opened up this morning because he knew I was having a rough time with everything that's happened, the toupee, the truth about—"

"He's been pining for you for years, Lilly," Faith interrupted. "Even after your family had their falling out, he still hoped you'd come back around, and lo and behold! Here you are!"

"Preposterous."

Faith stabbed a red-tipped fry at her. "Denial."

"Whatever." Lilly shook her head. "Back to the farm."

"Deflection!" Faith sang softly.

"What would be a good second business option for the farm? I know we have the milk from the cows, but there's not that many cows. I know I don't know a lot about farming yet, but I'm pretty certain that a few cows can't produce enough milk to make a decent profit."

"You are correct there."

"I'll have to talk to Ryan to figure out how much the farm is getting in rent from Earl and what we get paid for the minimal milk we ship. I know that's not going to be enough once the inheritance money and my grandparents' savings are gone."

"How long until that happens?"

Lilly cast a sideways glance. Even if small towns knew a lot about everyone's business, she wasn't sure she wanted to divulge that information. Especially in public. "We'll have a few years," she answered vaguely. "So what else could we do to bring in more money?" Lilly tapped a finger against her latte mug. "Lone Tree isn't really good for vineyards, right?"

"Nope. A guy came here from Mankato, or was it St. Peter? Anyway, he tried to start grapes and a winery and all that. The ground's not right for grapes, I guess. Or the guy blew all his money on marketing and building a fabulous winery before he had anything to sell."

"Gotcha, no wineries." Lilly tapped at the keyboard. "What about a creamery? Make our own cheese and yogurt?"

"You could..." Faith's voice trailed as she cast a watchful eye around the dining area. Lilly followed her, finally noticing the majority of the tables were vacated. She shifted her eyes back to her companion, unsure of what could have distracted her in the silent café.

Maybe it's the fact it is so quiet?

"Faith?"

"Hmm?" She turned to face Lilly quickly. "You could do cheese. I know that's really expensive to start up. The machinery alone could bankrupt you before you started."

"Gee, thanks," Lilly pouted.

"This might be way out in left field, but hear me out. I read online once about this one place that has yoga classes with goats or llamas running around on the yogaers... Yogaees? Yogees? Anyway, I also saw an article online about how someone started a llama yoga farm."

"Goat yoga?" Lilly didn't even try to hide her amusement.

"And llamas," Faith added. "Apparently, it's a big thing. City folks are paying through the nose to have little goats jump and poop pellets on them while they do their downward facing warrior dogs."

"Downward facing dog and warrior are two separate poses," Lilly corrected.

"Whatever." Faith waved a hand. "You could do that, although Ryan hates goats. You could possibly do that with calves up to a certain age. They'd be super cute and bouncy while people try to center their chakras."

Lilly flinched at the hard ch- that Faith used. She quickly typed "goat yoga" into her search engine and was surprised to find it actually was a thing, and a popular thing, too. Many websites and businesses proclaimed their new offerings of animal-based yoga classes, held at local farms or parks within range of the main yoga studio. She scanned a few articles and yoga studio sites, her skepticism slowly turning into cautious optimism.

"I'm putting that in the 'Maybe' column." Lilly bookmarked a couple of sites to look at later. "I have a background in yoga. I'm certain I could talk to my old instructor about how to get that going."

"You'd never get Ryan to go along with it," Faith interjected.

"And why do I care if Ryan would or wouldn't go along with it?" Lilly asked. "He can stick to the cows, and I can work on the other stuff."

"Because he's part of the farm whether you like it or not."

"I'm not going to get rid of Ryan or the cows!" Lilly shrank in the booth after she realized her voice was louder than she expected.

"You'd better not. It would break his poor heart and drastically shift the nature of his undying affections."

Lilly sighed as the other woman grinned. "Focus, Faith."

"How many rooms are in that house? What about a bed and breakfast?"

Lilly chewed on a fry. "There's not many extra rooms, could maybe do three to four guest rooms? But do I really want to basically wait on people hand and foot? How horrible would that be?"

"Hey, watch it." Faith flicked her fry at Lilly, splattering flecks of ketchup and salt on her keyboard.

"Present company's chosen profession excluded."

"See if I ever give you free fries again."

A voice shouted Faith's name from the kitchen. "I better go check on that." Faith scooted out from the booth. "I'll be back as soon as I can."

"Take your time." Lilly waved her off as she went back to her laptop. She ate fries absently as she searched for creameries and cheese machines. Her appetite waned as she looked up the retail price for some of the required equipment.

Ryan still has feelings for me?

Lilly balked at the sudden thought. She dismissed it quickly as she recalled current proof of the hired man's disdain for her. Except in the last day, he had barely said a kind word to her or treated her with any amount of respect. Especially if Lilly looked at their relationship as employer and employee. If an employee spoke to his boss in the manner that Ryan chose to speak to her, he'd have been fired long ago, if this had been any other job.

What were the employer-employee dynamics supposed to be like on farms?

And hadn't Faith just tried to awkwardly set her up with her cousin Joshua yesterday? Lilly shook her head and decided to not put much merit in Faith's proclamation. Her new old friend was merely trying to get her back in the dating game after the divorce.

The front door chimed open, the bells jingling loudly in the quiet café. "Ms. Schmidt, good afternoon."

Lilly glanced away from her laptop and fries and watched Maggie Swenson saunter over to her booth from the entry. Her crisp business casual attire contrasted sharply with the country chic décor of the eatery.

"Good afternoon, Maggie." Lilly returned her smile. "Having a late lunch?"

"Oh, no, just stopped in for a coffee to go. Office has been particularly empty today." Maggie stood next to the booth and surveyed the contents of the table. "No internet at the farmstead? I thought Bev and Harold got the service years ago."

Lilly shook her head. "There is internet at the farm. I just needed a change of scenery, that's all. And to pick Faith's brain."

The realtor's forehead creased. "May I ask what about?"

"I'm researching that ag-tourism I told you about earlier today. I hope it'll keep the small town feel of Lone Tree." Lilly cast a sly glance Maggie's way then. "You wouldn't happen to know who I'd talk to about zoning and permits for adding such ventures to the farm, would you?"

"Possibly the county or city property offices. I'd start with the city offices first. They'd know more about who to speak with about changing the business classification of the farm and property and whether or not you'd also need to log a business permit with the county."

Lilly grabbed a pen from her purse and jotted that information down on a napkin. "Thank you, Maggie; that will help get me going in the right direction."

She smiled. Though, the gesture was pulled taut across prematurely wrinkling skin. "I'm always at your service, Lilly. Now, I'll let you get back to your research. Gotta grab my coffee."

Lilly had barely picked up another fry and taken a sip of her latte before another shadow stood next to her booth. The sweet caramel flavors soured in her mouth when a wave of dried cow manure, straw, and cigarette smoke rolled over her table. Lilly shielded her nose and mouth with a hand and turned to confront the source of the offensive odor.

"Mr. Graves—?"

"You need to stop talkin' to that fool," the old farmer snarled, his words slurred by the lump of chew cradled in his lower lip.

Lilly took in his stained overalls and jacket, the sleeves of which appeared to have survived a fight with a blender. Shreds of fabric clung together somehow with the cuff of the sleeve.

"I'm sorry?"

"Stop talkin' to that woman," Graves repeated.

Lilly sat straighter in the booth. "I can speak with whomever I please, Mr. Graves. And for your information, she addressed me first."

"She's just sweet talkin' ya so she can get your granddaddy's land, too." Graves pointed a gnarled finger at her. "Those land salesmen, she's not much better than that Carpenter fool! That land belongs to me!"

Lilly took in a slow breath and held the man's watery gaze. Being this close to the older famer for such a prolonged time allowed her to see how weathered and haggard his face truly was. She wasn't sure of his true age. Though, she estimated he was around the same age as her grandparents, early to mid-seventies; but the sun, elements, and tobacco had aged him prematurely. If she didn't know any better, she'd have put Mr. Graves closer to ninety.

"According to my grandparents' will and the state of Minnesota, it's my land at the moment, Mr. Graves," Lilly replied, her voice tight.

Why hasn't Faith come back?

"That's a load of bull, blasted real'state salesmen, lawyers... politicians, the whole lot of them are damned fools," Mr. Graves railed, his gravelly voice threatening to crack. "Twisted Harry's words, made him sign that fake will, just 'cause he took to the drink. Thought him not in his right mind to make decisions. He made his decision, alright! He gave me that land fair! Told me to my face and shook my hand, like a man."

Lilly swallowed, the fries turning to stones in her stomach. "I'm sorry, Mr. Graves. I'm sorry if my grandfather told you that you could have the land, and it didn't make it into the will. Perhaps we can come to an agree—"

"I already had an agreement, missy!" A rheumatic fist thundered into the table top. "I've waited two months for you and your thieving parents to do right by me. You have a week to hand over my land."

"Or what...?" The words escaped her lips before she could stop herself.

"Reckoning," the old man growled, a dribble of tobacco juice trickled down his chin.

Lilly focused on the rust-colored line creeping down through grayed whiskers, keeping her unaware of another figure coming up from behind Mr. Graves. She started at the thudding of boots and a hand clamping down on Grave's hunched shoulder.

"Earl, I think it's time for you to let the young lady finish her meal." Ryan's face appeared over the old man's shoulder.

Mr. Graves yanked his shoulder from under Ryan's grasp. "Get your hand off me, you worthless cripple."

Ryan's face remained stoic; the only response to the man's insult was the darkening of his eyes. "Earl, it's time for you to leave."

Graves took a step away from Ryan and glanced around the café. The few patrons still seated now openly stared at the trio, their focus mainly on the disheveled farmer. He turned toward the main counter and found Faith standing by the register, arms crossed firmly across her chest. Lilly had never seen the woman with a stern expression, and the look on her face now was beginning to scare her.

"You're in on it, too!" Graves jabbed a finger into Ryan's chest. "One week, hear me? I want my land in one week!"

With his last threat still hanging in the air, the old man shuffled out of the café, blatantly bumping into chairs—occupied or not—on his way out the door.

Ryan watched as the man continued down the sidewalk until he was out of sight. He lowered himself into the booth across from Lilly. "Are you alright?"

His hand reached for hers and clasped it tightly. She opened her mouth to protest his gesture when she realized her whole body was shaking. Lilly let his calloused hand wrap around hers as the tremors continued. It took a few false starts to finally get the words out.

"No, I'm anything but alright." Lilly's voice barely reached a whisper. Lilly shook her head as she locked eyes with Ryan. "You owe me an apology."

"An apology for what?"

"For not believing me that Earl Graves is dangerous."

Chapter Eleven

"**I wish you would let me call Joshua,**" Faith insisted.

Faith, Ryan, and Lilly sat in the booth, the fries and laptop long forgotten after the scene caused by Mr. Graves. Faith and Ryan occupied one side of the booth with Ryan seated on the outside while Lilly remained rooted to her seat. She feared standing up, afraid her knees would still be unable to carry her weight.

"I don't know why we'd need to bring him into this," Ryan returned.

Lilly leveled her gaze on him.

"Because he threatened you and Lilly!" Faith interjected.

"That was barely a threat," Ryan huffed. "He's said more believable threats while soused at McGee's Landing."

Faith shook her head. "He wasn't at the bar. He was in my café, threatening my customers."

"Then *you* call Josh and make a report."

The siblings hadn't noticed Lilly's eyes burning into Ryan's skull. They continued to argue over Earl Graves' words. Faith's eyes darted to meet Lilly's occasionally, her expression growing more concerned with each pass. Either he was oblivious to her, or he had practice over the years ignoring such glares.

"We need to talk to the police." Lilly's clipped voice silenced the siblings' arguments. "Neither of you believed me when I said he was dangerous. First Carpenter, then the raccoon, and now this—"

"The raccoon that turned out to be a prop for some high school drama club, which is all alleged by you," Ryan pointed out. "And there's nothing linking him to Carpenter's death. You didn't bring up any of this to him, did you?"

"No, I didn't." Lilly sat straighter in the booth. "I wish I would have, though. See what his reaction would have been. If the man is alright with threatening someone in public, why wouldn't he be capable of doing something horrific like that? Killing animals is one of the signs of a murderer."

Ryan rolled his eyes. "I think someone's been watching too many crime shows on TV."

Lilly lashed out with her foot, grinning as the top of her shoe connected with Ryan's shin. He howled and bent to grasp his wounded leg. Only for a brief moment did she worry if it was his left leg. Faith bit her lip to keep from laughing.

"I'm talking to Josh whether you like it or not. This isn't a coincidence—Carpenter dying, the toupee, and his little stunt just now."

Ryan shifted in the booth to bring his injured leg up onto the bench. He glared at her as he rubbed his shin.

"I'm with Lilly on this one, Ry-Ry." Faith shrugged. "It's not like she's pressing charges or anything—"

"But I want to!" Lilly interrupted.

"—but any information, no matter how trivial it may turn out to be, is better than ignoring it," Faith finished.

"Fine, do whatever you want," he grumbled as he picked at the cold fries. "It'll be a waste of everyone's time."

"Why are you so against me talking to the cops?" Lilly demanded.

"It's not the cops, really. Just one in particular." Faith elbowed her brother in the ribs. "You're just territorial."

"Am not," he shot back.

Lilly eyed the siblings. "Territorial with Josh? How so?"

She couldn't help but think of Faith's matchmaking schemes.

Faith grinned, settling into storytelling mode. "The rivalry between Ryan and Josh goes back to middle school. They competed in baseball, football, basketball, 4-H, FFA—"

"FFA?" Lilly asked.

"Future Farmers of America," Ryan muttered.

"You'll get used to them, and the 4-H-ers." Faith tapped a cold fry on Lilly's laptop. "Bev and Harold did a lot of calf showing with those groups for county fair time."

"I don't know anything about... calf showing..." Lilly swallowed hard.

"Don't you worry, we'll help you out! Especially Ry-Ry here!" Faith rammed her shoulder into his. Ryan gripped the table to keep from toppling out of the booth. "Ry-Ry's had many a prize winning calf in his time."

Lilly smiled as a flush of red spread under the brim of Ryan's hat. "And did Josh show many calves?"

"No, calves weren't his thing," Ryan answered.

"You're territorial of the farm because he didn't stick with it," Faith chimed in. "Or maybe you haven't gotten over how he nursed you back to health."

Lilly watched as Ryan's face paled. "That's not it," He snapped.

"Nursed him back to health?" Lilly echoed.

Faith's face brightened as her brother's darkened. "After his accident, Aunt Maggie and Josh helped during his convalescence and physical therapy. Josh was a regular old Florence Nightingale!"

"Faith, be quiet," he muttered.

Faith's eyes sparkled with Ryan's unease. "Why?"

"Nevermind," Ryan segued. "Can we focus on Earl please?"

Faith pressed her lips into a thin line, victory over her brother clear on her face. "Fine. We'll talk to Josh about Mr. Graves. He might want to talk to you, too, you know. Since you were here."

"Fine, whatever," Ryan sighed.

Lilly looked at Ryan. She had a hard time figuring out his alliances. He had seen and heard how Earl addressed her; he himself had been threatened along with her. Why couldn't he see reason?

He glanced up and locked eyes with Lilly. After a long pause, he blinked. "What?"

"Why are you defending him?" Lilly asked.

"I'm not defending him," Ryan returned.

"Then, why not file a report?"" Lilly's eyes scanned his face.

"Because it's nothing," Ryan growled. "Earl is a cranky old man, harmless. His bark is worse than his bite. You're just blowing all of this way out of proportion because your big city sensitivities got triggered because someone just doesn't like you."

"Are we talking about Earl or you?" Lilly demanded.

Faith looked at one face, then the other, her lips a white line of antic-ipation with a healthy dose of morbid enjoyment.

"You really don't want Josh involved in this. That's what this boils down to," Lilly continued when Ryan remained silent. "Nothing to do with the threats or the dead animals speared to barns. You just don't want Josh pushing in on your farm."

"It's my farm, now?" Ryan's eyes flashed.

"The way you've been acting, it might as well be," Lilly fired back. "Who cares if someone gets hurt, as long as you get to play king of the farmyard, right?"

Ryan slammed his palms on the table and abruptly got to his feet. The few customers left in the café after Earl's grand performance turned in their seats to watch the trio. "I've got chores to do."

Without another word, Ryan left the café. Faith and Lilly watched him leave as Faith stifled an amused chuckle.

"How can you possibly find this funny?" Lilly asked.

"I was getting a little worried there for a second."

"Were you? Sure didn't look like it."

"He was being too nice."

"To me?"

"To anyone." Faith scooted out of the booth. "But he got that out of his system and is back to his old grouchy self. That talk about Josh must have been just too much to handle. And yeah, I might have gone too far. But sometimes, he needs to get shaken up a bit."

"Lovely," Lilly sighed and looked up at Faith. "I was beginning to get used to the more human Ryan."

"Don't. My kids call him Uncle Oscar now, cuz he's always so grouchy." Faith grinned.

Lilly tried to match the gesture. "Should I call 911 to report our suspicions of Earl? Or ask for Josh? I don't know how this works."

"No, I'll call Josh. I have to talk to him about settling up his tab, anyway. I'll just mention it that Earl was harassing one of my guests, and we'll go from there."

"Thanks, Faith, for everything." Lilly gave a tired smile. "It just really hasn't been my week."

"Don't mention it." Faith patted Lilly's shoulder as she turned toward the main counter. "In Lone Tree, we look out for our own."

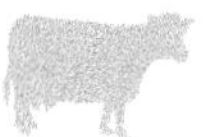

Ryan's truck was parked in its usual spot when Lilly pulled into the farm's driveway. She sat in her car and glared at the rusted truck, wishing to throw something at it or kick in a side panel. The thing was so beat up after years' worth of fun as only "good ol' boys" can have, she was certain Ryan would never notice a new dent or a missing Swiss-cheese-like section of rusted metal.

She envisioned a green and rust colored hunk of metal sitting atop her mantel in the den, only to be followed by a new souvenir added after each time he'd made her mad. Lilly grinned wickedly.

The poor man wouldn't have a truck left after I was done with it.

Lilly finally shook her revenge fantasies from her mind and pulled herself from the front seat and trudged up the front steps. As much as she wanted to learn more about the farm and its business plans, she couldn't stand the thought of looking at Ryan at that moment, let alone talking to him. Once inside the house, she felt some of her lingering anger ebb. She set up her laptop once more at the kitchen island, planning on following up on the ideas she and Faith had discussed before Earl Graves so rudely interrupted them.

Ryan for that matter, too. His presence after the altercation with Earl was no doubt meant to be comforting, assuring. Perhaps even a little of the brave man tending to the damsel in distress. It had only turned into Lilly reinforcing her previously held belief that Ryan did not like her, however, no matter what Faith said.

And the feeling was swiftly becoming mutual.

Lilly logged back into her search engine and began researching farm side businesses. Everyone had a side hustle nowadays, whether it was selling kitchen utensils, overpriced makeup, or being your own taxi service taking tourists around downtown. Why couldn't those in the rural sector have a piece of the action?

That proved to be her most fruitful search phrase yet.

Her vision blurred as she tried to surf through all the related topics that popped up. Many matched what Faith had suggested: a bed and breakfast, doing outdoor yoga or fitness classes; then, a handful of links appeared halfway down the page that perked Lilly's interest.

Multiple links provided a fountain of knowledge about making one's own soap, lotions, candles, and even cheese within the comforts of your home. This is exactly what she'd been looking for. Lilly clicked on one link after the next, skimming information from each page.

After her initial excitement faded, Lilly spent more time on each page. New age cottage industries and farm-to-kitchen or farm-to-bath side hustles were just a few of the newest in a long line of home industries to take off in the last few years and it appeared that the trend wasn't fading any time soon.

Lilly grinned as she opened a new tab in her web browser and brought up the Brown County Library website. After typing in various combinations of "how to," "homemade soap," and "make your own lotion," she had a list of potential books to scour the library shelves for the next day.

Tomorrow was Friday, the day rumored to be the head librarian's return from sick leave. Hopefully, she'd be of more help than moody Allison. Lilly hoped the young woman's boy troubles had been resolved.

As a fellow dumpee, Lilly knew pulling yourself up by your bootstraps was always the hardest part of healing.

Lilly scribbled down titles, author names, and Dewcy decimal numbers in a small notebook, hoping the website spoke true to the location and availability of each how-to book at the Lone Tree Library. If not, Lilly could make the twenty minute drive to Sleepy Eye to see if that branch held the necessary tomes.

As she continued to search online, bookmarking various sites with easy directions and recipes for soaps and lotions, Lilly felt the stress of the last week melt out of her. Even the memories of Max Carpenter's lifeless face drifted away into the background.

Why did she need to worry about dead bodies and potential murder suspects? Perhaps Ryan was on to something, not to get involved with finding evidence that Earl Graves killed Max Carpenter. If he was guilty, the police would bring him in for questioning. If he was responsible for the poor dead toupee on her barn door, they'd figure that out, too.

She wasn't Nancy Drew. Real life didn't follow the carefully plotted mysteries of the crime shows she binged on Netflix—scripted or documentaries.

All she had to worry about was keeping her family farm running. No amount of threatening from a crazy old man could change that. And no amount of mood swings from her hired hand would deter her either.

Suddenly inspired, Lilly bolted up the stairs to her bedroom. She dug through a handful of still-to-be-unpacked boxes until she found her drafting supplies. Grabbing a small pouch full of pencils and another full of various drafting pens, she piled them on top of her sketch pads.

Once back in the kitchen, she spread these new items out on the island. Her graphic design skills had suddenly sparked back to life, stirred by the "cottage industry" images and pages borne of her web search. Although the emerging sketch was rudimentary at best and far from being her final design, Lilly was pleased with the cornerstone she'd build her new venture on.

Encircled by a wreath of prairie flowers and hay stalks, a rough outline of Dandelion's head was the center of her piece. Settled around the various boughs of the wreath were small bars of soap, bottles, and an old-fashioned butter churn. Splashed across the top of the wreath was country-inspired lettering which read:

COOL BUSINESS NAME! CATCHY CATCH PHRASE!

Lilly smiled down at her hastily composed sketch.

She sat back from the island and felt her stomach twist. Now, how exactly was she going to pull this off? What was she going to do with soap, butter, and lotion?

She had to admit that coming up with a brand logo was going to be the easiest part of getting this venture off the ground. Her brain buzzed with ideas, some slipping away before she could fully form them, others building upon the suggestions from Faith and what she had seen during her time spent in the outer edges of the Twin Cities.

Turning the farm into some sort of bed and breakfast started to appeal to Lilly. Mrs. Swenson's reaction to doing something with ag-tourism brought a smile to her face, too. Lilly tapped a finger against her pursed lips, milling the B&B idea along with the make-your-own craft business. She didn't think that the farm would be good for an apple orchard or berry fields, so doing a pick-your-own option wouldn't work too well. And she didn't have time to wait for apple trees to mature.

"What about a bed and breakfast..." Lilly worked through her thoughts out loud. "A bed and breakfast... but I'd need something to grab the people in..."

Her eye fell on the crude sketches of soap bars and lotion bottles.

"With classes to make your own soap and lotions! And butter! I remember that butter's not that hard to make over a weekend."

Lilly filled another sheet in her sketch pad with a list of possible items guests could make at her bed and breakfast.

"This is a good start," Lilly informed the empty kitchen as she started doodling a new version of the logo.

She knew a logo would go through numerous revisions before she was satisfied. It would also change as she solidified her business plan and what she'd offer her bed and breakfast guests. Already, she noticed some design elements that needed alteration. She began touching up the image, adding some elements while changing others.

The somewhat unfamiliar chimes of the doorbell broke her creative streak.

"Now who could that be?" She glanced around the vacant room and frowned. "I'm going to need to get a pet. A cat or dog or something," she continued as she rose from the stool. "This whole talking to myself thing is going to get real old, real fast."

The doorbell rang again as she entered the main hall. "Coming!" Lilly called as she hurried across the hardwood floor. She slipped in her socks and collided with the heavy wood door, grateful that it was sturdy; perhaps whoever was on the other side hadn't noticed the collision.

Lilly opened the front door and was about to push open the screen door when flashing lights blinded her in the late afternoon light. Red and blue shadows flooded her porch, casting the two men who stood on the other side of the door in a back lit kaleidoscope.

"Mrs. Rhodes?" the taller man to her left spoke first.

"Cousin Mike—uh, Sheriff Brandford." Lilly's eyes adjusted to the discolored lights. She recognized his voice before his features came into focus. "What brings you out here? Did you get some new information on Mr. Carpenter?"

"All in good time, Mrs. Rhodes," Brandford returned bluntly.

She frowned at the formal, clipped response and turned to the man standing next to the sheriff. "Joshua, um, Officer Heimdall." Lilly knew she blushed at such an informal address of a police officer, especially when in the presence of one who she guessed was his superior. "Can you two tell me what's going on?"

"We're going to need to check out the tools in your barn, Mrs. Rhodes," Brandford answered.

"Sure, you can look through the tools." Lilly shifted her gaze between the two officers. "I believe Ryan's still down in the barn, finishing chores, he'll know more about the tools than I would."

Brandford directed a hard stare at Joshua. "Go find Klein and have him join you in the barn with Mr. Swenson. Make sure he doesn't leave."

Joshua didn't meet her eyes as he loped down the porch steps to the waiting police and sheriff cruisers to collect the requested officer.

"Doesn't leave..." Lilly's blood ran cold as she slipped out from behind the screen door and onto the porch. The sheriff barely moved to accommodate her presence. "Wait, what's going on here?"

"We found a link between Mr. Carpenter's death and the item left on your property," Brandford withdrew his notebook from the inside pocket of his long coat, "and it seems to involve your hired man."

"What?" The word exploded out of her mouth and echoed across the yard. "How does that figure?"

"We tested that tool found with the toupee and it wasn't just paint. There were trace amounts of blood, too. The preliminary blood evidence on that tool matches Mr. Carpenter's blood type. It appears the same weapon was used in both incidents," Sheriff Brandford continued, making notes in his book. "I spoke with Mr. Graves today, as it seemed he had some past run-ins with our deceased realtor."

"What does that have to do with Ryan?" Lilly asked again, her knees turning to rubber as her stomach hardened to stone. "The tool that pinned the toupee on the door was one of the ones Ryan said was stolen."

"We just need to take him in for further questioning, to clear up a few discrepancies in the stories we've been hearing." The sheriff's voice grew cold, as if he was bored with her questioning. "We're still narrowing our list of persons of interest."

"Does that mean Ryan is..." Lilly faltered on her feet.

"The tool used came from your barn, Mrs. Rhodes." Brandford turned toward the barn where a voice echoed. "We're just trying to figure out how it got from there to a murder scene."

Lilly slumped against the screen door, her eyes following as the Sheriff left the porch and strode across the yard toward the barn. She watched as the men assembled in her yard, the two officers flanking her hired hand as Sheriff Brandford joined them. Ryan's voice carried up to the house, though his exact words were lost over the distance.

She slid down the door and plopped ungracefully on the porch. Her mind buzzed worse than a kicked hornets' nest, the Sheriff's words stinging with each syllable.

Did Ryan give the tools to Earl?

He said they were missing, apparently stolen by whoever killed the toupee. He'd made such a fuss over their initial disappearance the other day. How could he have forgotten such a significant detail as lending them to the old farmer?

Was he having another bad day that day, too? Ryan had yelled at her, accusing her of moving the tools. She replayed that scene from memory. The anger and frustration in his face and demeanor certainly appeared genuine. His temper spiked on days when his leg was hurting more, perhaps the pain from his leg clouded his memory? He'd forgotten about lending the tools to someone and lashed out only from pain?

Earl had to be lying. If the Sheriff talked to him already that day, as he claimed, Brandford must have caught the old man after their last altercation at Grandma's Attic. The old man accused Ryan of being caught up in the alleged plot against him. The old man's mental and emotional states would have been anything but rational. And then being brought in for questioning by the police?

Why wouldn't the old man try to spin things to take some of the attention off himself and put it on someone else? Just long enough to cover up whatever else could be incriminating evidence. He'd stupidly used the same weapon twice, what other smoking guns does the man have to hide?

She watched as the police and Ryan continued their conversation, unsure if she should join them. She should know what's going on if her employee is involved in a potential murder case. Though, her presence probably wouldn't do anyone any favors, given Ryan was caught between an ornery sheriff and his own cousin—perhaps the less people involved, the better.

But if the police were here based on a tip from Graves, he must have reigned in his crazy enough for the sheriff to want to check out this new lead.

Ryan insisted that I not involve the police about Earl Graves...

Lilly swallowed hard, trying to keep her roiling stomach at bay.

"Earl has to be framing Ryan." Lilly barely heard her own words over the sound of the escalating questioning. "He stole the tools and is now lying to cover up his theft and murder, trying to throw the cops off his scent for a while."

She groaned and tilted her head back against the screen door, the taste of the clichés souring in her mouth. "Ugh, I do watch too many crime shows."

The farmyard grew quiet and Lilly's head snapped up at the sudden lack of yelling. Sheriff Brandford, Joshua, and the assumed Officer Klein walked back to their respective cruisers. She locked onto the patrol car with Joshua and the other officer in it. Joshua maneuvered down the driveway, his eyes focused on what was directly in front of the windshield. Perhaps he didn't see her sitting on the porch, or he chose not to acknowledge her.

Ryan's Chevy truck roared to life, the diesel engine mirroring its owner's current mood. Lilly watched as the vehicle's tires tore into the gravel, a plume of dust and rocks spraying out from under the tailgate as the truck disappeared after the patrol cars.

That's a good sign, Lilly decided. *At least he got to leave in his own truck and not in the back of a cop car.*

Chapter Twelve

Friday morning arrived to a bevy of disappointments Lilly hadn't expected.

She ticked the first item off the list when she awoke to the familiar sound of an angry diesel engine leaving the yard, signaling she had slept through morning chores. Lilly rolled over in bed toward the windows. Her plan to join in on the workings of the farm was off to a bad start.

Lilly planned to pick Ryan's brain that morning about the logistic and financial workings of the farm, having been inspired by her bed and breakfast and cottage industry ideas the day before. However, after the unexpected events of yesterday afternoon, she decided sleeping through morning chores wasn't as bad as originally thought.

After Ryan's surprise questioning by the police, she was surprised that he even came back last night to finish the evening chores. Being linked to a rash of crimes and alleged murder by the town crazy isn't always the best motivator for finishing one's work. Lilly propped herself up on an elbow to face the lace-draped windows and made a point to thank Ryan for coming back.

She didn't want to think about what would happen if she had to tend the cows by herself.

Lilly pulled herself from the tangle of warm bedclothes and worked on finding some proper barn clothes. Even if Ryan would be more cranky than normal, she planned to be out in the barn learning as much as she possibly could today. She also wanted to check in at the library to see if the head librarian was truly back from medical leave. There were still some unanswered questions about a certain disgruntled farmer and big-dreaming realtor that needed following through.

She stood in front of her new closet, a massive walk-in that could have passed for a small bedroom. In the months since her grandparents' passing, most of the clothes had been boxed away. Lilly wasn't sure if her Aunt Ellen had taken on that role, given she wasn't sure if her aunt and grandparents were on speaking terms. If they had been, she never heard a word about her grandparents from Ellen, her husband, or her cousin Tammy; Aunt Ellen had probably been trying to keep the peace

Now the left side of the closet's poles, shelves, and cubicles stood bare while the remnants of Beverly and Harold's clothes sat folded neatly in boxes along the right side. Lilly wondered if friends and neighbors from Lone Tree had come and helped tidy up some of the house while it waited for her arrival. She could see the ladies from her grandparents' church come and lovingly put their friends' belongings into boxes and plastic totes. Lilly now wondered what should be done with the remainder of the clothes. Perhaps she'd stop in to see Faith or Mrs. Swenson after her trip to the library and seek their advice on the next steps.

She stared at her few clothes, shoes, and accessories hanging on the left side of the closet, awkward invaders that tried to take up as little space as possible to not disrupt the natives. As she studied her clothes, it became painfully obvious to Lilly that she didn't have any proper barn clothes. Save a few pairs of basic jeans and some plain t-shirts—that once boasted hefty price tags for such simple garments—her wardrobe looked more at home at cocktail brunches than Main Street, USA.

"Perhaps I need to go shopping..." Lilly muttered to the cavernous closet as she picked out the most basic articles of clothing she owned. She remembered the spill in the barn from Monday and believed that her blouse and skirt would never fully recover.

After throwing on jeans and a bright yellow t-shirt, with a short stop in the master bath to tame her wild mane of bed head curls, Lilly made her way down to the kitchen. She polished off the last of Maggie's consoling sandwiches as she gathered her purse, keys, phone, and notebook filled with questions for the librarian. She scrambled through the pile of sketches to find her list of how-to books to look up at the library. The thought of lugging all those books around put another pin under her behind to get her home office set up. She could easily print off pdf files and other how-to instructions without needing to depend on a clunky physical book.

Lilly wanted to transform one of the spare rooms on the second floor into a workstation; however, she wasn't sure how she wanted to go about it. Did she clear the room completely out and start from scratch or gradually introduce her own furniture and electronics over time?

As she passed into the main hall, she glanced at the pile of boxes that had yet to make it up the stairs. Most of her clothing and personal items had made it up into the master bedroom as she worked slowly at unpacking her life, but her professional life remained packed away on the main floor, waiting for her to find direction.

Hopefully the motivation from the B&B and cottage business ideas would keep her moving in the right direction. Whether she ended up opening a bed and breakfast and making artisan butters with suburban housewives on a girls' weekend, or settling for a completely different undertaking, Lilly didn't want this drive to leave.

She feared the thought of growing stagnant.

Lilly walked down the porch steps and made her way toward her car. The library would be open and she could complete her research before the afternoon chores. Then, she could focus on getting to know her farm better.

She paused at the side of her Kia, fingers grazing the door handle, and surveyed the farm yard. The outbuildings stood stoic in the clear spring morning. She caught flashes of black and white moving about the sliver of pasture that she could see from that far up the yard. Sporadic grunts and calls from the cows drifted across the grass, only to be interrupted by Dandelion's telltale bellow.

Lilly smiled as she pictured the ornery matriarch moving about the pasture, ordering the younger cows around, ensuring order in her little bovine kingdom. Hopefully, the elder cow kept a close eye on the rest of the herd to ensure a repeat escape was far from anyone's mind.

Save for the muffled calls from the cows, the yard was quiet. A drastic change from her life in Lowry Park. The soundtrack to her day had once been city buses, traffic, various forms of construction, and the press of humanity in one of the largest downtown areas in the state. Now, she was lucky if she heard a passing car on the main gravel road. It was unnerving to be this removed from civilization. She didn't even know where her nearest neighbors were.

Another thing to ask Ryan about.

She climbed into her car and made her way down the driveway.

The second item on her list of disappointments coincided with the library.

Lilly parked her car in front of the library's well-manicured lawn and loped up the steps. She found it hard to reign in her nervous excitement; she was unsure what sort of information—if any—she'd get out of the librarian and her knowledge of town lore.

Once inside the library, Lilly noticed the marked change in atmosphere since her last visit. The study tables were now filled with groups of three to four elderly men and women, working hard on various puzzles instead of rowdy card games. Lilly walked slowly through the tables, noting that some tables worked on jigsaw puzzles and others worked on large crossword layouts. Overhead, from hidden speakers somewhere amongst the stacks, came soft classical music.

Mrs. Krzmarzick must be back from her medical leave.

Lilly made her way through the throngs of seniors to the main circulation desk. There, she found her assumption to be correct. The head librarian sat behind a pile of books that Lilly feared would topple on the woman. As she drew closer, Lilly believed the woman to be somewhere in her sixties, her silver and blond hair piled atop her head in tight, well-defined curls. A pair of bright red cat eye glasses, balanced precariously at the end of her nose, caught flashes of the fluorescent lights above with each move of her head.

Lilly watched the woman work in silence. She lifted one book from the overwhelming pile, opened the front cover with her left hand, and hammered down a metal stamp with her right. Then, she placed the stamped book on another growing pile to her right in what seemed to be one fluid movement. The fact the library still used old-fashioned rubber stamps fascinated Lilly. Hadn't the county library system upgraded to electronic catalogs and check out systems yet?

"Can I help you, Ms. Schmidt?"

"How did you—?" Lilly stammered at the direct question.

"I was convalescing at home after surgery, not dead. I heard of your arrival days ago." The librarian's voice, with spot-on, dry, and tired tones, made Lilly wish angsty Allison was on shift.

"Sorry, yes, I was wondering—oh, wait, no, it's Mrs. Rhodes, um, I mean, no, Schmidt." Lilly clamped her mouth shut at the exasperated gaze Mrs. Krzmarzick shot at her over the cherry red rims of her glasses.

"Do you need help finding something that can't be found in the computerized catalog?" The chill to the woman's voice brought forth flashbacks of Lilly's fifth grade teacher, Mrs. Levinson, who reduced her to tears after getting a division problem wrong.

"Sorry," Lilly offered, her voice softer. "I was wondering if there was a way to look up land titles for Lone Tree?"

"Land titles?"

"I'm trying to figure out who owns the farm lands around my grandparents' farm, Harold and Bev—"

"I know who your grandparents are," Mrs. Krzmarzick sighed as she stamped a book with a thunderous *thwamp*!

Who doesn't in this town?

Lilly took a deep, calming breath through her nose. She hoped the breathing exercises her yoga instructor taught her three weeks ago would help in this situation.

"Then you'd certainly know—"

"Plat books," the librarian interrupted.

"Excuse me?"

"Plat books," Mrs. Krzmarzick repeated over another crashing stamp. "They show the land ownership in the county. Upstairs, in the Reference section under Local Reference. We should have last year's copy."

"Nothing for this year?"

Steely gray-blue eyes burned into hers. "Last year's book is the most recent our library has. Land ownership wouldn't have changed that drastically in the last four months, save in your situation. If you want something more current, I suggest trying the New Ulm Library. Or the court house and ask for county land records."

Lilly took a step away from the desk and gave her best dealing-with-a-rude-customer smile. "Reference, upstairs, got it. Thank you."

Another raucous stamping cued her dismissal.

Lilly rushed to the stairs, thankful to be away from the ill-tempered librarian. Now having met her, she understood the sullen mood of Allison at the mention of the head librarian. *I wouldn't want to work for that woman either,* Lilly shuddered as she ascended the stairs. *Maybe she needs to up her post-surgery pain meds.*

Once on the second floor, Lilly made her way to the reference section. The less than helpful librarian didn't give her much else to go on, other than the section. Other librarians would have at least given a Dewey decimal number. Lilly hoped she'd be able to navigate the shelves enough to find the plat books. Perhaps she'd check the computers in the other room to see if the online catalog could point her in the right direction.

Even up in the quieter upper level, the booming stamps of Mrs. Krzmarzick traveled up through the stairs and floor boards in muffled whumps. Lilly shuttered at the thought of what internal demons the elderly lady was trying to excise via rubber and ink.

After a brief tour of the reference section, Lilly found a shelf full of maps and decided to begin her search there. However most of the books about maps were of Minnesota as a whole, the country, or world maps. Crouched down to scan the lowest shelves, she determined this venture was a wash. Lilly unfolded herself from the floor and, as she stood, she came face to face with a shelf marked "local reference."

"Oh, for the love of Pete..." Lilly moaned and let her head fall back.

This shelf held mostly spiral bound books and binders, like the kind one would make at a Kinko's or Staples store, that held meticulously researched family trees of prominent Lone Tree citizens, town and county history, and three ring binders containing recent town hall and civil meeting minutes. She scanned the spines of the binders and flipped them to read the covers with high hopes that the plat books would be plainly marked and not in some rural code that only farmers could decipher.

Thankfully, the plat books were in their own three ring binder with "Brown County Plat Books" neatly printed on the binder's plasticized cover in Sharpie. Lilly took the binder into the computer room and flipped it open as she sat. It took her a moment to process what she was seeing as the plat book was no more than a thin book, maybe the size of the A section of a telephone directory. The thin tomes were three-hole-punched along the spine and put into the binder, allowing the reader to flip through each book and year easily.

Lilly went to the back of the binder and found last year's plat book. Inside, the plat book had a layout similar to the old King's Street Atlas her father kept in the car, even after the invention of GPS and cell phones with built-in navigation apps. The plat book showed Brown County as a whole, then each quadrant of the county was further plotted out in grids with numbered columns and lettered rows to help pinpoint a certain area.

She smiled as she flipped through the pages, trying to familiarize herself with the county and where Lone Tree stood in relation to the other towns. Lilly sighed, thankful that something was finally going right for her that day. Now, to just take the binder home and do her research in a slightly less hostile environment.

That feeling quickly shifted once she closed the binder. At the bottom edge, produced with a dial-by-letter label maker, was the stern warning:

NoT FOR PUBLIc CHECKOUT. SEe LIBRARIAN FOR ASSISTANCE.

Lilly let out a breath as she pinched the bridge of her nose. She did not want to talk to Mrs. Krzmarzick again. She knew that "see librarian for assistance" was code for "pay for the librarian to make copies for you."

"It'd be adding insult to injury having to hand money over while getting verbally abused by her," Lilly muttered, fingers tapping the binder's worn cover.

She dug through her purse resting in the chair next to her and withdrew her cell phone. Lilly opened the plat book up to the pages that showed what she believed to be most of Lone Tree proper and the lands north of town, where her farmland and the lands that Max Carpenter was interested in were located, and started taking pictures.

If she couldn't take the book home, she could at least have these pictures as reference. Hopefully, Ryan would be back for mid-afternoon chores and in a receptive mood so she could ask him to help her decipher the information from the plat pages.

Lilly rose and placed the plat book binder back on its shelf, taking a picture of the shelf's location for future reference. She had a suspicion that the other books about Lone Tree's history were going to be just as important later on.

The final disappointment of her day was less of a disappointment and more of an utter fiasco.

Lilly dodged detection from Mrs. Krzmarzick on her way out of the library, though the percussion of the woman's continual stamping followed her out the door and down the sidewalk. She had the passing wonder about how the groups of elderly patrons could play their puzzles amidst all that clatter.

Out on the sidewalk and in the fresh spring air, Lilly's mood lifted, and any negative vibes from the librarian blew away with the breeze. She glanced at her watch and noticed it was close to eleven. Perhaps a quick stop at Grandma's Attic before the lunch rush was in order. Although, this being Small Town, USA, lunch rush probably did start at eleven in the morning or sooner.

Lilly started down the sidewalk toward the café, vaguely wondering when she should cross the street as she was currently on the wrong side of Main. On her left she passed Mrs. Swenson's realty office. Through the large front windows Lilly made out shadowy traces of figures moving around the office, though she couldn't pinpoint Mrs. Swenson. Thankfully, Maggie didn't look out and make eye contact; Lilly wasn't in the mood to get sucked into a conversation with the woman today.

The intersection loomed closer ahead and Lilly made her choice to cross the street legally instead of jaywalk, which still seemed to be a tolerated pastime in Lone Tree. She watched, with a faint smirk, as at least five men in grease stained jeans made their way lazily across the middle of the block toward the café.

She pushed the crosswalk button and spun idly in a circle as she waited for the little white LED man to bid her walk safely across the street. Lilly stopped with a jerk as she noticed the business on the corner. She stood before Prairie Pine Realty, Max Carpenter's office, biting her lip, waffling on whether she should go inside and offer her condolences to his former coworkers.

Lilly didn't waffle for long. She hopped up the single cement step from the sidewalk and pulled the door open. More jingle bells announced her arrival to the office workers, who were notably absent from the front desk. She took measured steps into the office, noticing the crisp feel of the space. Lilly hadn't been in many businesses in Lone Tree yet, though she had sneaking suspicions that the primary décor choice was somewhere in the wood family, giving the customer a little slice of down home Americana.

Despite its folksy name, Prairie Pine Realty was anything but folksy Americana. Sleek lobby chairs and coffee tables filled the small receiving area, the chrome and leather glinting in the late morning sun. Table lamps and ceiling fixtures sported abstract geometric shades of what appeared to Lilly to be imitation papyrus.

"Hello?" Lilly called, alarmed by how long she had been in the lobby and had yet to be greeted.

Maybe they're out to lunch and forgot to lock up?

Lilly stood by the front desk and leaned over the counter in hopes of catching someone's attention.

"Hello? Is anyone in?" Lilly waited a few moments and received no reply. She turned to go when movement behind her caught her eye.

"Hello."

Lilly faced the front desk again to find a petite woman emerging from a back office with a cautious expression.

Lilly replied gently. "I'm sorry, are you open now? I can come back—"

"Is he gone?"

Lilly frowned at the tremor in the woman's voice. "I'm sorry, who?"

"Mr. Graves." The woman crept back to the reception desk and dropped heavily into the wheeled office chair.

The hair on the back of Lilly's neck prickled. "Mr. Graves?"

"Yes." The woman shook her head. She tried to smooth out her rumpled suit jacket and pencil skirt, both a shade or two off from the chrome furniture, but failed to get a few stubborn creases out. "That man..." She shook her head again, then flashed Lilly a brilliant receptionist smile. "I'm sorry, I'm Tiffany. Did you have an appointment?"

"No. No, I didn't," Lilly answered. "I'm Lillian Schmidt, and I was just walking by—"

Tiffany's face blanched white under her foundation. "You found Max..."

Lilly nodded and swallowed hard. "Yes, I did. That's why I stopped by, to offer my condolences to the staff? I just felt like I should..."

Tiffany stood up and clasped her hands around Lilly's. "Thank you, dear. It was so hard to hear of Mr. Carpenter's passing and then to hear that that man had something to do with it."

Lilly winced when Tiffany's grip tightened when Mr. Graves was mentioned. "Mr. Graves? The police found proof that he did it?"

"Well... no," Tiffany admitted. "But it's only a matter of time. I don't know why it's taking them so long to get their act together. I mean, it's so obvious that he killed poor Max."

"He was here before I was, that's why you were hiding out in the back?"

The receptionist rolled her eyes. "Yes, he was here. Lurking outside the door and peering into the window like some sort of perv. He's been doing it every day this week, even before Max died."

Lilly looked over her shoulder at the front window. "Have you called the police?"

"I think everyone in the office has called them at one point this month. They say that since he's outside the building on a public sidewalk, he can't be charged with harassment or anything until he comes inside the office. And we'd never let that happen."

"You'd think the police would take it more seriously, since he's a person of interest in Max's death. I find it rather telling that he's creeping around the office of a man he's been accused of killing." Lilly chewed on her lip thoughtfully.

The receptionist gave a useless shrug. "Not everyone liked Max around here. As much good as he wanted to do for the town, he was more of a polarizing force than a uniting one, I'm afraid."

"How so?"

Tiffany shot her an expression that clearly said she wondered if Lilly was paying attention to any of the talk buzzing around town. "It really boils down to the opposition he got from the Chamber of Commerce."

"You'd think the Chamber would want him to bring new businesses in?"

The clerk laughed. "They do, but only if they are the ones bringing the new stores in. Each wanted the crown of 'Savior of Lone Tree.'"

"Interesting..." Lilly tapped her denim-clad leg thoughtfully. "Did Max have any business partners? I couldn't help but notice it's rather quiet around here."

She shook her head. "Max was the only realtor in the office at the moment. He liked it that way, strangely, to work by himself."

"Really?"

"He felt that other realtors in the office only made the work environment too competitive for his liking. Max really wanted a work space that fostered a family-type atmosphere."

"What will happen to you and the office now?"

"I haven't had time to think of that…" Tiffany gave Lilly's hand another firm shake, tilting her left arm slightly. "I'm so sorry, I'd love to chat some more, Lillian, but there's a twelve o'clock coming in soon."

Lilly mirrored the woman's pleasantly dismissive smile. "Oh, of course, and I should be getting on my way as well. Please tell the staff that I stopped by and if there's anything I can do…?"

"Certainly, Ms. Schmidt." Tiffany offered a little wave as she walked Lilly to the door.

Lilly stepped onto the sidewalk and hoisted her purse higher on her shoulder. She wasn't sure if her trip to Max's realty office accomplished what she'd hoped. Although, she had learned about Mr. Graves' chronic harassment of Max's workplace. With the man's history with the town, and especially with Mr. Carpenter, how could the police not suspect him?

She stopped at the crosswalk, waiting once more for the lights to grant permission to cross the street. Given the level of traffic, Lilly was tempted to just jaywalk. Everyone else in the town seemed to do it. But what did her mother say about other people jumping off bridges?

"What were you doing in there?"

She sadly recognized the grizzled voice behind her before she turned around.

Speak of the devil... maybe we said his name too many times and we summoned him.

"What can I do for you this morning, Mr. Graves?" Lilly turned around and copied Tiffany's customer service smile.

"You were talking to Carpenter's people, weren'tcha?" Graves stabbed a finger at her arm.

Lilly drew away from the man before he could touch her. "It's none of your business what I was doing in there, Mr. Graves."

"You're selling off my land!" The old farmer shouted.

"I was doing no such thing. I went in there to offer my condolences about Mr. Carpent—"

"I told you I want my land, missy!" Mr. Graves' dark eyes burned into hers. He rose up onto his toes to bring himself closer to her face. "You're sneaking around my back and trying to sell it before I figured it out!"

Lilly sighed. She missed the light for the crosswalk and now was stuck with the ill-tempered man for even longer. "Mr. Graves, please. I'm not selling the land. I haven't talked to anyone about it. I'd like to be able to sit down with you and discuss what we can do together to continue the contract my grandfather set up with you."

"Stop usin' your big city words to try and get away with this," the man growled.

Lilly pinched the bridge of her nose and exhaled an undignified grunt. "I'm done talking with you, Mr. Graves. You're not hearing a word I've said to you all week. We're done here."

She turned and made to cross the street, traffic lights and jaywalking be damned.

His malformed hand shot out and grabbed hold of her arm as she turned to step off the curb. "Don't turn your back on me, girly. You'll do what I say or I'll—"

"You'll do what, exactly, Mr. Graves?" Lilly snapped, yanking her arm from the man's grip. "It's pretty daring for you to be threatening me when you're a suspect for murder."

Mr. Graves stared up into her face dumbly and blinked his cataract-riddled eyes. He then burst out into laughter, a disjointed cackle that reminded Lilly of a hyena. "Suspect for murder?" He crowed, slapping his knee.

"Yes, for Mr. Carpenter's murder," Lilly pressed. "And for spearing that painted hair piece onto my barn door to scare me."

His disturbing laugh cut short. "Hair piece? I don't know nothin' 'bout no hair piece."

"A tool you borrowed, that was also used to kill Mr. Carpenter, was found plunged into my barn door, with a painted toupee on the other end, painted red to look like some bloodied raccoon or something." The words tumbled out before she had a chance to stop them. Warning bells went off in her mind that she was telling him too much of what she knew.

If he was really as dangerous as the evidence was leading her to believe, she needed to be more tight-lipped around the crazy old man.

"I didn't do nothin' with no painted raccoon on a barn door," Mr. Graves repeated. "I did borrow some tools from that cripple hired man you got. But I didn't touch Carpenter and I don't hurt a raccoon unless I'm prepared to eat it."

Lilly grimaced at the thought.

"You're so hell-bent on getting my land, why wouldn't you sneak onto my yard and send me a mob-style message?"

"Sneak onto your yard?" Mr. Graves's hyena laugh assaulted her again. "Missy, I can't do no sneakin' around nowhere. I've got arthritis in both hips, a bum knee, and gout in my left big toe. How in the world was I supposed to sneak onto your yard with a dead animal and sneak off again? I'd keel over before I'd get halfway up your drive."

Lilly pursed her lips together, mulling over her response carefully.

"If you're havin' any problems on your yard, I'd look no further than the cripple."

"Ryan. His name is Ryan," Lilly corrected.

Mr. Graves snorted. "He's not as innocent as you think, missy. Get your head out of the clouds and take a good hard look at'im."

"Excuse me?"

"I'm not the only one who had an ax to grind with Carpenter." Mr. Graves chuckled as he continued, "I've seen the way you look at that Swenson boy. Just cuz you're sweet on him doesn't mean he isn't capable of nasty things."

She chose to ignore the man's comments. "Ryan wouldn't do such a thing."

"He's around your yard more than anyone else, and he has access to all those tools and machin'ry." The farmer's lips pulled back in a tobacco-stained grin. "Don't be missing the forest for the trees."

Lilly frowned and put more distance between her and Mr. Graves. "I really must be going. If you want to have a civilized conversation about my grandfather's promise to you, you'll know where to find me."

"You think you got everything all figured out, don'tcha?" He snapped as he took a step toward her. "Don't get sidetracked from what you owe me. One week and I want my land."

Lilly stepped off the curb and ran across the street. She barely heard the yelling old man and blaring car horns as she hurried down Main Street.

Lilly followed the sidewalk and forced herself to be mindful of the cracked cement. The longer she spent in Lone Tree, the more she was convinced the town had never heard of high heels before. She sighed, making a mental note to check out more sensible shoes options the next time she logged into Amazon.

The Lone Tree Chamber of Commerce was housed in a squat, one-story building that, judging by the shape and sharp slants of the roof, Lilly was certain had once been a fast food restaurant of some kind. She could still make out the placements of beverage dispensers and the condiment bar by the shadows on the faded wallpaper as she glanced through the vast wall of windows.

She entered through the enclosed glass vestibule, snickering that the original women's and men's restrooms sat to her right, pock marked blue and white signs beckoning the proper patrons through their doors. Once through the second set of doors, Lilly found the dining area transformed into a cubicle farm. The space, once filled with hungry patrons devouring their orders of burgers and fries, now stood quiet seating areas with gray sofas and magazine racks. What certainly had been the kitchen area now stood closed off from the rest of the cubicles by a collapsible partitioned wall and a sign that designated upper management offices lay beyond the door.

Bells chimed above her as she moved through the door. What was it with this town and door chimes? Lilly bit her lip to keep her smirk in check as the occupants of the cubicles began inspecting the new visitor. Their heads popped up over the industrial beige walls just enough to spy the rest of the lobby, yet not long enough to draw too much unwanted attention, before sinking back down to continue their work.

"Hello and welcome!" A bubbly voice called from the former-kitchen-now-executive office, belonging to a middle-aged woman, an obvious bottle blond. Her hair did not match what natural skin tone Lilly could see through heavily applied makeup. The woman made her way over before Lilly made it ten steps into the lobby. "How may the Chamber help you today?"

"I'm looking for Lisa Munroe, head of the Chamber?" Lilly shook the woman's offered hand.

"You found her!" Lisa Munroe gave Lilly's hand one last hard shake before releasing her grip.

Lilly forced herself to match Lisa's overly perfect smile. She remembered those smiles from the fundraising events and celebrity galas that Alec insisted she attend. That smile that said "I will pretend to like you until I can determine your usefulness, or until the check clears." She couldn't count how many times a woman with that same smile, at those same functions, had turned away from her mid-sentence once they realized their data mining mission wasn't getting them anywhere.

And now, years later, Lilly found herself shaking hands with a small town wanna-be version.

"I was wondering if you'd be able to help me with starting a business."

Lisa's plastic smile softened with real emotion. "Oh! Please tell me you're going to be reviving Bev's market!"

"Um, yes..." Lilly hoped her smile and voice didn't waver too much. A farmer's market, that's an idea. "How did you know I was related to Bev?"

"Oh, dearie, I can see her in you. You have her eyes." Lisa smiled warmly. "And word of your arrival has been making its way around town. It's not hard to spot the newbies in Lone Tree."

Lilly forced her smile once more. She wasn't a "newbie." She was born and raised in Lone Tree. True, she'd had a decade and a half reprieve, but that didn't change the hard facts.

"How easy is it to start a business?" Lilly redirected.

"Well, depends, dearie." The Chamber head drew out each word. "I believe there are some permits and other legal forms to complete. Permissions from the county, the city council, food inspectors, and the like. The Chamber doesn't have any of those powers, unfortunately, but I can give you the names of those on the council and the county inspectors."

"County inspector?"

"You'll be having it on the original farm site, right?" Lisa asked and Lilly nodded. "Then you'll need a county health inspector to come out and look around, because of the livestock—you do intend to keep the cows, correct?"

"Yes, the cows are staying."

"Then, with the sale of produce and other consumables being that close to livestock and their... uh... byproducts, a health inspector is a must."

Lilly's stomach sank. That sounded like a lot of work.

"Come this way. We'll talk more in my office." Lisa gently directed Lilly by the elbow toward her office door. "We'll let the others have quiet to focus on their projects."

Lisa held the door open until both passed through, then shut it quietly behind her.

"What projects are they working on, if I may ask?" Lilly seated herself in one of the pair of stiff, high-backed chairs nestled before Lisa's enormous wooden desk.

"Oh, certainly!" Lisa nodded enthusiastically, settling in her own chair—a large green exercise ball nestled in a roller base. Lilly found herself studying the exercise ball chair instead of politely focusing on the Chamber of Commerce head. Lilly eyed the unique chair choice with piqued interest. Maybe I should get one of those for my home office...

"The ladies are busy getting donation and fundraiser letters completed by the end of the week. Even though Apple Dapple Days isn't until September, we need to do marketing, fundraising, and promotion now in April."

Lilly arched a brow. "Apple Dapple Days?"

"Don't you remember Apple Dapple...?" Lisa's voice trailed off as her eyes scanned her guest's face. "No, I suppose you wouldn't remember it under that name. You probably knew it as the Harvest Moon Festival."

Lilly nodded, memories of Harvest Moon Festivals long past popping up unasked in her mind. The last one she attended with Ryan crept to the forefront. They were inseparable on the hayride and probably displayed more PDAs than comfortable for some attendees.

She blinked and forced out a small breath to refocus. "Why did the name get changed?"

Lisa's eyes rolled back and she let out a beleaguered sigh, something Lilly was certain wouldn't be very dignified for a Chamber of Commerce head. "The Ladies' Auxiliary group at Our Lady's Grace raised such a stink about it ten years ago. Claimed that it sounded too much like a pagan ritual and that we were leading our young people to witchcraft or some cockamamie thing like that."

"Really?" Lilly tried not to snicker.

"They also had a field day with all those Harry Potter books, too. Those came out at the same time." Lisa shook her head and brushed some bottle-blond tresses from her face.

Lilly nodded in sympathy, memories long forgotten returning of the somewhat unfavorable reputation Our Lady's Grace Catholic Church had gained among her and her schoolmates. The overly pious women, who apparently had nothing better to do, would announce a new cause every other month it seemed, to save the souls of the town's youth. She left Lone Tree before the Ladies Auxiliary could foil many of her early high school memories.

She did recall that even the local Diocese was becoming rather annoyed with the women's numerous crusades.

"Sounds like nothing has really changed." Lilly offered a small shrug. "I remember those ladies protesting our freshman dance and the senior prom theme the same year. It's a wonder this place hasn't turned into a replica of the *Dirty Dancing town.*"

Lisa gave a small smile, and Lilly knew she didn't understand the pop culture reference, which was surprising because Dirty Dancing was not a new movie. "Those ladies have been a thorn in my side—really this whole town's side—for decades. This is the third name change the festival has had to endure."

"Third?"

"It used to be the Harvest Moon Festival, but even before that it had always been known as Thaddeus J. Longford Days."

"Thaddeus Whoford?"

"Thaddeus J. Longford, one of the original settlers and founders of Lone Tree. Helped the settlers escape during the Sioux uprising of 1862. There's a bit of town history that says he helped Chief Sleepy Eye with those refugees from that settlement that would eventually become the town of Sleepy Eye."

Lilly maintained her practiced smile as Lisa continued with her history lesson after a heavy sigh. "Apparently, Mavis Schumacher's daughter did a book report in the early seventies on Longford and discovered that he also took part in the lynching of Indians and slaves... that one black mark on his name was enough to erase all the good he did for this town. So, Mavis got her Ladies Auxiliary to launch a huge campaign to change the name of our founder's day festival. Now, we can't honor our founding father anymore."

There was so much wrong with what Lisa had just said that Lilly had had to bite her tongue to keep from interjecting. Rule One of data mining Lilly had learned from her years in complex upper-crust society: don't correct opinions of someone you need a favor or information from, no matter how glaringly inappropriate those opinions might be.

"Because of all these name changes and baseless scandals, donations and funding are leaner and leaner each year," Lisa concluded, casting a forlorn gaze upon the banners and posters of festivals past that decorated her office walls.

Lilly leaned forward, ready to redirect the Chamber head back to the business that had brought her there in the first place. As Lilly opened her mouth, Lisa found her second wind. "I thought Apple Dapple Days was a good name, until Sheila brought up the whole pagan thing again this week. I don't even remember how she linked apples to witchcraft but it was just hooey!"

Lilly's interest piqued at the over pronounced way Lisa said the woman's name—the amount of acid dripping from each exaggerated syllable seemed physically impossible.

"She had brought it up before?" Lilly asked, leaning back in the uncomfortable chair. She didn't know the people of whom Lisa Munroe spoke so poorly, but the gossip was intriguing and would possibly prove useful later. It was like being in her own little soap opera.

"She felt Apple Dapple was too childish..." Lisa's thought petered out into the ether as she stared down at her desk. "What were we looking for?"

"Health inspector and city council members?" Lilly prompted.

"Ah, yes!" Lisa slapped the top of her desk with one hand as the other worked on pulling open heavy drawers. "I know I have that information written down somewhere..."

As the Chamber head dug through her files, Lilly glanced around the office, trying to avoid just staring at Lisa in silence while she waited. The room was more time capsule than office, the walls and bookshelves lined with snapshots of Lone Tree's past. Old high school pennants from the '50s and '60s occupied one wall, proclaiming the might of the Lone Tree Braves, before giving way to antiquated Thaddeus J. Longford Days posters. All were yellowed and pocked with the passage of time.

Next to the unnecessarily large desk stood small bookshelves that held more picture frames than books. In one frame, Lilly spied a photograph of a much younger—and more brunette—Lisa Munroe standing next to an equally younger—though no less tanned—Maxwell Carpenter. He held up a smaller picture frame that Lilly determined was a dollar bill. Rising behind the pair was the storefront for Prairie Realty.

She found herself locked on that photograph. Maxwell Carpenter frozen in time, perpetually celebrating the opening of his real estate office. In spite of his overly processed and manicured appearance—past and present—Maxwell seemed genuinely happy.

Max.

"Why did Sheila give a suggestion for what to rename Apple Dapple Days? Who is Sheila?"

The words blurted from her mouth before Lilly registered she'd said them.

Lisa leveled a crisp blue gaze at Lilly as she said flatly, "Sheila Carpenter."

The name hung between the two like a rotten odor.

"Is that his wife?" Lilly guessed.

"His mother. She suggested renaming it Maxwell Carpenter Days"

"He must have done something noteworthy to be considered for that honor," Lilly ventured.

"He did nothing of the sort," Lisa snapped. "And I am not renaming the festival after him." She punctuated her oath with a slammed drawer. "Her son hasn't even been buried and she had the nerve to call me the other day and suggest changing the name again!"

"I never said—"

"I am sick of this town fawning over that man like he was some sort of hero. He was not going to be the savior of Lone Tree."

Lilly cleared her throat as the temperature seemed to rise in the office. The Chamber head didn't want to talk about Max anymore. She needed a distraction and quick.

"I'd think the Chamber of Commerce would like new businesses coming into town," Lilly's eyes strayed back to the photo of Lisa and Max and the first dollar. Bringing up that memory would not be a good way to bring Lisa back to her side. "Though, I don't think Max's way was going to be the best way," Lilly hastily added at a disapproving glance from Lisa.

Lilly glanced around the desk as Lisa absently thumbed through the papers she had momentarily forgotten about in another drawer. Lilly herself had forgotten why she had come into the office in the first place.

A pair of leather boots sat next to Lisa's desk, ankle-height and made of leather the color of a newborn fawn, with snarling lions stamped into the supple material above the thick wedge heel.

The same emblem stamped in the ground in that police photo.

"Are those *La Scarpas*?" In her excitement, she reached out and plucked one of the expensive boots from the floor.

"Yes..." Lisa's icy voice sank deep into Lilly, setting off a new set of warning flags.

Never, never touch a woman's pair of *La Scarpas* without permission.

"Oh, I'm sorry..." Lilly swallowed. She knew Lisa watched her every move, and would as long as the boot remained in her hands. Lilly turned it over slowly in her hands and studied the lion stamp. "It's been so long since I've seen a pair outside New York, I got a little excited."

"I see." Lisa's plasticine smile reemerged.

"I didn't think anyone in Lone Tree knew of La Scarpas, let alone owned a pair!" Lilly flashed her own practiced smile when she glanced up at Lisa for a moment. Her eyes went back to the lion logo.

Her excitement faltered a bit as it sunk in—if these boots really were the ones that made the impression at the crime scene, that meant Lisa probably had something to do with Max's death. *Is this bottle blond a killer?*

"I'm sorry, really..." Lilly forced a girlish giggle as she placed the boot back down next to its mate. "It's not every day you see a pair."

"Those were a gift from my husband, last summer when we went to Italy," Lisa said.

"Beautiful shoes. And lucky woman," Lilly gushed. "My husband—well, now ex-husband—wouldn't get me a pair when we were in Paris two years ago. Super jealous of you right now."

A small, pleased smile graced Lisa's face for a moment. "Well, consider yourself lucky then, to not have such gorgeous shoes tainted by such memories."

Lilly glanced back down at the boots and felt a tight pang in her gut at the memory of her time in Paris. The Chamber head was right. She didn't need any more bad memories.

"Can... I look at them just one more time, please?" Lilly asked.

Now having the proper request, Lisa nodded as she brought a stack of papers up onto her desk.

Lilly picked up the same boot and made a show of turning over the boot, inspecting the sole and the intricate logo stamp, the snarling lion jumped out from the brushed leather. The legendary logo didn't seem right. There was something missing from the lion's mouth.

"How does a real estate agent get involved with setting up new businesses? Thought they just sold the buildings to the business owners and then moved on to the next sale."

"He'd often neglect to mention a certain permit or zoning requirement when he'd show potential business owners locations around downtown to rent for their stores," Lisa began, pinching the bridge of her nose. "Then, once the space was leased or purchased, the city and county inspectors would pay a final visit. They would find seemingly easy, yet important, steps were missed, the new owners, or even some citizens, would protest the city council trying to shut down the business due to failure to comply with permits. Not wanting to damage our already hurting downtown, the city would have to fast-track forms and permits. It was easier for Maxwell to beg forgiveness after the fact than to ask permission for these new ventures. Same thing with those big box stores he promised were coming. He was promising all sorts of prime real estate to investors before the ink even dried on the sale agreement. He promised the same land to multiple buyers and then took the best offer."

"Playing them against each other, and they didn't even know there was another player," Lilly muttered. "Perry has a theory that Maxwell wasn't working the land deals by himself, that he had a silent partner, so to speak."

"I see you've done some homework." A wry smile parted Lisa's heavily colored lips. She leaned over her desk, fingers steepled in front of her face, "Or should I say you've been snooping. Why are you so interested in Max?"

"I'm not snooping," Lilly returned, though she felt her cheeks flush. As she took a seat in the high back leather chair in front of the desk, she added, "I'm trying to get a better picture of the man who died on my property."

"Yes, died on your property," Lisa stressed. "You've been in town, what, barely a day and you were already alerted to Max's big box schemes. And yet, he's found dead on your property a day or so after you show up. I wonder, Ms. Schmidt, have the police spent this much time snooping around you as you have around town?

"Remember, word travels fast here in Lone Tree. The disgraced granddaughter of Harold and Bev asking about a dead man is prime gossip fodder. You must realize that you're not off the hook as a person of interest. He was found on your land, land that he was eyeing as his next conquest."

"I didn't know that..."

"Why else was he found that close to your property, Ms. Rhodes?"

With each patronizing word, Lilly felt as if the high backed chair had started to swallow her whole. "I had a brief interaction with Mr. Carpenter before his death. I can't be that interesting to the police. I heard about his dream for the town and I think it could really work."

Lilly hoped she sounded more confident than how she felt.

Lisa remained silent, her eyes scanning Lilly.

"You didn't drink his Kool-Aid, did you?" Lilly asked.

"At times, but overall, I knew that his plans would fair about as well as his schemes on Main Street. All flash and pizazz but no substance.

Really did imitate the man who proposed them. The Chamber head absently shuffled the papers on her desk. "So you're playing detective now? Running down your list of suspects, seeing who hated Max the most. That must mean I'm a suspect?"

It was more of a statement than a question.

"I'm trying to figure out who could have done this to Mr. Carpenter." Lilly's voice shook. "He died on my land, and I feel I owe it to him to figure this out. His death is somehow linked to my land and I'm tied to his passing whether I like it or not."

Lisa's mouth pressed into a hard line, slowly growing into the plastic smile from earlier, and Lilly knew she said too much. "Are you sure you're here to resurrect your grandmother's market?"

"Yes"

Lisa Munroe placed a stack of papers on her desk blotter and held Lilly's gaze, almost against her will.

"Well, I'm sorry, Ms. Schmidt, but I seem to have misplaced those numbers you were looking for. I'm sure if you hurry, you could make it over to city hall before the clerk closes for the night."

Chapter Thirteen

Lilly took a round-about way back to her car from the Chamber of Commerce, then took the long way home. As she drove, she realized that her covert escape scheme was all for naught. Mr. Graves wouldn't need to lay in wait for her to leave town to follow her home; he already knew where she lived.

That realization only soured her mood all the more.

Her stomach growled as she parked her car in front of the farmhouse. In her escape from Mr. Graves and the impromptu stop at the Chamber of Commerce to escape the crazy old man, she hadn't actually gone to the café for lunch as was her original plan. Now, she was not only cranky but hungry.

The presence of Ryan's truck in the yard almost went unnoticed in her unnerved state. Lilly paused on the front porch and gazed thoughtfully at the rusty Chevy. Mr. Graves's words echoed back to her and the replay of his upsetting laugh sent chills down her spine. Again, the old farmer had thrown blame onto Ryan. He tried to deflect attention with the ownership of the tool used to murder Mr. Carpenter. Now, he claimed he couldn't have spiked the toupee onto her barn door.

Lilly entered the house with a huff as she found herself believing Mr. Graves's claims. Her annoyance threatened to boil over to pure anger by the time she opened the freezer door and pulled out a frozen pizza. It wasn't the home-style meal she'd been planning on at Faith's place, but it would have to do for now. She didn't have enough mental or physical energy to actually make something.

After the pizza was in the oven, she plopped down at the kitchen island and stared at her hands. The last thing she wanted was to give anything that cranky old man said credence. Ryan may be more than distant with her and not very welcoming of the new boss, but that wouldn't lead someone to such atrocious acts.

Right?

What if the old man was right? Lilly drummed her fingers on the counter, deciding to play devil's advocate. Somehow, she had to work out Mr. Graves's accusations to see if they held any validity.

Ryan did have more access to the farm and all the tools and equipment on the grounds. That point did check out. Mr. Graves was older and had said he had arthritis and gout, so that did raise some doubts in Lilly's mind whether he'd be able to sneak around her farm undetected. *Could... could it be possible Mr. Graves or Ryan is lying about how well they can move? People don't lie about stuff like that, though.*

Unless they've got something to hide.

"What was that one movie where the bad guy pretended to have disabilities to cast off suspicion?" Lilly asked the empty kitchen. She came back to herself then, however, and shook her head. "This isn't the movies, Lillian," she muttered. "Need to stop using movies and television shows to prove your points."

"The Usual Suspects."

"Holy cripes!" Lilly faltered on the stool, grabbing the island counter before she fell to the floor.

Ryan walked into the kitchen from a forgotten door behind her that led to one of her grandmother's walk-in pantries. She hadn't had time to explore that room. She stared wildly at him as he made his way to the island, wiping his hands on dirty jeans.

"What are you doing here!?" She cried. "You scared the crap out of me."

"Sorry." The shadows from his hat brim couldn't hide the smirk pulling at his lips. "Wanna pop one of those in the oven for me, too?"

"What?"

"A pizza; that sounds good for lunch."

Lilly gaped at him as he retrieved his own pizza from her freezer. "What are you even doing in my house?"

"I had to take a leak." Ryan jerked a thumb over his shoulder toward the pantry. "There's a mud room in there with a commode and a half-stall shower. I use them all the time."

"You take showers in my kitchen!?" Lilly's voice rose a few octaves.

"Not in the kitchen. Mud room," Ryan corrected. "And yes, I do use it. I don't want to get my truck all full of mud and manure."

Lilly's jaw dropped. "You're worried about getting that truck dirty?"

Ryan opened the oven and withdrew her pizza before sliding his onto the rack. He looked over his shoulder with an incredulous expression. "Yeah, I am."

"Whatever." She shook her head and settled herself onto the stool cushion.

She watched Ryan as he maneuvered around the kitchen, pulling open drawers and cabinets on a mission to collect utensils for lunch. He placed a plate before her and the opposite stool, then put a cutting board with her chosen pizza next to her plate. Ryan handed her the pizza slicer.

"Thank you," she said softly, heat rising in her cheeks as she realized she hadn't offered to help.

He answered with a sharp nod and went back to collecting another cutting board and pizza slicer for his lunch. Lilly gazed at him, watching how he moved. He had informed her that some days were better than others. Was today one of his better days?

After a few more minutes of quiet tension, he checked the oven before bending down to retrieve the personal sized cheesy pie. In spite of his stained clothes and rough manners, he conducted himself with the ease of a master chef in the kitchen. With a stocky build that spoke of hours working with heavy equipment and animals, Lilly marveled at his fluid movements as he took a glass down from a cabinet. He seemed so at ease in this house.

"What are you looking at?"

Lilly blinked, realizing that Ryan had already moved to sit across the island from her. Her face blazed crimson. She had been staring at him, and not just his leg. Mr. Graves's snide comment about her and Ryan bounced around her brain.

She lowered her eyes and quickly bit into a slice of pizza. The melted cheese and red sauce burned the top of her mouth, but she managed to avoid spitting it out. As she choked down the scalding food, her eyes drifted over to her left hand and the still pale circle around her finger.

Her heart constricted, momentarily overpowering the pain in her mouth.

"Nothing," Lilly breathed around a blistered tongue.

Ryan narrowed his gaze at her for a moment, then shrugged and dug into his own pizza. The two ate in silence. Lilly consciously avoided his stare while trying to eat as quickly as her wounded mouth and pride would allow her.

"What's wrong?" Ryan broke the silence.

"Hmm?"

"You're not normally this quiet—something's up," Ryan pressed, gesturing with a slice of pepperoni. "Spill."

Lilly swallowed a mouthful of pizza. "And why do you suddenly care if something's bothering me?"

"Humor me."

She finally met his eyes and instantly began to replay her run-in with Mr. Graves. She got to the part where the old farmer had thrown suspicion onto Ryan and froze, which only piqued the hired hand's interest all the more.

"And... then what?"

"Nothing," Lilly lied, shoving more food into her face.

"What else did he say?"

"Ah cant tok wif mah mouf full, it's roo," Lilly informed him, words slipping around melted cheese and crust.

"Sheesh," Ryan shook his head. "I thought you Uptown girls were supposed to be dainty and refined and stuff. Billy Joel lied."

She swallowed and grinned. "Hah, shows what you know."

"So, now that you're done doing impressions of my five-year-old nephew," Ryan pulled another slice onto his plate, "what did Earl say? Honestly."

"He said that I should be looking at you as a suspect for the toupee prank and even Mr. Carpenter." Lilly's food turned heavy in her stomach.

Ryan chewed his food in silence, his head bobbing up and down slightly, as if he was mulling over the new information. "Makes sense."

Lilly coughed, almost choking on her pizza. "What?"

"He tried to pin the tools on me, so why not keep that going?" Ryan's voice was even and steady, the exact opposite of how Lilly felt.

"How can you be that calm? He basically accused you of murder!"

He shrugged again. "You basically accused him. Besides, it's Earl. He's crazy. He'll say anything to either get attention or keep suspicion off him. I'm not worried."

His nonchalant attitude about being accused of murder didn't sit right with Lilly. She watched him carefully as he sat across the island from her: someone who was connected to a murder, yet he ate calmly as if it were just another day.

"Earl said you also had something against Mr. Carpenter," Lilly began, watching how he reacted to the statement.

"I guess I did."

"Did?"

He swallowed. "I dated his daughter for a year or so, right after high school."

Lilly's brows shot up. "You and his daughter?"

Why did that make her stomach flip?

Ryan grinned. "I do date, amazingly. There are plenty of girls who can appreciate the whole down home on the farm thing. I dated Emily for about a year. I know Max didn't approve of me dating Emily. I think she did it to get back at her daddy for whatever reason, and I was okay with being part of that plot for a while. When I had my accident and things got too serious for her, though, she bailed."

"Wow, really? You were cool with her letting you use you like that?"

"Hey, I was twenty and didn't care. Emily Carpenter was hot, and who wouldn't want to date one of the few hot girls in town?"

"Unbelievable." Lilly massaged her temples. "Then why would Earl say you have a problem with Max and not his daughter? Being dumped by the town hottie must've been a hard blow."

"If you're trying to imply that I killed Max Carpenter ten years after his daughter dumped me... you're about as crazy as Earl. I'm going to tell you this one last time, like I've been saying all week: Earl is crazy. He likes to cause trouble, stir up the rumor mill from time to time, but he's not dangerous."

"He's threatened me, multiple times," she pointed out.

"Again, he's all bark, no bite. I wouldn't be worried about him."

"Should I be worried about you?"

The question crossed her lips before she could censor herself.

Ryan's blue eyes locked onto hers, his iron gaze unwilling to let her look away. "Do you think you should be?"

"That's not fair." Lilly's palms slapped the counter. "Don't turn this around on me. Earl flips things onto you, and then you flip things back. Someone has to be telling the truth! Answer my question. You have been linked to a dead man, and the police have questioned you. As much as I hate to say it, Mr. Graves does make a valid point. You have complete access to this farm. You could have put the toupee up on the barn door while you claimed to be getting the cows in. I barely know you, so who should I believe?"

"Barely know me?" A flash of hurt sprang up in Ryan's face but was gone almost before Lilly could register its presence. "You know me. At least, you knew me."

"Ryan... that was... fifteen years ago," Lilly stammered. "People can change a lot in that amount of time. And not always for the better."

He held her stare in silence. Lilly was quickly becoming tired of his silences.

"Right." Ryan pushed away from the island. He took the last slice from his pizza and walked out the back door.

Lilly pushed her plate away with a frustrated grunt. She picked up the cutting board and placed it on a shelf in the refrigerator; she'd deal with the leftovers later. For now, she needed to get out of the house and clear her head.

The early afternoon sun reduced her to squinting as she walked down the back porch steps. She thought about going back inside to get her sunglasses, but she pushed through the temporary glare and continued her mindless walk. She heard the cows calling and shuffling in the barn, their bellowing louder as they were released out into the pasture.

Part of her mind insisted she go to the barn and find Ryan. Try to make amends for basically accusing him of murder. The other part, the stubborn portion of her DNA that maintained she had done nothing wrong, kept her feet pointed away from the big red building.

She was trying to solve a murder. She had to suspect everyone until the evidence excluded them. Even if she'd rather they be innocent until proven guilty. Someone had to be guilty.

Or could all parties be guilty?

Lilly made her way towards a smaller, squat building that was the family's long-unused chicken coop. She stooped lower to glance into the darkened building. Chicken roosts, long vacant and now only housing a various community of mice and other vermin, spread down the long building in rows, awaiting the return of clucking hens, peeping chicks, and a crowing rooster. Lilly smiled sadly, remembering the mornings she and her grandmother had collected eggs.

Well, her grandmother had collected eggs. Lilly had spent most of the time chasing the big Rhode Island Red rooster around the roost rows.

Then, being chased by the enraged rooster, tail feathers splayed and wings furiously flapping as it tried to run her down. Lilly only found a safe haven behind her grandmother, who apparently topped the rooster in the coop hierarchy.

Maybe I'll get chickens, Lilly thought as she retraced her steps back toward the barn. Another thing she could do to help make the farm profitable. Maybe eggs and broiler chickens instead of soaps and lotions. Everyone needed to eat. Not everyone needed overpriced artisan toiletries.

She reached the barn, but decided against going in; she didn't want to deal with Ryan. She wasn't ready to talk to him just yet. Knowing him, they'd have another argument instead of coming to a civil agreement.

She walked down the slight hill to the bottom part of the barn and along the pasture fence. She considered what Ryan had said, now that her willfulness had begun to wane. Small towns and rumors went together like peanut butter and jelly. Just because a handful of people said the same thing didn't make it true.

So, Ryan had dated Carpenter's daughter for a while. That didn't automatically make him a killer. Ending a relationship usually ended one's relationship with their ex's family too, didn't it? Lilly was a prime example of that. After Alec had announced the dissolution of their marriage, she found herself cut off from any contact with Alec's parents, who she'd thought adored her. She'd found it difficult to reach any of his family, even right after the separation.

I didn't really need those Jimmy Choos back anyway. Let Olivia try to squeeze her chubby cankles into them.

If Ryan did harbor a grudge against Carpenter for not being one hundred percent for him dating Emily, why wait until almost a decade after the fact to exact revenge? In crime fiction lingo, she believed that was what detectives called a "long con" or "long game," to plan a crime that didn't have a payoff until many months—if not years—into the future. In this case, it'd be an exceedingly long game. And she was having a difficult time figuring out what the payoff at the end would even be.

Lilly shook her head and rubbed the back of her neck. All this overthinking was giving her a headache and creating knots in her shoulders. She had to stop thinking about the murder stop being suspicious of Ryan. It was ridiculous, really, to think that Ryan had something to do with Carpenter's murder.

In spite of her intentions, however, she couldn't shake the farmer's rantings. He did make a valid point that stuck no matter how hard she pushed. What he had said about the logistics of Ryan being able to put the alleged-raccoon-turned-toupee on the barn door without detection made too much sense to Lilly, even if she hated to admit it. It made more sense than an old man sneaking onto the property, nailing a fake carcass to the barn door, and leaving without a trace.

He might not have killed Max, but that didn't mean he was happy about her being there. Was the "bloodied" toupee supposed to have scared her away? Be some sort of message to her?

Doubt gnawed at her stomach.

And then there was the unknown identity of Max's supposed business partner to consider. Perry was the only one who felt strongly about that theory. Lilly was having a hard time coming up with a potential second man... woman... person. Max's own employee had said he liked to work alone. He hadn't liked competition. If someone had the same ego and self-importance that Max had, the likelihood of them working together on such high-money deals was slim to none.

Unless he had an ex-business partner—someone Max had cheated out of a deal and a hefty payday. That felt like a plausible motive for murder.

That still didn't get her any closer to a name or face for this mystery partner, though.

Lilly let out a frustrated sigh and tried to focus on the meandering cows. She appreciated that Ryan let them out during the day as much as possible. Fresh air and exercise were important.

Dandelion lumbered over, her substantial frame surprisingly graceful. She came right up to the fence and gave a short *whuff* in greeting before bobbing her muzzle into Lilly's hand.

Lilly smiled as she scratched the top of Dandelion's head. "Hello, old girl."

Dandelion swung her great neck away from Lilly and bellowed over her shoulder.

"What's wrong now?" Lilly followed the elder cow's gaze.

Behind the matriarch bovine walked one of the younger cows, one whom Lily had yet to learn the name of. One of these days. she'd have to force Ryan to write all the cows' names down. The cow's faltering gait drew Lilly's attention. Another bellow from Dandelion seemed to encourage the younger cow to turn around. When she did, Lilly saw two pale white hooves poking out.

"Ryan!" Lilly shrieked.

She backed away from the fence, much to the confusion of Dandelion.

After what seemed like ages, Ryan finally emerged from the barn. "What?"

"There's... there's hooves sticking out of that cow!" Lilly gestured wildly in the general direction of the cow.

Ryan had joined her at the fence and followed her frantic flailing. "Huh, Emerald is calving." Ryan sounded more annoyed than alarmed. "She's about two weeks early."

"Help her!"

He stood calmly and watched the cow named Emerald move around the pasture. Lilly followed Ryan's example and tried to settle her breathing and heart rate. The other cows, Dandelion included, moved out of Emerald's way or gave her gentle sniffs or head bumps, seeming to encourage and comfort the new mother.

"She'll be fine," Ryan remarked as he turned away from the pasture.

"You can't just leave her out there!" Lilly cried as she followed him to the barn. "She's having a baby!"

"Yeah? And?" He shot her a smirk over his shoulder. "Cows have been giving birth unassisted by man for thousands of years. I don't think the fate of the Holstein breed rests on Emerald and her calf. I'll check on her in a bit and see how she's progressing, but the best thing I can really do for her now is to let her be. The other mamas will help her out, too."

Lilly stopped short as he continued into the bottom of the barn. She hated to admit it, but he was probably right about this one.

She jogged after him. "So what do we do now?"

The barn appeared larger without the constant noise and motion of the cows. Another sound, this one an ominous metallic scraping, filled the lower level. Lilly watched as Ryan evaded her question by slipping into the office. She decided to explore the barn without him since it seemed he was done talking to her at that moment. She went down the middle of the cement walk that separated the two rows of stalls, making sure to avoid stepping in any questionable piles along the way.

Between the walk and the stalls ran a long trench, roughly a foot deep. Along the bottom of the trench was a large chain with slatted panels at regular two foot intervals. Lilly watched in disgusted fascination as the chain and panels churned up the slurry of cow waste along the trench down to the far end of the barn.

"Ugh..." Lilly grunted.

"Be careful, don't want to have to fish you out of the barn cleaner."

Lilly jumped at Ryan's voice. She whirled around and scowled at his amused expression.

"You didn't answer me."

His eyes rolled under the cap brim. "Now what?"

"What are we going to do about Emerald?"

"I told you already, nothing for now." Ryan passed by her and Lilly followed out of morbid curiosity. At the end of the barn was a large open space with steps that led down into a small vat. He stood on a stair and looked down into the open space. The chain—what Ryan had referred to as the barn cleaner—emptied its repugnant cargo into the vat, spun on a massive wheel-and-cog to continue along the other side of the walkway to pull that waste in turn.

Lilly followed suit and leaned into the open space. She groaned and staggered back after inhaling a concentrated breath of manure stench.

"This is the barn cleaner." Ryan gestured to the chain and cog system. "The manure gets scraped into this vat and it drains out through an underground tunnel into the lagoon beyond the pasture."

"Lagoon?"

"A large pit where all the manure sits. Then it gets pumped out and put on the fields for fertilizer."

Lilly swallowed dryly. "Oh."

"C'mon, you wanted to know more about the inner workings of the farm, right?" Ryan asked as he clapped her on the shoulder.

Lilly frowned, not sure if her stomach was souring at the pungent smell of cow poop or because Ryan had thrown her own words back at her. She took a step back. "Cow poop removal wasn't that high on my list."

Ryan narrowed his eyes at her, a corner of his mouth twitching upward. "Normally, Earl hires out a company to come and empty the manure pit out and spread it on the fields. However, I'm not sure how that's going to work now since you got his undies in a bunch."

Lilly knew her face darkened at the mention of Earl and his undergarments.

"You should get back to the front of the barn, the air's better up there." Ryan gripped her shoulders and spun her to face the barn doors. "I don't need you fainting or getting sick on me."

Lilly didn't need further convincing. She moved quickly to the main doors. As she put more distance between her and the barn cleaner vat, the stench thinned and her color returned.

Finally, she stood in the double doorway, sucking down gulps of fresh air. Her distress over the manure smell overpowered her unease at being so close to the door that once held the helpless fake raccoon. Even though it hadn't been a real dead animal, Lilly couldn't shake the horror of what she'd first believed it to be. She sniffed in a vain attempt to get the manure smell out of her nose. Lilly ran her hand over her face as the trembles of nausea began to pass.

She heard Ryan's boots thud on the cement behind her and groaned. *Great, I bet I look like a weak city girl.* "What witty phrase are you going to regale me with now?" Lilly growled.

"You should go up to the house, get away from the barn for a bit," Ryan suggested. "We'll continue your acclimation to the farm when you're not going to keel over at any moment."

She cast him a sideways glance and studied his face for a moment to make sure a verbal sucker punch wasn't close behind. He held her gaze and arched his brows the longer she stared at him, as if to silently ask why she wasn't moving yet. Lilly gave a final undignified snort—either to rid her sinuses of the lingering stench or to signal she didn't fully believe Ryan's altruistic motives, she wasn't sure which—and slowly trudged up to the farmhouse.

Over an hour later, after using up all the hot water and at least two shower bombs, Lilly had finally rid herself of the concentrated poop stench. To finish her de-stinking and re-humanizing, Lilly even treated herself to an at-home manicure.

Lilly admired her newly lacquered nails, the deep green shade glistening in the mid-afternoon sun. The color pleased her, a darker metallic hue she wouldn't have normally chosen for herself. The label on the bottom of the bottle declared the color "envious emerald." The polish was a remnant of an informal goodbye party her girlfriend Chloe threw for her the week before she left Minneapolis.

Her friend insisted that just because she was going to be living on a farm now didn't mean she had to forgo her basic feminine upkeep.

Lilly sprawled out on a couch in the living room, relishing the quiet stillness of the house. The grandfather clock ticked away in the hallway, adding soft punctuations to the muffled hum from the kitchen appliances. An early spring bird's song even made its way through the window, adding to the relaxing vibe. As she practiced deep breathing techniques that would do her yogi proud, Lilly felt her queasiness from earlier finally finish ebbing away.

Again, Ryan was right. Lilly had needed to get out of the barn. Perhaps she would make a point of staying out of the barn during the heavy cleaning.

Lilly stretched her arm off the edge of the cushion. Her dangling fingers hit the box of her grandmother's journals. She rolled over and, after a quick check on her still-drying nails, considered the box, knowing that eventually it would have to return to the attic where they would be safe from any future renovations she'd eventually get around to planning.

Or any prying eyes.

Lilly remembered Ryan's confession of coming into the house randomly. What else was he helping himself to besides the lavatory? She would have to discuss boundaries with him in the very near future.

Before the box returned to the attic, she needed to read the more recent journals. Lilly had to find proof of her grandfather's promise to Earl Graves. That way, she could show the old farmer that it was written down somewhere. Maybe it wouldn't be legally recognized like her grandparents' will, but it would hopefully get her in Earl's good graces.

"If the crazy old coot would just listen to me," Lilly muttered.

Lilly wanted to let Earl Graves keep running the fields. He could even buy them off her if he wanted. She didn't care much about the crop fields. She just wanted to make sure the farmstead remained hers.

She'd have to check with Ryan to see if any of the crops planted benefited the farm in any way, or if any and all profit went to Earl and all she'd see would be rent checks. Lilly sighed and rolled back onto the couch.

More questions with not enough answers.

Lilly must have drifted off into a light sleep, as she found herself waking to the sound of the back screen door slamming shut and those telltale boots clomping through her kitchen. She glanced over at the living room entry with drowsy eyes.

Ryan's form burst into the living room. "Lilly, I need you back out in the barn."

The intensity of his dark eyes brought her to full attention. "You're not afraid I'll pass out? Or has the barn aired out?" Ryan reached for her hand and pulled her from the couch. *"Hey—!"*

He pulled her through the house without a word. Once they reached the back porch, Lilly wiggled her hand free from his grip. She wanted to ask him what the matter was, but his stern expression kept her mute. "Get your shoes on." Lilly didn't argue with his command.

Ryan led her into the barn, which to her relief was indeed aired out of the offending stink, and brought her to a small pen on the far left side of the barn. Lilly hadn't seen this area in her recent explorations of the barn.

In the pen was the young Emerald. She was untethered and stood in the middle of the space. Lilly watched as the cow rocked her weight from side to side and her black and white mottled flanks trembled. Emerald faced away from them, giving her and Ryan a clear view of her backside and the still protruding hooves.

"What's wrong?" Lilly felt an invisible fist clench her chest.

"She stopped pushing." Ryan climbed over the metal gate. "This is her first calf. Not only is she going two weeks early, but the calf is still a little too big for the birth canal."

Lilly ducked through the openings of the metal gate to get closer. "What does that mean?"

Ryan walked to Emerald's head and started tying a heavy piece of twine to her collar. "We have to pull the calf out."

Lilly froze. "What do you mean, 'we?'"

He finished tying Emerald to the metal pen and came around to where Lilly stood. "What it sounds like. You and I have to help Emerald's calf. Otherwise, it's not going to make it."

"You said that she'd be able to birth this baby on her own!" Lilly cried.

Ryan pushed his arm through the metal gate and grabbed what looked like an old Christmas decoration—*was that a candy cane?*—and more twine.

"Hold this." Ryan tossed Lilly the candy cane. She nearly dropped it into the straw.

"I... I..." Lilly stammered, her fingers fumbling with the heavy plastic cane. "I can't, Ryan..."

"It'll be fine."

Lilly stared stupidly as Ryan wrapped the twine around the two hooves. He then took the cane back from her limp hands and attached the twine to the long handle. She shook her head, still damp tendrils of hair striking her cheeks. Suddenly, she held up a hand and stared at her nails.

"I just did my nails!" She blurted frantically.

Ryan raised his head and pushed the brim of his cap back. The two locked stares for a moment, her eyes wild and his a mix between disbelief and amusement. "I'll buy you a manicure." He laughed and thrust the cane back into her hands, "And you're still helping me."

Emerald swung her head back and bellowed. The fist gripped at her heart tighter as Lilly saw the fear in the large animal's eyes, now bulged out and rimmed with white.

"Okay," she said softly, "tell me what to do."

Ryan took her hand once more and led her closer to Emerald. He put both her hands on the part of the cane closest to the curve. Ryan stood next to her and gripped the plastic rod, his fists staggered with hers. "When she has a contraction, we need to pull on the feet. That'll help the calf come down the birth canal, alright?"

"How will we know when she has a contraction?"

"I'll let you know." Ryan gave her a sharp nod. "I've done this enough to know when they're coming."

The rod trembled in her grasp. "Shouldn't we call a vet?"

"He's on standby." Ryan nodded toward the cow. "A contraction is starting, when I tell you, pull."

"Wait, wha—"

"Pull!"

Both pulled against the cane. Lilly focused on the two white hooves at the other end of the twine. After what seemed to take forever, Ryan eased up on the cane and Lilly followed suit.

Lilly gestured to the still stuck hooves. "Nothing happened."

"It might take a few pulls to get things moving."

"You should call the vet!" Lilly turned to Ryan and she felt the tears burn against her eyes. "I can't do this!"

"You've got this, Lillian." Ryan's stern, yet calm, voice brought a tear down her cheek. "It's time to pull again."

Lilly screwed her eyes shut and yanked on the plastic rod with all her might. Her shoes started to slide on the straw but she caught her footing before she dropped. With Ryan's staggered hold on the rod, she was able to lean against his arm for added leverage. She felt the slack as she heard a wet splort from the far end of the cane.

She blinked her eyes open and staggered back. More of the calf's legs had slid out. Lilly believed she was looking at its knees. And what appeared to be two wet nostrils at the end of a black muzzle.

"Ryan... I can see the baby..." she whispered reverently. She heard him stifle a laugh which turned into a snort.

"We're not done yet." He adjusted his hold on the cane. Lilly followed his lead, hoping she was correct in her hand placements. "Mama's pushing a bit more, so the next couple pulls should do it."

Lilly glanced over at Emerald. The cow swung her head down and appeared to be sniffing the straw for something to eat. The panicked look in the animal's eyes had lessened considerably. She saw the sleek flanks tremble and then pulse once. Lilly knew another contraction was on its way.

Ryan and Lilly continued the rhythmic pulling on the calf for the next half an hour. She focused on the slowly emerging baby and didn't realize the passage of so much time. The little velvety snout had finished materializing before her eyes and the whole experience turned surreal for Lilly.

Am I really helping birth a baby cow?

Beside her, Ryan let up on his grip of the cane. Lilly followed him and watched mutely as he moved up alongside Emerald. He pressed his hands on her sides and continued down to her rump and tail.

"Something's not right," Ryan muttered. "She stopped pushing again. You're going to have to pull as I push down on mama's uterus."

Lilly gaped at him as the cane fell from her hands. "I'm going to do what now?"

He shot her a grin. "You're doing pretty well for a first time calver, you'll be fine."

She took a deep breath and picked up the fallen cane. "Just let me know when I need to pull," Lilly informed him as she dropped into a braced stance.

Ryan laughed and shook his head. "You're pulling out a calf, not blocking a defensive tackle. Okay, another contraction is coming. Get ready."

She gripped the cane and wrapped some of the extra twine into her fist to maximize her pulling. Ryan told her to pull as he leaned heavily into Emerald's side. The cow grunted at the unexpected pressure and tried to dance away from Ryan. He followed her movements and continued to push against the baby still inside her.

Lilly heaved against the rod and the twine, grimacing when the rough twine bit into her skin. She kept her eyes locked on the calf, both front legs and most of the head now revealed. She stared hard into the two black eyes, appearing more like a doll's eyes, pure black and glazed.

The calf's eyes blinked and the nostrils flared.

"It blinked at me!" Lilly shrieked, her handholds and feet slipping in her excitement.

"They tend to do that," Ryan grunted. "Keep it up, it's almost out!"

The next few moments sped by. She pulled and Ryan pushed. The calf's blank gaze locked onto Lilly's as it steadily slid out into the world. Head gave way to shoulders and a rib cage, then everything went sideways.

Lilly suddenly slipped on the straw bedding, but because she'd still been pulling on the cane, she slid right underneath the emerging calf as its ribcage cleared and it fell free of its mother.

Spindly legs, knobby knees, and a bewildered face all plummeted onto Lilly. She swore loudly as she found herself entangled in the newborn, straw and unmentionable slime falling on her. She finally pushed back from Emerald, giving the animal room to move, holding the calf to her chest. Lilly stared down at the new animal in her lap, surprised by how heavy the little beast was.

Ryan squatted down next to her and started wiping at the calf's face with a less than hygienic rag. As the gunk was removed from its mouth and nose, the calf started calling out. Emerald looked back at the group behind her, gave a soft mrrrooooowwwww, and went back to nibbling at the straw bedding.

"What is it?" Lilly asked breathlessly.

Ryan lifted a back leg quickly. "A heifer calf."

Lilly stared down at the little black and white face, too amazed at what had happened to notice she was covered in the unpleasant aftermath of helping to birth a large animal. "I helped bring a baby into the world..."

"Good job." Ryan gave her shoulder a quick pat as he stood. He moved over to Emerald and started palpating her sides once more.

"Can I name her?"

"Huh? Yeah, sure."

Lilly looked up at Emerald and then back at the little spindly bundle in her lap. The calf laid across her legs, fumbling hooves and legs trying to push herself to stand. She caught a glimpse of her ruined nails underneath the grime of delivery, then looked back at the mother cow.

"Envy."

"What?" Ryan poked his head around Emerald's large rump. "Envy?"

Lilly nodded. "Yes. It suits the same letter naming scheme my grandparents' started; baby's name starts with the same letter as mom's. And her mother matches my nail polish."

"Oh, lord," he groaned and went back to checking on Emerald.

"It's a sign," she grinned. "And this is going to cost you way more than one manicure, I'll tell you what."

In nearly as many hours, Lilly took her second shower of the day. Ryan sent her back to the house to clean up with the stern order to report straight back to the barn afterwards to help with Emerald and her new baby. No matter how many times she reminded him, he refused to call the calf "Envy."

Lilly tread lightly into the house, careful to not spread any of the birth gunk over the kitchen. Once in the mud room she'd previously believed to be a pantry, she stripped down to her undergarments and put her soiled clothes in a pile. She wasn't sure what she should do with those clothes, covered in such unsavory grime. Perhaps she'd try to wash them at least once and see what happened after that.

Maybe the burn pile would be a good spot for them to end up...

Even though she knew Ryan was down in the barn, and this was *her* house, Lilly still felt self-conscious hurrying to the upper floor and back to the bathroom. She took a condensed shower and dressed in what she felt were her second best choices for barn clothing

She pulled her hair back into a ponytail as she descended the back porch steps. As she approached the barn, Lilly heard more commotion and figured that, after the birth, Ryan had gone to get the other cows back into the barn for their evening meal and milking. Lilly entered the barn and was immediately greeted by a chorus of cows.

"Hello, ladies," Lilly called to the cows, even if her words were lost in their commotion. She found Dandelion in her front stall and tried to catch a quick pet of the cow's head. The large cow reared her head away from her hand, straining against the stall harness. The matriarch pulled against her binds and tried to slip through the stall and toward Emerald and Envy's pen.

"What's gotten into them?" Lilly asked Ryan as he walked down in the front of the right sided stalls. He checked their harness chains as he passed each cow.

"They know Emerald had her baby," he responded. "Some of the experienced mothers get a little goofy when there's a new baby. They all want to see her, like women cooing over a new human baby."

Lilly narrowed her eyes at the back of his head as she followed him. "And it's a mystery why you're still single."

They made it to the last cow, each one properly secured in their stall, and then he turned the way they had come. Lilly followed, feeling like a dog.

"I need you to help me feed the calf," he informed her.

"Envy," Lilly corrected.

"I'm not calling a calf after a *nail polish*." Ryan stabbed a finger toward her.

"And I'm not changing her name," she returned in a sing-song voice.

"Whatever." He shook his head and led them to one of the supply closets. "I need you to watch the calf and keep her out of the way while I try and get Emerald up."

"Up?"

"After I sent you to the house, she laid down and hasn't been on her feet since," Ryan explained, as if that would mean anything to her. "A cow needs to stay on her feet after birthing. It's not the best sign when they lay down and stay down."

"She just had a baby, give the poor woman a break!" Lilly countered as he held open the door for her. "My cousin Tammy had a baby and she stayed in her hospital bed until it was time to leave. And then she stayed in bed for a week after she got home... although I think she might have taken it a bit too far—"

"A cow is not exactly the same as a human woman when it comes to birth. There are lots of similarities, and yet a few glaring differences." Ryan walked to a wall of metal shelves. "I need to get her up so I can milk her and feed the calf."

Ryan stood before the shelving unit and scanned the items on the middle shelf. He ran his hand over various tubs and boxes before he picked one that looked more like a bulk tub of mayonnaise. He extended his arm behind him and waved the large tub at Lilly until she took it from him. She glanced at the top of the lid and scowled.

"Milk replacer?" Lilly read. "Milk replacer? Why not let Envy nurse off mom?"

"Because we want to get the calf off to the best start. We will feed her mother's milk, just with that added in. Think of it as vitamins for the baby," Ryan explained as he gathered more supplies from the shelves. He cradled a comically oversized bottle with a nipple as thick as two of her thumbs. "You can have a decent diet, try to eat all the right things, and still be lacking certain nutrients. This way we ensure the baby has the good stuff from mama's milk as well as some extra."

"Hmmm."

Lilly tapped the container's lid.

"Don't go all animal rights activist on me," Ryan warned, using the bottle to point at her. "Do I tell you how to eat your avocado toast and do your Occupy Wall Street protests? No, because I don't know anything about it. You don't know anything about livestock husbandry, so don't tell me how to do my job."

"Alright, alright." Lilly held up a hand in surrender. "And for your information, I didn't protest during the Occupy Wall Street movement. Alec and I were in Cabo."

Ryan grunted, shaking his head.

"And I'm not a fan of avocado," Lilly continued. "If it was guacamole toast, then that'd be a different story."

"Guacamole is avocado," Ryan corrected.

"It's so much more than avocado." Lilly waved the milk replacer jug dismissively.

"Anyway, Emerald could have milk fever or mastitis, which might explain why she's down. Hopefully, it's not something else wrong. I noticed some swelling starting before the calf was fully out."

"And that milk fever will hurt Envy?" Lilly asked, following obediently as he collected a single milker from their holding rack and a length of tubing.

"It shouldn't, it doesn't transfer from mom to baby. I'm more worried about Emerald. She might need antibiotics for the fever, and then Envy will need to be on full milk replacer until mom's off her meds."

He left the supply room and returned to Emerald's pen. Lilly watched with rapt attention as he hooked the milker up to the overhead milk line. She glanced over at Emerald and frowned. The large animal was laying on the straw, head tucked against her side, her massive ribs expanding rapidly with shallow breaths.

"Is she going to be okay?"

"If I can get her on her feet, she'll have a better chance." Ryan moved to the far side of Emerald and started leaning into her side. "C'mon, girl, get up," he grunted.

While Ryan attempted to get Emerald on her feet, her calf Envy stood on shaking legs. Lilly smiled as the little calf struggled to walk. Knobby knees and unsure feet made her first steps hilarious and endearing. The little calf gave her best bellow, a feeble sound compared to the adult cows.

"Don't worry, Envy, we're going to get your mama up." Lilly stroked the calf's broad forehead. Her black and white fur was still damp and littered with straw, but Lilly was thankful the gruesome aspects of birth had been cleaned away. "Did you clean off Envy?" Lilly called over to Ryan.

"Not completely. Emerald licked her clean until she went down, then I finished up," Ryan answered through gritted teeth. He was still working on getting Emerald to her feet but didn't seem to be getting anywhere.

Envy made her way over to Lilly and lowed once more. Lilly held her hand out to the little calf. The muzzle bumped into her fingers before velvety lips parted and sucked Lilly's fingers into her vacuum of a mouth.

"Hey now!" Lilly giggled. "You're not going to get what you want out of those!"

"Calves like to put anything in reach in their mouths." Ryan glanced over at her briefly. He stopped pushing against Emerald and slid down her flank to the straw bedding. "She's not budging. Dammit, I don't want to get the lift."

"Lift?"

"It's a harness that straps around the cow and I'd have to use the winch to lift her up, get her legs back underneath her but without so much pressure on the legs." Ryan scrambled up from the straw and brushed the seat of his jeans off.

"Sounds like you should've done that first," she commented as she tried to pull her slobbered fingers from Envy's mouth. "C'mon, give those back!"

"If I put her in the harness she might not stand on her own." He took off his cap and scratched vigorously at his hair. "And with how hard she's breathing, I don't think it'll do much good."

"Do you know what's wrong with her? Is this the milk fever?"

"I have two ideas of what it could be and right now the worst one is winning."

"Worst?"

"Her uterine artery is on the verge of rupturing."

Lilly shuddered at the flat tone to his voice.

"Call the vet!" she urged.

"I did, he's on another call. And the second vet is on vacation."

Lilly looked at Envy then to the fallen cow, her stomach filled with boulders. "What can we do?"

"Try to get her on her feet using her own power." His shoulders sagged. "We should get the calf a bottle ready, since I can't get Emerald positioned to milk."

"She won't get her mother's milk?" Lilly stepped in between Ryan and the calf.

"She will, eventually," he sighed. "She needs to eat, first and foremost. If I can get Emerald up and milked, we can do a second feeding later with the colostrum milk."

Lilly nodded. She watched as Ryan took the bottle into the supply room and returned a few moments later with it full of hot water. He worked the nipple over the top and handed the warm bottle over to her.

"You want me to feed her?"

"Yes. I need to work on Emerald." Ryan waggled the bottle in her direction.

Lilly took the bottle, and in the instant she turned toward Envy, the calf was thrusting her head up at the red rubber nipple. After a few false starts, Lilly finally got the nipple into the calf's mouth and the animal started to suck greedily. Despite her best intentions, more milk dribbled out onto the bedding than what ended up going down the calf's throat. Suddenly, Envy wrenched her mouth away from the bottle and bolted around in haphazard circles, trying to nurse from anything that had the unfortunate fate of coming into contact with her mouth.

"Hey, goofy, the bottle is over here." Lilly followed the calf around the pen, trying to shove the nipple back into its mouth.

"Watch out, calves get stupid around the bottle," Ryan warned.

"A little late for that," she called.

Finally, Envy rediscovered the bottle and glommed onto the red nipple. Lilly fought to control the bottle as the calf jerked her head up and down. Quite a bit of the milk replacer-water mixture ended up on Lilly's clothes.

Another donation to the 'farm clothes' pile...

From behind her, Ryan swore loudly.

She managed to face him, a struggle with a directionally challenged calf trying to headbutt the bottle into her navel. "What's wrong?"

Ryan took several steps back from Emerald, his hat rumpled in his fist, gaze laser-focused on the downed cow. Emerald's legs twitched in what Lilly thought were valiant attempts to stand. Her lungs sucked in breaths like a forge bellows, her exhalations labored. The cow's legs stopped moving as her thick neck gave out, her head dropping to the straw heavily. Emerald's jaw slacked and her eyes never closed.

"Ryan, what happened?" Lilly shouted.

"Her vein ruptured," he answered, voice hard as steel.

"She's..."

"Dead." Ryan swore under his breath and kicked at the straw. He jammed his hat back on his head as he stormed out of the pen and the barn, the wooden doors thundering against the walls as he left.

Lilly stared at the swinging barn doors. Her mouth dried and her throat constricted. She slowly turned her gaze back to the cow laying mere feet from her.

The cow couldn't be dead. She'd just had her calf. From what Lilly remembered, she was one of the younger cows in the barn. This wasn't supposed to happen.

An insistent bleat came from the little calf in front of her. Lilly blinked away burning tears as she looked down at Envy. The baby had grown bored with the bottle, now only a third full of milk replacer, and started to venture around the pen. That invisible fist from earlier was back and it punched Lilly in square the heart as she watched the calf amble closer to her mother.

"Envy, come... come back over here..." Lilly's voice caught in her throat. She tried to entice the calf with the bottle once more.

The calf bent her head down to the straw and sniffed at the bedding, expelling bits from her nose with loud snorts. Her lips grasped at the straw, already trying to eat even though she wasn't old enough.

"Here baby, come get your bottle. You still have milk left." Lilly tried in vain to lure the calf back to the far side of the pen. "No, no, not over there, Envy. Stay away from there..."

The little creature circled closer to Emerald's prone form. Envy's dainty hooves connected with one of her mother's hind legs, causing the calf to stumble. With what little grace she had, Envy righted herself and stood alongside her mother.

With innocent curiosity, the calf softly headbutted her mother's side. She nuzzled her flank and eventually found what she could access of the cow's udder. After several failed attempts to nurse, Envy moved further up Emerald's side and bumped against the still form.

"Envy, over here, baby…" Lilly's voice dissolved into tears as the calf lowed softly and continued to budge at her mother's dead body.

The flicker of the old television set gave the only light to the living room as the sun began its descent. Lilly stared at the ancient RCA screen nestled within its large wooden housing—the fact it still worked a sheer miracle in and of itself—and barely reacted to the tinny laughter that filled the room as Hawkeye pulled another fast one over on Charles Winchester the Third. As the program faded to end credits, the grandfather clock declared the hour six o'clock.

Despite her best efforts, Lilly couldn't shake what had happened in the barn.

She fought to stay with the calf after Ryan's blustery departure but Envy wanted to settle down next to her mother for a rest. As she tried to pull the calf, who weighed a lot more than what Lilly was expecting a newborn to weigh, Ryan returned and ordered her back to the house. He had finally reached the veterinarian and he didn't want her around for the autopsy. Lilly demanded to know what would happen to the calf now that her mother was gone. Ryan insisted she not worry about it.

His distant attitude after the death of Emerald rubbed her the wrong way. For someone who proclaimed to love the animals he worked so closely with, his reaction to a death was disconcerting to Lilly. Maybe she was overthinking Ryan's behavior. It would be safe to assume he has seen more than just one cow die while working on a farm. He could sadly be desensitized to the whole unfortunate matter.

Lilly sank further into the couch and absently picked at her nails, the green lacquer chipped after the day's events. Would she become desensitized to the deaths of cows? Her stomach sank at the thought.

When she and Alec were first married, they had rescued a Bichon Frise from a puppy mill. Lilly named her Princess and loved that little dog with her whole heart for three months. One morning, she came home to find the front door of their loft open and Princess missing. After a week of frantic searching to no avail, Lilly gave up hope of ever finding her precious puppy. She was inconsolable for another two weeks.

Even up until the bitter end of their relationship, Alec denied any knowledge or responsibility for Princess's disappearance, swearing he had no clue how the door to their home had been left slightly ajar. He mourned with his then-wife, surely; though, Lilly knew he wasn't nearly as shaken by the dog's sudden absence as she had been.

Seven years later, Lilly now doubted her ex's innocence she had once so easily accepted.

She compared Princess's departure to today's death of Emerald. Lilly hardly knew the cow, really had only fully understood her presence on the farm just that day. Now, she sat watching old TV reruns in the dark, mourning an animal she'd known for one day.

What would happen when she got to know the animals more? Living on the farm, she would undoubtedly spend more time with them, develop relationships with them, and see each as a sort of farmyard pet.

Much to the dismay of Ryan.

The cows were livestock, meant for food production via milk and, eventually, meat at the end of their lives. They weren't meant to be seen as pets. They had a job to do. How often did cows die on a farm from disease or difficult births like she had witnessed? She didn't even know the average lifespan of a cow.

How many more cows—or heaven forbid, calves—could she stomach losing on a regular basis?

Lilly chewed on the edge of her thumbnail, blinking in the flickering light of the television. For the first time that evening, she acknowledged what was on the screen. The grandfather clock down the hall announced the bottom of the hour as a new program flashed across the screen.

Accordions and tubas belted out nostalgic polka oom-pa-pas as elderly couples in brightly coordinated Bavarian-inspired outfits twirled around a dance floor. The band consisted of portly gentlemen of a certain age in Lederhosen. Many of the band members and those in the audience sang, their voices warbling out unfamiliar words in the very distinct tones of the German language.

Lilly scrambled from the couch and launched herself at the television set, clawing for the channel controls. Vivid memories from years long gone, of her and her family sitting around that same television set watching that very same show, came rushing back so violently she could almost taste the freshly popped popcorn drenched in real butter and salt her grandma dished out into huge bowls for each to snack on while enjoying the show. As the music disappeared with the changing of the channel, so did the memories.

She sat cross-legged on the floor, relieved she could now focus on the local evening news. Although, once she heard the leading story, Lilly wanted to turn back to the polka.

The anchor mentioned a brief update on the unsolved death of Lone Tree realtor, Maxwell Carpenter. A memorial service was planned at Mueller Family Funeral Home that upcoming Monday, as the coroner had yet to release the body due to the ongoing investigation. After the investigation, the family would plan a private ceremony at United Faiths Free Church. Any information regarding the death of Mr. Carpenter should be directed to the Lone Tree Police Department, while any memorial gifts should be delivered to Mueller's Funeral Home in Lone Tree.

Lilly frowned. The memorial was in just a few days. Should she make an appearance? The least she could do was send a card to his family. She felt she had to do something; the man died on her property after all.

"What's this? You're not watching *Band Wagon?*"

She sighed and rolled her eyes toward the living room entry. "If you're talking about the trippy polka version of *American Idol,* then that's a solid no."

Ryan leaned against the wood framing the entrance. "That's a Brown County institution, how can you not watch that?"

"Like this," she replied deadpan, gesturing at the television.

"Hmmm."

"How's Envy?"

"The calf is fine. Got her out of the pen and will put her out in her hutch in a few days."

"She's not going to stay in the barn?" Lilly frowned.

"We don't have proper pens for calves in the barn. Most of our calves will be bought by kids who need 4-H projects or show animals." Ryan shrugged. "Will have to wait and see if the kid's parents who bought Envy still want her."

"Still want her? Why wouldn't they take her?"

Ryan tilted his head, as if planning the best answer. "She might not be big enough, have the right qualities they are looking for in a 4-H project or to add to their own herd. Dairy farmers can be quite picky when it comes to herd genetics."

"And if they don't want her..."

"We'll have to refund daddy's money, and she'll stay here and join the herd."

Lilly shook her head faintly. There was so much she had to learn about this foreign world she found herself in. "At least she won't be killed."

"Killed?" Ryan arched a brow at her. "Is that what you city folks think happens to cows? We just kill them if they don't serve an immediate purpose?"

"Well, I... no..."

"The calf will grow up, either on this farm or another farm, and live out a full life as long as the farmer and nature allow." He pulled on the brim of his hat roughly. "For someone who spent almost half her childhood on this farm, I'm disappointed that's what you think would happen to the calf."

"In my defense, after my parents and grandparents had their big falling out, anytime a farm was mentioned, my dad would go off on these rants. Eventually, I came to think of farms as bad places. And when you live in downtown Minneapolis, you find quite a large community of people who support that line of thinking, that farms are bad for the animals, farmers are no better than murderers... and with how my parents treated any mention of this place, I had no reason to doubt them."

Ryan shook his head. "Unbelievable. You're not going to report me to PETA, are you? You're not hiding undercover cameras on my farm?"

"My farm," Lilly corrected. "And no, I am not hiding cameras around the farm. I'm not part of PETA. Though, I have done graphic design work for many animal rights nonprofits around the Midwest."

"Wonderful."

"You could see this as an opportunity to help change my mind, then."

A sharp snort.

Lilly cleared her throat. "What did the vet find out about Emerald?"

His mouth pulled back into a faint smirk as he caught her attempt to change the subject. "It was her vein that ruptured. He was surprised she lasted that long with how she was bleeding out."

"I'm sorry."

"Not your fault. Not my fault. Sometimes, cows die. It happens."

Lilly frowned. "That's a little cold."

"I've seen lots of cows die over the years. Some deaths make sense, some don't." Ryan pushed his shoulder away from the wall. "If I let every death get under my skin, I wouldn't have been able to last this long in this industry, honey."

"Honey?" Lilly's back bolted straight, the hairs along her neck and arms bristling. "I'm going to chalk that little misogynistic gem up to you having a bad day and being ineffective at expressing your grief."

Ryan laughed, a grating sound that cut down her spine. "People actually talk like that? Wow, I thought that was just social media hype."

"Excuse me?"

"Did you get those lines from one of your nonprofits? I'm sure now you've helped more than just animal rights groups. Probably some off-their-rocker feminists, too, right? Is that printed in a little pamphlet on how to speak to heartless, murdering farmers and big scary men?"

"What?"

"You might not belong to these groups who hired you, but I'm certain their doctrine leached into your brain while you designed their little lie campaigns."

"I think you need to leave."

"No, really, I think it'd be really enlightening for you to actually hear how ridiculo—"

In a blink Lilly was on her feet, barely an arm's length away from Ryan, her finger pointed like a spear at the front door. "You need to leave. Now."

The immovable object stared flaming daggers at the unstoppable force.

Ryan's unspoken last words continued to slice into the silence long after the front door slammed behind him.

Lilly waited until the rumble of his diesel engine drifted into silence. With measured movements, she gathered herself and turned the television off. She grabbed a pillow that had slipped from the couch during her race to change the channel, brushing unseen dust and lint from the edges.

Lilly slowly released a pent-up breath and then hurled the pillow at the front door with an anguished scream.

"Of all the horrible things to say..." Lilly paced the length of the living room, her fists clenching and unclenching at her sides. She was too angry to stay put, though. She stormed up the stairs to the master bedroom, releasing her wordless exasperation with each step until her voice went raw.

She continued to pace her bedroom. "Did he get drunk since I left the barn? Why would he... what was he... *aaaarrrrruĝĝĝĝhhh!*"

That was the last straw.

She didn't care that she had barely spent a week on the farm. Nothing had gone right for her since she'd arrived. Harassed and threatened by the town crazy. Belittled by a hired hand who at one point in their history had been her friend and more. Only hours before she and Ryan had worked together to bring a new life into the world. Now, his vile words burned like acid in her ears.

And on top of all that, a dead body was found on her property, and the most likely suspect was the same town crazy who had now set his sights on her.

Lilly was done.

No more would she be under the distressing terrorizations of a delusional farmer threatening her over something she didn't want. No longer would she allow herself to be toyed with by an unstable hired hand.

The farm wasn't worth this stress. She wanted to recover and rebuild after her divorce, not fight constantly for her mental and even physical wellbeing. This was her family farm, and she wanted to stay, but if this was what she'd have to put up with to stay there, to hell with that.

Either Ryan was out of there, or she was.

Chapter Fifteen

Lilly made her way up the front walk of the Mueller Family Funeral Home, not knowing exactly what she would find once inside. From the outside, the funeral home appeared to be a repurposed turn-of-the-century home, set back from the street to showcase elaborate landscaping. Like most funeral homes, this one was off the main drag of the town by a couple of blocks and was happily camouflaged in a residential neighborhood. The home looked structurally similar to the Victorian that now housed the Lone Tree Library. Perhaps this was the Mueller's family home, from the time of Lone Tree's pioneering days, now renovated to serve the family's macabre business in a second life.

She paused before the main door and double checked her appearance. Lilly was pleased to have an occasion to wear some of her more upscale clothes. After a day in dirt and manure splattered jeans, her pale olive tie-waist pleated Georgette skirt and dark olive floral blouse felt heavenly. Lilly bent and straightened her cream stilettos before opening the door.

Once inside the funeral home, beyond the initial entry flooded with a riot of color from all the stained glass that framed the door, Lilly felt as if she had been transported back through time. The interior décor of the main floor had been painstakingly restored to its original nineteenth century glory. Dark floral wallpapers—which she knew without a doubt to be fabric instead of the modern vinyl—complemented the dark mahogany of the wooden paneling when they met at the middle of the walls. Built-in bookshelves and stained-glass cabinets all held items that harkened back to the Victorian era. Though, most of the museum quality bric-a-brac were lost amongst the forest of floral arrangements.

The majority of the arrangements proved to be fake flowers, permanent fixtures of the funeral home's Victorian décor. The more modern arrangements brought in with the flood of mourners and well-wishers had been crammed in whatever available space was left. Small plastic signs declaring the deceased as *Father, Husband, Son, Friend,* dotted the sea of flora.

Rooms once set aside as formal receiving rooms or sitting parlors for the lady of the house now had a modern purpose as gathering areas for the bereaved. Overstuffed arm chairs and loveseats lined the walls, allowing guests to walk easily through the interconnected front rooms, unconsciously leading everyone back to the main viewing chapel. What had once been the kitchen, servant's areas, and the formal dining room had now been gutted and transformed into the main chapel of the funeral home.

Lilly allowed herself to be drawn along with the crowd of mourners. Fellow Lone Tree residents milled around in the staging areas, a calming murmur filling all the rooms and hallways. She recognized many faces from Grandma's Attic even though she didn't know their names. She caught a few furtive glances from small clusters of elderly ladies. Lilly could tell they knew who she was.

How hard would it be to not know the newbie in town? The prodigal granddaughter came home after years of disgraced exile only to find a dead body on her property, no less? Lilly was growing tired of being the primary supply for the town's rumor mills.

She stepped away from the main throng of people and found the guest book. She stared at the names on the pages but none seemed familiar. Many of the entries held sympathies and memories of Mr. Carpenter. She grimaced. Lilly hadn't known Mr. Carpenter all that long. All she could remember of the man was his impeccable fashion sense despite living in a small town.

Would Max's silent land development partner be amongst this list of names? If this mysterious business associate was a local, perhaps. Lilly pegged this associate to be from out of town, a foreign investor perhaps. Her penchant for jumping to conclusions took her far beyond the borders of Minnesota or even the United States. But what foreign land developer would be interested in lots of farmland in the middle of Nowhere, Minnesota? Was Max that much of a snake oil salesman to con an international businessman to invest in a bunch of corn fields?

And if Max cheated this partner out of money, leading to his death, why would this person come and sign a guest book at the funeral? That would be a clever way to throw off suspicion, Lilly mused as she picked up the pen. She fumbled to get the pen at a comfortable writing angle due to the little chain that attached it to the podium.

More importantly, how did Max manage to keep his patent leather shoes clean while being murdered?

Lilly almost let a chuckle escape as that thought crossed her mind while she signed her name. A group of elderly women, many she remembered from the library's puzzle groups, raised their collective head and shot her a critical stare. She met their gaze as she shuffled slowly toward the main viewing room. From the corner of her eye, she saw the group waddle to the guest book table overwhich they crooned softly about the latest addition.

She turned her attention back to the décor and tried to ignore the lingering feeling of being watched. A large velvet rope hung between the two posts of a grand staircase, similar to the one in her own farmhouse. Attached to the rope was a sign that stated the upper level was closed to the public at this time. That only piqued Lilly's curiosity. A sudden urge to jump the rope rose in her chest like a kid who'd just been triple-dog-dared.

Why was the second floor closed? Because of the viewing today? Were the offices up on that floor and the Muellers didn't want any intruders during such a busy event? Private rooms for the immediate family to mourn in peace before meeting the masses? Or were those rooms now where the embalming happened?

Her stomach dropped a bit at the thought. She shook her head and tried to focus on the dark green wallpaper with golden fleur-de-lis accents. More likely than not, the embalming happened in the basement. There's less likelihood of snooping old women sneaking down into the basement than up a grand velvet staircase.

Now to the task at hand, Lilly reminded herself. I just need to pay my respects to Mr. Carpenter's family, and then discretely duck out and get to the realty office...

The main chapel area was standing room only, not only due to the number of people but also largely because a flower shop's worth of bouquets at the far back wrapped down each side wall. Lilly wondered if the whole town had closed down for the event. She wouldn't put it past the small hamlet to call for an unofficial shut down to honor one of their own.

A small altar stood at the back of the room, draped and overflowing with bouquets of roses and showers of baby's breath. Amongst the flowers, resting on a wrought iron stand, stood a gilded picture frame with a blown-up photograph of Maxwell Carpenter, whose store-bought smile fought for dominance with his bottle tan—a perfect blend of professional and gaudy.

Lilly hadn't known the man long; though, the few minutes she'd spent in the funeral home were all she needed to form a clear picture of him.

Under the muted fluorescent glare from the recessed lighting, the gold of the frame turned Maxwell's carefully maintained skin more orange than the healthy, sun-kissed bronze he sought after in life.

"Ugh," Lilly groaned and turned away from the ostentatious display.

"It is such a shame, isn't it?"

Lilly jolted at the sudden voice at her side. She turned and eventually lowered her gaze to find the owner.

She was a small, elderly lady, her chin just above Lilly's elbow. Lilly knew she was on the shorter side of average height, but seeing the tiny woman next to her made her feel positively Amazonian. The woman had a nest of tightly curled hair, alternating silver and purple in the chapel's lighting. She wore a pantsuit that Lilly assumed was about as old as herself, the navy blue polyester having kept up well over the last thirty odd years.

"Um, yes, it is a shame," Lilly stammered.

"Such a shame..." The woman's face turned up and Lilly couldn't help but gape at the owl eyes that peered through bottle cap glasses. "How are you handling things, dearie?"

"Uh... what?"

"To have found him like that, really. That's not something a young lady like you should have to see, a dead body and all that." She tsk-tsked and shook her head.

"How did you know—"

The elderly woman patted Lilly's arm. "I know you, Lillian Schmidt. Your grandma and I went way back."

"Oh, I see, uh, Mrs., um..."

"Mrs. Robertson, dearie. Elvira Robertson."

Lilly smiled down at Mrs. Robertson, but her eyes were drawn to a small navy blue flower tucked in her silvery curls. Vaguely, Lilly knew this woman had a whole closet of coordinating pantsuits with a hair flower designated for each one. "It's nice to meet you, Mrs. Robertson."

"My husband, John, he's over on the other side of the room, talking to Mavis Neumann."

"Oh, okay...?"

"He's right over there, in the hat and boots," Mrs. Robertson explained as she took hold of Lilly's arm and pulled her through the crowded chapel. "I'm sure he'll be tickled to meet you, dearie. He and Harold and Beverly and I always got together to play five hundred. Do you know how to play five hundred, dearie?"

"I, uh, no—"

"Oh, I'll have to teach you. It's a good game. That, and Sheep' s Head. Not everyone likes Sheep's Head, but that's just because they never learnt to play it right."

"Um, Mrs. Roberts—"

"I had to leave John over on this side of the room because I wanted to talk to Adeline Remus, but John was still talking to Mavis. And Adeline and Mavis still go at it like cats and dogs, even though that whole business with Lloyd was over fifty years ago. I mean really, I don't know why they go on so. The way I see it, Lloyd's not worth getting into such a tizzy over, so it has to be that both have forgotten what they've gotten so mad about. Now, if it was Cary Grant, oh, now that's a man to start a lifelong feud over!"

Lilly fumbled behind Mrs. Robertson as she continued her hurried shuffle through the crowd. She was amazed at how strong the woman's grip was on her arm. There was going to be some level of bruising, she was sure of it.

"So I've had to wait until John stopped talking to her, that cheatin' hussy, so that I can finally go back over to him, 'cause if Adeline saw me even standing near Mavis, I'd be in the dog house too! John! Look who I found! It's Lillian, Harold and Bev's grandbaby!"

The pair came to a stop amidst a sea of glares. Lilly wished the floor would open up and swallow her. It seemed once everyone recognized it was Elvira Robertson hollering, however, they all went back to their own conversations.

Before Lilly stood a tall man in cowboy boots, a crisp button-down shirt, and a bolo tie. His eyes matched the turquoise pendant of the tie, though they darkened as they narrowed at his wife. A midnight black Stetson hat was held firmly in weathered hands before him, though Lilly knew that once it sat atop his thick patch of snow white hair again he'd strike an even more imposing figure.

"Elvira, consarnit woman!" Mr. Robertson's voice rumbled from deep within his barrel chest. "We're at a funeral home, keep your voice down!"

"John, say hi to Lillian Schmidt, Bev and Harold's granddaughter."

"I heard you the first time."

"She found Carpenter's body in the ditch."

Lilly kept praying the floor would swallow her. One of the deities had to be hearing her request; seriously, Buddha, Jesus, the Giant Flying Spaghetti Monster—she didn't really care which one answered at this point just as long as this public embarrassment ended swiftly.

His eyes rolled under bushy eyebrows. "Really, Elvira."

"Well, she did." Elvira sounded rather proud of herself.

"Hello, Mr. Robertson." Lilly thrust her hand out to the elder cowboy. "It's nice to meet you."

He returned the gesture with a strong, firm shake. "Ma'am, the pleasure is mine."

Now that's how it should be done! She felt her knees go weak at the good manners and gravelly country drawl.

"I hear you and your wife knew my grandparents."

"Yes, ma'am, we did. Mighty damn shame to lose both of them so suddenly. My sympathies are with you and your family, Ms. Schmidt."

Mrs. Robertson popped up between the two, her owl eyes glancing at each one in turn. "Have you gotten rid of Earl yet?"

"Elvira, please, this isn't the place," Mr. Robertson cautioned.

"Oh poo, it's not like no one knows." Mrs. Robertson slapped her husband's hand away from her shoulder. "The whole town knows he's the main suspect."

"Have the police made an arrest?" Lilly's hopes rose. If he was out of the way, then maybe she didn't need to be in too much of a hurry to get to the realtor's office.

"No, not yet." Mr. Robertson shook his head, his impressive Fu Manchu mustache wagging.

"Even if he didn't do it, you should get rid of Earl. He's no good," Elvira insisted.

"I know what you mean. I have yet to have a pleasant encounter with the man," Lilly offered. "Though, I wouldn't mind letting him run the land as he has been doing. I know my grandparents wanted to give him the land to run, and I'd like to honor that agreement. If he'd just listen to me."

"Oh, no, no, no, no, no, no." Elvira's tight curls bounced vigorously. "Not to Earl! To the other one..." She began to snap her fingers in an attempt to jog her memory. "Oh, what's his name...?"

"The other one? Who else ran their land besides Earl?"

"Not just the land, dearie, but the whole farm!" Elvira's wrinkled hand clasped her arm.

"Elvira, you're confusing the poor girl," Mr. Robertson huffed through his mustache. "Oh, I think Tullah Davenport finally arrived. Hadn't you wanted to speak to her if she showed?"

"Oh! Tullah!" The elderly woman wrenched Lilly's arm in excitement before she bounced off through the crowd.

"I apologize for that." Mr. Robertson gave a strained smile. "My wife's a good woman, but sometimes... she gets a little addlepated."

"It's alright, no harm done." Lilly stepped closer to the man as another mourner without appropriately defined boundaries of personal space wedged passed her toward the main altar display. Elvira's bluntness turned out to be a blessing in disguise. "So... you wouldn't happen to be able to clarify some of what Elvira was talking about, would you?"

"I'm not one to speak ill of the dead."

"I would appreciate any information you can give, Mr. Robertson."

He sighed. "Since you're kin, I suppose it'll be alright. Harold and Bev were at odds over what to do with the farm when their time came. Given that your father and your aunt had become estranged all those years ago, they weren't sure who in the family would want the farm. I know Harold had talked to Earl Graves about taking over not just the land but the building site as well, though I believe that Earl just wanted the land to run. He didn't need another homestead to worry about—"

"Who is this other person Elvira mentioned?" Lilly clamped her lips shut after she realized she'd interrupted. "Sorry."

The bushy mustache arched in what Lilly assumed was a smile from the elderly man. "The other party interested in the farm is your hired hand, Ryan Swenson."

"Ryan." Lilly stared openly at the man.

"I'm guessing you know about the man's accident with the bull?" At Lilly's nod, Mr. Robertson continued, "Not much opportunity for an injured man to get jobs in a rural community like this, especially not on the farm. Farms and fields are demanding places for those who work them. A man can't be anything less than one hundred percent if he wants to get the best out of crop or beast."

"My grandparents offered him the herdsman position on their farm."

"True enough. But that wasn't enough for Ryan. And what if Earl did take the livestock along with the land? He had no guarantee that Earl would keep him on. Those two got along as well as oil and water. So Ryan put his offer in to buy the farm from Bev and Harold."

"Just for the building site or the whole thing, land and all?"

Mr. Robertson shook his head. "I don't know that much, ma'am. All I know is that a lot of people wanted that land and he would do anything to beat out his competitors."

Do anything? Like kill? Lilly strained to keep her expression neutral. "It sounds like there's another player in this bidding war that you're not mentioning."

"The recently deceased Mr. Carpenter was aiming to get the land and building site as part of his grand renovation of Lone Tree."

Lilly nodded. "I've heard bits and pieces of his development idea, to get more stores and houses built out on the north side of town."

"Not everyone was a big fan of that idea, though it did get a green light from the Chamber of Commerce and city hall. That's one of the reasons Mr. Graves is looking to be the main one responsible for Mr. Carpenter's death. Earl has been the loudest in his disagreements with the selling of the land. Many of his neighbors have already sold, and his farm was next on the chopping block, at least according to him."

Lilly made a mental note to look back at the plat book pictures on her phone when she got home. "Graves's land butts up against my land, correct?"

"That's right," the mustache bobbed in agreement. "Which made it an obvious choice for Earl to run the land and to take it over if kinfolk didn't come back and claim it, assuming Earl outlived Bev and Harold."

"He's the same age as my grandparents, so I guess it would be a bit of a coin toss, huh?"

"Oh no, Ms. Schmidt, Earl is younger. About fifteen years I suppose."

"Really?"

Time did not treat that man well at all.

"Oh, I'm sorry, Ms. Schmidt, but I must go save Mrs. Carpenter from Elvira," his voice rumbled again in his chest. "I must cut our conversation short."

"No worries, Mr. Robertson. It was a pleasure talking to you."

Lilly followed Mr. Robertson with her eyes as he made his way over to the far side of the chapel and into one of the small sitting rooms. How he had seen his short wife in that crowd, and almost a room and a half away, Lilly wasn't sure. That was until she paused and heard Elvira's distinct voice bubbling over the normal din of the crowd.

Mrs. Carpenter... Lilly wondered if she should be so bold as to make her presence known to the widow. Meeting the person who found your deceased husband may not be high on the list of things to do at a memorial service. It wouldn't hurt to at least sneak a peek at the family as she made her way to the door.

She needed to fact-check Ryan's assessment of Emily Carpenter's "hotness."

Why did she even care about catching a glimpse of Ryan's old girlfriend and whether she was as attractive as he said? After their explosive last meeting Friday night, she had barely seen hide nor hair of Ryan. The only way she knew he was on the farmyard doing his chores was when his truck's engine polluted the calm country air with its horrible noise. She spent most of her weekend avoiding going anywhere near the barn, or outside for that matter, and she definitely avoided spending any extended time in the kitchen so she wouldn't have to look at the big red building that had become a stand-in for the abrasive farmhand. Or risk being around if Ryan came inside to shower, God forbid.

Ryan wants the farm.

Lilly walked through the funeral chapel and out into one of the side waiting rooms that had recently been vacated by a group of mourners. She glanced at the jungle of flower arrangements as she passed into the room, but her brain was too focused on other matters to take in the beauty of the bouquets.

Maybe Lilly could sell the whole farm to Ryan. Even if they had butted heads recently, he proved to be more level headed than Earl Graves. If she let Ryan take the farm off her hands, he'd also take the cranky old farmer along with it. With that plan, those two could harass each other until they were both blue in the face.

She'd finally be free to take her rightful inheritance in the form of money and start her life over somewhere else. Again. This time, in a less stressful environment. No half-crazy farmers, no moody farmhands, and no dead bodies.

"Ooof!"

"Excuse me!"

Lilly jolted back into the present when her elbow clipped the arm of a woman who entered the small seating room.

"Oh, I'm so sorry!" Lilly apologized.

"Watch where you're going!" The woman narrowed her dark eyes at Lilly, their steely gaze scanning her quickly. "Oh, it's you."

"I'm sorry?" Lilly drew back from the acid in the woman's voice. She was tall and seemed to have fallen straight out of a fashion magazine. The woman brushed back long raven hair over her shoulder.

"You're that Schmidt woman who just moved into town, my father spoke about you recently."

"I'm sorry to have bumped into you, I wasn't paying attention." Lilly drew her shoulders straight. "I hope I didn't hurt you."

"Not at all."

"I believe I'm at a disadvantage, you seem to know who I am and I don't know your name."

"Emily Carpenter-Hayes."

"You're Maxwell's daughter." Lilly suddenly found herself conflicted; should she show sympathy for the woman's loss or blow her off in the same manner she'd behaved toward Lilly so far?

"I'm sorry for what happened to your father." Lilly decided to take the high road. For now.

"Yes, yes," Emily sighed, her eyes scanning the sea of faces in the main chapel area. "Everyone has been telling me you were the one to find him."

"Is there anything you need? I feel well...well 'responsible' isn't quite the right word, but I feel somehow connected in all of this. If there is anything I can do for your family, please let me know."

"Thank you for your offer." Emily held up an elegant hand. Gold and colorful stones glinted off nearly each finger. "But I'm certain my family is fine."

"Oh, okay."

Lilly fidgeted with her hands, unsure of where to put them. Had she been dismissed by this woman? Should she stay? Technically, she had been in that room first. Being that close to Mr. Carpenter's daughter brought back uneasy memories of the day she stumbled upon him. She tried to think of when he had helped her get unlost from that muddy ditch.

"I love your dress," Lilly said offhandedly after performing her own scan of Emily's person. "That's Burberry, their panel slip dress, right?"

Emily did a double take. "Yes, it is."

"I love what you did with it, adding the pashmina wrap? Inspired." Lilly smiled, pleased to have thrown the woman off guard.

"Thank you." Emily nodded with a soft smile. "I didn't think anyone here would have a clue about good fashion."

Lilly laughed and pushed her shoulders back, puffing her chest out a little. "Well, it takes one to know one."

Emily's face actually revealed a genuine smile. "Burberry as well, I see."

"It was the last thing my husband bought for me," Lilly added. "I tried to get him to spring for the dress you're wearing, but he had a tight wallet."

The two women shared a pleasant, although forced-familiar, laugh before falling into silence again as Emily continued to scan the crowd of faces.

Lilly made note, Emily or someone in her family must have traveled to England for her to be wearing such fine clothes. True, with the advent of the internet and world wide two day shipping, anyone could have European fashion without having to leave their couch. Nevertheless, Emily didn't seem to be an armchair shopper to Lilly. When it came to high fashion, Emily would go to the source.

Would Emily know of a silent business partner of her father's? Or could her husband and his family be the associates?

"So, how's Ryan?"

She blinked, coming back to the present. "Excuse me?"

"Ryan Swenson. I believe he's still working on your grandparents' farm."

"Yes, he's still working on the farm, though now for me."

"I suppose I should offer my condolences to you, as well, for the recent death of Beverly and Harold."

Lilly bit her tongue at the offhanded tone to Emily's voice. "Thank you."

She watched Maxwell's daughter. The woman seemed distracted, perhaps even leaning toward appearing bored. Emily languidly scanned the crowd beyond the sitting room. She turned each ring on her fingers at least once before starting over again.

"Are you looking for him?"

"Him?"

"Ryan."

Once preoccupied eyes, now ablaze, turned on her. Emily's once porcelain face marred into a creased, flushed mess. "No. I am not looking for Ryan."

Lilly knew she'd be paying for that boldness, but she just couldn't help herself. She could see why Ryan wasn't too broken up about Emily. Apparently, there was no love lost between the former couple.

"You were the one who brought him up."

Why can't I keep my mouth shut?

Emily's nostrils flared, and Lilly was reminded of Dandelion suddenly. "Why? Are you afraid I'm going to steal him from you in my hour of need?"

Lilly couldn't hold back her laugh. "Wow, watch many telenovelas much? I'm not afraid of anyone stealing Ryan. Again, you asked me about him."

Emily drew a breath and regained some composure. "Obviously he hasn't changed if that's how you responded."

"What is that supposed to mean?"

"You clearly know we used to be an item eons ago." Emily shot a calculating glance over her shoulder.

"Yes, he said you broke it off with him after his accident," Lilly pressed. "Said that things got too hard for you to handle after that."

"Not just things, Ms. Schmidt. He got too hard to handle. And it wasn't just because of his injuries. I could have dealt with those."

"Why did you end it then?"

"It was like a switch flipped. He became a completely different man."

"He was in a lot of pain and he had to adjust to life after the accident."

"Please," Emily scoffed. "At first, I thought so, too. Possibly even a mild brain injury or something. That bull really did a number on him. No, he became erratic, impulsive, and violent at times."

"Violent?"

"I didn't want to be with an abusive man, so I ended it. Moved to Madison and went to college, where I found a good man." Emily flexed her left hand purposefully, making sure Lilly noticed the large shining rock on a certain finger.

"I'm glad you were able to move on," Lilly said softly.

Emily looked at her, and the stoic face softened around the edges. "You offered help to my family in our hour of need, and I will return the favor."

Oh gee, thanks.

"If you're planning on staying here and staying on that farm, you need to get rid of Ryan."

"Get rid of him? Why?"

"Haven't you been listening?" Emily gave a patronizing, almost motherly smile. "Oh, I do believe you have some kind of a school girl crush on the hired help, no?"

"That is none of your business!"

"No need to get up in arms, Ms. Schmidt. It's not easy to resist him when he really pours the charm on thick. I should know better than anyone." Emily Carpenter-Hayes patted her on the shoulder and started to walk to the main chapel. "Just get rid of Ryan, before he fools you anymore than he already has."

Chapter Sixteen

The air had cooled considerably during the time Lilly had spent in the funeral home. Overhead, the sky began to darken as clouds rolled in from the south. Last autumn's leaves blew down the sidewalk and the first buds of spring strained against the rising wind. She folded her arms over her stomach and wished she had brought a light jacket or a hoodie.

Lilly winced as she realized she sounded just like her mother. She was eternally grateful that her mother wasn't there. Otherwise, she'd never hear the end of it.

She had driven her car from the funeral home back onto the main drag of Lone Tree and parked as close as she could manage to Grandma's Attic. Lilly caught whiffs of burgers grilling and the fryers working overtime over a block away. After the surprisingly draining morning, Lilly found herself craving something greasy, cheesy, and possibly deep fried. Wouldn't Alec and all her clean-living friends back in Minneapolis be horrified?

After the week she'd had, Lilly felt that she had earned those extra calories.

Had it truly only been a week since she first drove out to Lone Tree? It felt like a lifetime had passed since she walked out of her Lowry loft and drove away from Minneapolis. It had been only last Monday when she pulled her little Kia in front of Lone Tree Reality and introduced herself to one Mrs. Margaret Swenson, the realtor assigned to finalize the transfer of ownership by the lawyers of her grandparents' estate.

How much things had changed in just seven days.

As she continued to the diner, Lilly's mind struggled to focus on one thought, though her skull seemed full to bursting with unwanted judgments.

Emily Carpenter-Hayes' last words hung in the forefront of her mind as she walked. Should she take them at face value or consider the source? A scorned lover with over a decade to sit and stew over the past who had also recently lost a parent...

Lilly had to admit that Emily knew Ryan better than she did, and knew him in the more recent past. Lilly had known Ryan back when they were barely teenagers, and her time around him had been relegated to weekends on the farm. Emily had grown up with Ryan, seen how he was when she wasn't around, on and off the farm, and beyond the formative teen years.

Hadn't she recently told Ryan that fifteen years is a long time for people to change, and not always for the better?

She stopped before the door to Grandma's Attic, the promise of artery-clogging comfort food only mere feet away. Lilly drew a deep breath of chilled late April wind and opened the door, letting the aroma of fresh brewed coffee and biscuits push her previous, unwanted thoughts into the back of her mind. The diner's seating area wasn't as full as it normally was this close to lunch time. She quickly scanned the small eatery and was shocked to find hardly any patrons in the diner.

"Lilly! It's been a while!"

"Hey, Faith." Lilly waved at the main counter as she walked to a vacant booth. "It's pretty quiet around here today."

"Yeah, most people are going to the memorial service today," Faith called over the counter. She stood at the register, numerous piles of what Lilly assumed were receipts spread out before her on the chipped Formica counter.

"Did you get a chance to head over there?"

"Not yet. I'm waiting for Tobiah to come and watch the Attic for me while I pop over there, sign the book, and say my condolences, all that jazz."

"I don't suppose I could bug you for some food?"

"Of course!" Faith's face popped over the register. "What would you like?"

"I think I'm overdue for a bacon cheeseburger and fries."

"Oooh, good choice! Comin' right up!"

Faith's form disappeared into the kitchen, leaving the already quiet dining room deathly still. Lilly could hear the clatter of skillets and cutlery from deep within the kitchen. She found the relative silence of the diner unnerving, like a precursor to a bad omen.

The bell above the door clanged as someone entered. Intrigued as to who her fellow diner would be, Lilly turned toward the front of the café and immediately regretted it.

Earl Graves shuffled among the empty tables, his weathered face permanently drawn into a scowl. He still wore battered overalls and a jacket that Lilly was certain only continued to hold itself together because it feared the wrath of the old man should it finally fall apart.

"Oh, crap," Lilly hissed and scooted deeper into the booth, hoping that the old man had yet to catch sight of her.

"Faith, the usual!" The old man barked as he made his way to the front counter and hauled himself up onto a stool.

Lilly grimaced at the order and wondered how Faith withstood that type of treatment from Earl. With any luck, her other customers more than made up for his poor manners.

"Earl, is that you?" Faith's cherubic face appeared in the order window. "Give me one second, I'm just finishing up an order."

"Who in the Sam Hill is in here?"

For the third time that day, Lilly begged for the Earth to swallow her whole.

She bent her head toward the wall, hoping her face and other identifying features were hidden as Earl turned on his stool to survey the diner. He grumbled under his breath and Lilly knew he was cursing whoever was holding up his service. How dare there be other people who need assistance before him?

Faith exited the kitchen and headed straight to Lilly's table. "Do you want coffee as well, Earl?"

The old man answered with an unintelligible grunt.

Lilly looked up just as Faith's body blocked her from the direct view of the dining room. Her stomach gave an undignified growl at the sight of the bacon and cheese hanging out from under the toasted bun that seated precariously alongside a mountain of golden fries.

"Here you go." Faith grinned as she placed the food before Lilly. "Did you want a pop? I'll grab you a pop, be right back."

Lilly was too focused on her food to realize that, once Faith had retreated to the kitchen, she was exposed. She grabbed the bottle of ketchup and started to make a small lake of sauce next to her fries before a tingle shot up her spine. Someone was watching her. Intently.

Crap.

"You!"

Footsteps that alternated between thuds and scuffs advanced toward her booth. Lilly squeezed her eyes shut as she lowered the ketchup bottle.

"Your time's up," Earl Graves growled wetly around a fresh pack of chew in his lip.

She suddenly didn't have much of an appetite.

"Earl, please—"

"Enough talkin'! I want my land!" He thundered a fist into the table.

"Hey, Earl! Back. Off." Faith's timing was perfect. She stood behind the old man holding Lilly's drink. "You need to back away, now."

Earl whirled on Faith, his eyes flashing. "This doesn't concern you."

Faith met his gaze. "It does too concern me if it's in my diner, Earl."

Briefly, Lilly felt sorry for the woman's kids if that was "The Look" they received when they misbehaved.

"Go back to your seat, or I'm going to ask you to leave."

"She's going to give me my land. Just like her granddaddy promised me." Earl leveled his eyes back onto Lilly. "I gave her a deadline to do as she was told, and her time's up."

"Earl, I'm not going to take the land from you!" Lilly blurted out. "I don't want to change whatever arrangement you and my grandpa had. Really! How hard is it for you to understand?"

His eyes narrowed and he chewed his tobacco thoughtfully, moving the wad from one side of his mouth to the other. Lilly's stomach lurched. He said something, but the words were lost in the chaw.

"Earl, there's a better place to have this conversation," Faith interjected, placing a hand on the man's tattered coat sleeve. "Maybe we can set up a meeting with you, Lilly, and Aunt Maggie, since her realty company handled the estate with the lawyers."

"Bah! Lawyers!" Earl yanked his arm free. "This is nothin' but a bunch of womanly treachery!"

"What?" Lilly all but jumped out of the booth.

"Earl—" Faith began but an arthritic finger jabbed at her face cut her short.

"This isn't over! By the end of the day, I'll have my land." Earl glared at Faith, then turned at Lilly.

"Maybe if you asked the lady nicely, you'd get a better response to your request," Faith rubbed in.

The old man snorted and pounded on the table once more before he shuffled toward the door.

Lilly sank against the back of the booth as Faith sat across from her. The ice clinked in her glass as she tried to line the straw up with her mouth. "Thank you. That's the last thing I needed today."

"I don't need him harassing my customers." Faith gave a small shrug. "Are you okay?"

"No. I'm not. I don't know what I'm going to do with that lunatic. He won't listen to me. I've tried to tell him I'll let him run the land like he has been doing—hell, I've tried to tell him that he can have the land. But he just won't listen!"

Faith nodded slowly, tucking an errant curl behind her ear. "Everything with Max has had him spooked for months."

"He should be over that, with Max dead," Lilly snapped.

"Max wasn't the only developer looking to buy up land. He's still afraid he's going to lose the acres he was working along with his own farm. Cropland is going for a steal now."

Lilly ran her fingers through her hair. "Is there anyone who can talk to him? As you've seen, he won't listen to me."

Again, another shrug.

"Lovely." Lilly picked at her mound of fries.

The front bell clattered again and Faith was on her feet before Lilly had a chance to register the arrival of new eaters. She chose to ignore any newcomers and tried to focus on the food before her. As she stared at the burger and fries her appetite steadily returned.

Today wasn't going to be a complete waste after all. If she could at least enjoy this meal, the rest of the day didn't matter.

"Lilly! Hi, Lilly!"

She rolled her eyes as she lowered her burger, mouth thankfully full of cheesy goodness. Lilly wasn't sure who was the worse dinner guest, Earl Graves or Maggie Swenson. At least Maggie meant well in her own overreaching way.

Maggie hurried over to Lilly's booth, New Balance shoes squeaking against the age-shined wood floor. The sneakers looked fashionable with her pencil skirt and blazer, yet Lilly knew no one else could pull that look off. The realtor's oversized purse knocked into empty chairs as she weaved through tables.

"Oh, Lilly, dear, how are you?" Maggie slid into the bench across from Lilly.

"Hi, Maggie," Lilly returned after a long drag from her pop. The carbonation burned down her throat, causing her to grimace.

"Are you okay?"

"Yeah, just drank too fast," she waved off the question.

"I'm so glad I bumped into you here. I've been just beside myself the last few days thinking about you and all your troubles." Maggie shook her head, hands flat on the table top. "I hope you've been managing out there in that big house by yourself!"

"I'm fine," Lilly nodded, thankful that she had food to shove into her face. That way her conversation with Maggie could be legitimately cut short. She didn't think she could handle any more dinner guests. "I have the cows to keep me company."

"The cows?" Maggie blinked.

Lilly nodded as she dug into her burger once more.

"What about Ryan?" The realtor added.

She shook her head and held up a finger, indicating she would respond once her mouth was clear. "Ryan? What about him?"

"Is he watching out for you?"

"I suppose," Lilly left her answer to that. No need involving a mother hen in the awkward idiosyncrasies of their turbulent relationship. She and Ryan were both adults and could have their disagreements, fights, and falling outs without any outside interference.

"I'm really glad that he's able to stay working out on the farm. It helps to keep him out of trouble."

"Trouble?"

"Oh, goodness, don't look at me like that! It was nothing too serious. You know how boys are when they're younger, out being rambunctious and trying to prove themselves to their friends and all that."

"Uh-huh."

"Although, now don't tell anyone I said this, I'm thankful for that accident of his. It really reigned in his rebellious side. Made him mature and think about what he really wanted out of life instead of going out with his friends on the weekends at the bars."

"I guess that's one way to see it. Though, I don't believe he'd see it the same way," Lilly bit into a ketchup loaded fry.

"After the accident—"

"Auntie Maggie, I didn't hear you come in." Faith sauntered out from behind the register. "Did you want your usual turkey wrap to go?"

"Oh, yes. Please dear, thank you." Maggie waved at her niece and nodded enthusiastically.

"Coming right up." Faith turned and disappeared into the kitchen once more.

A moment of silence hung between the two as Lilly ate more of her burger. She arched a brow and tilted her head, finding it strange that the woman fell suddenly mute. "You were saying?"

"Hmm?"

"About Ryan. After the accident..." Lilly prompted.

"Oh, yes." Maggie waved a hand in front of her face, as if to banish whatever had distracted her. "His parents and older brothers were too busy with their own farm to really help Ryan out after all his surgeries. So Robert and I offered to convalesce him in our house. Since Robert and I don't have a farm or children of our own, we had more than enough room and time to spend helping poor Ryan heal."

Lilly frowned. "What about Josh?"

"Josh... oh yes..." Maggie's voice drifted off again. "At that time, he was busy with the police academy. So it was like we didn't have any kids in the house, so Ryan had space."

Lilly chewed thoughtfully. "Faith told me a little about how Josh came to live with you."

Maggie nodded. "No family is immune from scandal, sad to say. My younger sister, Teresa, got mixed up with an unsavory crowd. She got pregnant and poor Josh was thrust into that horrid life. Teresa was able to keep him until he was five when she went to prison on some drug charge. None of our other family wanted or could take Josh in, and, like I said, Robert and I weren't blessed with our own children, so we took Josh in and gave him the kind of safe home he sorely needed."

"That's very generous of you."

"Nonsense! What is family for if not to be there in your hour of need?"

Maggie chuckled. "What about your family, Lilly? Are they going to help you out with the farm now?"

"Uh, no." Lilly placed her burger back on the plate. "My parents don't exactly know I'm out here."

"What? Why not?"

"I thought you'd know why. Because of the falling out between my father and grandpa."

"Oh, he's still hung up on that. I forget sometimes."

"I was going to tell them, but I was still getting back on my feet after Alec left, and well, I didn't need any more drama in my life by bringing that up to my parents." Lilly took a quick drink. "And it might not be a thing to worry them about, anyway."

Maggie sat straighter. "Oh?"

"I'm leaning toward selling the farm in the future."

"Oh, Lilly, no!" The realtor leaned forward, her ample chest pressed into the table top. "You just got here. Why would you ever think of doing a thing like that?"

"I'm tired of being threatened by Earl Graves." Lilly heard the old man's words still echoing in her ear. That, and the sight of his chew slopping around his mouth. She put her burger down to allow the nausea to pass.

"Don't worry about Earl Graves. His bark is worse than his bite." Maggie tapped the table with a fingernail. "And with... and who knows, with the investigation into Maxwell Carpenter's death, he might not be around for much longer."

"Have you heard anything more about that? I'm surprised he's still able to roam around the town if he's suspect number one."

The realtor tsk-tsked. "Things happen at a slower pace in small towns, Lilly. It's not quite the bustling metropolis the Twin Cities are."

"I suppose." Lilly locked gazes with Maggie. "You wouldn't happen to know any of Max's old real estate buddies? Coworkers from Prairie Pine?"

Maggie's eyes narrowed. "He doesn't have any coworkers at Prairie Pine. He was the only agent there."

"I know he didn't have any other agents now, but before," Lilly explained.

"Most of those agents have moved on to other towns, maybe Sleepy Eye or St. James," Maggie offered. Her words sounded hesitant and concerned as she continued, "Are you looking for another realtor for the farm...?"

"No, not for the farm." Lilly shook her head. "I just had a crazy idea in my head that maybe a former agent of Max's killed him to avenge some perceived wrong."

Maggie gaped at her, and Lilly forced a laugh. "I know, sounds crazy, right? I think Ryan's right. I'm watching too many true crime documentaries. Puts weird ideas in my head. There's just been too much going on that that's all I can think about."

Faith exited the kitchen and approached Lilly's booth, holding a hefty brown paper take out bag. "Sorry about that, Aunt Maggie. Curtis rearranged the walk-in again and I had a heck of a time trying to find the turkey."

Maggie took the brown paper bag from Faith with a smile. Lilly eyed the expression as she took a long pull from her straw. There was something patronizing in that smile, and it didn't sit well with Lilly.

"No worries, Faith. The office is slow today with the memorial service. It's not going to matter if I'm a few minutes late." Maggie started to scoot herself out of the booth. "But duty still calls, even if it takes its sweet time. You two have a good day. And Lilly, please do reconsider. It'd be a shame to lose you."

Faith watched as her aunt left the diner, then plopped down on the empty bench the instant the bell above the door signaled she was out of ear shot. "What did she mean by that?"

"Have a good day? I guess she wants us to enjoy ourselves?" Lilly gave a shrug and buried her face into her burger once more.

"You putz." Faith flicked a fry off Lilly's plate. "You can't shove food in your face forever. Eventually, you have to breathe. And then you're going to tell me."

"Fine," Lilly yielded around half-chewed bacon and cheese. "I'm going to sell the farm."

For the first time in a week, Lilly watched as Faith's mouth opened but no words came forth.

"You're joking."

"No, I'm not. I've been here a week and I've had to deal with a dead body and a crazy old man threatening to do who knows what to me. That's not what I signed up for when I accepted the farm."

"I do suppose the lawyers should have put a full disclosure in the will. 'By signing here, you do hereby take possession of the Schmidt family farm as well as the crazy neighbor and all his baggage.'"

"Yeah, that would have been nice to know ahead of time."

Faith was silent for another moment. "I'll echo Aunt Maggie and say I wish you'd reconsider, too. It's been fun having you around. And it'll be a shame to see the farm go."

"I know." The hamburger and fries settled heavily in her stomach. She wasn't up for a guilt trip double shot. Her celebratory burger was quickly turning sour and threatened the rest of the day's outcome. "I'm not doing anything yet with the farm. Hopefully, things settle down with Earl once the police get to the bottom of Max's death."

"You still think that Earl killed him, huh?"

"Who else could it be?" Lilly twirled a fry in the remnants of the ketch-up lake. "Most of the evidence points to him. And it's not like he's doing much to try and clear his name, is he? Publically threatening me, harassing the people at Max's realty company. Why he's not in police custody is beyond me."

Faith formed a steeple with her fingers and rested her chin on her thumbs. "I see."

"Don't tell me he's harmless." Lilly stabbed a fry at Faith. "You've seen how 'harmless' he actually is."

"I'm not saying he is. Why don't you explain your theory of Earl's involvement with Max's death? Then we can see how far fetched it is or isn't."

Lilly frowned. She had a sinking feeling that revealing her thoughts about Earl's guilt would backfire spectacularly. Nevertheless, she needed a sounding board. Perhaps Faith was right and, by saying it aloud, all the thoughts in her head would start making sense.

"Fine. Okay, so Earl and Maxwell have been having this feud—"

"Really, it's just Earl."

"—A one sided feud, but a feud nonetheless. Max is buying up farm land for a big revitalization of Lone Tree's economy. Earl's not happy because, soon, his land will be up for sale next. Then, my grandparents pass away, and to Earl, it looks like more land is going to be sold off. Land he's been using to supplement his income, land he's been running for decades. Not only does he have to deal with the realtor trying to buy up land, now he has me, the city slicker granddaughter who will go back on all the promises that were put in place long before I was even born."

"Okay... so far, so good." Faith stole a fry from Lilly's plate.

"And, instead of acting like a civil human being, he just starts being more crazy than usual. More bite to his bark, to spin what Maggie says about him. It's the final straw, and he finally snaps. Kills Max since he was the main person to start throwing wrenches—real or imagined—into Earl's long term plans. Whatever those might be. Now that Max is out of the way, the land buying will slow down. Thinks he put some fear into the big bad real estate machine."

"You'd make a good mystery writer."

"And you should get your own fries." Lilly snatched a fry from Faith's thieving fingers and popped it into her own mouth. "As I was saying, now that Max is out of the way, Earl figures he just has to scare the granddaughter off the property. Then, he can continue running the land as is. If I give up the land, he can just have it or buy it from the estate for nothing."

"I don't think that's how that works."

"I know, that's not exactly true. There was a clause in the will and estate documents saying that I—or any family member listed in the will—had so much time to take full control of the property before it would be forfeited over to the county and state and auctioned off."

Faith arched her brows, "And when is that cutoff date?"

"May, I believe." Lilly took a long drink from her pop, the straw gurgling as she reached the bottom of the glass. "And since it's the last week of April, Earl is down to the wire to get me off the property. Which leads up to the lovely accessory he harpooned onto the barn. That wasn't enough of a scare tactic, so now he's resorting to verbally threatening me."

"Okay, so let's just say this is what's actually going on. How does a decrepit old man like Earl kill Max, who is about fifteen years younger than him?" Faith asked.

"The police said he was killed by blunt force trauma to the head. With all the farm equipment around, and Earl's long history doing hard labor, he'd still be able to weld some sort of wrench or blunt object hard enough to take out Max."

"But why kill Max at all? He could have just focused on scaring you off and still kept things the same."

Lilly shrugged. "It does seem rather risky to kill someone, but this man isn't firing on all cylinders. Like I said before, it was just the last straw and he snapped."

Faith shook her head and inched out of the booth. "I don't know, Lilly. It's a nice theory and all, but I don't think Earl killed Max."

"Who else in town would have a motive to kill him?"

Faith's shoulders slumped. "I don't know. At least no one I'd like to think ill of."

The front door chimed open and Lilly watched as her friend rushed back behind the counter as a group of elderly men and women came in and began staking out the prime eating spot. Lilly recognized them from the funeral home. She glanced at her watch and noted that the memorial service would be winding down now. The morning was gone and the afternoon had crept up on her.

She dug into her purse for her wallet. As she pulled out some bills for lunch, Lilly realized that Faith never quoted her an amount due for lunch. She guessed at what the burger and fries cost and threw down what she believed would cover her bill and also left a sizable tip. It was getting late and she still needed to swing by Prairie Pine Realty before heading back to home.

Home. It wouldn't be home for her much longer. Lilly tried to shake the thought from her mind. She was doing the right thing, protecting herself from the old farmer and a potential killer. If they killed once on her land, who knows if the killer would make that a recurrent dumping spot.

Lilly stepped out into the brisk air, and a revelation pushed her back.

Killers often come back to the scene of the crime. Television and movie criminal profilers had taught her that much. Something about taking pride in their work, seeing the act of murder all the way through. Like some sick ego boost.

Lilly's gut turned to ice as she played over Faith's words. Then, Emily Carpenter-Hayes' words followed close behind. Warnings of an unstable man, motivated to have the farm, and who shouldn't be trusted.

A man whom she'd been alone with out in the middle of nowhere on more than one occasion.

Chapter Seventeen

Ominous clouds built heavily in the southeastern sky. Lilly watched the thunderheads churn and darken as she drove north out of town. She felt that the sky matched her mood, steadily darkening since the memorial service.

Her mood worsened even more as she maneuvered up the driveway and caught sight of Ryan walking from the house to the barn. Lilly slammed on the brakes, stopping just as the Kia was set to plow into her grandmother's unkempt flower bed. The weed-choked sprouts begged for attention. She grimaced, realizing more plants and flowers would start blooming and demanding to be tended soon. Lilly knew she hadn't inherited her grandmother's, or even her mother's, green thumb.

Lilly could kill a plastic succulent.

Or maybe that was Alec again...

She sat in her car and listened to the engine tick while it cooled down. Her fingers flexed around the steering wheel, knuckles alternating between flushed and pale. She called upon her yoga breathing techniques to slow her mind. Too many thoughts about too many unpleasant things pinged around her brain like a deranged game of Pong.

Ryan couldn't be a killer. He may be a Class A jerk, maybe more than just a little unhinged—what was with the horrible things he said Friday night?—but those things alone didn't make one a murderer.

Right?

She couldn't put together a plausible motive for Ryan to kill Max Carpenter, not one as "beyond the shadow of doubt" as Earl killing Max. Except for the explanation that Ryan is a clinical psychopath who is able to hide his murderous tendencies so well no one would have any clue.

Lilly could hear the news reports now. A cherry-picked selection of Lone Tree's citizens would be paraded in front of the news cameras. They'd each give a slightly varied version of the same old "He seemed so quiet, maybe a little odd, but that was because of his accident..." That cliché line every killer's friends and neighbors give about the accused while the police in the background are rolling stretcher after stretcher of remains out the front door.

She laughed as she thought of little old Elvira Robertson in front of the camera with a big microphone shoved in her face. What town secrets would she spill live on the air? She'd most likely tell Madeline and Adeline to just stop it already; Lloyd just wasn't worth it.

A sharp knock on the passenger window shook Lilly out from her daydream. She glared over at Ryan's mud streaked face as he rapped a knuckle against the window again.

"Yes?" She asked.

He spoke again, repeating what she believed to be his previous question. She knew the words dripped with exasperation despite sounding like the teacher from Charlie Brown through the window.

Lilly allowed herself an exaggerated sigh as she opened her door and stood. "I couldn't hear you through the window, dummy."

She bit her lip to hide her grin at the quick widening and narrowing of Ryan's eyes as she stepped into full view. She knew she looked good. That was why Alec offered to buy it for her when they were in London last fall. Then, he had to go and serve her divorce papers before she had a chance to wear it for him.

Now, the only man Lilly could flaunt it for was the temperamental hired hand. *Who said I had to wear it for a man...* Lilly's lips spread into a satisfied smile. What had men done for her lately besides cause a whole lot of headaches?

Ryan turned, casting his face in shadow from his hat, and jerked a thumb to the front porch. "Aren't you going to collect your package?"

"Package?" Lilly echoed as her eyes followed to the front of the house.

"Yeah. A package. Parcel. Mail. You can't remember if you ordered something?"

Slowly, her memory clicked as her eyes fell upon the familiar Amazon logo. "My milk soap!"

"Milk soap?"

Lilly ignored Ryan's question as she hurried up to the porch. She picked the shoe box sized package and shook it, pleased with the weight. "When did it get here? This morning?"

"No, Saturday."

"Saturday?" She whirled on him, eyes bright. "Why didn't I know about this until now?"

"You were too busy sulking in the house all weekend, I didn't want to interrupt the fun."

Lilly shot daggers at his smirk. "I'm still waiting for an apology for those horrible things you said Friday." Lilly declared.

"Don't hold your breath." Ryan turned and headed toward the barn.

"Hey! Hold on one hot minute!" Lilly bolted down the stairs, as fast as high heels and dirt would allow, and caught up with him. "I need to talk to you!"

"When don't you need to talk?" Ryan faced her.

"Do you have an explanation for Friday? What you said was entirely out of line."

"Jeez, you sound like my mother."

"I thought we were friends—or at least we were learning to be civil again. And then, out of the blue, you said nasty things to me. Why?"

Ryan met her gaze, though his eyes were shielded by the hat brim. "Friday wasn't a good day." He turned on his heel and continued to the barn.

"Is that all you have to say about this?" Lilly stormed after him, Amazon box clutched to her chest. "It wasn't a good day?" Instantly she cursed not taking off her shoes right away as her ankles threatened to snap with each awkward step.

"That's all I have to say." Ryan trudged up the earthen ramp to the hay loft.

Lilly began to follow. Her right stiletto sunk into the soft dirt and threw her off balance. Her arms flailed as she began to violently tilt backwards. She, her purse, and the Amazon box tumbled into the grass and down the incline. Eventually, all came to a stop before the lower doors of the barn.

She sat in the dirt and grass, bottom lip trembling as she surveyed the dirt and grass stains on her shoes. The high end, delicate fabric of her skirt had torn during her tumble, and a section of hem and inner lining had pulled loose and hung down her scuffed knee.

Satiny blouse, untucked and rumpled, billowed in the wind. Her package with the soap-making kits came to rest in a patch of early dandelions, while her purse—bought along with the London outfit—rested in a still-drying mud puddle.

The thought that this was the perfect way to send off a painful reminder of her marriage briefly passed through Lilly's mind. This, and being worn for the first time to pay respects to a dead man.

A few yards beyond her, Dandelion, who was out for the afternoon while the chores were being completed, stuck her head over the pasture fence and bellowed loudly in her direction.

"Oh, shut up." Lilly narrowed her eyes at the gentle bovine. "No one asked you." She swiped angrily at a wet cheek, knowing her dirtied hand left a large smudge, and sniffed.

"You alright?"

Lilly looked up and spotted Ryan, who had poked his head out from the hay loft door. She noted ruefully that he did not make any visible motions to come out of the hayloft to assist. "No, I'm not alright!" She cried.

"You should get yourself a nice pair of work boots. Red Wings are great for the farm. Then you won't fall like that."

Lilly pounded her fists into the grass and screamed out her exasperation.

Ryan chuckled. "Need help?"

"Not from you!"

Lilly struggled to her feet, adding more mud and stains to her knees and clothing. She faltered once up on both feet and threatened to fall again but she caught herself. She couldn't put her full weight on her right foot. Lilly hobbled over to the Amazon box and then her purse, stifling a whimper at the mud stains on the hand-tooled leather.

Even if it was a horrid reminder of her cheating ex... it had been a really beautiful purse.

She made slow progress to the farmhouse, her soiled goods cradled in each arm and her head held high as she knew Ryan watched every unsteady step she took. Her backside ached and her right foot screamed with each step. More than just the shoe had been damaged in the fall.

"Hey, your ankle doesn't look too good," he called after her. "Do you want—"

"There is nothing I want, especially from you!" Lilly shouted as she pivoted around to face him. He had come a few feet down the loft embankment. "I've had it with this farm! I've had enough of this dumb little town! And I've had more than enough of you!"

"No one's forcing you to be here, you can leave anytime."

"I will! After the buyer's check clears the bank, I'm outta here!"

"Well, good riddance—wait, what buyer's check?"

"Surprise!" Lilly threw her hands over her head, her box and purse falling to her feet once more. "I'm selling the farm."

Ryan hustled as fast as he could from the barn to her. She gathered up the box and purse and started toward the house. Now that she was hindered by a broken shoe, he closed the gap between them quickly. He caught hold of her elbow, but she wrenched it free.

"You can't sell!" He shouted.

"I can, and I will." Lilly turned from him once more and, after collecting her parcels once more, stormed across the lawn.

Finally, the pair made it to the back porch. Lilly clomped up the stairs joltingly. She barely made it to the second step before she bent and tore off her stilettos and threw them into the yard. Ryan dodged the flying shoes as he attempted to follow behind her.

"Hey, wait a minute. We need to talk about this." Ryan grabbed at her elbow once more.

"Let go of me," Lilly hissed through clenched teeth. They locked stares until he finally released his grip. "And I'm done talking about this. There's nothing more to say. No one in this whole town wants to listen to me anyway."

"Why are you selling? At least tell me that much!"

Lilly opened the screen door to the kitchen and paused. She took a deep breath and turned, revealing an overly friendly smile. "Today was a bad day, and that's all I have to say."

She left Ryan on the porch with the gunshot slam of the screen door.

Lilly stared at the unopened Amazon box in the middle of the kitchen island. The mud splotches had dried while she took a shower and changed. Now dressed in lululemon leggings and an oversized T-shirt, she felt comfortable albeit still uneasy.

Emily Carpenter-Hayes' words regarding Ryan echoed in her head, an unwelcome earworm she wished she'd be rid of sooner rather than later. Her stomach flipped as she replayed the scene in the farmyard barely an hour before. How could she have blurted out she was selling the farm before the plan was even in motion? And to Ryan of all people?

What's done is done, Lilly thought bitterly as she traced the address label on the box. He was going to find out soon enough. Aunt Maggie could have filled him in about her new plans the instant she left Grandma's Attic.

That was one thing Lilly missed most about living in a bigger city. For the most part, people didn't know your business unless you wanted them to. She was certain that, over the last week, she had yet to meet someone who wasn't tied to her family farm or part of the Swenson family to some degree.

"Like the country version of Six Degrees to Kevin Bacon," Lilly muttered. "I'm pretty sure my connection is that I've landed in a backwards, nosy town and Kevin Bacon is nowhere to be seen. Pity."

Lilly fidgeted with the Amazon box. "Now what to do with these soap making kits? I guess I could return them. Or I could use them. I suppose I could surprise all my friends with artisan, handmade soaps for Christmas. They'd appreciate it, I'm sure. Those kinds of things go for big money in the Cities..."

Her words died away as she glanced around the empty kitchen.

It had been a grand dream, thinking she could run a farm and make it into a cottage industry. If it hadn't been for a few sour experiences, she believed her idea had hope. There was enough inheritance money left over from her grandparents, dog-eared in certain bank accounts for paying any property taxes and loans still out on farm equipment, Lilly could have taken her time figuring out what her final vision for the farm would be before finances became an issue.

Now, she was being driven off her family land by a cranky old man and an unbalanced hired hand—both of whom could be murder suspects.

Lilly ripped open the Amazon box and withdrew the two soap kits. Prairie Pine Realty was closed early, so she had to wait until tomorrow to get the sale process going. Most of her life was still packed to move, so why not play around and make some soap?

She grabbed the soap kit and surveyed the bold notice on the edge: "For children ages 8 to 12." Lilly had a sudden flashback of watching Fight Club back in college and the painful soap-making process Edward Norton's character had suffered through and shuddered.

Lilly paged through the directions and separated the plastic-wrapped bundles of soap base, fragrance bottles, and silicone molds into piles on the counter top. In short order, she determined that, after the pieces of soap base were melted via the microwave, preferred scents and colors were added, and the whole concoction had been poured into a mold shape, the soap would need to set for at least six hours.

She prepared her first bar of soap, choosing to create a pink lavender-scented butterfly from the limited choices given by the kit. Perhaps she'd go with the unicorn shape next and give that to Ryan. Lilly smirked at the thought as she squeezed the right amount of lavender fragrance into her pink soap. As she poured the finished mix into the butterfly mold, Lilly wondered if any grown woman would pay for the chance to do this on a larger scale, and if so, how much?

A knock at the kitchen porch door pulled Lilly from her musings. She glanced at the screen door as it opened, more focused on keeping the liquid soap moving. The last thing she needed was the soap to start hardening. The instructions didn't explain how to reheat the soap once the coloring and fragrances were added.

The last thing she needed were dyes exploding in her microwave.

"Lilly?"

She looked up at her name, not immediately recognizing the voice. Thankfully, she was done pouring the soap so she could gape openly at her new visitor. "Josh, what are you doing here?"

Joshua Heimdall walked carefully into the kitchen, his boots scarcely making a sound. Lilly took a second glance to confirm it was the friendly officer. Instead of his LTPD uniform, he was dressed in jeans and a dark gray hooded sweatshirt. Even his hair, normally combed back and slick, had a more casual look.

Lilly stood from the kitchen stool and held her breath. Panic gripped her chest as worst case scenarios involving loved ones flooded her vision. "Is something wrong?"

Josh smiled sheepishly. "No, nothing is wrong."

Lilly allowed herself a pause to push the panic away. "Then, to what do I owe this visit?" She sat back at the island and continued tending to her freshly poured soap.

"I wanted to check in on you." He stood at the opposite side of the island. "Faith told me that Earl has been making himself a stronger nuisance to you recently."

Lilly looked up at him through her lashes and didn't bother hiding her strained smile. "I'm glad people are so quick to take continual, multiple threats so seriously around here."

"I'm sorry we didn't believe you right away." Josh rested his elbows on the counter. "I'm here to make up for that now. Is there anything I can do?"

"Either help me get that man to actually listen to me, or get a restraining order out on him."

"I'll look into both."

Lilly scraped the last of the pink soap into the mold and set down the dish. Josh picked up one of the unused soap molds and turned it around in his hands. She wasn't sure if he'd ever been so closed off around her, even bordering on shy.

"Is there something else on your mind?" she asked.

He finally met her gaze, his eyes searching hers for an answer before he even spoke. "Maggie told me you were thinking of leaving and selling the farm."

She sighed. "And are you going to tell me to not leave as well?"

"Well, no, not entirely." Josh picked at a wrapped bundle of blocks of pure soap base and began to fidget again. "More like, some friendly advice if you do go through with it, who not to sell to."

"Well, Max is out of the way, so I can't sell to big scary land developers." Lilly huffed, plucking the package of soap from Josh's fingers. She placed three chunks of soap into the melting dish and walked to the microwave. The beeps and whirl of the microwave preparing the soap were the only sounds in the kitchen.

"Max was the least of my concerns around here." Josh watched as she sat at the island once more and began adding pink dye to the melted glycerin. "Has Ryan made an offer?"

"An offer? No, he just found out about the possibility not thirty minutes ago. I doubt he's had time to process what I told him, let alone anything else."

Josh looked down at the counter and then met her eyes once more. He appeared almost apologetic. "I know you and Ryan have a past. Just make sure that doesn't get in the way of telling him no if he makes an offer."

Lilly frowned. She'd had enough with the cryptic messages and warnings; it's all she had received since setting foot back in Lone Tree again. "Why do I need to tell him no?"

"He'll tell you a sob story about his leg and his injury, it being hard to get work and all. Might even throw in some lines about your grandparents for good measure. But the Swensons have enough land for all their kids—his parents aren't keeping him from any jobs."

Lilly held Josh's gaze, trying to pick his statements apart. She remained silent for a moment, choosing her next words carefully. "Yet Maggie and her husband helped take care of Ryan after his accident. Helping family out."

"It was more like his parents dumped him on Maggie and Robert," Josh replied. "They didn't have the time or patience to take care of Ryan with so many properties to run. Ryan's dad took advantage of his brother and sister-in-law. Treated them as second-class, especially Maggie, ever since she married into the family."

Lilly shifted in her seat, unsure of how she felt hearing this account of the Swenson family. True, the last time she'd had any extensive contact with them was fifteen years ago, but, at the time, her family and the Swensons seemed to get along well. Of course, who was she to doubt Josh's words? Her own family had kept huge secrets from each other.

"Because Maggie's sister... your mom... had her problems." Lilly tested each word slowly. He nodded. "Were there a lot of problem children on the Heimdall side?"

"Enough to make the good ones guilty by association." Josh leaned back from the island and continued to fidget with a soap mold. "And when Maggie and Robert took me in, the shunning increased. Ryan and Faith's parents always looked down on us. So much so they got their grandparents to change the will around."

"Change the will?"

"So Robert and his immediate family would get less than the other siblings, cousins, grandkids, all of it. Robert and Maggie may as well have been completely written out of the will with the short stick they got."

She set down the soap she was preparing and stared at the counter top. "That's horrible."

"Robert and Maggie did what they could to get by." He traced his finger along the counter, lowering his eyes. "Maggie wasn't always a realtor. She and Robert worked at the high school for a few years; he was a teacher and she helped in the cafeteria. Then, she got her realtor credentials right when the recession hit. No one was wanting to buy houses and things got tough again. I helped out where I could—joining the police force helped. But Max was our family's saving grace."

"Max?" Lilly blurted out. "But Maggie didn't like Max."

"She didn't like what he wanted to do with the developing, and some of his business practices were a bit shady, true." Josh shrugged. "But he'd send prospective clients to Maggie's office, to her specifically. Got her extra accounts that normally wouldn't have come her way. And now he's gone..."

"Maggie's afraid all that Max helped build will go away, too?" Lilly ventured. "I would think that the established clients would stick around. And Max isn't her competition anymore. So that can only be good."

He looked up and smiled. "I keep telling her that, too. I think she's just worried about all these big things happening one after the other. Bad news comes in threes, isn't that the saying?"

"I thought that was just deaths."

"Well then, I hope that's not the case. One death is enough for this town at the moment."

Lilly gave a small chuckle. "I don't think the gossip-mongers would be able to handle any more excitement."

Joshua glanced down at his watch and slowly pushed away from the island. "I suppose I've taken up enough of your time. I should be heading home."

"It was nice to see you without dead bodies and faux raccoons." She grinned.

He made his way to the back porch door and smiled. "I thought we could use a change from our usual hang outs."

Lilly couldn't help but laugh, only to mentally kick herself for giggling like a schoolgirl at an obviously corny joke. But she had had a bad day and he was cute and why couldn't she be a little twitterpated around him?

Joshua opened the door and took a step out onto the porch. She noticed a strange expression flash across his face. "Just remember what I said, okay? About selling?"

Lilly nodded, her lips pressed into a firm line.

"I'll catch you around, Lilly."

The screen door banged shut and thrust the kitchen into a complicated silence. Joshua's revelation about the Swensons and their treatment of family sat heavily on Lilly. Family secrets and soap opera level drama seemed to run rampant in Lone Tree. Her mind churned over his words, which took away precious concentration from her soap making endeavors.

Soon, spilled dyes and fragrances turned the kitchen island into a poor man's version of Bath and Body Works. Broken and misshapen soap bars littered the counter. The survivors of the experiment sat curing in the whimsical mold trays. Lilly smiled at her progress. Thankfully, the age limit on the box had a plus sign after the number. Lilly had set up a contingency plan that included a long night of bad movies and a bottle of wine if she failed directions aimed at a grade schooler.

Maybe having a bottle of wine with supper was called for after the day she'd had, especially after conversing with Joshua.

The back door opened once more, and her brief rush of excitement of it being Joshua returning was dashed by the muttered curse and wafting scent of dirt and cow. "What happened in here?" Ryan exclaimed.

Lilly raised her eyes to meet Ryan's gaze. "Making soap."

"You haven't gone all Fight Club on me, have you?"

She pressed her lips into a tight line to hide her smirk. Why was it when she was the most vexed with him, he somehow found a way to be annoyingly endearing?

"Was Joshua making soap with you?"

Lilly laughed. That explained the strange look on Joshua's face right before he left. He saw Ryan approaching. "No, he wasn't making soap with me. He just came by to chat."

Ryan grunted. "Why?"

"Why wasn't Joshua making soap?"

"No, why are you making soap?" he snapped.

She sighed and shoulders slumped. "It was going to be my great cottage industry for the farm. Artisan soaps, lotions, stuff like that."

Ryan's dark eyes blinked. "Artisan... cottage... cottage cheese?"

"No cottage cheese, although that would have been interesting to make. I researched making cheese and the like, but the logistics are way out of my league at this point." Lilly shook her head. "No, I planned to do farm-to-consumer marketing, cut out the middleman and sell directly to the consumer. Bring the wholesomeness of the farm back into the home. Even with agro-tourism, people come to the farm and experience the country life for a weekend, sign up for classes to make homemade soaps and lotions and the like. I even planned to figure out how to make some with real milk!"

"That explains your milk soap comment from before." He scratched his chin as he picked up one of the failed first soap forms. "But why bother with this now that you're selling?"

Lilly felt the hardness in his voice. "I bought them, might as well get my money's worth."

"I don't understand how you can sell." Ryan dropped the misshapen soap and went for a half-empty bottle of perfume next.

"And I can't understand how you can't understand me wanting to sell." Lilly snatched the bottle from his fingers. "This last week has been anything but welcoming."

"What would your grandparents think?"

"My grandparents?" Lilly sputtered, voice raising. She had expected the question to come at some point, but she wasn't prepared for how she'd react to it actually being said. Joshua's warning echoed sharply in her ear. "I'd like to think that they'd be worried about my safety first! A dead body and a suspected murderer with a grudge takes higher priority than the farm."

Ryan snorted, whisking the bottle away from Lilly again. "Then it's better that you're leaving if you care so little for this place."

She closed her eyes and gripped the edge of the island counter. Lilly focused on inhaling positive intentions and exhaling her anger. Her anger, she quickly realized, was stronger than any yoga breathing technique she knew.

"I'm not going to apologize for having a strong sense of self-preservation." Irritation pushed each word through clenched teeth. "And if you love this place so much, I'll extend to you the first chance to make a bid on buying the farm. I will gladly let you take this farm and the crazy neighbors off my hands."

He narrowed his eyes at her. She knew he was mulling over her offer as he stared intently from across the island. It seemed that, in each of their interactions, he had tried his best to intimidate her. Lilly shuddered under the weight of his gaze.

Echoes of Emily Carpenter-Hayes' and Joshua's warnings drifted through her ears once more. Was he as dangerous as his ex-flame made him out to be? Was he just out for more land? Emily did know him as the man he became, not the teenager Lilly knew. What reason would Emily have to lie?

"How much?"

His question shook her back to the kitchen. "What now?"

"How much for the farm. Are you selling just the building site or crop land along with the building site?"

Lilly blinked. "I, uh… hadn't gotten that far yet. I suppose the land and the buildings."

"How much an acre?"

"How much?"

"Are you going with the current market price or more, make a little profit from the deal? It'd be better if you gave a bit of a discount, since I've worked here for a long time and knew your grandparents so well."

"A discount?" Lilly's voice broke. "Why would I give a discount?"

"That's the neighborly thing to do. Someone who's worked long for the family, either renting the acres or working in the barn, they get a deal on the asking price. Shows that you respect the relationship and the work the other has put into things."

"Right."

"That's what Bev and Harold would have done." Ryan shrugged as he fidgeted with a broken piece of glycerin. "And it's traditionally done that way around these parts."

Did my grandparents have this conversation with him before they died? Lilly narrowed her eyes.

"Well, I'm sad to say this, but Bev and Harold aren't here. You're dealing with me now." Lilly fought to keep emotion from rising in her voice. "And tradition is just peer pressure from dead people."

"You were more than willing to give into Earl's demands for you to honor his agreement with Harold!" Ryan countered. His fist struck the island top soundly, warping the glycerin still in his grasp. "If you're going to honor one, you have to honor all."

How many verbal agreements did my grandparents make to these people?

"Oh, I do, do I? Once you start getting as violent and threatening as Earl, then maybe we'll talk!"

A strange shadow passed under the brim of his hat.

Lilly cleared her throat as her spine trilled. "But I'm certain that we can be civil adults and come to our own arrangement." Her words tripped on her tongue.

A cool smile spread across Ryan's whiskered face. "I'm glad to hear that you're willing to negotiate. But I'm going to have to pass on your offer. I can't afford this place, discount or not."

Then why did you make such a fuss? Lilly's chill of apprehension flashed into the heat of vexation.

He turned away from her, much of his face hidden under his blasted brim. Lilly saw the brief flash of worry wash over his face. Her stomach knotted. He depended on this farm for not only income but for a sense of purpose. Now, she threatened to snatch that all away. Although, if his cousin was to be believed, Ryan wasn't as hard up for opportunities as he apparently wanted people to think.

What would Grandma and Grandpa do?

"I bet I could talk to the realtor, put a clause in the buyer's contract that you are to be kept on as a hired man when the farm is sold. You already know so much about this place and have a great rapport with the cows—"

Ryan cut her off with a wave. "Thanks, but no thanks. I'm not a consolation prize. When Walmart gets built here, I'm sure I can get a job as a greeter."

"Ryan—"

"Can't you see it? Propped up on a stool in the entryway, welcoming shoppers in to experience the low, low prices."

"Wait a minute, Ryan—"

"No, I'm done getting handouts."

"From what I've heard, you don't need handouts. Your family is pretty well off and, if you wanted to, you could go back to daddy and be set for work."

"Who told you that—never mind." Ryan yanked his hat from his head and dragged his fingers through his hair. "It was Josh, wasn't it? What did he say?"

"You should know—"

"What did he say?" he shouted.

"Your father got them cut out of your grandparents' will," Lilly spat.

They sat in the kitchen, the hum of the appliances the only thing breaking the heavy silence. Ryan popped a fragmented soap failure from its mold and turned it over in his hands. Lilly fought for something to say. All her words fell flat before they even formed on her tongue.

"Right." Ryan finally broke the silence. He sounded tired, defeated. "Of course he would say that, and of course you'd believe it."

"Why shouldn't I believe it?" Lilly asked. "I've been unearthing a lot of family drama over the last week, why wouldn't I think he's telling the truth?"

"Maybe you should get both sides of the story before you start making assumptions."

"Like you did about me when I left?" Lilly leaned over the island. "Faith said that ever since I left, you still pined for me. I think it's safer to say that you've been nursing a grudge for fifteen years based on faulty information. Even after you found out why I had to leave, you still trudge around here in your perceived righteous anger and take it out on me like it was my fault!"

"Faith said what?"

"So, even if what Joshua said isn't completely true, how you've treated me this last week is reason enough to never sell the farm in any fashion to you, ever. I wanted to stay here, make my family proud, but excuse me if a dead body and a crazy old man have taken all the joy out of being back home!"

He shook his head. She wasn't sure if he was disagreeing with her or if this was a signal he was done with the conversation.

"The main factor in you wanting to sell is Earl."

His blunt statement caught her off guard. Lilly stared blankly at him, her brain-mouth connection still not functional at full capacity. "Yes, I suppose so..."

"If Earl left you alone, then you'd stay. Not sell the farm, right?"

"Yes..."

Apprehension drew the word out longer than necessary.

He gave a sharp nod and bounced away from the island and off the stool. The movement was so sudden and fluid Lilly did a double take. Ryan put the soap fragment back on the counter and headed toward the back door.

Lilly watched him move. As she held an uneasy breath, her blood ran cold. "Ryan... what... where are you going?"

"Over to Earl's."

So casual.

"Ryan—"

He glanced over his shoulder and gave her a brilliant grin. She froze, never having seen such an expression from Ryan before. She could believe now what Emily had said about laying the charm on thick.

"Don't worry, Lilly." His voice flowed like warm honey as he opened the screen door. "Old Earl and I are just going to have a little chat."

Chapter Eighteen

Lilly sat in her grandfather's leather chair, surrounded by the boxes of her grandmother's journals. The boxes had been shuffled from second floor to kitchen, from kitchen to living room, now finally from living room to den, but never quite getting back up where they belonged as Lilly planned. She couldn't quite make herself put them back up in the dusty attic. By tucking the journals away, she felt she would be losing her grandparents all over again.

A few more days downstairs wouldn't hurt anyone.

She thumbed through a more recent volume of her grandma's diaries, trying anything to get her mind off Ryan, Earl Graves, and Max Carpenter. The journal she held contained entries from the last few months of her grandparents' lives, ending two weeks before their deaths in February. Perhaps she'd be able to glean some clarity of mind and a direction for her life.

It was hard to look through this journal. Her grandma's handwriting wasn't as neat and precise as in previous journals. The last entries she read were from the early seventies, when her grandmother had been a new mother and younger woman. Suddenly, Lilly was thrust forward almost fifty years and the changes were jarring.

January 8

Earl came by again to talk with Harold about the land rent agreement. I'm not sure how much longer he can work our land. He has almost as many health problems as Harold.

I spoke with our lawyers about the land and our will. One doesn't want to think or dwell on such things, but at our age it is inevitable. I know Harold refuses to speak of the matter, since the children left. How can he still hold this grudge after all these years?

Harold doesn't know I've been in talks to change the will. Our land should stay in the family. Not in the hands of strangers. He's gotten us into this mess, so it's up to me to get us out.

She couldn't imagine being in her grandmother's shoes, trying to keep the farm afloat while her husband drank himself into a stupor. Somehow, she had managed to keep enough income filtering through the accounts to pay Earl for his assistance and to keep other creditors at bay.

Lilly shook her head as she flipped ahead a few entries.

February 2

The word got out that we're looking to transition off the farm. I'm not sure how people found out but it's bound to happen. Of course Harold got wind of it and he's fit to be tied. I just don't know what I'm going to do with that man.

On top of all that now we are dealing with the vultures. Land developers who always come sniffing around when farmland is rumored to be for sale soon. Hopefully the will changes go through soon. Maxwell had promised the transitional paperwork would go through without a hitch. He has been such a help during this transition. The farm and the land will all go to Lillian in five years' time, or when we both pass.

Lilly held the journal at arm's length, as if the book had somehow bit her. She reread the last passage three times and still couldn't believe it.

Maxwell Carpenter had helped her grandmother set up the change-over of the farm. Her stomach churned. Was this another one of his schemes to get the land, like how he had conspired poor Perry out of his desired lot? Although, the will came to her via certified courier from her grandparents' lawyer. So the arrangement he made with Bev appeared to be on the level.

There was that comment he made, about the timeframe. If an heir didn't come forward to claim the land, it went on the market. Was that part of Max's plot to get the farmland, sneaking that clause into the agreement? Everyone in Lone Tree had written Lilly's parents off as deserters. They had left without a word fifteen years ago, why would any of that family come back now? It was a perfect set-up. However, Lilly did come and claim the land, by some cosmic accident, and messed up Max's plan.

Lilly frowned as she reread the February entry once more. According to her grandmother, Max had helped in setting up the transition process. The will and deed claimant paperwork came from a lawyer's office that Lilly didn't recognize, from Sleepy Eye, the next town over. But when she came to Lone Tree, she had to stop at Maggie Swenson's realty office to get the transfer officially notarized and completed.

I just wish the vultures would stop hounding us. I get so many phone calls from neighboring farms, looking to add to their land. And that Tessa woman. She is the worst of them. Constantly badgering me for an answer. Not to work with Maxwell. For some reason she is so determined to know who will run the land when we're gone.

The land will still be run by Earl for as long as he wishes. That is spelt out in the will and transition paperwork. I put copies of it all in our safety deposit box.

She gaped at the last paragraphs. Who was this Tessa and why was she harassing her grandmother? Lilly didn't recognize the name from any previous entries or journals. She fumed against her grandmother's lack of writing down a last name or more identifiers. Perhaps this Tessa was Max's alleged partner in the development deals.

But more important than a possible lead to the mystery partner, Lilly had proof that her grandparents wanted Earl to run the land. It was written down in official documents at the bank. All Lilly had to do was get a hold of the safety deposit box and Earl would be off her back for good. He'd have his proof that Bev and Harold were taking care of him after he was gone, and that she would honor their wishes. Maybe then, he would listen to her about any plans to let him buy the croplands if that was his wish. Anything to make the pedantic old farmer complacent.

Lilly glanced at her watch, painfully unaware of how much time had passed in the den. When did Ryan leave for Earl's? She clutched the journal to her chest as she raced to gather her purse and car keys. Maybe if she hurried, she could reach Earl's farm before Ryan did too much damage.

Lilly paid little attention to the thunderheads churning and darkening as her Kia bounced along Earl Grave's driveway. Even though she applied the barest amount of pressure to the accelerator, she felt as if her car—and herself—would rattle to pieces. The gravel path looked more like a forgotten mining quarry than a driveway. Her stomach pitched into her throat with each jarring pothole.

Earl's farmstead was across two fields from her grandparents'—her—farm. She could see the outline of the grove and the barn from his drive, but she felt a million miles away from any point of civilization.

As her car shuddered to a halt in front of the main house and its detached garage, Lilly took in her surroundings. She was parked next to an ancient silver truck, one older than herself. It must be Earl's vehicle, though she'd never seen the man actually drive. She frowned, annoyed at herself for not paying attention to what the man drove.

That's important information dear old Nancy Drew wouldn't have left unnoticed.

An A-frame house sat behind an unkempt hedge of lilac bushes and a barely there lawn. She recognized dog runs and half-heartedly filled in holes. She wished she'd brought some sort of backup as the very real possibility of being accosted by off-leash farm dogs settled like a rock in her gut. If the temperament of their owner was any indication, these dogs would not be so welcoming to unexpected visitors.

Fat, heavy rain drops splattered erratically on her windshield, early heralds of the upcoming storm.

The farm yard stood silent and abandoned, appearing more like an on-location set for a zombie movie than a working farm. Rusted out equipment, a riding lawn mower, and an assortment of tractors poked out from overgrown patches of grass and weeds. Lilly figured the lawn hadn't seen any sort of mower in years due to the thick, dead undergrowth that threatened to choke off this year's grass.

To her left, the house loomed. Despite its horror-film worthy look, it was in better repair than the other outbuildings. Slabs of asphalt shingles signaled the final resting places of a machine shed and granary, their roofs laid flat on the ground with the walls beneath them long rotted away. The barn, nestled further back from the house and drive, looked soon to follow in their mode of demise—the faded, red wood pocked with what Lilly could only assume were many rounds of buckshot.

Why would he shoot at his own barn?

The oppressive silence from the barn made Lilly's stomach roil with the assumed answer.

She shook the dark thoughts from her mind and made her way slowly to the house. A lack of a certain green Chevy truck bolstered Lilly's faltering hope. Perhaps she had beat Ryan to Earl's farm. Now, she had the chance to talk to the cantankerous farmer before her hot-headed hired man made a bigger mess of things. Her grandmother's journal rested on the passenger seat. Its mere presence gave her the extra boost she needed to exit her car.

A rumble of thunder startled a scream from her lips. Lilly clapped her hands over her mouth and flicked her gaze over the yard anxiously, awaiting either a swarm of barking dogs or a very ticked off old man. The silence ticked by, punctuated by more heavy drops from the angry skies overhead.

"Let's get this over with before I get drenched," Lilly muttered to herself as she stomped up to the front door.

Her knock echoed dully within the house. As hard as she strained her ears, she heard no stirrings from Earl's home. She knocked once more, with her fist instead of just knuckles. The same emptiness greeted her.

She moved around the side of the house and deeper into the yard, toward the one shed that remained upright.

"Earl!" Lilly shattered the silence of the farm yard with a quaking yell. "Earl! I've come to talk to you!"

Given how quickly he had accosted her all the other times their paths had crossed, Lilly wondered if the old man was indeed not at home.

"Earl!" she shouted, her voice gaining strength. "I came to talk to you about the deal my grandparents made with you. I found proof, so you don't have to worry about the land anymore."

Maybe she should have told someone she was coming over to Earl's home, like Faith, Maggie, or even Second Cousin Twice Removed Sheriff Michael. Earl was a person of interest in the death of Maxwell Carpenter. He had made numerous public threats to her over the last week. The whole town knew Earl was not the most stable man.

Lilly had hoped that coming to his home would throw him off his crazy enough to possibly get through to him, and to stop the madness he seemed hell-bent on fostering. Though now, as she tip-toed around his yard, she was second guessing her plan. Perhaps coming out to a suspected killer's deserted farm without ensuring backup was not the smartest decision Lilly had made.

A flash of lightning lit up the farmyard, freezing the following moment's worth of sound and action in its eerie strobe.

From behind the house rose a strangled cry followed quickly by an animalish yelp.

Through the tall, dead grass, a blackened figure ran through the maze of neglected machinery, only feet from where she stood. Lilly wasn't sure if the figure saw her or just chose to ignore her.

Rumbling thunder and a diesel engine combined into a sickening roar. Swollen clouds finally let loose their overdue payload, a torrent of heavy drops pummeled Lilly's head and shoulders.

Lilly turned as the silver truck screamed off down the driveway, each pothole the tire encountered threatening to render the vehicle down to its frame.

Did Earl just leave? Why would he leave without confronting her? He'd spent the last week going out of his way to tell her what was on his squirrely little mind. Lilly knew her presence on his land would be enough to encourage the old man to talk to her; whether it was a productive talk was beside the point.

She turned in time to see a black retriever plod through the grass to her side. Lilly braced herself for an attack but was surprised to find the old dog lick at her outstretched hand, its rough tongue grazing her palm. The dog took her hand in his mouth and Lilly choked back a scream.

The black dog tugged on her hand gently and whined.

"What's wrong, boy?" Lilly pulled her hand from his mouth and scratched behind a floppy ear. He licked her hand again before turning and retreating the way he came. Her gut told her to follow the dog.

With the other weird events that had just happened, why not follow a strange animal into a downpour?

Lilly barely registered her drenched clothing and hair by the time the dog had finished leading her behind the house. He plodded up onto a small back porch and sat down next to a lump of blankets. She sighed and smiled, wondering how lonely the old dog must get while his owner went around terrorizing the town.

"Is your bed getting soaked, buddy?" Lilly cooed. She took a step on a porch stair and reached out to the wet fabric in hopes of pulling it away from the edge of the porch and maybe under the awning.

She screamed as the lump groaned and moved.

"Earl!" Lilly knelt down next to the old man. His clothes, already ragged and worn, hung from his fragile frame and made him almost shapeless. He laid on his stomach, face side-pressed painfully into the rough hewn wood boards. "Earl, oh, goodness, what happened?"

Earl's visible eye flicked up to her face then closed. His dog laid down next to him and began to whine.

"Stay here!" She pointed to the dog. "I'm going to get help! Everything is going to be okay."

She wasn't sure if she was reassuring the dog, the man, or herself.

Lilly backed away from the porch and fumbled over her own feet. She landed hard on a knee in the growing mud. She took that as a sign to slow down and collect her thoughts. Lilly looked at the ground through the long grass and heavy rain, willing her heart to return to her chest and stomach to leave her throat. She wasn't going to help anyone if she went running around the cluttered yard and ended up getting injured on a hidden piece of machinery.

Lilly pressed her hand into the dirt and steadied herself to rise. She had a plan, simple yet foolproof: get to her car and call for an ambulance. Come back out to the porch to make sure Earl is safe and breathing. Make sure the dog is safe. She also had to alert the police to the silver truck and the figure that had just left. They must have knowledge of how Earl got hurt—if they weren't responsible for whatever happened to him in the first place.

She glanced at her mud splattered hand and froze once more, even though each second was precious. Next to her thumb was a boot print. A fresh boot print—the dirt had barely turned to mud from the rain.

Her stomach sank at the snarling lion rising out from the mud.

Lilly scrambled to her feet, careful to not disturb the boot print and hurried to her car. She skidded through the mud, limbs getting tangled in the dead grass, and finally slammed into the side of her car. Numb fingers and a dazed mind made it difficult to open the door. Once inside and the phone acquired, Lilly punched the emergency numbers and locked her door. In fits and starts, Lilly relayed the information to the dispatcher, urging them to hurry out to Earl's farm.

She turned the key and her Kia clunked to life. The windshield wipers didn't stand a chance against the rain, but it allowed her to see some of the yard behind her car. Lilly knew she had promised to go back to the old man and his dog, but the thought of being out in the open soured her stomach.

The pounding rain and thunder made it harder to see and hear if, or when, the diesel pickup returned.

Chapter Nineteen

"**If I never see another cop car**, it'll be too soon." Lilly trudged up onto her porch, sodden shoes leaving clumps of mud with each step. She pulled off the ruined shoes and let out a defeated whimper. Another pair destroyed. One of these days, she needed to get on Amazon and buy a whole pallet of work boots she wouldn't care about covering in mud or various animal by-products.

The recent storm rumbled in the distance as it moved slowly on its southeastern path. Lilly pushed through the front door and dropped her shoes and purse, and then immediately kicked the door shut with a wet, socked foot.

She went upstairs with squelching feet and made a beeline for the shower. As she soaped up and tackled shampooing her hair, she willed the hot water to wash away not only the dirt and chill, but also the memories of the last few hours. If only the hot water heater could reach that desired temperature.

It had taken fifteen minutes for the fire department's first responders to arrive at Earl Grave's farm. Although, Lilly figured five of those minutes were spent navigating the minefield that was his driveway; the muddy ruts created hazards for the large rescue vehicles. The ambulance hadn't been far behind, also delayed due to the uneven gravel, made worse as the rain expanded each pothole. With the emergency personnel there, Lilly had left the safety of her car and led them back to where Earl laid on the porch.

Earl's faithful hound hadn't left his side. He even tried to follow his master onto the stretcher as the EMTs loaded him up. Lilly had held the dog back to allow the paramedics and first responders to finish their work.

She recalled the sequence of events as best she could to the police who had just arrived as Earl was being loaded into the back of the ambulance. Thankfully, Sherriff Second Cousin Twice Removed hadn't shown up with this new batch of deputies and officers. Lilly believed that, before the week was over, she'd have met the entire Lone Tree Police Department. She also didn't want to explain to her distant relation why, yet again, she was at the scene of an accident slash potential crime.

An unknown officer had taken her statement and contact information. Lilly wished she'd seen more of the strange person who fled Earl's farm just as the storm broke. The officer hadn't seemed pleased with what information she did provide. She hadn't seen the make, model, or license plate of the truck. Apparently, "old truck" wasn't exactly promising; that description probably fit most of the farm vehicles in and around Lone Tree. Though, knowing it was silver helped... a little. It's likely "black shadowy figure" wouldn't produce much of a suspect sketch. The officer grew even more dour when she insisted on showing him where she had seen the boot print. Well, where it had been. The rain storm had not only obscured any details of the mysterious figure, it had also washed away the boot print with the lion logo. The distinct Las Scarpas emblem had become nothing more than a muddy smudge in the middle of a boot-shaped puddle.

Lilly knew she had tripped on the officer's last nerve when she'd asked if they would let her know how Earl was after he got to the hospital. The officer had replied sternly that only next of kin would be privy to that information. As far as Lilly knew, however, Earl Graves didn't have much in the way of family.

"Tell Micha—uh, Sheriff Brandford about the boot print. It matched the one found near Max Carpenter's body," she insisted as she had followed the officer to his squad car.

He looked at her as if she, too, had been hit upon the head like the cranky old farmer.

Lilly stepped from her shower and toweled off, relishing the warm, clean fluffiness on her skin. Sadly the shower did nothing to calm the thoughts racing in her head. It did the exact opposite. Lilly went into post-shower autopilot as she tried to piece together the evening's recent events with all the previous information. Somehow, there was a connection.

Wasn't there?

Earl had been hit over the head, much like how Max had been struck. She hadn't seen the wound when she initially found the man, and he had been in no condition to give a report of his injuries. She overheard the EMTs as they assessed Earl and stabilized him for transport to the hospital. No clear evidence remained at the porch or surrounding yard to give a concrete theory of how the farmer had been attacked, or what the cause of the wounds was. The phrase "blunt object" was tossed around the sodden farmyard. That description would have to suffice until a further inspection was done at the hospital.

Had he indeed been attacked? The fleeing figure in the truck seemed to be a dead giveaway. Lilly scrunched a towel through her hair as she worked through the facts and theories. Maybe the stranger had seen Earl fall, it was all an accident, and they went for help, so focused on their mission they didn't notice Lilly's presence. That theory was plausible. Earl, being an older man living alone, could have suffered a fall.

Lilly could still hear the plaintive wail of the ambulance siren echoing in her ears. As the EMTs had prepared to depart, she had caught one of them telling the driver to "step on it." Even the emergency technicians knew his prognosis wasn't favorable.

Lilly shuddered as a drop of cooling water trickled down between her shoulder blades. She forced out a loud breath in an attempt to dislodge the memories that continued to flood her mind. It was getting late, and nothing more could be done about Earl tonight.

What she needed now was to eat and try to focus on things she could control. Lilly, towels wrapped around body and hair, flopped back on her bed and ran through a mental checklist of what food remained in the house. None of it sounded appealing.

Suddenly, she was up and moving around the master bedroom and closet like a woman possessed. She supposed she was one. Lilly needed to get off the farm and away from all the dirt, drama, and death for one night. She needed city lights, crowds, and whatever culture Brown County had to offer.

Lilly dressed in one of her favorite outfits, one that she reserved for casual entertaining of Alec's friends and her mimosa brunches with her girlfriends downtown. Thankfully, Olivia hadn't caught sight of this number in her closet during all her closed-door trysts with Alec. The *Other*

Woman would have made it a point to make sure Alec secured it in the divorce proceedings, as she had with nearly everything else in their loft.

Including her husband.

The Charleston-inspired dress hung hidden in the back of her current closet. A modern update on the style of the Roaring Twenties, the powdery gray-blue dress consisted of gauzy fabric dappled with silver sequins and beads along the bodice to end in a graceful bow slung low at the hip. The asymmetrical hem fluttered around her knees, giving it that quintessential "flapper" air. When she slipped it on, Lilly felt a sudden pang for her friends in the Cities

She and her girlfriends had been obsessed with the television series Downton Abbey, convinced they lived in a modern day version of the period drama: rich families, old money, and no responsibilities save for who would host the next luncheon or fundraiser. They held watch parties for the British melodrama and, naturally, decided they needed to dress the part. Every week, the gaggle of millennial girls would don their flapper-style dresses, sipping on drinks with giggle-inducing names like the Bee's Knees, Mary Pickford, and of course, the Hanky Panky. After the series had ended, the group continued with their cocktail hours in full costume at a bar in downtown Minneapolis.

Lilly finished the ensemble with her favorite pair of sling-back heels in a steely blue that not only complimented the look but made her legs and butt look fabulous.

Her hair, too wet from the shower to be properly styled, went back in a lazy yet stylish braid. She toyed with the idea of digging out her bucket fascinator hat to really complete the modern flapper motif, but decided against it. Maybe next time she went out, she'd make it a point to go all out. Lilly didn't want to shock the good people of Lone Tree too much;

she'd already made a less-than-stellar impression her first week in town, why not give them a little break at the gossip mill.

She knew Lone Tree didn't have much for "upscale" eating establishments and Monday night wasn't prime, but she remembered an Asian restaurant when she drove through New Ulm last week. If not that spot, there were always the old standbys of The Lamplighter or The Kaiserhoff. Though she might be just a tad overdressed, she'd even settle for Happy Joe's Pizza at that moment. Anything to get away from the farm.

"I wonder if they still have the viewing window," Lilly wondered aloud as she drew on her Mackinaw jacket.

Lilly smiled at memories of the countless hours she'd spent staring at the chefs on the other side of the window, marveling at the large discs of dough being flipped and stretched to impossible sizes before being slathered with tangy marinara sauce.

Jacket secured and impractical yet fabulous shoes strapped, Lilly headed to the door for a much-needed night out. She reached for the door just as the knob turned seemingly upon its own accord. She frowned. *Who keeps coming into my house like they own the place? Couldn't be Ryan, his mode of entry is the back kitchen door.*

Lilly grabbed the knob and yanked the door open to reveal a startled Maggie Swenson on the other side.

"Maggie?"

"Oh, hello, dearie..." Her gaze fell upon Lilly's clothes and her eyebrows arched even higher on her forehead. "Am... am I interrupting something?"

"I was on my way out to get a bite to eat,"

"Really... so soon?"

Lilly's brows furrowed. "Soon?"

"I hurried over after hearing Merlin's scanner about what happened to poor Earl." Maggie shuffled her way by Lilly and into the entry.

Lilly's only choice was to follow the woman. She sighed. Supper would have to wait. "Someone should really tell Merlin that listening to the scanner is a bad use of his time."

"Oh, let the old man have some fun," Maggie chuckled. "I had to come by to see how you were doing. You seem to keep getting mixed up in ugly things since you've come to town, but I see you've gotten over this rather quickly."

Maggie stopped in the kitchen and busied herself with checking the countertops and random utensil drawers. Lilly stood next to the island and watched her guest's movements. She kept her purse and keys in plain sight, hoping the overt hint would be received by the busy-body realtor. Maybe this would end up being a short, painless visit.

"I just need to get out of the house for a bit," Lilly responded, unsure of how to read Maggie's odd remark.

"What were you doing over at Earl's, and especially during a storm?" Maggie asked.

"It wasn't raining when I got there," Lilly said. "I went to go talk to Earl about the land deal between him and my grandparents."

Maggie shook her head. "Poor man, the years of isolation have done a number on his mind. And now, with losing Bev and Harold, he's just a mess."

"That's what I thought too, but I found proof of the deal in Grandma Bev's journal. Here, let me show you—" Lilly announced as she glanced around the kitchen. "Oh, I must have left it in the car. That's why I went over to Earl's. To show him that we can work this whole thing out."

"That's marvelous, dearie." Maggie smiled. "I'm certain Earl will love to hear that when he gets home from the hospital."

Lilly settled a hip against the kitchen island. "Finally, I can put this whole drama behind me and move on with my life."

Maggie eyed her closely. "Have you made a final decision if you're staying or going?"

Lilly shrugged. "Not yet. Grandma wanted the farm to stay in the family, but between Max's death, Earl's craziness, and now Earl being attacked... I guess I'm taking it one day at a time now?"

"Well, sounds like all your big obstacles are out of the way now." Maggie busied herself with checking the tidiness of the kitchen counters and cabinets.

Lilly chewed on her bottom lip. "Not necessarily. There was something in grandma's journal, when she was talking about transitioning off the farm. All these people kept calling and asking about the farm."

Maggie shrugged. "It happens more than you know out here. Every farmer is looking to add to their acreage. If they can just swoop in at the right time, they can sometimes get land for a steal."

Lilly nodded, digesting what Maggie said. "I guess the only obstacle now would be if Tessa tries calling again."

Maggie walked around the island and stopped opposite Lilly, her brows raised. "Tessa?"

"Grandma mentioned this Tessa calling her a lot, almost harassing her about the land. Didn't put a last name in the journal." Lilly shrugged. "At least now, if she starts calling again, I know to shut any of her inquiries down."

The two fell silent for a few moments. Lilly fought the chill that crept up her spine. She had only known Maggie for just over a week, but this was one of the longest stretches the woman had gone without talking. "Hey, did you hear anything on Merlin's scanner about how Earl is doing?

Is he over at Sleepy Eye Medical? The police didn't tell me his condition before the ambulance took him away."

Lilly knew she was rambling. She couldn't help it. The awkward silence of the kitchen grated on her nerves, and she needed to fill the void.

"I don't think you need to worry about that any more tonight. You've been through so much, Lilly." Maggie's eyes narrowed as she continued to walk to Lilly's side of the island. "I think a solo girl's night out is just what you need."

"That was the original plan." Lilly glanced down at her outfit, suddenly feeling naked in spite of yards of fabric. "I was going to go to New Ulm."

Maggie chuckled. "I hope you can find some suitable nightlife, dearie. Things aren't as fast paced in Lone Tree as they are in Minneapolis."

"I'm certain I'll find something. As long as I'm away from this farm,"

"Then why don't I take you to the Attic?" Maggie whirled around, her eyes bright. "It'll be my treat!"

"Oh, well, I had really wanted to..." Lilly's smile strained. She couldn't come up with a polite excuse to save her life.

Before she knew it, Maggie's arm was laced with her own and the elder woman was ushering her down the hall. Lilly gave herself a raincheck on the solo night out. Maggie was only looking out for her, and had been since the moment she arrived in Lone Tree. She supposed one dinner with the realtor was a worthy price for all the kindness the woman had shown.

"And we can have a lovely discussion about your plans for the farm," Maggie said as they descended the porch steps. The rain-soaked gravel of the drive gave way under their feet. "Hopefully, we can change your mind about leaving. Faith was telling me that you were thinking about doing yoga for goats?"

Maggie's question was momentarily lost on Lilly as she glanced down at the porch steps. The hole was missing. Ryan had fixed it. *Huh*, I guess I'll have to thank him. Lilly frowned at the thought, not ready to play nice with him yet.

"Not yoga for goats. Yoga with goats," Lilly corrected. "People will be doing the yoga while baby goats run around and jump and play. It's very popular right now, and I thought it'd do well down here, since there's bound to be a few goat farmers in the area. That, or some kind of bed and breakfast where you can make your own milk soap."

"Hmmm."

Lilly wanted to convince herself the damp air was responsible for the chills going down her spine.

"Sounds positively avant-garde, no?" Maggie forced the pair to turn at the top of the driveway U-turn and headed toward the barn. Lilly turned back to the parked cars, wondering at the odd detour. That's when she noticed a truck parked next to her little Kia.

An older model, silver truck that looked to have lost a battle with more than a few mud puddles.

Lilly's feet fought to take the next steps forward.

"Careful, dearie. It's pretty muddy, and those aren't the best shoes for the farm," Maggie warned.

"I wasn't planning on walking around the farm," Lilly reminded her. "I thought we were going to go have something to eat at the Attic? Why are you taking me to the barn?"

"Oh, I figured you could show me what you have planned for goat yoga. It'd be interesting to see how you'd like to change things around. Perhaps walking around and envisioning your soap and yoga class space will help you make up your mind a little quicker."

Lilly gingerly snaked her arm free from Maggie's hold. With each step, tingles of alarm shot out from her spine and threatened to cloud her brain. She reminded herself that now was not the time to start on her wild theories. Her guard was still up from earlier at Earl's farm. She just needed to shake her overactive imagination and get her nerves under control. There had to be a perfectly normal, and not nefarious, reason why Maggie had a silver truck instead of her normal sedan. How many people in the area drove similar trucks? Silver was a common color.

"Shouldn't we wait until it's a little drier?" Lilly asked. "I haven't had a chance to really get many ideas down on paper. Most of them are still up in my head, really. You could come back maybe later next week, and I'll have a big spread for you; a whole presentation of branding and sketches for how the outer sheds will be upgraded. I've been toying around with a logo and everything. The whole nine yards."

Maggie turned to her and smiled. A smile that looked more at home on one of Lilly's old debutant friends or Lisa Munroe. Plasticine, fake, forced. A smile used to hide behind.

"You sound just like Max, you know?"

Lilly swallowed hard. "Oh, really?"

"I think you two would have had a lot in common, had you known him longer," the realtor continued. "Always thinking big. Always coming up with the next answer. Always wanting to fix people's problems... even when you weren't asked to help."

"That's what makes small towns so great, I guess; everyone wanting to help their neighbor out."

"I suppose." Maggie's smile faded.

"I think merging the ideas I have about make-and-take classes with yoga would go well with reviving Grandma Bev's farmers' market. Have a whole area where people, local and not, can come and experience all that Lone Tree has to offer." Lilly realized she was rambling before it was too late.

Something in Maggie's demeanor made her nervous.

The silver truck made her nervous.

Maggie sighed. "Beverly did want to share all her land's bounty with the citizens of Lone Tree."

"Then it'll be a perfect way to honor Grandma and Grandpa's memory. A marriage of the past with the present, even the future. I had an idea of what to do with the hayloft. Though, I'm sure Ryan would have about one hundred reasons why I can't touch the hay loft."

Stop talking, Lilly, and get to your car.

Maggie nodded. She held back a moment and fell in step with Lilly. "Ryan has put a lot of time and energy into making things just the way he wants them on his farm."

His farm?

"My farm," Lilly corrected.

"Oh my, what did I say?" Maggie laughed, her hand falling on Lilly's shoulder. "Goodness, I suppose I thought of this place more as Ryan's. Since, like I said, he's spent so much time here with your grandma and grandpa. Unlike you."

Lilly took a hard turn and stared at Maggie. "What did you say?"

"Let's go up to the hay loft and you tell me what you want to turn it into. Maybe I can convince Josh to go easy on you." Maggie's fingers dug into Lilly's shoulder briefly before she walked up the soft incline to the loft doors.

"Josh?" Lilly sputtered. "Don't you mean Ryan? Why did you say Josh?"

Maggie's smile faded.

Lilly swallowed hard, her throat suddenly arid. Every red flag and alarm bell in her screamed wildly, yet she couldn't stop herself from following Maggie. Mrs. Swenson's behavior came from out of nowhere, but so had Ryan's. Perhaps the Swenson and Heimdall clans were prone to mood swings, behavioral issues, or were easily affected by the full moon or planetary alignment.

Where was Mercury... was it in retrograde already?

Lilly cleared her throat and tried again. "I think we should really wait until it's drier out... and not so dark..."

That's when she looked down and saw a lion snarling up from the muddy earth.

"I know of a contractor in Sleepy Eye who would do miracles with this place, Lilly," Maggie called over her shoulder as she worked on pulling the door along its track.

Lilly was too preoccupied with thoughts of *La Scarpas* to think about renovations. The muddy boot tracks Maggie left as they made their way into the hayloft were identical to the ones found near Maxwell Carpenter's body and the injured Earl Graves, down to the raised paw and the famed snarling fangs.

But Lisa Munroe also had *La Scarpas* boots. Maggie having the same boots meant nothing. Just two women in a small town who both had great taste in shoes. How many women in Minneapolis had the same pairs of designer shoes in their closets? That didn't make them all murderers...

The fangs.

Wait a minute. These boot prints of Maggie's had fangs.

Her legs froze mid-step as the rest of her caught up to what her subconscious had already figured out.

Lilly recalled Lisa's shoes and tried to compare her mental snapshots. It was the fangs. Lisa's lion was missing his fangs. A telltale sign of a knockoff pair of La Scarpas. Bootleg manufacturers could never get the fangs right.

Lisa's boots were counterfeit. Maggie's were the real deal.

Lilly fought the shiver that spilled down her spine.

"Something wrong, dearie?"

Maggie's simple question turned her cold. She looked up at the woman and gave her best customer service face. "Nothing, Maggie, just lost in dreaming up my new business space."

The realtor matched her smile and stepped aside to allow Lilly to enter the loft before her.

Lilly's mind spun into overdrive as she walked by Maggie and into the loft. Before her was the large edifice of hay bales Ryan insisted on keeping in the middle of the floor. The shaft of light from the open door fell upon the myriad of farming tools, their cool metal blades refracting the evening sun into deadly slivers of light. Instead of imagining the future homes of her cabinets full of yoga mats and homemade soap, Lilly focused on finding the nearest exit while avoiding standing anywhere near the readily available instruments of death.

If I survive this, I'm making Ryan bury all of those in the grove.

Even as she made escape plans, Lilly found it hard to believe what her eyes had told her. How could Maggie be the killer? What did she have to gain from getting rid of Maxwell and Earl? True, the two men were hard to get along with at times, but murder?

Lilly turned to keep Maggie in front of her at all times. Her mind raced with possibilities and theories that soon left her with her guard lowered. She was overreacting. If Ryan was here, he'd tell her the same thing. She'd been playing detective for over a week, chasing ghosts and half-theories. What had he called her again? Oh yeah, Nancy Drew.

She was just a spoiled, sheltered divorcé who just wanted her life to matter. So why not play detective? Lilly shook her head to clear her thoughts and keep the tears from falling.

Were they tears of fear or clarity?

"I'm truly excited for this next stage in your life, Lilly," Maggie said as she slid the hayloft door closed. "I know the last few months have been hard on you. But now, I believe things will finally turn around."

"I hope so, too." Lilly swallowed hard. She attempted to disguise the quaver in her voice with a brief coughing attack. "I'll be glad to get rid of all this hay. It just is murder on my allergies."

The door clammered shut with a metallic clicking. Maggie's smile flattened as she turned to Lilly, revealing the door handles had been strung through with a red bike rope.

"What... what are you doing?" Lilly stammered as Maggie snapped a padlock through the braided metal hoops.

"I have a bit of a confession to make, Lilly." Maggie clasped her hands behind her back and started a slow walk toward Lilly. "I actually really don't like your ideas for the farm. Never liked them from the first insipid idea that came out of your mouth."

"Maggie, I—"

"You should have kept your nose out of things, Lilly," the realtor continued. "All of this had nothing to do with you, but like every other blasted hipster filth that arrives from the city, you think you know better. Our way of life isn't good enough for you so you need to come in and bulldoze centuries of history to make the world fit into that little lemming brain you have."

"Maggie, please."

"You should have stayed in Minneapolis!" Maggie shouted. Her voice bounced off the rafters. "I almost had everything in place."

Lilly swallowed and backed away from Mrs. Swenson. "In place for what?"

"To keep this farm in the rightful hands," Maggie declared.

"Yours? You don't even farm!"

"Not mine, you lemming," Maggie hissed. "Joshua."

"Joshua?" Her stomach sank into her feet. "Wait... what did Joshua have to do with the farm? He doesn't want it, Ryan does... right?"

"True, Ryan has given years of his life to this farm—to keeping that drunkard's accounts in the black to keep the bank off their backs. It wasn't his fault that no one else would hire him after the accident. And those surgeries and pain pills did a number on poor Ryan. The pain pills made him a completely different person."

Pain meds... Lilly's back collided with the far wall of the hay loft. Bits of straw and cottony cobwebs clung to her. That explains everything! His mood swings, those horrid things he said to me, Emily's warning...

"Maggie, Ryan can stay working here!" Lilly gasped. "You don't have to do this."

"This isn't about Ryan!" Maggie shouted. "That spoiled brat... no. Joshua! This was all for Joshua!"

Lilly kept her eyes locked on Maggie as they did a twisted dance around the hay bales. "His inheritance..."

Maggie nodded, a glimmer of motherly love shining through her anger. "That poor boy has been through so much. The rest of the family shouldn't have thrown us aside like they did."

Lilly's brain scrambled to keep up piecing the puzzle together. "How were you going to get my farm for Josh?"

"I had things all lined up and he had to go ruin everything!"

"He ruined... Max. You were Max's partner in the land deals, weren't you?" Lilly demanded.

"Yes. We shared the profits of the sales," Maggie answered, puffing her chest out. "He knew my family was struggling, so he offered me a cut of his profits if we helped each other out with choice deals."

"Max set up the farmland transfer to me. I wasn't supposed to show up."

"In wanting to help Bev and Harold's transfer papers look more on the up and up side, he accidentally put a huge roadblock in for the two of us. Once Harold and Bev passed, it was only a matter of time before it would go up for sale, the estate and bank would take it over and auction it off at the right price. None of their children wanted anything to do with the farm, especially that hardheaded father of yours. I didn't expect that Bev would change the will at the last minute to give everything to you!" Maggie snapped. "He promised it wasn't going to be an issue, and then you actually laid claim to the land. His slip-up cost me almost half a million dollars! That would have helped me and Robert out, helped Joshua."

"You killed Max." If she was going to play detective, why not go all in? She didn't have anything else to lose.

"Yes, I did," Maggie nodded.

"How would you get your money if your partner was dead and the land was claimed by me?"

"He still owed me money. He promised me the sale of your land would go through. But he wouldn't pay me what was mine. What was due to my family after all these years!" Maggie stood firmly at arm's length in front of Lilly. "I thought it was serendipitous that you stumbled upon his body. What better way to get rid of the flimsy slip of a girl than have a dead body on her property? You'd get scared and run back to the Cities where you belonged. You'd forfeit your claim and then the land would go to auction as planned, and this time I wouldn't have to split any of the profit with Max."

Maggie closed the gap between them with one swift stride. Lilly jerked back against the wall. "That's what you were supposed to do. Then, you started thinking you could start over here, turn this place into some modern, perverted Green Acres. And your talk of rural tourism? You sounded just like Max. Made me sick every time I looked at you."

"Then why Earl? How does he play into this?"

Maggie's smile was cold and patronizing. "He was a thorn in my side as well. As long as he continued on claiming that Bev and Harold had left the farm to him, it would draw out the process of the bank and the estate to foreclose on the property and put it up for auction—the longer Joshua would have to wait for his rightful dues. I had planned it all for Earl to be convicted of killing Max. It was perfect. Those two have been feuding and bickering for years."

"Then, Earl lived up to his reputation and started bringing Ryan into the investigation," Lilly finished. "Which would bring police closer to your family and, eventually, bring your involvement with Max to light."

"How was I to know those tools I took out of Earl's truck were borrowed from this farm?" Maggie seethed. "The stupid police even followed through with the insane conspiracy Earl was concocting. So, naturally, he had to go."

"You don't need to add more blood to your hands, Maggie," Lilly pleaded. "I'll leave. I'll go back to Minneapolis. I'll even go farther away. Josh can have the farm. It doesn't have to be like this."

"I know, I know." Maggie shook her head, her voice sounding genuinely remorseful. "But, you're a loose end that can't be ignored. You know too much. I can't risk you turning noble, trying to be the savior of Lone Tree again."

"I promise, I won't!"

"Stop talking." Maggie stretched out a hand and wrapped her fingers around a hand-held scythe. She drew the tool close and cradled it gently before her. A strangled cry escaped Lilly's lips as she focused on the tool. She could feel its cold sting already.

"Maggie! Please!"

"It's a shame, really." Maggie lifted the blade before her face, eyeing it with a detached air. She picked at a fingernail with the tip of the scythe. "Since you've been back, he's been happier. Joshua... oh, my Joshua. He really did like you, Lilly, back when you were younger. Even when you and your horrid family ran out of town unceremoniously. Broke his poor heart, it did." Maggie gave a small, yet overly dramatic sigh. "I suppose he got over your departure once, he'll have to get over you again."

Lilly inched along the wall until she hit another stack of hay bales, these mottled green and gray with mold and moisture. With her eyes locked on the blade between her and Maggie, her mind churned to a halt with each escape plan she tried to formulate. Maggie stood too close to allow for her to dodge around the blade or any grabbing fingers. She didn't know the layout of the rest of the loft to be able to run and hide.

She was stuck on the upper level of the proverbial house while the masked murderer made his way up the stairs, blocking the only exit.

Lilly's hands dug into the hay behind her, the ancient silage crumbling into rank dust and debris in her fingers. The pungent aroma of the hay brought her back to the present, although still without a plan.

The woman who slowly advanced toward Lilly turned into a complete stranger. Gone was the affable realtor—now replaced by a calculated killer who moved with the stealth of a large cat. Lilly swallowed dryly while she studied the new Maggie, hoping to predict her next move.

As Maggie advanced, Lilly threw her fistfuls of smelly debris into Maggie's face. The realtor's hands flew up to her face, fumbling the scythe to the floor as she tried in vain to get the grit from her eyes. While Maggie worked to clear her vision and recover her weapon, Lilly bolted.

Of course, her Louboutin heels were meant for meetings with the CEO or Sunday morning mojito brunches at Hell's Kitchen, not running for her life in a hay loft. The time-worn wooden planks, along with a strategic layer of silken straw, failed to give her slick heels any traction. Lilly's step faltered as a heel warped under the strain and her legs splayed out from under her like a newborn calf.

A cloud of dust and curses exploded from her lips as she slammed into the floor. Lilly coughed out bits of straw as she laid half prone on the floor, staring down a knot hole in a plank. She could see clearly down into where the cows rested comfortably, blissfully unaware of the life and death struggle happening only feet above their heads.

Dandelion's distinct call rose through the floor.

She scrambled to find purchase with her hands and feet, her expensive and utterly useless shoes failing to get grip. She rose on shaking knees just as fingers sunk into her hair and yanked back. Lilly swore from the pain and both hands reached up to dislodge the fingers' grip.

"My, my, Lillian, such language," Maggie chuckled. "What would Grandma think?"

"She'd think you're crazy!" Lilly spat.

Maggie's grip tightened as she pulled Lilly backwards through the straw once more. "Come, Lilly, let's not make this harder than it has to be."

With one hand still entwined in Lilly's braid, Maggie leaned over to one of the tool racks and picked out a medium sized claw hammer.

Lilly found herself being dragged by her braid toward the sliding doors. Maggie relaxed her hold on her hair long enough to undo the lock she had previously placed on the door and shove it open. The older woman sent Lilly tumbling down the muddy embankment with a powerful shove. Lilly rolled to a stop at the bottom of the incline, shoulders and head sore from bouncing down the ramp, her arms and hands battered from skidding along the gravel and dirt. Maggie was on her again in an instant before Lilly had the chance to gather her bearings. The woman roughly hauled Lilly to her feet by an arm. She cried out again as Maggie wrenched her already battered shoulder.

"Come on, Lilly, we're going for a little walk," Maggie announced.

Lilly shivered at the cool detachment in her voice.

She allowed Maggie to lead her toward the grove behind the barn. By allowed, she really just stopped fighting against her captor in hopes of staying alive a few moments more. Lilly's mind struggled to formulate a plan through the panic.

Too much farmyard lay behind her and the relative safety of the farmhouse. One would think the open and flat terrain of the yard would help her escape by providing an obstacle free shot to her car or house. The soft dirt of the farmyard would hinder Lilly in her broken and useless heels and unfortunately benefit Maggie, who had the forethought to wear sensible shoes when she left the house this morning to go on her murder spree. The openness of the yard and surrounding fields beyond only made the thought of escape all the more daunting. Not to mention that her nearest neighbor was at least a mile away. That would leave Maggie more than enough chances to catch her if she tried to flee. Her best option, for now, was to let Maggie bring her to the next location and reassess the situation then.

She'd have to make her stand there and hope it worked.

They walked past the calf hutches, the half dozen white shelters seeming out of place and alien given Lilly's current predicament. Only three of the hutches were occupied; Envy stuck her head out of her hovel as they walked by. The small calf lowed at them, which caused the other two calves—whom Lilly hadn't met yet—to emerge from their homes and join the chorus. Their plaintive cries were daggers in Lilly's chest.

"I'm sorry, babies," she called to them in a thick voice. "I know you're hungry—"

Maggie pushed the head of the hammer deep between Lilly's shoulder blades, prodding her forward and making her stumble. "Keep moving," she growled.

Lilly managed to look over her shoulder, calling out once more, her voice cracking. "I'll be back to feed you, I promise!"

"Don't waste your breath. They're dumb animals. They'll forget you by tomorrow."

Lilly lowered her eyes to the ground and focused on walking instead of Maggie's harsh words.

Maggie pulled on her braid to force a stop. Lilly hissed through her teeth as, through her pain, she realized where the woman had brought her. She really smelt it before it even came into view.

The manure pit.

She had declined Ryan's invitations to see the end of the line for the barn cleaner, and she could now say she was glad she did. The manure pit, or "lagoon" as Ryan called it, sat in a raised pit the size of a swimming pool. Lilly could only guess at its depth. The earth embankment rose at least knee high and just past the edge sat what appeared to be well plowed dirt. The manure had a crust under a fresh layer of mud that helped to curb some of the offensive smell.

"What are we doing here?" Lilly asked as she held a hand over her mouth and nose. Despite the lagoon being a small pond of super concentrated manure, the aroma wasn't as overpowering as she'd expected. Maybe she was finally getting used to it, or maybe the adrenaline pumping through her made her immune.

"This is your last stop on your farm tour." Maggie pushed the head of the hammer into the middle of Lilly's back. She nudged her up the embankment and closer to the edge of the pit. Lilly stumbled with her flimsy shoes until they caught purchase on the slope.

She trudged up the embankment, with some less than gentle persuasion from the hammer, until she stood on a thin ledge of earth surrounding the mottled brown mass of congealed poo.

"Alright, now in you go," Maggie said.

"In? You can't be serious." Lilly whirled around to face her attacker and a foot dipped closer to the surface of the lagoon. The topmost layer crumbled under the slight pressure of her foot. Liquid manure seeped through the crust opening like she'd stepped on Satan's Pot Pie.

"Yes, in," Maggie repeated and pressed the hammer into her sternum.

"How is manure going to get rid of me? Fumigate me to death?"

"You're not too far off."

Maggie struck her shoulder with the hammer. Lilly screamed and her foot sunk deeper into the liquid stink. "Many a farmer has succumbed to the lagoon, unable to crawl out onto the crust of their manure pits. If the concentrated ammonia fumes along the crust don't force them to pass out, the unknown thickness of the crust has been their undoing. It's much like ice on a lake, you never really know how thick it is until it's too late."

Lilly tried to free her foot from the lagoon and was unsuccessful. The putrid sludge sucked harder at her foot until it finally relinquished her of her left shoe. She stared helplessly as the lagoon claimed her Louboutin; within moments, it was lost to the putrid horrors below.

She glanced up and over Maggie's shoulder to the back of the barn. It appeared miles away. The faint sounds of the cows barely penetrated the distance, save Dandelion's insistent bellowing. Lilly had never felt so alone and helpless.

She knows there's something wrong, Lilly thought sadly. That realization was quickly replaced by the hope of rescue. If Dandelion was bellowing like that, it meant that feeding time was close at hand. Ryan would be coming to start chores any moment.

"Maggie, please stop this," Lilly pleaded. "Ryan will be here soon. You don't want him to find you like this!"

Maggie smiled balefully. "Oh, poor Lilly. I sent Ryan off on an errand. He won't be interrupting us any time soon."

Lilly's heart sank.

"Now, get moving." Maggie waved the hammer.

Her foot sank deeper into the muck, which threatened to pull the rest of her along into the lagoon. Lilly fell onto the thick, putrid crust, her body making a minimal dent. She shifted her weight tentatively as she was unsure how far her luck would be able to last. Cracks erupted at the pressure points under her knees and elbows, allowing more rancid brown sludge to seep up.

She breathed a sigh of relief as the cracks ceased spreading. Maggie had underestimated the strength of the manure. This bought her some more time.

Lilly looked up at Maggie and couldn't suppress her chuckle at the woman's bewildered expression.

"So, was there a Plan B?" Lilly quipped.

Maggie's face flushed crimson as a strangled cry burst from her mouth. She flung the hammer at Lilly. The tool landed head first in one of the oozing cracks, but had little of the desired effect the crazed woman hoped for. The hammer slowly sank into the crack, and both women watched as it soon disappeared into the pit.

"Plan C?" Lilly raised her brows.

"Shut up and just die already!" Maggie lunged into the lagoon at Lilly.

With the added weight, the lagoon's compromised crust buckled. The brown mire rose up and surrounded Maggie's feet and legs, getting as high as her knees with each thrash. Lilly scrambled away from the woman and the growing poop quicksand before she became more entangled in the crumbling mess. Loud, wet sucking noises popped and gurgled around her as she struggled to find traction on the crust to reach the grass embankment.

Maggie's thrashing and cursing spurred Lilly to fight the pull of the manure even harder. Thankfully, her weight had already been spread out, making escape possible. Her feet and hands still broke through the brown skin of the lagoon, but she finally grabbed a fistful of grass and hauled herself up out of the muck.

She crested the embankment, sticky, wet, and foul smelling, but she was free from the lagoon and from the wild woman. At least for a moment. She stared at Maggie who continued to thrash and fight the pull of the manure. Lilly bit her lip, suddenly torn over whether she should help Maggie to safety.

Even if she had gone off the deep end, death by manure pit was not the way to go.

"Get back here!" Maggie shrieked, "Die!"

Lilly swore and twisted frantically up the embankment as the once-lost hammer sailed through the air and landed only feet from her knee. She fumbled to her feet and took off as best she could with only one shoe, running toward the barn with Maggie's shrill curses filling her ears.

Her heart pounded in her throat as she burst into the barn. She struggled to get her mind working. A small, yet loud, part of her brain yelled at her, berating her for having gone into the barn once more. An enclosed structure with limited exits.

Did she learn nothing from watching horror movies?

Lilly slammed the door shut and ran toward the office. Each step sent bolts of fire down from her head and shoulder into the chest. The office door grew fuzzy behind a veil of red hot pain and nausea. Dandelion bellowed when her hand reached the door knob. Lilly shot a wild glance at the cow over her shoulder and pulled her hand away. The office was small and it'd be easy to find her. It was an even more confined space with only one way out. She needed somewhere with lots of nooks and crannies for hiding.

And possibly with make-shift weapons.

Thanks, Dandelion, old girl.

Taking the cow's "advice," Lilly switched trajectory and headed for the supply room. She knew Ryan kept a multitude of medicines and needles in there for treating and vaccinating the cows. She'd be bound to find something to defend herself in there. Again, as her fingers wrapped around the door handle, Dandelion grunted. It might have been Lilly's overstimulated brain, but that moo sounded awfully patronizing.

"What?" Lilly hissed. Locking eyes with the large bovine, she gestured wildly at the door behind her. "What's your great idea?"

The cow pulled against her chain and threw her head toward the empty maternity pen. She lowed softly as she caught Lilly's gaze again.

"Crazy cow, why would I want to go to the back of the barn? I'd be a sitting duck for sure!"

The old cow rolled her eyes and huffed out a strong breath.

Somehow, Lilly knew she needed to be quiet. She caught her own breath at the sound of footsteps winding their way across the hayloft floor.

That couldn't possibly be Maggie, no way she'd have gotten out of the lagoon so fast... unless...

"Ryan?" Lilly gasped.

Dandelion shook her head and grunted loudly.

"Shut up, stupid cow." Maggie's voice dripped acid.

Lilly's stomach sank.

Damn, that woman is persistent, Lilly thought with a hard, dry swallow.

The logistics of how Maggie freed herself from the manure would have to wait. Lilly's addled brain struggled to concentrate with all the noise from the cows.

Dandelion.

The hefty cow bumped her girth into the neighboring cow, which set off a domino effect of perturbed bovines. Soon, the whole barn was filled with belly-aching cows, clanking chains, and snapping tails.

Lilly glanced up at the ceiling and tried to determine if any of the shadows she saw were Maggie's. The noise from the animals effectively covered her movements in the barn, which Lilly was thankful for. It also destroyed any method of tracking Maggie's movements, though. Lilly's stomach twisted as the commotion from the cows began to die down. She strained her ears to pinpoint where the realtor had gone off to.

The hayloft fell silent.

Maggie could be anywhere now.

Behind her, the barn door rattled.

"How in the world did she get there so fast?" Lilly hissed. She glanced at Dandelion, as if for some last minute advice. "Well?"

The large bovine's eyes rolled back to show mostly white as if to say the obvious thing: "You blew it."

Lilly headed over and flipped off the main lights, sending the lower level of the barn into dark shadows. The overcast skies and damp air added to the gloom—perfect for hiding. She crowded down between Peony and Pansy, nearly crawling under Peony's swollen belly and udder.

Jeez, is Peony pregnant or something? Lilly shouldered her way around the animal's bulk.

The barn door swung open slowly, the old hinges creaking from the wetness. Lilly shuddered and held her breath as a small gust of wind blew through the barn down the main walkway. Some of the cows stirred. The air in the barn chilled suddenly, and it was not just from the breeze. Lilly poked as much of her head around Peony's leg as she dared, not wanting to catch Maggie's attention or spook the cow.

She hadn't survived death by hammer and manure pit to only be trampled by a jittery, fifteen hundred pound cow.

Maggie moved stealthily down the main walkway. From what Lilly saw through legs and shadows, Maggie appeared more manure and mud than human.

"Lilly, please, let's just end all this silliness," Maggie cooed. "You're only prolonging the inevitable."

Lilly wondered briefly how long Maggie had prepared this. The elder woman sounded more Bond villain than small town denizen, and it became hard to take the woman seriously.

Maggie's muck encrusted leg passed into Lilly's field of vision. Lilly held her breath and shifted along with Peony. The cow decided to turn length wise in her stall at a pivotal moment. Maybe the cow sensed the danger Maggie posed, much like Dandelion and her bovine caterwauling, and shielded her. She pressed against the cow and mirrored her moves the best she could.

Maggie paused, her nose pointed to the ceiling as her eyes scanned the stalls. She sniffed loudly then moved to the next stall and melted into the shadows.

Lilly waited until the shuffled footsteps fell fainter toward the back of the barn, close to the barn cleaner. She reached under Peony's neck and unhooked the chain link that held her fast within the stall. The cow flicked her large glass eyes and whuuufffed in Lilly's face, like she understood what Lilly wanted her to do. She backed out of her stall a few steps and stopped, waiting for Lilly's next move. As quietly as she could muster on her shaking limbs, Lilly ducked behind Peony's neighbor, Pansy, and unhooked her chain. She grasped each chain to keep the links from clanging, Lilly didn't want to risk Maggie knowing the difference between a normal chain clink and an escaped cow chain clink.

Peony didn't match her sister in understanding Lilly's plan, content to lay down in her straw and chew her cud.

Lilly scrambled away from the lounging cow, now more exposed than before. She stopped behind Dandelion. She fought to crawl in close to the cow, but Dandelion shifted back and forth, huffing in agitation. Apparently, the matriarch of the herd figured out Lilly's plan and was ready to get on with it.

Stop it, you daft heifer, you're going to squash me! Lilly cursed as she dodged Dandelion's dancing hooves. The cow settled down enough for Lilly to work her way to the neck chain. One soft click later, Dandelion was free of her stall.

Maggie managed to come back down the row of cows, returning to the front of the barn after her inspection of the back of the barn. Now, she saw Lilly scoot out of Dandelion's stall.

"There you are!" Maggie crowed as she hurried down the main walk, a new weapon brandished high. Even in the thick shadows of the barn, Lilly could make out the form of another hammer. Although this one appeared to have been forged for Thor instead of an average farmer, Maggie welded it as if she were from Asgard herself. The straw and dust on the floor caused Lilly's feet to slip with each fumbling grasp for safety. She curled into a tight ball as Maggie and her hammer loomed over her. Lilly prayed for the end to be quick.

And then all hell broke loose.

Dandelion's roar echoed in the barn. The large cow backed out of her stall and put her massive body between Lilly and Maggie. The woman slammed full force into the solid wall of bovine flesh. Dandelion's war cry spurred on the other cows to action—untethered or not. Peony and Pansy bucked in their stalls and collided with the far wall, penning Maggie in. The other cows raised their voices in distress, pulling on their chains with such force Lilly feared their necks—or the iron poles—would break before their bonds did.

"Blasted cow!" Maggie shoved at Dandelion's flank. It had the effect of a bug trying to move a windshield. She attempted to duck underneath, but the cow seemed to be one step ahead.

The large bovine swung her massive rear end toward Maggie and knocked her to the floor. Lilly finally made it to her feet while Dandelion continued to move in reverse. Lilly feared for a moment the cow would keep moving until she stepped on the deranged woman. Dandelion started to lower herself down to the floor with Maggie in the way.

"Dandelion, stop!" Lilly shouted.

Maggie pushed against any cow that came too close, swinging her hammer at any leg or hoof or head that dared to enter her personal space. She managed to get to her knees with the intention to stand, when Dandelion's impressive derrière loomed over her.

"Get away from me!" She screamed as the large animal started to lower her back half and lay down. A hind leg swung around and clothes-lined Maggie at the knees, knocking her back on her own rear. Lilly flinched and turned away as Maggie screamed again when Dandelion put her whole weight down. Right across the woman's legs.

The realtor shouted and cursed, swatting at Dandelion with the side of the hammer until Pansy's frantic back kick relieved her of the weapon. Dandelion settled into her new spot and stared off into the shadowy barn, seemingly oblivious to the shrill commotion happening under her.

Lilly blinked and forced herself to snap out of her minor level of shock she felt herself slipping into. She didn't want to test her luck by hanging around the barn any longer than she needed to. Maggie escaped from the manure pit, who knew what superhuman strength her rage would grant her. She might be able to dislodge herself from under a half ton cow.

Lilly bolted to the open barn door and out into the damp, chilled evening. Freedom was only a few strides across the farm yard. She envisioned herself getting into her car and driving to find help. Call the police and hope they'll believe her story, and then continue to drive, and drive far away from Lone Tree and the farm forever...

A black figure stepped into her path as she exited the barn. Strong hands caught her arms as the two collided, warm arms wrapped around her. She screamed and swatted at the unknown hands to free herself.

"Hey! Lilly! Stop!"

A familiar voice stilled her flailing hands. Fear fell from her eyes and she finally saw clearly for the first time in what seemed like hours, days.

"What is going on here?" Ryan asked. His voice and face held none of the normal anger or exasperation she expected from him. Only concern came from him, with maybe a touch of fear behind his John Deere brim.

Lilly tried to speak to relay her harrowing events, and demand to know where he'd been. Her breath failed to even say his name, but all her strength faded. She collapsed against his chest and cried.

Chapter Twenty-one

For the third time in less than two weeks, Lilly's yard was awash in swirling blue and red lights and people in various uniforms. Multiple emergency response vehicles and rescue vehicles shouldered for space on the driveway and grass. Two ambulances, one from Sleepy Eye and the other all the way from New Ulm, sat on the edge of the chaos.

Lilly sat on a stretcher in the back of the Sleepy Eye ambulance, awkwardly half dressed. An EMT inspected her shoulder and back, and she winced with each palpation as the medical technician poked fresh bruises with squeaky gloved fingers. The technician, called Murphy—"But my friends call me Murph!"—apologized with each sharp intake of breath she made.

She kept her body as straight as she could muster, her ruined Mackinaw jacket hugged tight to her near-bare chest. Lilly worked to focus on what the EMTs said about her injuries. Instead, her mind replayed the events of the last few hours over and over. She vaguely heard something about an X-ray for her shoulder, the one Maggie so graciously slammed with one of her many hammers.

"I hope nothing's broken," Lilly muttered.

Second-cousin-twice-removed Sheriff Brandford walked up to her ambulance, his face aged even more since the last time they spoke. Lilly frowned at his grim expression.

"How are you holding up?" Michael scratched at the five o'clock shadow along his chin.

"I'm alright—" she began but her words devolved into a pained hiss. "Although, my arm might fall off."

"Sorry," EMT Murph chimed in from behind her.

"Adrenaline is a hell of a thing, isn't it?" Michael finally cracked a small grin.

"Especially when it wears off," Lilly growled. She hurt in parts of her body she didn't even know she had. Muscles in her arms and legs randomly spasmed as she sat on the gurney. Her involuntary movements made Murph's job a little more difficult, and Lilly didn't feel one bit remorseful.

"We might want to take her to Sleepy Eye for monitoring," Murph announced. "I'd feel better if we got a few images down of that shoulder and back."

"Is that where she went?" Lilly's eyes widened.

Michael shook his head. "Mrs. Swenson went to New Ulm Medical. Her legs were pretty messed up from that cow. And they have better resources for guarding her."

"Dandelion."

"What?"

"Dandelion," Lilly corrected. "The cow's name is Dandelion."

Her second cousin twice removed nodded gently. "She'll be there, recovering under guard until she's stable enough to be charged and transported to a holding cell. Then, on to court."

She nodded absently and hugged her jacket tighter, ignoring the pain in her shoulders. The chain of events after Dandelion laid on Maggie merged into a blur for Lilly. She remembered crashing into Ryan after leaving the barn. The next moment, police and sirens flooded her yard. For the next two hours, she was asked a flurry of questions by Michael and other officers, EMTs, and medics. During all that commotion, she lost track of Ryan's whereabouts.

Ryan, being the nephew of the accused, most likely had his hands full with his own interrogations. There is a lot of red tape to muddle through when your aunt turns out to be wanted for two murders and one attempted murder. Or was that one murder and two attempted murders? Had it only been mere hours since she saw Earl Graves off to the hospital? When she last saw him, he still breathed. But a lot can change in that amount of time.

"How's Ryan?" She asked softly.

Michael glanced over his shoulder and nodded his chin toward the barn. "He's finishing up in the barn with some officers. Those cows messed up the bottom of the barn, probably destroying a lot of evidence. Ryan had to help the guys get the cows under control before they could do any work. Hard to get anything done with cows trampling over part of the crime scene."

Her eyes narrowed. "That didn't answer my question."

The sheriff shrugged. "I haven't talked to him since another officer took him aside for questioning. Had to make sure Heimdall wasn't involved, for fear of biases. Then, the crime scene guys needed him to tame the savage beasts."

"Oh." Lilly lowered her gaze to her knees. She picked at soiled holes in the embroidery of her dress.

No more mimosa brunches for you, old friend.

A sad Louboutin slingback heel still clung to her right foot, more forced into place by muck than actually staying on of its own accord. Yet another high end outfit destroyed by the farm.

"How is Earl?" Lilly asked.

"Earl?"

"I didn't hear how he was when they took him to the hospital," Lilly yawned. Her body started to slow down, all its energy spent. Her brain slowly followed suit.

Sheriff Michael nodded. "He'll pull through. No serious injuries, but the docs want to keep him a few nights just to be sure."

"I want to know when he gets out, I have some news he's been wanting to hear," Lilly said as firmly as her sluggish mind would allow.

Michael gave a ghost of a smile and patted her uninjured shoulder. "You'll be the first one to know."

"Good."

Moments later, Lilly nodded as EMT Murph recommended she see her doctor first thing in the morning. He insisted that she ride in the ambulance to Sleepy Eye Medical for X-rays just to be safe, and suggested that picking up a prescription of painkillers might not be a bad idea. She nodded as he gave her his advice. She did like the idea of heavy narcotics. Perhaps that would let her forget any of the last week or so had ever happened.

"Are the cops done with me? Can I go inside and change now?" Lilly interrupted Murphy's litany of medical terminology.

"How am I supposed to know?"

Lilly blinked, realizing that neither Murph nor Second Cousin Twice Removed Sheriff Michael had responded to her question. The sheriff had moved on to another group of officers and Murph was filling out paperwork on a clunky metal clipboard.

"You're not Michael," Lilly stated, pointing dumbly at Ryan.

"Thank the lord for that." Ryan stood beside the textured metal bumper of the ambulance, looking amused. He took half a hobbled step from the ambulance, his countenance shifting so drastically that it made her woozy. "Do you need the EMT? I can go get him."

"No, thank you," Lilly waved off his offer. "I just need a moment of peace and quiet."

"You and me both." He dropped hard onto the metal bumper-slash-step of the ambulance.

"Hey! You're making me screw up on my report!" Murph whined from within the ambulance.

Lilly and Ryan snickered.

She studied him as their laughter faded away. His face remained a near-impenetrable mask, save his eyes. They appeared lost and unfocused under his curved hat brim. "How are you holding up?" She asked, certain that silence marked the longest between the two to date.

He turned sharply and pushed his hat back. "Me? What about you?"

Lilly shrugged and immediately regretted it. She might take Murph up on that ride to Sleepy Eye to get those feel-good drugs. "I'll manage. Once I get some pain killed in me."

Ryan grunted. "Careful with those, they sneak up pretty quick."

"Oh, I didn't—"

He elbowed her shin gently. "Stop."

They fell into another silence; though, this one was more comfortable than the last—a mutual agreement to just be still and observe. Lilly glanced at the sky, out beyond the barn and the grove. A chilled wind blew in from the southwest, one last push to get the storm system safely out of the area. An overcast sky obscured the sunset as it sank behind the grove.

"Wind's changing," Lilly muttered.

Ryan shot her a look over his shoulder, a hint of a smirk pulling at his scruffy face. "Is that a hint of the old Lilly finally making her way out?"

Lilly felt her chest and cheek flush as she flicked her gaze away.

"I hope so," Ryan continued. He leaned back with his elbows. "I've missed her."

She cleared her throat, tongue suddenly dry and stiff. "Ryan, I—"

"So, see you tomorrow at six o'clock?" He cut her off. "Unless the cops take my herd in as evidence."

"My herd," Lilly corrected.

"Hmm." He grinned. "I suppose I need to start brushing up on my resume? Or is it too early to ask that question?"

"No." Lilly hadn't expected to answer so quickly. Yet, the answer felt so right on her lips.

"No?"

"I think I'll stick around a little longer," Lilly replied. "Can't let a little thing like attempted murder keep me off the family farm."

Ryan chuckled. "I don't know if this is too little too late, but... I'm sorry... for what... for what my aunt did. If I had known what she was up to... why she..." Lilly rested a hand on his shoulder, gave a gentle squeeze, and waited for him to continue.

"I feel responsible for all this," he concluded.

"Nothing for you to apologize for," Lilly said. "Have you heard from Josh?"

"No." Ryan shook his head.

"One thing I don't understand, Maggie started to get squirrely when I mentioned the name Tessa. Guess I was trying too hard to not die to ask Maggie who that is. Does that name mean anything to you?"

Ryan shifted on the bumper. "I heard some of the cops in the barn talking. All hearsay, mind you, but they were doing some digging into Max's books and he had duplicate sets of books for everything. Some of the books mentioned a Tessa."

"Great, that still doesn't explain who she was or why she was harassing my grandma about the land," Lilly huffed.

"Tessa is Josh's mom." Ryan said. "Well, her nickname. Real name was Teresa."

"Were the sisters working together, or did Maggie just use her sister's name as a cover?"

"Slow down, Nancy Drew." Ryan held up a hand. "Let the actual police do the actual police work. I'm surprised you didn't get into more trouble going around asking questions. Not the best way to reintroduce yourself to Lone Tree."

Lilly sat and let that sink in for a moment. "Do they think Josh was part of this, or just Maggie?"

He sighed. "I doubt he'll be allowed to leave town for a while until things are sorted out." He took his John Deere cap off and scratched the back of his head. "I hope Aunt Maggie worked alone, for his sake."

She squeezed his shoulder one more time, unsure of what else she could say. What do you say to someone whose family member tried to kill you? All she knew, at that moment, was the two of them now had something to work through, together and on their own.

"I want to get chickens," Lilly announced.

Ryan eyed her, then turned to face her fully. "Chickens."

"Yeah. Chickens. Add some farm fresh eggs to our milk soap and goat yoga." Lilly beamed at his confused expression. "And, it might be a while before I'll be ready to go back into the barn again, so I'll need something to do."

Ryan continued to stare at her in silence, the same odd look on his face.

"What? I've heard that neighbor's rooster crow in the morning for about two weeks now. I think every good farm needs at least a handful of chickens."

"We do."

Lilly blinked at him. "We do what?"

"Have chickens." His smug grin reappeared. "That's not the neighbor's rooster crowing. That's ours."

"What!" Lilly shouted. A handful of officers paused in their investigation and turned to the ambulance. "Where are they?"

"In the little shed, back by the old chicken coop, kinda near the calf hutches." Ryan pointed behind the farmhouse and Lilly knew exactly what little fenced in shed he referred to.

"I hadn't seen them out..." Lilly whimpered.

"They'd been locked up in the shed for most of the winter. Chickens would sit face first in a snowstorm and drown if we didn't coop them up. Stupid birds. It was getting nice enough out, and you were here, I was going to let them out of the shed so they can eat stuff off the ground instead of waste money on feed."

"They weren't in the main coop..."

Ryan couldn't contain his laughter. "You really weren't paying much attention to the farm if you missed we had chickens all this time. Was solving Max's murder really that time consuming that you didn't see your own chickens?"

Lilly silently pouted.

"So, if you're not going to do barn duty anytime soon, that means I hereby pass all chicken and egg-related duties on to you." Ryan grinned.

Lilly cleared her throat and sat up as straight as she could without too much pain. Which proved to be not very straight at all. "Fine, I accept. What's their normal schedule like?"

He chuckled. "In the spring, fed by six o'clock, let out by seven-thirty for egg check. Back in the fence and shed by dusk before the coyotes and foxes have their way with them."

Lilly groaned. "Why do they need to be up and fed that early? Can't they be checked on later? And why can't I just do egg checks when I'm in there to feed? Seems like a lot of extra work."

"The rooster is territorial of his ladies, and is especially cranky before breakfast. I think you city folks call that 'hangry?'" Ryan answered. "You dig under his hens while he's in there and he'll make you second guess your desire to keep chickens."

She had started second guessing her announcement already. She didn't like the sound of such a territorial bird on her property. Maybe it wasn't too late to back out of her announcement and see if Faith would want to put fried chicken as next month's dinner special.

Ryan caught her distraught gaze and laughed. Lilly's mouth dropped. "I don't know why this is so funny to you! I've been here for how long and had no idea there were chickens on the property?"

"Those aren't your chickens," Ryan admitted through his laughter.

"But you just said..."

"I had to get you out of your head, Lilly," he said, elbowing her leg once more. "The rooster you hear is my parents' rooster. Our farms are close enough, and he's just loud enough that you can hear him in the morning."

"So we don't have..." She felt her panic start to ebb. Lilly slapped his shoulder. "You are so mean to me! Why did I agree to keep you on?"

"'Cuz you won't be able to find another hired man who could stomach your constant talking."

Lilly slapped him one more time, this time hard enough to make her own hand sting. Her pain was worth knowing he felt it too. "And you'd never find someone to hire you with your thick-headed stubbornness."

"I bet Earl might need some help now..."

Lilly rolled her eyes. "You two would kill each other before lunchtime. So, one last time, because the shock and adrenaline are really wearing off now, and I'm tired and hungry. Tell me the truth. There are no chickens?" She glared at him, though she couldn't rid herself of that blasted smirk.

He matched her grin. He held up hand with two raised fingers. "Scout's honor. We don't have chickens on the farm."

"We don't have chickens on the farm... yet."

In response, an unseen rooster crowed.

THE END

Lilly Schmidt will return in Fowl Play

Book 2 in the Accidental Farmer Mystery Series

Acknowledgements

I'd like to thank the following people who helped make this book possible!
(In no particular order...)

The fabulous leaders of Fox Pointe Publishing, LLC, Kiersten Hall and Chelsea Farr, who (as a newly hatched publishing house) took a chance on me and gifted me time to work on this manuscript through financial hardships, a freaking global pandemic, and personal roadblocks, in order to spend the time I needed to get myself, as well as my book baby, in order.

Thank you to Sarah Olson, my patient editor, who gave me direction and pointers to get this book ready for the readers. I enjoyed reading your notes and suggestions, I truly believe they helped me get out of my own way to see this work with fresh eyes. Sorry it took all summer to get these revisions done!

A special thanks to my beta readers: Ann Horrmann, Jennifer Neve, Brittany Olson, Matt Goers, Chelsea Farr, and A.J. Sullivan. You guys were the first eyes to look at this manuscript other than me and I thank you for being gentle with me, as well as truthful in your feedback. You helped make this book what it is today!

My technical advisors: Brittany Olson, Carrie Mess, and Tim Stender. I appreciate the time you took out of your busy days to answer my numerous (and let's face it, elementary) questions about cows, bovine anatomy and medicine, agriculture and farming in general, and equipment terms to ensure that this book, though a work of fiction, stays true to the career and livelihood of farmers (crop and livestock) who put food on our table, fuel in our cars, and clothes on our backs.

To my RRS BP crew! A huge shout out to you, because without you this book probably wouldn't have been written. And a special thanks to Karlene, for being the best boss lady ever for turning a blind eye all those times a Word Doc was up on my work screen...

Huge thank you to Krista Johnsen for being the best graphic designer friend I know! I can't thank you enough for your generosity and creativity, and for bringing this fabulous cover to life.

And to family and friends who are too numerous to name, and if I try to name you all I'll forget someone and then that person will get mad and I don't need that negativity in my life; thank you for all your overt and covert support, inspiration, swift kicks in the pants to get going on deadlines, and good mojo over the years I've been working on Farmed & Dangerous, and writing in general.

Thank you.

About the Author

Amy Gregg is an author of several books, including *Relic Chosen: Magic and Madness* (Minnesota Book Award nominated), *Through the Woods*, and *Next Weekend*. When not writing, she enjoys true crime docs, knitting, and spirited discussions of all things Marvel. A native Minnesotan whose childhood was spent both on the farm and in the suburbs, Amy now splits the difference and lives with her family & 10lb cat near the edge of the Twin Cities.

Keep up to date on future books at:

facebook.com/AmyGreggAuthor

@amylgregg

@amylgregg

www.ingramcontent.com/pod-product-compliance
Lightning Source LLC
Chambersburg PA
CBHW050438200726
48295CB00024B/664